LIBERTY STREET

Liberty Street is a book of warning, for America does not know what is being done in her name. Laid in the exotic setting of a Caribbean town, it is the story of a hunt where paradoxically the hunted and the hunter change places, where the prosecuted becomes the prosecutor. That, in brief, is the book's plot, but no outline can suggest the rich variety of the story, swiftly-moving, dramatic, and dealing with a subject of uttermost significance to every American.

In the tropical capital of Santa Rosa an oddly assorted lot of people had gathered. Some of them, like Marie-Té and Konrad and young Bubi, had just arrived and found the gaudy little place, with its air of lost civilization, gay and diverting. Others, like Nestor Kerjanian, the frantic little Armenian with his shabby suit and flaming red necktie, had been there, it seemed, since the beginning of time—or, if not there, in other places like it, where he spent endless days and months waiting for some miracle that would lead to the fulfilment of cherished hopes.

Kerjanian, for example, had wandered over the face of the earth for thirty years, wanting only to get to his brother who lived on Liberty Street in Brooklyn. In one way or another he symbolized them all.

There was Marie-Té, the beautiful Austrian girl, ardently sought after by two men whose natural animosity, heightened by jealousy, led to a sensational climax. There was Siegfried Stumpf, typical of the intellectual German, ever torn between conflicting loyalties, Nazi and anti-Nazi in one. There was Baron Falkenborn, rich in wisdom and in gentleness, and his nephew Bubi, who spoke five languages at the age of eight, and was the owner of a pet armadillo.

The destiny of nearly all these people lay in the hands of Warfield Harrington, the suave American diplomat—one of those men of ill will to whom we owe so much of the chaos of our world. It was because of him that they waited and saw their dreams fade. John Camberly alone had the understanding and the determination to oppose him; for Camberly, a true American, saw the danger to his country in men like Harrington, who believe that America should exist for the benefit of a chosen few. Camberly had dedicated himself to a war to the death with these "native fascists".

Liberty Street is peopled with memorable characters like these. It is a novel to touch the heart and the imagination. Beautifully written, it is both timely and unusual, a story told with humor and gayety. I. V. Morris has caught the spirit of high courage, intelligence, and essential kindliness which must in time triumph over the faint-hearted and spiritually poor of the earth.

LIBERTY STREET

By

I. V. MORRIS

HARPER & BROTHERS
PUBLISHERS
NEW YORK AND
LONDON

TO THOSE WHO WILL KEEP THE
STAUNCH HEART OF AMERICA ALIVE

LIBERTY STREET

Chapter I
I Am Kerjanian

MARIE-TÉ FALKENBORN FOUND SANTA ROSA EVEN more alien than Lisbon, the Azores or Havana—the stopping off places on her long journey to New York. There were orange-colored birds that screeched like rusty hinges outside her window; there were trains of burros munching beatifically at each other's tails; there were Indian beggars who proudly exhibited their deformities and accepted alms with casually muttered benedictions. The atmosphere of a lost civilization hung over this Central American capital, where adobe hovels bracketed pink stone buildings that represented Spanish Colonial architecture at its best. The ensemble went to the Austrian girl's head like a rich sweet wine.

"Santa Rosa may lack plumbing, but it certainly has charm," she said to her Uncle Konrad as they sat at breakfast in Pension Hilda the day after their arrival. "Somehow it reminds me of Vienna— so gay, so carefree. It's a revelation to find a city with so much real gaiety in the year 1943. I wouldn't at all mind spending a few weeks here."

"Probably," said Uncle Konrad, biting into a bright yellow mango, "your wish will be realized. We are refugees. It is our profession to wait, as it is another person's profession to sell umbrellas or to practice law."

"Don't be pessimistic, *Liebling*," Marie-Té exclaimed. "A pessimistic refugee might as well be dead. Only settled, wealthy people with bona fide passports can afford the luxury of being downhearted nowadays. I have an appointment this afternoon with the American

3

Minister and I am going to bring you back a nice present for your birthday: United States visas."

Later that day she changed into her white linen suit, did up her blonde hair on the top of her head, as she wore it when she wanted to impress people, and set off for the American Legation. She was feeling happy as she picked her way over the cobblestones, between pastel colored houses gleaming in the sunlight. There was the sound of laughter and of high-pitched voices and of a mechanical piano jingling out a tango behind the shuttered entrance of a café. Marie-Té whistled the tune between her teeth as she strolled along.

A few moments later she was climbing the steep hill that led to the Legation, then giving her name to a native porter in a dark-blue uniform. As she passed into the waiting room, a shabby little man jumped to his feet.

"Have you," he said, addressing the porter in bad Spanish, "told the Minister that I was waiting? It's over a month now that I've been coming here. I insist on seeing the Minister at once!"

Oh goodness, here he was again! thought Marie-Té with a sinking of the heart. The eternal little man who was to be found in every passport office throughout the world. In consulates and legations from Vienna to Havana she had come across his like; she might have known that he would bob up again in this Central American capital, still demanding an appointment, still waiting for his visa to the United States, the ultimate goal of every person fleeing from persecution and hunger and despair.

Now the little man whipped out his pocketbook, searched through it, and produced a soiled calling card. "Please give this to the Minister," he said in a peremptory tone. "I am Kerjanian. Nestor Kerjanian."

Obviously the sleepy-eyed doorman didn't understand a word, but he smiled obligingly, his white teeth standing out magnificently against his dusky skin. No doubt he was used to these frantic callers, thought Marie-Té as she watched him amble off down the uncarpeted hallway. Then she brought her glance back to the man

4

called Kerjanian, who stood with arms folded on his chest, gazing at a poster of Niagara Falls with its waters painted red and green and blue in the gleam of colored searchlights.

Despite that brave pose, there was something desperate and pathetic about the visitor. His shiny pale-blue suit, his carefully laced shoes, his black town hat all had an exhausted air. He looked as if the long periods of waiting had sapped his strength and consumed his last ounce of patience. If something did not happen soon, he would in desperation do violence to himself or to others, thought Marie-Té. And in her mind's eye she saw millions of frantic, harried men like this one rising up at last and *demanding* the attention which they had so long begged for without avail.

There came the sound of approaching footfalls, crisp and loud. The little man swung around, and his fingers went up to straighten his crimson necktie, an elegant looking article which contrasted signally with the rest of his garb. Then he took a step forward to face the young man who had appeared in the doorway, immaculate in cream shirt and gray flannel suit. On this newcomer's face was an aloof, utterly bored expression as he studied the caller; he held Kerjanian's card gingerly between two fingers as if he disliked to touch the tired-looking pasteboard.

"I'm sorry," he said, talking *at* the visitor rather than to him, "the Minister can't possibly see you today. He can't see you any day this week. Anyway, visa matters are handled by the consulate on the second floor."

Marie-Té, who was watching Kerjanian, noticed that he was trembling. He stretched his short body upward, and tried to impart an imperative tone to his voice.

"It is most important that I see the Minister in person. I have business with him—special business."

The young man patted away a yawn with his well-tended hand.

"I know, I know," he said in a listless voice. "But just go to the consulate—they'll take care of you. Mr. Harrington sees no one without a previous appointment."

5

Marie-Té was surprised at the effect of these last words. The visitor's eyes flashed in his pale face, giving him a completely fanatical air; when he spoke, his voice shook as if he were on the verge of hysteria.

"Harrington?" he cried. "Did you say Harrington?"

"Why yes," replied the young man, on whom Kerjanian's excitement had made no impression. "The Minister's name is Mr. Warfield Harrington. What of it?"

Marie-Té saw the little man step forward and with an impetuous movement snatch away his calling card. His nostrils were quivering; his every feature expressed rage and horror. "What of it?" he shouted. "Why, only this—that I happen to know your Warfield Harrington. I am Kerjanian! And this is what I think of him." He spat furiously on the floor. Then he deliberately replaced the calling card in his pocketbook, pulled open the front door, and flung out of the building.

The young man smiled faintly as he followed the figure of the stranger swinging down the hill. He took out of his breast pocket a folded handkerchief and carefully wiped the fingers that had held the card. Then, turning to leave, he caught sight of Marie-Té and his self-satisfied countenance expressed both male admiration and solicitude.

"Oh, this is too bad! You are Miss Falkenborn, no doubt? Imagine our idiot of a doorman bringing in that dirty card and never even saying that you were here! I'm Mr. Baker, the Third Secretary. The Minister's been expecting you—er—for some time."

"I know," said Marie-Té, laughing. "Don't rub it in. Punctuality isn't one of our Austrian virtues."

She could tell that he admired that easy manner of hers that came from centuries of breeding; it never failed to impress these young diplomatic pups. Obviously he liked her looks too, to judge from his sidelong glances as he accompanied her down the corridor. Oh yes, my friend—it's good, all of it, she thought with the

6

self-assurance of a young girl who has been much admired in her lifetime. My slender legs, my blonde hair, my graceful figure—I've been hearing about them since I was old enough to know the meaning of a compliment. Thank you all the same. She smiled at him before stepping through the doorway that led to the Minister's office.

Warfield Harrington was seated behind a large desk, on which stood a flagpole with a miniature American flag. Despite this show of patriotism, Marie-Té's first impression of the man was that he looked distinctly un-American. He might have been taken for an Englishman, though when one came to analyze his looks, one found nothing typically English about them either. Tall and thin, he was exceedingly well preserved for someone who must have been approaching fifty. The dark suit and gray necktie were discreet, giving him the dignified appearance that one felt he was anxious to achieve.

"How nice to meet you," said Marie-Té, taking his hand. "Our friends in Havana told me to be sure to look you up."

"I'd have been very angry with them if they hadn't." He gave her a charming smile as he drew up a chair. "I've been expecting you for quite a while. You had no difficulty finding the Legation?"

"None at all." She laughed mischievously. "I was late—well, I was late simply because I started late."

The Minister seemed taken aback by this unusual frankness. "A very logical reason," he said, recovering himself quickly. "Anyway, I am pleased that you finally came. We have very few European visitors in this year 1943. Are you staying with us long?"

"That depends upon you. I applied for my American immigration visa a year ago, but I am still waiting."

"Ah," said Harrington, and now that she had divulged the purpose of her call, a subtle change had come into his manner. "Regulations are regulations, you know."

"Oh yes, I know. I learned all about them during my three-months' stay in Havana. The thing I don't understand is why in 1943, with far more people than ever in need of refuge, those restrictions seem to be getting tighter all the time. How do you account for that, Mr. Harrington?"

The diplomat shrugged his shoulders. "These are war times, Miss Falkenborn."

"Ah! I see that you're a real diplomat, Mr. Harrington. I've never yet known one of you who wasn't terrified of coming forth with a concrete statement." Marie-Té gave a little laugh. "As you say, this is wartime. But is that any reason why hospitable America should close its doors to people so terribly in need of haven? Do you know, Mr. Harrington, I sometimes see an awful picture: rows of dead people hanging by the neck, with the nooses that strangled them fashioned out of red tape. Ugh! Their faces look awfully white next to that official color. Do the generous Americans really know what's going on, Mr. Harrington? I wonder."

Warfield Harrington had recourse to a little nasal chuckle which expressed nothing and could be interpreted howsoever the listener desired.

"For a charming young lady, you seem to have a very lugubrious turn of mind," he remarked. "Did you—excuse my asking—leave Austria for reasons of . . . of . . ."

"Race? No, Mr. Harrington, I'm not Jewish, if that's what you mean. And I'm not a political refugee either. Perhaps I left Austria simply because my instincts told me that my future lay in the United States. I believe every one's future lies there for the next decades."

"H'm. Very interesting," said Harrington. "I asked because— well, because we like to know exactly whom we have to deal with nowadays. We've quite enough undesirables in the United States as it is—Semitics and others."

"We used to think," said Marie-Té, a hint of hostility in her young voice, "that in America undesirables became desirables. Won't a little plot of earth and a steady job turn a raving anarchist into the most law-abiding of citizens?"

Warfield Harrington did not seem interested in this argument; he examined his nails, while a little smile played about his lips. A breeze blowing through the open window swung the curtains into the room and fluttered the little American flag upon the table. When he spoke, it was with the obvious intent of changing the subject. "Are you here alone, Miss Falkenborn?" he inquired.

"Except for my kid brother and my uncle," answered Marie-Té. "Today is my uncle's birthday, by the way. We are going to celebrate at a night club called Chez Boris. Would you care to join us?"

"Unfortunately that's impossible," said the Minister with the air of having suffered a major disappointment. "But I shall see you there in any case. The De Castros—the Portuguese Minister and his wife—are giving a party. The British Chargé d'Affaires and his wife are going to be present, and a number of diplomatic people."

"Oh, you'll be much better off with them," said Marie-Té. "Our table isn't going to be nearly so smart: a down-and-out Pole from our pension, a gay little French lady, my shabby uncle and my shabby self. Still, we do mean to have fun! Come and say hello to us. No one will speak to you about visas—you needn't worry."

"I am not worrying," Warfield Harrington replied drily. And anyone noting his astute eyes and the smile with which he punctuated these last words would have vouched for the truth of one of the diplomat's rare positive statements.

She ran down the steps of the Legation, and kept right on running the whole length of the hill, with her hat in her hand and the light hair flying up at every stride. Offices depressed Marie-Té Falkenborn; they gave her a feeling of claustrophobia. And if one type of office was drearier than another, it was a legation office!

But at the foot of the hill she saw something that put her back into high spirits. Coming down the road was a very fat old lady riding sedately on a burro, the burro's head and that of its owner both covered by identical sombreros. Two holes were punctured in the donkey's headgear, through which his long twitching ears protruded. Unaware that people and animals simply could not allow

9

themselves to look so ridiculous, they jogged merrily down the main street of Tegucagua, the old lady smoking a cigar and absent-mindedly kicking at the donkey's stomach beneath her billowing peasant skirts.

Marie-Té laughed delightedly. She felt that she was going to like this city, which was so vivid and so alive. In the gutter an Indian as small and wiry as a monkey was selling honey-covered cakes, while his neighbor extolled the merits of his stock of merchandise, which consisted of a single egg. Alternately he spat upon it and polished it on his sleeve, or threw it high in the air, to catch it miraculously in his sombrero. *"Huevo! Quién quiere un huevo?* Who wants an egg?" he half shouted, half sang to the passers-by.

Yes, who? thought Marie-Té, and though she was still smiling, she couldn't help thinking of those millions of people in Europe who would be glad to stand in line all day to purchase such a luxury. That is the way it was nowadays—at any moment her thoughts would go flying back to the same subject: the famished people of what had come to be the wrong side of the Atlantic. Mr. Harrington had implied that they had better stay over on their bank, and if worst came to worst starve to death there. Marie-Té hoped fervently that he did not represent the views of the American people.

Pension Hilda, Marie-Té's German-run boardinghouse, possessed a quality of Teutonic ugliness that set it apart from every other building on the street; in this graceful Spanish-Indian town, where no construction seemed to have taken place since colonial days, it stood out like a telegraph pole in a grove of willows. Once you had shut behind you the spotless white door that fronted the thoroughfare, you realized that you had stepped right back into Europe, leaving the land of Indians, of coffee plants and waving banana trees thousands of miles away. There was a pair of varnished antlers in the vestibule, hung on the wall between the lithograph of Goethe and a water color of a group of smug-looking cherubim. Peering through the glass doorway on the right, you could glimpse the parlor, with a number of gilt chairs, three clumsy little tables covered with lace cloths, and at one end a plush sofa of an immensity and ugliness that could only have been tolerated in a Germanic household.

It was on this sofa that Marie-Te saw a young man lying as she passed through the vestibule on her return from the Legation. Standing beside him was Hilda Stumpf herself, the refugee owner of the pension, in the act of sliding a hideously embroidered leather cushion beneath his head. There was something infinitely tender in the big clumsy woman's gesture, and in the smile with which she gazed down into his exhausted face. Her warm brown eyes shone; her face, that resembled the big, puckered face of a lion, grew magnificent with love.

Embarrassed at having been the witness to such an intimate little scene, Marie-Té was about to walk on when Hilda Stumpf caught sight of her through the glass door. Instantly the exalted look vanished, to be replaced by the placid, cheerful expression of a German *hausfrau.*

"Ah, come in, come in, Fräulein Falkenborn," she called out in her deep voice. "I would so much like you to meet my brother."

The tall young man jumped to his feet and hurried to open the door. Marie-Té now saw to her surprise that he had on a full-dress suit, though the bright sunshine was pouring through the windows. She remembered having been told the night before that Stumpf used to be a teacher of philosophy in Munich University, and more recently had been incarcerated in a Bavarian concentration camp. Certainly his high forehead and visionary eyes were the hallmarks of an intellectual, but his attire could scarcely have been called appropriate.

"Siegfried," Hilda Stumpf said, "this is our beautiful new guest, Fräulein Falkenborn. Let us hope that she and her uncle will stay with us a while."

"I sincerely hope so," said Stumpf, and he made a formal German bow.

"Speaking of your uncle," Hilda Stumpf went on, "would he

take it amiss if I asked him to play his violin a little softer? He has been at it ever since you went out, and I hate to say anything to an artist, but some of the boarders have been complaining."

"Oh, don't feel badly about it! We've been told the same thing in every boardinghouse and hotel since we left Paris two years ago. My uncle loves music and, like a child, he always wants to play as loudly as possible."

"I understand that," said Hilda Stumpf, nodding her great head, whose tawny wild hair and furrowed brow kept reminding Marie-Té of the head of a lion. "I am an artist too—that is, I am a writer—and I always want to shout loudly because I feel I have so much to say. But no one cares to listen to me," she added a little sadly.

"Oh, they will one day," Marie-Té assured her, and, remembering the depth of emotion in Hilda's face when she bent over her brother, she had a feeling that her words might come true.

But Hilda Stumpf shook her head. "I fear not," she said. "I've written for as long as I can remember, and so far my audience has consisted of the few kind friends who come to listen when I read my new work each year. I have done eleven novels and not one has yet been published." She smiled at Marie-Té, then with an impulsive moment, took her arm. "I am so pleased to have you with us, dear Fräulein Falkenborn! It will do my brother good to look at such a beautiful girl each day."

Siegfried Stumpf gave a laugh which made his tortured-looking face seem boyish. "Ah, Fräulein Falkenborn," he said, "It's clear that you are going to find a place in my sister's new book. Her heroines are always incredibly beautiful and her heroes miraculously brave. In fact everyone is very definitely one thing or another, which isn't at all as people are in real life. Perhaps that's why my dear sister's books don't get published."

Marie-Té laughed too, and a little feeling of happiness surged through her. What genuine human beings these were! She wouldn't give the world up for lost when even in an out of the way spot like Santa Rosa one could run into two such pleasant, cultivated people—people whom one instinctively knew to be of the same kind as oneself.

"I am off to the night club in a few moments, so please pardon this attire," Stumpf went on, indicating his dress suit, which was shiny with age. "I am headwaiter at Chez Boris."

"Are you really?" Marie-Té tried not to show her surprise. "In that case we will probably be seeing you this evening. It's my uncle's birthday and we are having a little party at your night club."

"I'll be delighted to welcome you," said Siegfried. "I can promise you a good table, and," he added practically, "a thirty-three per cent discount."

In the meanwhile Hilda Stumpf had stepped over to the console by the window. Now she came up to Marie-Té, holding a bronze statuette.

"Please give this to your uncle from Siegfried and myself. A little birthday present."

Marie-Té pressed Hilda's hand in thanks, while her eyes passed over the gift. It depicted a little shepherd boy blowing on a flute and was in the worst possible taste; nowhere could it have fitted better than in the atrocious baroque setting of Pension Hilda's parlor.

"I thought he might like it—seeing that he is a musician," the big woman explained. "It belonged in our old home in Munich and was one of the few things I took with me when I left Germany eight years ago."

"Oh, it's just what he would like," Marie-Té assured her.

"And seeing that it is his birthday, please don't tell him about the violin playing until tomorrow. Promise me that," said Hilda earnestly, taking a handkerchief from the pocket of her white starched blouse and flicking a speck of dust off the shepherd.

Marie-Té leaned forward quickly and kissed Hilda on the cheek. "How nice you are! Do you mind my telling you that I like you very much?"

Hilda Stumpf blushed. "And I like you, Fräulein Falkenborn.

13

In these times one can't afford to wait for years before telling people what one thinks of them."

Marie-Té left the authoress and mounted the staircase to the second floor. Before her stretched a row of doors as identical as the doors in a sanatorium, behind which the least imaginative could have pictured the tidy bedrooms, a little exhausted-looking from having been swept so often and so well, the series of white wooden beds with feather bolsters, and the bedside tables in which reposed the classical receptacles, as unchipped and carefully polished as though they had been rare examples of Dresden china. It was through one of these doors that there drifted a series of screechy notes, repeating themselves time and again as a certain movement was attacked, courageously yet ever without success. At exactly the same point the player would break down, and then, after a few seconds' silence, the process would recommence.

As she listened, with one hand on the doorknob, Marie-Té's lips curved in a smile. With a quick shove she had pushed open the door, and was standing in the entrance, laughing gaily.

Uncle Konrad was sitting on the edge of his bed with the violin tucked under his chin and his eyes fastened on the notes, pinned to the near wall. One strand of his blond hair had fallen down over his right eye, accentuating the air of concentration with which he studied the music; the large chin gave evidence of determination and the naturally soft mouth was pinched into a thin line.

Lying stretched upon the bed was a very beautiful little boy in a blue shirt and leather shorts. He had Uncle Konrad's soft blond hair, but with him it stood out like a cloud around the well-molded head. At Marie-Té's entrance he ran up to her to fling both his arms around her waist.

"Oh, Marie-Té, why have you been away so long? Did he say that we could go to America? What's that you are holding?"

Marie-Té laughed and squeezed him back. "Oh Bubi, you always ask three questions at the same time and as I've told you

14

before, I'm only going to answer the last. This is a birthday gift for Uncle Konrad—from the Stumpfs."

Uncle Konrad jumped up with amazing swiftness for such a tall, heavily built man; on his face was a look of boyish curiosity. When Marie-Té put the little statue in his hand, he stood gazing at it in delight.

"What kind people!" he murmured. "What wonderfully kind people!"

"What do you think of it, Bubi?" Marie-Té asked her brother.

The little boy went up to peer at the bronze shepherd.

"It is very ugly," he said. "But it isn't really ugly, because they gave it."

"Yes, that is what I think," said Marie-Té. "Nothing's ugly that is given in love." She put her arm around Uncle Konrad's shoulder. "And I haven't given you anything at all, darling! You are sixty years old today, and your only birthday present has come from strangers."

"You give me a wonderful present every day," said Uncle Konrad. "Every time you smile at me, you are giving me a present."

"I haven't given you anything either, Uncle Konrad," Bubi said. "Not even a jack-in-the-box, like last year in Lisbon."

Marie-Té reached out for Bubi's hand, and she put her arm tighter about Uncle Konrad's shoulder. Suddenly she knew for certain that never in her life would she be closer to any two people than she was at that moment to a man more than double her own age and a little boy less than half of it; the bonds of exile that united them were stronger than any other bonds on earth.

"We may not be able to buy each other anything," she said. "But we're still together, aren't we? That's something. And to-night you and I are going to have a real splurge, Uncle Konrad! Did you ask the French lady to your party?"

"Of course, Maria-Theresa," answered Uncle Konrad, who was

the only person who still declined to use the abbreviation Marie-Té. "A charming woman to find living in this pension in this God-forsaken town. Gay and witty too! The idea that such a cultured person should have had to flee her country because she had Jewish blood is nothing short of ludicrous. Madame Legervais a member of an inferior race! I could laugh myself sick over that."

"Is the young Pole we met last night coming too?"

"Count Oronoff? Of course. Have you ever known a Pole to refuse an invitation?"

He walked to the mirror to straighten his butterfly tie and flick a hair off the lapel of his corduroy jacket. His appearance, if negligent, had about it something vaguely aristocratic, like that of a figure in an old Viennese etching. Already he was humming a little tune, delighted at the prospect of an evening's jollity, but Bubi, with the tenacity of a child, insisted on having all his questions answered.

"*Are* we going to America soon, Marie-Té? Did you see the man at the Legation? Tell me what he said."

"You really want to know? Well, he said—exactly nothing! Bubi, child, you still have much to learn. If a diplomat ever said anything . . . why then he wouldn't be a diplomat. Even in talking of the weather, Mr. Harrington managed to keep back any definite information. Just fancy if I were to quote the American Minister as having said that the rainy season began the tenth of July, and it actually began the twelfth! Grave complications. International complications, perhaps!"

Uncle Konrad, standing before the mirror, was laughing uproariously. His glance met hers in the glass.

"Oh, Maria-Theresa, you are an *enfant terrible!* Thank goodness that even the collapse of a whole world hasn't changed you. Your grandfather, with all his ambassadorial decorations, would rise in his grave if he were to hear you speak like that of the American Minister."

"He should have done some rising up while he was alive," said

16

Marie-Té. "If he had, perhaps that collapse of the world wouldn't have taken place. But what did he do instead? Twirl his mustaches! That's what they all did—those gentlemen with decorations on their chests. As a result we are here today, planning to celebrate your birthday at Chez Boris."

"I admit that Sacher's in Vienna would be more congenial," said Uncle Konrad wistfully.

"Of course it would. But don't worry, Uncle Konrad. You'll be back in Vienna soon, and having dinner at Sacher's too!"

"Well, that's something to live for. I shall order one of those famous schnitzels. Do you remember how they used to melt in one's mouth? I'll have a *Sacher-torte* for dessert."

"Probably more than one, if I know you, darling! And after dinner, you'll take your lady friend for a drive down the *Ring*. The street lights will be blazing, and everywhere you'll see gay faces and hear laughter. There won't be a single swastika in sight."

"And how about you, Maria-Theresa. Where will you be?"

"Oh, my fate lies on another continent," said Marie-Té, laughing. "But I will come to visit you and Father sometimes. I promise."

"Do you really believe all that—or do you just say it to make me happy?"

"Yes, I do believe it. And if all us Austrians who have been kicked out of our land, and all the Dutch and the French and the Greeks who have been kicked out of theirs, keep believing that the day of their return will come, then that day *will* come. As sure as fate it will, Uncle Konrad! For if enough people hope with enough strength, then no power on earth—not even the Nazis—can deny them."

Chapter II

Chez Boris

SIEGFRIED STUMPF ALWAYS MADE A POINT OF getting to the night club several hours before the arrival of the guests. His reasons for this were twofold: to stop Boris Popoff, the Russian owner, from getting drunk so early in the evening, and to make sure that enough waiters had showed up for duty. Their arrival being dependent on the amount they had received in tips the night before, it often became necessary to round up the delinquents at their homes, the local brothels, or the jail, where they were apt to land whenever they had made enough money to buy liquor. Thanks to the ex-teacher of philosophy from Munich, Chez Boris was nowadays run in a comparatively orderly fashion. The floor was swept, the tablecloths kept clean and the waiters made to dress in neat red and white striped native costume instead of an odd assortment of American sports sweaters, jockey caps and ripped trousers bound around with bicycle clips.

Tonight Siegfried was pleased to find that most of the staff had put in an appearance. Four of the boys were playing poker at a corner table, presided over by Boris himself, who was the best player of the lot. The proprietor always figured on taking away half of his staff's tips—in fact counted on this as part of his legitimate income. His blue-black beard and great mop of hair gave Boris an uncouth appearance, and though he wore full dress, he had the unfortunate habit of taking off his shoes and socks when drunk and paddling about in his bare feet, the toenails of which harmonized with his black garb. All in all, it was doubtful if he would have been allowed inside any night club if he did not own it.

On the raised dais the orchestra was practicing a new tune. Gomez, their leader, stood with his back turned, conducting with his violin bow. He was the type of man who looks as if he hadn't slept since he was a baby and as if his only nourishment since then had been a few flicks of cocaine, washed down with absinthe. Yellow-green was his complexion, and he had a pair of shiny black eyes, like the markings of one of those exotic orchids that grew so abundantly in this country. Had he been just a trifle smaller, one really might have thought of reaching out one's hand to pluck him and put him in one's buttonhole, there to languish, there to die.

Gomez's orchestra was one of the best jazz bands in Central America, and their numbers were comparatively up-to-date. A new batch of sheet music had just arrived from the United States, in the playing of which they were now perfecting themselves. Piano, violin and three saxophones were rendering, each in a different key, "The Lambeth Walk."

Boris looked about from his poker game and clapped his great dirty hands as the orchestra crashed into the finale.

"Ah-ha, that's the stuff. Real swing, eh what, Stumpf? We're catching up to 1943 at last."

"Yes indeed," agreed Siegfried. "Before we know it we'll be doing the Turkey Trot."

"Eh? What's that? Speak to Gomez about it—he probably has the music on order right now. By the way, we have a very smart party tonight. Señora de Castro called up from the Portuguese Legation to reserve a table. Let's give them number six, right next to the music."

"Not unless you wish to supply ear muffs, Mr. Popoff. Better put them at number ten; they'd be happier there."

"You think so? Well, you arrange it, Stumpf—that's what I hire you for," said Boris, reaching under the table for his *aguar-*

19

diente, which he always drank out of the bottle, like a peasant. It was, he said, the nearest thing that he could get to vodka, and to judge from the proprietor's usual bearing about 2 A.M., it must have had almost as much effect.

That pleasant hour saw the night club enjoying a busy session. Word had gone about that Gomez's orchestra were to play some brand-new American numbers, so all the chic people of Santa Rosa were present. There were a number of young society ladies with their chaperones; there were several parties of young married people; and at two large tables the gay blades of the town had congregated. The young men had on a variety of costumes, ranging from full dress to reefer jackets and plus fours, a garb that rumor said was the height of elegance in England. For the most part they had ordered coca-colas, which they mixed with red wine to form a concoction weird enough to turn any squeamish stomach.

Señora de Castro's party lent a distinguished flavor to the assembly, and apart from them, there was at least one other table composed of foreigners. Boris Popoff sat wriggling his bare toes underneath the counter as he pleasurably computed the evening's takings; both tables had ordered champagne and there seemed a good chance of disposing of a few more bottles.

"Have another glass," Uncle Konrad was urging as he refilled the goblet of his Polish guest. "Really, my dear Count Oronoff, I am beginning to quite like it here in Santa Rosa."

"That is because you have been here twenty-four hours, not as I have, for twenty-four weeks. Thank God I have got my American visa at last! The town is insignificant and sordid, my dear fellow, like this whole hemisphere. When I think of the charm of an old-world country like Poland . . ."

"If you speak of charm, speak of Austria," said Uncle Konrad, who had some difficulty expressing himself in French.

"Well, Austria too," admitted the Pole grudgingly. "Our countries at least are civilized; they have culture. But look at those waiters—their expressions, their bodies. They are serfs, neither more nor less—no higher than were their forefathers under the Mayan Empire. You may have them! I give them to you gladly."

He made a lavish gesture and drained his glass to the last drop.

"These countries," said the little Frenchwoman, Madame Legervais, "are like truffles: you either appreciate them—or not. But as a steady diet. . . ." She put her daintily manicured hands to her stomach symbolically.

"Ha, ha!" Uncle Konrad was delighted. "*Quel esprit!* Madame Legervais, allow me to tell you that you are a very charming creature!"

Suddenly they all noticed that a man in evening clothes was standing by their table. It was Warfield Harrington, come over from the diplomats' gathering to ask Marie-Té to dance.

"May I?" he said, smiling charmingly.

"Why, of course!"

Doing the Lambeth Walk . . . Gomez's orchestra was screaming as Warfield Harrington steered his partner about the floor. He did not dance at all badly, she thought, but in an automatic manner, as if he had been wound up with a key; there was about as much music in his body as in one of Boris Popoff's aluminum chairs. The orchestra ceased playing and he absent-mindedly applauded.

"You are looking charming tonight, Miss Falkenborn."

"Ah, so you actually remember my name!"

"Of course I do," said Harrington, chuckling up his nose. "There aren't so many attractive ladies in Santa Rosa."

"Still being diplomatic, Mr. Harrington?"

"Not at all. When you walked into my office this afternoon . . ." Harrington broke off as two people from his table danced by close beside them. Only after he had maneuvered Marie-Té and himself into a corner did he continue, ". . . I really felt quite overwhelmed. And that blue velvet dress, if you don't mind my saying so, definitely suits your type of beauty."

Ah, so the dress had done the trick once more, thought Marie-Té. Good old dress! If it finally got her an American visa, she would never wear it again, but preserve it preciously, as one might preserve a trusted old weapon of combat. She leaned back her head to smile at Harrington, and felt his arm pressing tighter about her waist. Oh, how easy it was to make a man fall in love with one! Easy, yet always thrilling. Marie-Té felt stirring within her that old spirit of flirtation that was an integral part of her Viennese nature.

They were dancing near the diplomats' table now, where Señora de Castro, Harrington's hostess, sat watching them with an anxious eye. Here was a rival, thought Marie-Té, and a chic and pretty one to boot, if somewhat on the faded side. Mischievously she pressed her cheek against Harrington's as they danced past, causing the lady at the table to wince. Harrington's reaction, also, was decisive.

"Would it," he asked, speaking rapidly because the dance tune was coming to an end, "would it be presumptuous to ask you to have dinner with me some night? Tomorrow, for instance?"

"But I'd simply love it!"

"And would it be too much if I asked you to wear that same blue dress?"

"Certainly not. Particularly as I have no other."

She felt him stiffen a little, as though she'd made a slightly obscene remark, but then he forced a laugh as he escorted her to her table.

"He at any rate seems civilized," remarked the Pole as he watched Harrington making his way back to his own party. "A charming man, I should say, with impeccable manners. Now even in Warsaw this Harrington would not seem out of place. Yes," he added reflectively, taking a little more champagne, "if many

22

Americans were like him, there might be some hope for this un-
cultured hemisphere after all!"

It was while dancing with Harrington that Marie-Té had first
noticed the man at the corner table. She did not recognize him at
once. Only when he kept staring at them did she recall having
seen before those burning, fanatical-looking eyes, and the red silk
cravat, whose flaming elegance contrasted with the rest of his
attire. Why, of course! This was the same little man who had insisted on seeing the Minister in person, and who, upon hearing
Harrington's name, had spat so furiously on the Legation floor.
Now his eyes, as they followed her partner about the room, expressed an infinity of contempt and hatred.

Count Oronoff also had remarked on the fellow's rudeness, as
Marie-Té learned when she came back to her table. Even in Santa
Rosa, he said angrily, a man ought to have better manners than to
gape at a pretty woman, especially when he sported a week's
growth of beard and obviously belonged to the lower classes.
Whereupon he craned his neck and glared furiously at the offend-
ing party.

"That's right," agreed little Madame Legervais, "Poland's
honor must be upheld."

Oronoff nodded glumly, not sure whether or not she was making fun of him.

"Vive Paderewski! Down with the unwashed!" cried the little
Frenchwoman. Her dislike of Oronoff was obvious, and presently
there took place an incident which caused the rest of them to
share it. While dancing with Marie-Té, the Pole passed close by
the table where the little man sat alone, moodily contemplating his
empty glass. Perhaps Oronoff's awkwardness was to blame, perhaps the fact that the other man's legs protruded on the floor. In
any case, the Pole stumbled and only kept himself from falling by
snatching at a chair. Red in the face, he swung around, letting go
of his partner.

23

"Keep your legs where they belong, idiot!"

The little man's reaction was instantaneous and unexpected; jumping to his feet, he gave a little bow, then picked out a calling card from his pocketbook and handed it to the Pole.

"Nestor Kerjanian, at your service," he announced in French. "Name the time and place. It will be a pleasure for me to give you satisfaction."

Oronoff was so astonished that at first he did not grasp what the fellow meant. In Poland, to be sure, he once had fought a duel, but that had been with someone of his own class and each combatant had been reasonably sure that the other would not try to hit him. This was something quite different. The idea of this uncouth-looking individual daring to suggest such a thing made him furious, besides scaring him quite a bit. It was—why, it was nothing less than an insult to Poland!

"You're—drunk," he said, turning away arrogantly. "I have a good mind to have you thrown out on the street."

"What! You refuse?"

Kerjanian was standing on the dance floor, waving his calling card in the air as though it were a weapon. He had drawn himself up to his full height, which was about a head less than the tall Oronoff. He glared after him in fury.

"You refuse?" he shouted again. "But you can't refuse! I demand an apology."

"Oh, keep still. You bore me," said the Pole as he put his arm about his partner's waist and made to dance off with her.

Marie-Té became stiff as a rod. It always gave her physical pain when she saw one human being hurting another who was beneath him. If this overbearing Pole had had his way, he'd have turned out everybody from the night club—excepting, of course, Warfield Harrington, whom he had recognized instantly as a kindred spirit.

Without the slightest hesitation she left Oronoff in the middle of the floor and turned to address Kerjanian. "I apologize in my

24

friend's place," she said to him in French. "But do you really think a duel is necessary—Mr. Kerjanian?"

A pleased look came into Kerjanian's face as she pronounced his name. He hesitated a second, but then his anger flooded back. "I insist on a duel!" he shouted so loudly that Siegfried Stumpf, the headwaiter, came running up to see what was the matter. People at other tables were peering around, and some of the diplomats in Señora de Castro's party seemed ill at ease. Marie-Té noticed that Warfield Harrington was carefully looking in the opposite direction, as though unacquainted with her, even though they happened to have had a dance together.

"Yes, yes, you're absolutely in the right," she said, touching Kerjanian's arm and trying to make him sit down.

He shook her off. "Coward!" he shouted after Oronoff. And then, switching to Spanish, *"Cobarde! Cobarde!"*

The Pole paid no attention but turned his back and began walking to the exit, leaving Marie-Té beside Kerjanian.

"May I sit down?" she asked him.

Kerjanian, still stationed at the edge of the dance floor with his card in his hand, flashed her an unseeing glance. Then he looked away again toward the retreating enemy, and folded his arms on his chest in a Napoleonic gesture. When he finally resumed his seat, he gave a start on finding a young woman at his table. He scowled.

"What do you want?" he asked ungallantly. "Are you still making fun of me?"

"Why should I be making fun of you? There's nothing funny about you that I can see," Marie-Té assured him. And she thought, Oh how lonely, how scorned, he must feel to take offense so frequently and with such vehemence! Her whole heart went out to the little man.

Kerjanian seemed partly conciliated by her courteous manner, though he was brooding over his grievance. "Yes, yes, he despised

25

me," he muttered angrily. "He wanted to humiliate me before all these people. Before your friend Harrington too!"

"My friend Harrington! So you know him?"

"Oh yes, I know him," Kerjanian cast a sharp look at Señora de Castro's table with the gathering of diplomats. He lowered his voice and assumed a mysterious air. "To tell the truth, it's because of him that I came here tonight. I saw him stepping out of his car outside."

"Is that so?" said Marie-Té, hiding her curiosity.

"It's ten years since I saw him last," Kerjanian volunteered. "He was American consul in Aleppo then. I am an Armenian and I used to live in Syria once upon a time."

"So it was in Aleppo that you two met before?"

"Well, not exactly. In the country, rather, but not far from Aleppo. Moreover, we didn't really meet, to tell the truth. It was a fine Sunday morning, I remember, and will you believe it that the same sort of thing happened between us as this afternoon? That's what's so amazing: that it should repeat itself after all these years. I don't know you nor anything about you, but I tell you here and now—" Kerjanian's eyes blazed up and his bony forefinger fanned the air. He looked all at once completely fanatical—like a Biblical prophet of doom. "—I tell you here and now that this Harrington cannot go on as he is doing; retribution will overtake him."

"And what happened that other time—in Syria?" she asked, not knowing herself why she stayed on here talking to a stranger.

Kerjanian's eyes narrowed. He seemed to be peering at the past through those tiny slots beneath his eyelids, and what he saw filled him with distress. His little body twitched; the hand lying on the table closed involuntarily around the handle of his glass— so tightly that the thin stem snapped and the rounded top smashed into splinters.

"What happened?" he repeated. "Well, I will tell you what happened. Just this: one man mortally insulted another. Now as

26

long as those two live, that insult also is a living thing. It's like a third person that sprang into being that day in Syria and lives a life of its own, independent of either one of us!

"At that time I was teacher in the Armenian school in Aleppo," Kerjanian went on, obviously pleased at this opportunity of talking about himself. "I am, you see, a qualified schoolteacher, second class. One Sunday I was walking in the hills outside the city when a car swept by so close to me that I had to jump into a ditch. As I gathered myself together, I saw that the automobile had stopped, and also that an American flag was flying from its bonnet. At that my anger died away, for, I must tell you, I have always loved America. Yes, I'm a great lover of that country, where everyone is as good as everyone else, and everyone is everyone's friend. So when the American gentleman inside the car lowered the window and asked me to point out the way, I politely offered to accompany him."

Kerjanian broke off to light himself a cigarette. These memories of the past had excited him tremendously, and his little hand shook so that he had difficulty striking the match. When he had taken two puffs he crushed out the cigarette against his plate and continued, speaking rapidly and with vehemence,

"I only made that suggestion to oblige him, and because of my great respect for the country of his origin. Just imagine my surprise—yes, my surprise and horror—when this distinguished gentleman with the American accent, instead of inviting me to sit beside him, pointed to the front seat next to the chauffeur. Naturally I couldn't understand it. Even so I decided to swallow my pride, convinced that there must be some explanation for his rude behavior. From my front seat I turned about and addressed him in the fluent English which I had taught myself, and will you believe it that he answered me not in English, not even in French, but in Syrian—of which he knew exactly ten words. But ten words are enough to speak to a dog! Then he leaned back on the cushions, closed his eyes, and apparently forgot all about me.

27

"There I sat next to the chauffeur," Kerjanian told her, "my eyes glued to the American flag—that flag which for me has meant more than the cross on churches or any other emblem of brotherhood. And all the time I was thinking one thing only: this man cannot be a real American! You see, I have a brother who owns a carpet shop on Liberty Street in Brooklyn, near New York. He writes me often, and this wasn't the kind of American my brother writes about. Not the kind of American who gave my brother a loan when he was in trouble. Not the kind of American who risked his life to save my brother's little daughter when she fell into the East River in New York. No, this was the cold-hearted man of power whom we in the old world have slaved under for centuries. This wasn't a real American!"

"I think you are right—at least I hope so," said Marie-Te, remembering that her first impression of Harrington had been his un-American manner and appearance. He had struck her as being a typical diplomat of the old school—noncommittal, suave, calculating—and that certainly wasn't the sort of man fit to represent a virile new America to which the whole world was looking for guidance. But Kerjanian, absorbed in his own story, was unmindful of her interruption.

"Much worse was to come," he said, scowling darkly and staring at Harrington at the other end of the room. "Our destination was the house of the French colonel who was in military charge of that whole district. When we drove up, the colonel and his lady came out of the house to welcome the foreigner, while I climbed down from the box, naturally feeling like a fool. What did the American do? Listen and I will tell you. Casually he took out his wallet, searched through it, and ended by handing me a five-franc note! Yes, that is how he insulted me in the presence of the French officer and his wife!

"For one moment I remained speechless," said Kerjanian, and the glance of his fanatical black eyes burned Marie-Té. "Then anger overcame me, and I crumpled the note into a little ball and

28

threw it at the American's feet 'I am Kerjanian!' I called out. 'Keep your money.' Everyone looked frightened, and the lady, turning to her guest, said, 'Will you come into the house, *Monsieur le Consul?*' That is when I knew for the first time that this man was the consul of the United States, and when I made inquiries later on, I was told that his name was Harrington. Now you can understand how I felt this afternoon when he insultingly refused to receive me. There's something strange in his turning up in my life a second time—yes, there's something ominous in it."

Kerjanian sat staring out into space with his tragic black eyes, his mouth set in a hard bitter line. Marie-Té felt like taking him into her arms to comfort him, he seemed so lonely, so miserable. How pathetic, she thought, that an insignificant little action, should seem to him of such vast importance! But then she corrected herself. No, it really was not insignificant at all. A callous word, a slighting or brutal deed, could never be called insignificant; its seeds lived forever and might grow into huge trees that overshadowed a person's life.

"Wien, Wien, nur du allein . . . sollst stets die Stadt meiner Träume sein . . ." sang Uncle Konrad's violin, borrowed from Gomez, the orchestra leader. He stood on the platform of the darkened night club, bending his big body toward Irène Legervais in the manner of night club violinists; the gay and sentimental tune soared into the smoke-charged room. A long lock of blond hair had fallen down over his massive forehead and the great bow tie, become unknotted, dangled down like two ends of a scarf. It was very late and, if truth be known, Uncle Konrad was more than a little drunk.

"Ah, très bien, très bien," cried Irène Legervais, applauding. "You take me right back to Vienna, or what's even nicer, to that chic Austrian restaurant in Paris where I used to go. Play it again, Konrad! Please!" Her vivacious brown eyes were sparkling and the pretty little rouged mouth was smiling, smiling. How lovely

29

it was to be gay again, to drink champagne, to be with light-hearted, carefree people! Not since she escaped over the Pyrenees into Spain had she felt as happy as tonight, and she was falling rapidly in love with Konrad. Ah, that delicious sensation when one feels oneself slipping irresistibly into love! Perhaps, she thought, things would go better from now on and she would remember how to laugh and sing, as she used to do in those days that seemed as far away as her own childhood—those golden days before terror was let loose in the world.

". . . *Wien . . . mein Wien.*" The last notes of the melody lingered in the air, caressing her as softly as the feather-light lingerie she wore next to her skin, and of which she had to be so careful because she would never be able to afford another set.

"Look out, Konrad," she said. "In a little while I shall be growing sentimental."

"Do, my dove, do," said Uncle Konrad. He stepped down from the dais, violin in hand. "I am feeling sentimental myself tonight."

"With your permission," interrupted Gomez, the owner of the violin, following Uncle Konrad and reaching out his pale hand for the instrument. "With your kind permission. . . ."

"A little later," said the Austrian with an impatient gesture. He sat down at the table, tucked the violin under his chin and began to play, *Ich möchte in Grünzing sein* and *Du bist mein ganzes Herz.* "Do you like that?" he asked the Frenchwoman.

"Ah, *cher ami . . .* it's lovely!"

"*You* are lovely," said Uncle Konrad, laying down his violin on the table. "As to my fiddling tonight, why it really doesn't count. I'm a classical violinist; you ought to hear me perform a Brahms concerto. Now that's something to listen to! But these popular tunes. . . ." With an airy gesture he dismissed them and reached out for Irène Legervais' little hands. Gomez, who had been biding his opportunity, snapped at the instrument as a tropical orchid snaps at a fly; his petal-like fingers closed over it. Then he flitted away and disappeared in the thick smoke. Uncle Konrad did not notice him. "And to think," he was saying, "that I had to travel over thousands of miles of ocean to find you in this hole of a city. The ways of the gods are indeed beyond comprehension." He carried her fingers to his lips and, with the air of a gourmet sampling a fine dish, he kissed them one by one.

While Uncle Konrad was devoting his sixtieth birthday to flirting and to playing the violin, Marie-Té remained sitting with Kerjanian. Gradually she drew him out about the past, for she was fascinated by this intense little man who tried so hard to hide his pain and loneliness behind a mask of superiority. She learned of his constant wanderings since he had fled Armenia after the massacres, twenty-five years before, of his vain search for stability and respectability, of his present attempt to enter the United States with a dated passport issued by a country that no longer existed. Here, she thought, was the eternal refugee, the man who had been a refugee so long that he could remember no other existence.

"What do I want of life?" Kerjanian said, still speaking as though he were alone at the table and were asking the question of himself. "Not much. Just what is wanted by millions of men like me—my brother refugees tramping the earth north and east, south and west: hard, honest work, the respect of my fellow men—a little peace of heart. That's all I ask. That's what I've never had. But when I get to America at last"—his eyes brightened—"I am going to buy myself a little plot of land—just an acre, or maybe half an acre. I shall plant things and see them grow up, and I shan't have to run away just as they are sprouting. I shall sit on a bench and watch my vegetables grow, and the neighbors will pass by and politely take off their hats to me, and I will bow and take off my hat to them. Perhaps I'll have a wife and a little boy."

"How well I understand you—oh, how well!" said Marie-Té. But, as usual, Kerjanian didn't listen to her; his momentary tone of exultation faded, and he went on in his old bitter voice,

"But there's still a long way to America! Perhaps I'll never get there after all. I'm tired—very tired. And my throat is parched. I sometimes think the dust of all the roads I've tramped has lodged there and that I'll never be able to wash it away. Here, waiter!"

A waiter who had been sitting fast asleep with his head on a table, woke up and shuffled toward Kerjanian.

"No, no, I don't want you," the Armenian said. "I want the headwaiter."

"What is your order?" asked the sleepy attendant, who had failed to understand Kerjanian's Spanish.

"The headwaiter!" commanded Kerjanian, and he repeated in a strange mixture of French and Spanish, *"El primero garçon! El primero garçon!"*

The bewildered waiter disappeared and Kerjanian turned to Marie-Té to explain. "I never have dealings with subordinates. For a refugee it's absolutely necessary to maintain one's dignity, otherwise one might as well give up at once. That's why I always insist on going to the top."

Siegfried Stumpf, who had been sitting behind the bar, profiting from some quiet moments to look into a volume of Kant, sprang to his feet. "At your service," he said, appearing beside Kerjanian and assuming the stiff stance typical of any German official.

"Bring me," said Kerjanian, with the air of a millionaire ordering a steam yacht, "bring me a glass of soda water and make sure that it is iced. . . ."

A few moments later Señora de Castro's table broke up, the guests making their way to the entrance door and into the warm night outside. Marie-Té noticed that Warfield Harrington affected a big circle so as not to pass near her table. As if galvanized, Kerjanian jumped up, his eyes blazing.

"Excuse me!" he cried. "I must go. I must follow that man and see where he lives. I shan't let him out of sight."

He threw some money on the table, grabbed his hat and rushed out of the night club. Marie-Té found herself sitting there all alone. Looking around, she saw that Uncle Konrad and his lady love had both disappeared, a circumstance from which certain conclusions might have been drawn. As she started for the doorway, Siegfried Stumpf hurried up, the volume of Kant in his hand.

"If you will wait for me, *gnädiges Fräulein,* I will escort you back to the pension. I wouldn't like you to go alone so late at night. In the meanwhile you can sit comfortably at this table and read my Kant."

Marie-Té seated herself again and perused *The Critique of Pure Reason* to the accompaniment of "The Lambeth Walk." Everything seemed completely absurd and incongruous—as incongruous and absurd as was the whole world nowadays.

Oh Lord, oh Lord, thought Marie-Té, as she watched a gentleman in a riding habit doing the rumba with a young lady in a dress of sequins. Where are we going? What is going to happen to us all? Even Kant might feel confused if he had the misfortune to be alive today.

The night club was almost clear of guests by the time Siegfried Stumpf rejoined her. "It's too bad," he said, shaking his head. "Señor Popoff is completely drunk tonight. Most of the waiters too. I've locked the whole bunch up in the back room to sleep it off, otherwise they certainly would have got into trouble and been arrested by the police. Then tomorrow night I'd have been without waiters! I must remember to drop around in the morning and let them out."

They walked together through the narrow streets of Santa Rosa, tall Stumpf in his full-dress suit, which looked shabbier than ever in the early light of dawn, Marie-Té in the long blue evening gown that she had put on to celebrate Uncle Konrad's birthday. She felt foolish walking by the beggars lying sleeping in the roadway. A family of Indians, come to town to sell their merchandise, approached along the street with their heavily laden burro. They

33

stopped to stare at the two foreigners, and long after she had passed, Marie-Té could feel the gaze of the amazed Indians following her.

"I suppose," she said to Stumpf, "we could not look funnier to them if we were wearing fancy dress."

"No," he replied, "but they mean no harm by staring. Besides, they don't stare as much as the tourists stare at them, and they haven't the incredible tactlessness of producing cameras to take our pictures! No, these are charming, considerate people. When my own country threw me out, I found a second home among them. By now I almost feel that I belong here."

"But not quite?"

"Of course not. I am a German, now and always. My only hope is that one day there will be a Germany to which I can return."

"Oh, there will be! Perhaps sooner than one thinks."

"Perhaps. Or perhaps the forces that drove us both abroad will catch up with us over here. Who knows? The powers of evil are strong."

"Don't give up, Siegfried Stumpf!" said Marie-Té. "Personally I never shall give up."

"It's good to hear you say that, Fräulein Falkenborn. I admit that there are times when I've been sorely tempted to. If it hadn't been for my dear Kant"—he tapped the book beneath his arm—"and for my sister Hilda, I'm not sure that I'd have had the courage to resist. She's a great woman, Fräulein Falkenborn—a tower of strength she is, though I know that it must sound boastful to talk like that of one's own sister. She herself doesn't realize her magnificent strength and courage."

Over Siegfried Stumpf's emaciated face there flashed a look of exultation. Marie-Té, remembering the scene between brother and sister that she had inadvertently witnessed, thought, How those two must love each other! What a blessing for them to have each other in their exile!

"Yes," Stumpf went on, "life is difficult nowadays. There are

34

times when a man reels very tired and—well, the truth is that I was never born to be a headwaiter at Chez Boris. I'm a teacher of philosophy—*Privatdozent*, Heidelberg, 1927. What have I to do with politics? I'm not even of Jewish extraction. But all at once they locked me up in the concentration camp, simply because I refused to teach Nazi doctrines in my classes! That I couldn't do, Fräulein Falkenborn. You agree with me?"

"Of course I agree with you," she said, feeling that his clear blue eyes were peering at her hopefully through his spectacles. "You have saved your soul."

"Not yet, Fräulein," he said, running his hand nervously through his thinning hair. "Don't forget that the Nazis are as persistent as the devil himself, and like the devil, they can offer high inducements. There's a German school here—still a center for the Nazis, even though this country has broken relations with the Reich. I've had a letter suggesting that I apply for a post there. It would be nice to talk German again. A pleasanter job than serving drinks in a night club!"

"Not," said Marie-Té, "if you never dared look at your face in the mirror. In that case, Herr Stumpf, I'd prefer to keep on wearing a headwaiter's uniform."

Siegfried Stumpf did not answer; they walked on in silence. Suddenly it had become clear to Marie-Té that this man with the clear honest eyes was in reality a torn soul—as torn as the German race always has been. In spite of all—in spite of the concentration camp, and his ruined career, and exile—he was first and foremost a German. Perhaps it was because of the multitude of Siegfried Stumpfs that the Nazi party had originally gained power.

A moment later they had turned a corner and found themselves beside Independencia Park, from which led the main street of Santa Rosa. In the eucalyptus trees the birds were just waking up, and there was a mad twittering and fluttering in the branches; it sounded as if every bird in Central America had made its home

35

among the leaves. The dawn bathed in limpid light the fronts of the tired old buildings that faced the plaza.

"It is beautiful!" said Marie-Té, standing still to look.

"Oh yes, it is beautiful. But you forget to appreciate it if you come home at this hour every morning." In the voice of Siegfried Stumpf could be detected a note of exhaustion—or might it have been despair?

Running toward them across the park was a little boy with a huge sheaf of newspapers beneath his arm, as fresh and gay looking as the morning itself. His black hair was cut in a bang low on his forehead, and his rich red mouth was laughing. On his head he wore a coconut shell as a hat, and as he ran, his patched jacket flew apart, disclosing the naked brown body underneath.

"Los Americanos toman Tunis! Americans take Tunis," he was calling out happily.

"You see, Herr Stumpf. You mustn't be discouraged," said Marie-Té. "The dawn is in sight at last. Even this little urchin seems delighted."

"Oh, that fellow's always laughing," said Siegfried. "I see him here almost every morning when I'm trudging home and I've heard him announce the greatest catastrophes in tones of jubilation. Do you know why he's so happy? It's because he's a great artist. Would you like to hear him sing, Fräulein Falkenborn?"

"Of course I would," answered Marie-Té.

"Paco, sing something for the lady," said Siegfried Stumpf, taking a twenty-centavo piece from his pocket.

Paco slid it deftly underneath his coconut shell and climbed up on one of the park benches, his newspapers still clutched under his arm.

"I sing 'Star-Spangled Banner.' Like?"

"Yes, like," said Marie-Té. "It's my favorite song nowadays."

"O.K. Fine," said Paco in American. "You listen, lady."

Very pure and very strong came Paco's voice as he swung his arms in time to the music, on his face the ecstatic expression of a

36

real singer, oblivious to everything but the music he is creating. First one and then another of the newspapers slid out from beneath his arm and went fluttering to the ground, but Paco sang on without paying any attention—sang the words of that song which is like a message of hope to free men throughout the world.

AMERICANS LIBERATE AFRICA, ran the headline of the paper lying at Marie-Té's feet. Would it be Europe next? Was there hope for the world again? As she listened to Paco's strong young voice, a wave of relief and happiness swept over Marie-Té.

Chapter III

Portrait of a Diplomat

NEXT MORNING, AS ON EVERY OTHER, WARFIELD Harrington was awakened at seven-thirty. No sooner had his Chinese servant, Ah Sing, touched his shoulder, than he had leaped from his bed and was doing setting-up exercises, his torso and members moving in a mechanical, staccato fashion; he looked like one of those wooden men whose arms and legs jerk out when you give a tug at the string.

"One—two—three—four," he counted aloud in Spanish, thus killing two birds with one stone, for he was accustoming himself to think in the foreign language. *"Uno—dos—tres—cuatro."* Even his voice sounded wooden, as though the automaton had been equipped with a device for speech.

Seven minutes later he was standing in his tub, letting an ice-cold shower drum on his body without registering the slightest sign of shock, and two minutes thereafter was stepping into well-pressed trousers and reaching for one of his unobtrusive neckties. Quarter before eight saw him sitting in the alcove of his sitting room, nibbling a piece of toast while his eyes skimmed the headlines of the paper. No item of news evoked either surprise, pleasure or chagrin; doubtless had he read of the imminent annihilation of the planet, it would not have prevented his carefully folding the newspaper, replacing it on the tray and walking to his writing desk to pen a letter to his mother.

This rite occupied exactly fifteen minutes from the setting down of the invariable "My dear mother," to the signing of his name below the microscopic script. He wrote daily not because he loved his mother, or was even particularly fond of her, but for a reason allied to the Swedish exercises. For Warfield Harrington was painfully conscious of the stiffness, outside and within, that made his movements and thoughts seem mechanical. By flexing his limbs each morning, he might eventually achieve a certain suppleness of movement, and in the same way, by devoting fifteen minutes daily to a human relationship, he might end by limbering up his creaky emotional joints.

Of course it was difficult to write three hundred and sixty-five letters a year to someone whose life differed so utterly from one's own. In the middle of a sentence he would sometimes pause abruptly, aware that what he had just written could not possibly be interesting, or even comprehensible, to an old woman living on the coast of Maine who still thought of Boston as a distant and rather wicked city. Well, small matter. Why shouldn't one write a letter for one's own satisfaction, rather than for the pleasure of the recipient?

He let his glance wander to a snapshot of his mother on his writing desk, and sat for a moment gazing at the haughty mouth, at the cold eyes under the thin brows. It occurred to him to wonder if those glasslike eyes ever had recorded images that did not already exist in their owner's mind. She was a proud woman, he thought—proud as all her race were proud. And the eyes of the proud are unseeing.

His glance moved to the background of the photograph, showing the white colonial building, with the rock-bound coast in the distance, and a field, literally sown with rocks, in the foreground. That was the soil in which lay his own roots, and perhaps he had its very meagerness to thank for his tenacity and his toughness. Where would he have been now without the shrewdness and—he admitted it to himself—the ruthlessness, which went with his New England blood? Why, still in a consular office, no doubt, like old

39

Philpotts, whose sweet nature had earned him the august position of consul general in Santa Rosa after thirty years of service.

That was not the consummation that he, Harrington, had set for his career! He was not a plodder, nor was he an altruist, though he knew how to work hard, and how to be nice to people too— if it advanced him toward his goal. But if it advanced him further to use a knife—well wouldn't he have been a fool not to do so? It was a hard road that he had taken, a road scattered with the bodies of competitors over whom he'd had to tread. But once he'd started on it, he'd never looked back. Eyes front! Forward! He knew that he would be made an ambassador one day.

At eight-thirty to the dot, he drove up in his car before the steps of the Legation. Jesús, the *mozo,* ran out to open the door, on whose surface was painted a white circle enclosing the United States emblem. Harrington gave him a nod, and his quick eye noted that the man again had failed to shave. Well, whether or not he had been with the Legation for twenty years, he would get the sack next time, the Minister decided. And he made that decision as casually and impersonally as he had settled on his choice of necktie.

It was still half an hour before the official opening of the Legation. Harrington always liked to arrive quite early, both so as to check the arrival of his staff and to savor the sensation of authority that he experienced on being alone in the official building. He, Warfield Harrington, once known as the most unpopular boy at school, had eventually risen to this! Through manipulation, through perseverance, and above all through his New England shrewdness, he had attained a position where he issued orders and drove about in a Packard with the United States emblem on the door. Not so bad! No, not bad at all for the young man from Stoneborough, Maine, who had dedicated himself to success for the primary purpose of proving himself to others.

It wasn't yet nine when he heard Baker's light footfalls on the

Legation steps and his superficial good-morning greeting to Jesús. Bright fellow! Harrington thought approvingly. Unless he was mistaken, he would go far in the service. The knowledge that Baker came early with the specific object of making a good impression upon him, flattered and pleased the Minister. In many ways Baker reminded him of himself when he had first started in the service, and it was natural that the young New Yorker had become his favorite among the staff. He knew that one day Baker might very well find himself in a position where he could be useful; Harrington didn't stand to lose anything by stretching him a helping hand.

"Good morning, Baker," he called out as he walked back through the corridor to his office. "How's everything?"

"Pretty fine, thank you, Mr. Minister," answered Baker. And he ran ahead to open Harrington's door.

One by one the rest of the staff arrived—first Señorita Baricala, the typist, then Hermosillo, the Legation clerk, then Ted Kelly, the vice-consul, who stopped on the front steps to exchange a few words with Jesús and was laughing as he came through the door. Harrington, watching from his window, felt his usual disapproval of the red-cheeked young Irishman, who was wearing his straw hat on the back of his head in a jaunty manner altogether unworthy of a diplomat. Now that old Philpotts was away on leave, Kelly was directly responsible to the Minister, and Harrington knew that sooner or later that young fellow would have to be taught a lesson.

At any rate, they were all here now, excepting only John Camberly. Camberly's frequent lateness was a great worry to his punctilious chief, and seeing that the man was First Secretary, the situation was rather ticklish. Harrington knew that the idea was ridiculous, but it sometimes seemed to him that Camberly came late on purpose, simply so as to annoy him! With all the others he could deal without great difficulty, the iron hand of authority ever covered by a velvet gauntlet. It was different with Camberly:

the man had a dignity of his own which Harrington had sensed at their first contact, and to make matters worse, he had an excellent standing in Washington. Still, it was absolutely necessary to do something about his late arrivals.

"Tell Mr. Camberly when he comes that I would like to see him," he said to Baker, who had brought in a paper for his signature.

"Yes, Mr. Minister. Yes sir. If I'm not mistaken, that must be Mr. Camberly now."

A moment later Harrington's door was opened by a tall man in a white drill suit. Though his movements were slow, almost deliberate, there was an alert intelligence in the glance which sought Harrington's evasive eye. His voice was low and pleasant with a trace of a southern drawl.

"You wished to see me, Mr. Harrington?"

"Yes, Camberly. Sit down," said the Minister, indicating a chair. "I wanted to speak to you about a little matter that's been troubling me: the staff are not arriving so promptly as I would like. Have you remarked on it?"

"No, I can't say I have."

"You haven't really? Sitting here at my desk this morning, I noticed that hardly anyone except Baker came on the dot. The others were anywhere from five to fifteen minutes late. One would think that we'd all gone native!" He gave his usual dry chuckle.

Camberly nodded without answering; he didn't even pay the Minister the compliment of smiling. Harrington could feel the Southerner's latent hostility, but he went on in a confidential tone, "Personally I've been coming ahead of time so as to give them a good example, but it doesn't seem to help. What do you suggest that we do about it, Camberly?"

Camberly tugged at his ear lobe in a characteristic gesture. "I haven't the faintest idea, Mr. Harrington."

A hot feeling of irritation assailed the Minister. To be sure, the fellow's answer had been polite enough, but it was the implication in the voice that Harrington disliked—the implication that it was comparatively inconsequential in the momentous year 1943 whether or not a few Legation clerks in a small Central American town arrived before or after the clock struck the hour. Then there was the further implication that instead of bringing up this triviality, Harrington might well have discussed with Camberly any of a number of important matters pending at the moment—for instance, the resurgence of German propaganda in Santa Rosa. Harrington's policy of discussing only details with his subordinates was a subtle way of keeping them in their place and bringing out the fact that in matters of policy and decision he dealt directly with Washington.

"Well," he said, smiling politely, "if you haven't any objection, Camberly, I propose that you say a word to the offenders. I don't want the men to think that I'm after them all the time, and they'd take it better coming from you. Hope you don't mind?"

"Not at all," Camberly said coolly. "But now that I'm here, do you mind if I speak to you about a passport matter? There are some German-Jewish refugees due from Cuba who've applied for visas to the United States."

"Ah, the same old story," said Harrington in a bored voice. "We'll discuss it some other time. Terribly busy this morning, Camberly."

"Excuse me for insisting, Mr. Harrington, but this matter is pretty urgent. I understand that these people are in extreme want, and ought to be admitted to the United States as soon as possible. What's the point of our going through the motions of public sympathy if we never intend to do anything about it when it comes to specific cases?"

"Oh, don't worry, Camberly. Someone will always take care of the Jews," said Harrington.

It gave him a certain satisfaction to note that Camberly's mouth tightened as he turned to go. But as the Minister sat there and reflectively watched the broad shoulders moving toward his door,

43

a fresh wave of animosity toward Camberly swept over him. Here, he thought, was the perfect representative of that new type of Foreign Service officer with whom he had no patience: a man of action without respect for established procedure and formal usage —an individualist who wanted to judge each case on its own merits instead of classifying and pigeonholing it in the usual way. Harrington had met several of that kind lately and, old-school diplomat that he was, he resented the fact that they had broken into what used to be a closed organization. He didn't quite know how to deal with a man like Camberly. Indeed, he found him a most disagreeable type.

That night he sat waiting for Marie-Té in the lobby of the Hotel Imperial, and profoundly regretted his rashness in inviting her. Of course she was late again! He might have known it. He hoped that none of his acquaintances would see him sitting there alone in his dinner jacket, an untasted cocktail before him. Perhaps he oughtn't to have suggested dressing, even though he felt so much more at home in stiff evening clothes than in loose-fitting garb.

Harrington didn't like the lobby of the Imperial anyway, and he regretted that the dearth of suitable quarters had forced him to make his residence in this hotel. It was in the worst possible taste, for one thing, with two conflicting motives vying in the decorations. Modernism was to the fore, but as Santa Rosa was an overnight stop for the Pan-American planes bound for Panama, a dash of local color had been supplied out of deference to the passengers. Examples of local peasant art crammed the ultra-modern showcases, while on the hotel desk reposed a huge basket filled with the outsize fruit extolled in every travel catalogue. How could the gullible tourists guess that fruit at most seasons of the year was by no means plentiful in Santa Rosa? Only old inhabitants of the city like Harrington realized that these luscious grapefruit and outsize oranges were all flown down from Florida and rushed to the hotel from the airport just before the passengers' arrival.

Damn! said Harrington to himself. Oh damn! And he picked up his cocktail, sniffed at it, then put it down again. What an exasperating girl she was! On the point of going off to telephone her pension, he caught the faint scent of mimosa, and glanced up to see Marie-Té standing beside him. She looked more attractive than ever tonight in that blue velvet dress which she had admitted laughingly was her sole evening garment. It suited her molded figure remarkably and was just the right color to set off her light hair. Despite her low *décolletage,* she gave him the same impression of dignity and breeding as the day before when she had walked into his office.

"Heavens! I'm late again. Isn't it dreadful?"

"Only about twenty minutes," said Harrington, rising and drawing out her chair.

"Don't be pompous, my dear. You know that it didn't do you a bit of harm to wait a little. What have you got there? A cocktail? Do order me one."

Harrington clapped his hands for the waiter. "Have a bacardi," he said. "They make them quite decently."

"One wouldn't think so. You haven't even sampled yours."

"Oh, I don't care for cocktails myself. I only ordered it for appearance's sake," explained Harrington.

"As you do most things. Or am I wrong?"

"You seem to go in for psychology, Miss Falkenborn," he answered with his little chuckle. "But I'm not such a bad psychologist myself. If I make a point of being conventional, then it's just as true that you make a point of being unconventional. Last night at Chez Boris you deliberately sat down beside that unshaven tramp so as to shock people!"

"Apparently I succeeded."

"Oh no. You remain a lady whatever you do," said Harrington. "Most of my women friends in the diplomatic corps could envy

45

you: they behave like queens and unfortunately look like cooks."

Marie-Té laughed, and even Harrington gave an appreciative chuckle; he always had enjoyed his own humor more than anybody else's.

"I hope that you are hungry," he remarked when they were seated in the dining room a little later, with the dusky headwaiter who had addressed him as *"Votre Excellence"* hovering in the background.

"I am always hungry, my dear." Marie-Té smiled, disclosing her strong white teeth. "I love eating and drinking and everything nice. Isn't it a pity that you suffer from indigestion?"

"How did you know that?" asked Harrington, surprised.

"Oh, I just felt it."

She burst out laughing, and Harrington found himself laughing along with her. All at once he felt definitely pleased to be sitting here with this attractive girl having dinner.

"Pardon me, *Votre Excellence*," the waiter broke into their conversation, "but if I may make so bold as to suggest"—a dark finger, rimmed with dirt, descended on the menu—"the 'Imperial Ragout' is very nice—and perhaps some diplomat pudding for dessert."

Marie-Té smiled at the waiter in her friendly way, but Harrington's eyebrows lifted in an icy stare.

"Thank you," he remarked dryly. "We will order for ourselves."

After dinner they sat in the bar, Marie-Té with a Scotch and soda, Harrington with a liqueur. He was feeling mellow and on unusually good terms with life; that inner stiffness of which he was constantly aware had melted away in the warmth of conversation. In Marie-Té he had found someone not only young and handsome, but actually clever enough to appreciate his special brand of humor.

"I am," she told him, "almost completely happy at this moment. I have enjoyed an excellent meal; I have laughed and talked

46

a lot; and now, to be quite honest, I am the tiniest bit spiffed. What more could one ask?"

"It's wonderful to see someone who enjoys things so much. You know, you have a real gift for life," Harrington told her.

"I've developed one," she answered. "Nothing like uncertainty about tomorrow to make one appreciate today. You see, I've been supporting myself since I was nineteen years old."

"Have you really? And how?"

"Why, I had a job in a dress shop," she said, and burst out laughing at Harrington's expression; he looked as if he had been stung by a hornet. "Yes, my dear, you have been entertaining a Paris model. Aren't you shocked at yourself?"

"Well, I admit that it is a new experience," said Harrington, forcing a smile. And he thought, What a fool I have been! It just shows how one can be mistaken about these foreigners. But then he looked at her fine profile, with the sensitive lips and aristocratic nose, and he felt puzzled.

"I know just what you are thinking," she said, and laughed again. "You're right: I'm not really a tramp—just a penniless Viennese, like so many others. I didn't actually have to take a job, but it was better than living on a shoestring on my great-aunt Stephanie's estate. And I didn't have to flee from Austria either, but it was better than living under the Nazis. I stayed in Paris almost three years with my kid brother, whom Father sent to join me after Mother's death. When the Germans came, I fled westward again, this time with my uncle, who, fortunately, had a little capital abroad. My story's uninteresting—I'm sure you've heard it a hundred times. Refugees are commoner nowadays than American tourists in the twenties."

"Yes, you're right there," said Harrington a little nervously, for he was afraid that she might begin to talk to him about her visa.

It was a welcome diversion when the door opened to admit a little group who seated themselves at the far end of the bar.

"Why, there's your hostess of last night—old Señora de Castro," remarked Marie-Té. "She must have been handsome once upon a time."

"How cruel youth is!" said Harrington smiling. "Carola de Castro doesn't consider herself old, I assure you—and besides, she is the best-dressed woman in Santa Rosa. She was the queen of the city before your arrival. Will you pardon me a moment, Miss Falkenborn? She's beckoning me."

Harrington made his way over to the other table and said good evening to Señora de Castro and her fat little husband, who was Minister of Portugal. He bowed to the other people.

"My friend," said Señora de Castro plucking at Harrington's sleeve in a semi-intimate, semi-formal way as she fixed him with her beautiful soulless eyes, "I want to ask you a great favor. You must lend me your wonderful servant Ah Sing for my party next Tuesday night. I want to put him in charge of the drinks. At my last party, you'll recall, all our servants became dead drunk and put us to shame."

"Oh you can have him, with pleasure," said Harrington, nothing in his voice betraying the fact that he had seen through that feeble ruse and knew that Carola de Castro was eaten up with jealousy. For Marie-Té had been right in surmising that the Portuguese lady was not without interest in Harrington. De Castro was old, and he suffered from heart attacks. Who in Santa Rosa would have made a more suitable successor than the bachelor Minister of the United States?

"Well, that's all settled then; Ah Sing will mix our drinks." Señora de Castro flashed Harrington one of those half-intimate smiles which she had been perfecting for almost thirty years. Instantly it faded away and her face resumed its usual masklike expression. "Who is the young lady?" she asked in a flat voice, raising her lorgnette and submitting Marie-Té to a quick but piercing survey.

48

"An Austrian girl who has just arrived in Santa Rosa," Harrington explained.

"A refugee no doubt?" said Señora de Castro wrinkling her nose a little.

"More or less." Harrington passed over this point lightly. "I was thinking of asking you if I might bring her to your party."

Harrington saw a fleeting look of annoyance in the Portuguese lady's face, but not for nothing had she been a diplomat's wife for twenty years; she replied almost enthusiastically, "Delighted. Delighted, my friend. Anyone you vouch for is welcome in my house."

"Yes, do bring her by all means," put in old De Castro, adjusting his monocle to get a better look at Marie-Té. "A delightful creature—so fresh, so insouciant! She is like Vienna itself. Ah *Weiner Wald*! Ah *Grünzing*! Ah Vienna!" He lapsed into platitudes.

"*Taisez-vous, mon cher*," said Señora de Castro dryly. "You are boring us."

Harrington took his leave, pleased that his judgment of Marie-Té had received confirmation; nothing could have testified so eloquently to Marie-Té's attractiveness as Carola de Castro's jealous attitude.

The rest of that evening he was riding on the crest of the wave. He joked and recounted anecdotes in his best manner, and it seemed that her very presence sharpened the rapier of his wit. As he drove Marie-Té to her pension and dropped her at the door, this sensation of satisfaction was still with him. At the next corner he rapped on the window and had the chauffeur wait until he saw a light flash on in one of the first-floor windows. So that was where she lived! At this moment she would be stepping out of the blue velvet dress and reaching for her nightgown. He imagined her standing there naked, seeing before him her long slender body with the narrow waist and the high full breasts. Yes, he told himself, she was certainly an attractive woman. Even he, with

49

whom sexual desires were so well controlled as to have almost disappeared, was keenly conscious of her female charm.

It wasn't until he had driven back to the Hotel Imperial that something happened to mar what would have been a perfect evening. As he stepped across the sidewalk and was about to open the front door, he grew conscious of a pair of eyes upon him. Turning his head, he caught sight across the street of a little, shabbily-dressed man whose appearance was distinctly familiar. He gazed at him a moment before the recognition came. Why, it was the same "unshaven tramp" at whose table Marie-Té had seated herself in the night club Chez Boris!

Very unpleasant, Harrington found it, to be watched by this disreputable creature, on whose face, illuminated in the glare of a street lamp, lay an unmistakable look of hatred. What did it mean? Why should his sensation of well-being have to be disturbed tonight? With an angry step the Minister passed through the open door, closing it behind him to shut out of his well-ordered existence everything that failed to benefit himself. When he looked out of his sitting room window a moment later, he saw the little man's figure receding down the street. He was walking rapidly with arms folded on chest and his glance wandered neither to right nor left.

Chapter IV
Love in Santa Rosa

KERJANIAN OCCUPIED A ROOM IN ONE OF THE poorer parts of Santa Rosa, behind the market place. When he awoke, just after dawn, the square would already be astir, with Indians from the countryside arriving on their burros, sacks of carrots or bunches of gaudy flowers dangling from the saddle-bows. Even at that hour discussions and bickerings could be heard and, strangest of all at five in the morning, brilliant laughter. As difficult would it have been to go to sleep again as to convince these fantastic people that this was no hour to do business. Day and night they would doze, accomplishing no more than a grass-hopper, then put on a great burst of activity at dawn.

And so Kerjanian's new day of suffering had begun. Terrified of the stale thoughts that came swarming back with regularity each morning, he would attempt in vain to fix his attention on one or another object, as a drowning man might seek to grasp a log. He studied the crude unpainted dresser, and counted for the hundredth time the parallel veins delineated in the woodwork. Then he switched his glance to the ceiling, trying to decide whether the coffee-colored blotch upon the plaster looked more like an elephant reaching out his trunk or a picture in one of his childhood schoolbooks of Don Quixote tilting with the windmill. But sooner or later these efforts broke down; he felt despair stealing over him again, like the effect of a powerful narcotic.

What was he doing here? Why was he being detained in this outlandish spot in the midst of Indians, filth and sloth? Why did

Warfield Harrington stop him from traveling to North America? These and a host of similar questions presented themselves in a rush, overwhelming Kerjanian with their urgency. He lay as if chained to the rickety bedstead while the din of the market place grew ever louder outside his window.

And behind all his suffering and all his loneliness was an agonizing feeling of homesickness for a country that he had never had—a country that he had lost before he was old enough to know its meaning. For a quarter of a century now he had been a refugee, yet that feeling of homesickness was still with him. Sometimes as he lay there a sound would come to his ears, or a smell to his nostrils, and his mind would fly back to his earliest childhood in the Turkish city south of the Caucasus. He would see before him the village street, the bazaar at one end, the church at the other, and in between the row of trim, brightly painted Armenian houses; he would see the interior of his parents' home, with the big carpet on the wall and the crossed scimitars underneath it.

Yet never once had he been sure that the sound or smell which sent his thoughts winging back really had been sensed for the first time in the village of his birth. Might he not have known it in Aleppo many years later on? Or perhaps in the port of Baku on the Caspian Sea? It was difficult to say. He had been an exile too long; he had lost track of his own background. Oh lucky refugee, he thought, who could weep on remembering the noise of pattering rain on some special roof once loved! Oh happy refugee whose heart contracted at the sound of a voice in his own dear language! He, Kerjanian, had no beloved voice to remember, only the dry voices of various consular officials saying, "Come back tomorrow . . . write for an appointment." A medley of stilted official phrases, all meaning exactly the same thing: that he was not wanted.

Yes, he was not wanted—he was not wanted anywhere! Perhaps he would have given up his search for happiness long ago if it hadn't been for that brother of his in Brooklyn, near New York, who had found for himself what Kerjanian so desperately sought. The United States of America was the one spot where the homeless were welcomed, where the foot-weary were given rest! Every one of his brother's letters written from the carpet shop in Brooklyn reposed in Kerjanian's little tin trunk. He knew by heart passages in which his brother extolled the merits of his adopted land, and especially of his adopted city, Brooklyn.

Brooklyn, beautiful Brooklyn, thought Kerjanian, finding pleasure in pronouncing the name aloud—399 Liberty Street, Brooklyn, he repeated, smiling to himself. To think that his brother's address might one day become his own! What joy it would be to say to yourself, when you were out in town in the evening, "I am going home to 399 Liberty Street, Brooklyn." Then later, when you inserted your key in the lock, clean, fresh smells would come toward you, together with the laughter of children, who had learned to laugh loudly and gaily because they had always lived in this street called Liberty.

Weak and undernourished as Kerjanian was, the tears used to rise to his eyes. He wiped them against the pillow. Oh, he knew that all these daydreams might never be realized, that after tramping and tramping for years, America was not much nearer than before. There had been times in the past, too, when it had seemed that he would get there, and at the last minute something had always intervened. Once his brother had been unable to send the passage money; another time, in Marseille, he had been detained because his papers were not in order. And here in Santa Rosa, Warfield Harrington, enemy of the defenseless, representative of the mighty, had appeared upon the scene. Kerjanian could be sure that he would follow the usual procedure of procrastinating and of turning an official blind eye on every form of human suffering.

Harrington! Harrington! The name hammered in Kerjanian's ears as he lay in bed in the sordid room above the market. By now it had become associated in his mind with the host of people who had insulted or foiled him in the past: with the official in Marseille who had refused him a French passport and the haughty Pole at Chez Boris who had declined a duel and the purser on the boat in the Black Sea who had forbidden him the first-class deck. All these people might have been called Harrington, for all possessed the same arrogant expression borne by "the false American." They were his enemies and the enemies of mankind, finding their greatest joy in the humiliation of their brothers. He hated them with a hot implacable hatred.

The morning after his visit to Chez Boris, Kerjanian experienced an even greater despondency, an even sharper sense of desperation, than usual. He felt like a salt-water crustacean which after the recession of the tide has been left stranded high and dry on a foreign element. The knowledge that even in the year 1943 there were people with well-pressed, spotless clothes who drank wine and who laughed, caused his own scrappy meals, his own shabby wardrobe, to seem especially repugnant. As he put on his shirt, his socks, his one and only suit, he experienced for the garments such a distaste that it cost him a real effort to touch them with his hands. How long before he could replace that shiny blue jacket with patches on the elbows? Or invest in some pretty flowered handkerchiefs? To judge from present indications he would still be wearing these garments when they put him in the grave; they were like an additional layer of skin, to be rid of only through the decomposition of the body.

Not until he reached for his necktie did a glimmer of satisfaction come into the Armenian's eyes. That handsome red cravat was his badge as a man of taste, a man who appreciated (though he had never owned) the beautiful things of life. Yes, the purchase of that necktie had been a success—if truth be known, one of the most successful and definite actions that he had accomplished in years. When he looked at himself in the mirror, it seemed to him that it almost compensated for his otherwise disastrous appearance:

for the cheap shirt and the unshaven cheeks and the fingernails which he knew to be dirty without caring sufficiently to clean. Pride in his appearance was a thing of the past, and Kerjanian knew that that was just what the Harringtons of the world wanted. They treated you as if you were dirty and slovenly and low—and in the end you came to believe that they were right. Thus they managed to widen the breach between themselves and you. Oh, how clever they were, those slick politicians and diplomats, who ever had governed, and ever would govern the world!

Out on the street the day's heat struck him like a blast from a steam furnace. The crowd on the market place was already dispersing, everyone seeking shelter from those murderous rays. The old women cowering behind their stalls looked as desiccated as their own fruit and vegetables. A crateful of turkeys left standing in the blistering sun had their beaks open, gasping for air. But it occurred to no one to move the crate into the shade.

Kerjanian in his pale-blue suit and black town hat felt just like one of those turkeys. As soon would he have gone about without his jacket as to switch to a sombrero, for though he had sunk far, he was determined to maintain his position before the natives. With dignity he walked about the market place, avoiding the piles of refuse which had collected by the stalls and in which rats and vultures were picking. From the cheapest wares he selected here a few vegetables, there a piece of meat or a fish—foods which he later would carry home to cook on a spirit stove. Everything about this market place and about the town disgusted him; he saw only squalor, filth and ugliness and had one thought alone; that because of Warfield Harrington he was being detained here, unjustly and against his will. How could he escape? How much longer must he endure this? The wearisome old questions recurred to him as he walked about beneath the beating sun, head down and dazed with misery.

Now he was bending over a basket of mango fruit, haggling in his wretched Spanish with the vendor. About to produce his pocketbook to pay for his purchase, Kerjanian heard close beside him a

55

little boy's gay laughter. Free and golden it was, like the very spirit of gaiety. And it was like a song at the same time, rising and falling in cadence.

Kerjanian glanced over his shoulder and saw the laughing boy standing beside a stall. He was perhaps eight, dressed in leather shorts and sandals and wearing a huge sombrero. On the sombrero in colored crayons was drawn a red cow jumping over a train. Beneath his hat the child's hair fell softly, honey-colored and wavy.

The Armenian stood and stared at him. He thought that never in his life had he seen a creature so utterly delightful; among the dark-hued natives this beautiful blond child seemed more like an apparition than a flesh and blood human being. There he stood, bright red lips curling in laughter, legs spread, hands sunk deep in the pockets of his leather shorts: a flash of sheer beauty among the refuse piles.

Now the old woman at her stall was polishing the reddest apple and handing it to the boy. He reached out for it and sank his teeth in the tender pulp, still giggling, every inch of his lithe body exuding gaiety and animal spirits. Kerjanian had an imperative desire to go up and address the lad, but shyness forbade him. Instead he simply stood there watching while the boy finished his apple and with a gesture that had in it the grace of a ballet artist, flung the core far away.

Suddenly he turned and went skipping off between the stalls, his sturdy legs moving freely and lightly beneath the leather. Kerjanian, forgetting about his mangoes, followed. For some reason it seemed to him tremendously important not to let this happy boy out of his sight, and once when a peasant's cart got between them, he broke into a run. He kept some distance behind, and whenever the boy stopped, he stopped also. Any idea of speaking to him he had now abandoned; he wanted only to keep looking at the child and to listen to his laughter.

They left the market place and entered the lower stretch of Calle de la Independencia, Santa Rosa's main street. Here the traffic was

56

fairly heavy, occasional automobiles mingling with the bullock carts and pack donkeys. There were no sidewalks, and Kerjanian watched nervously as the boy made his way along the unpaved road. But he managed very well. Walking along without seeming to pay much attention, he would neatly sidestep the oncoming vehicles, his every movement controlled with exquisite grace. Presently Kerjanian stopped worrying about him; this boy, who moved with the ease and alertness of a wild animal, could take care of himself.

He was whistling a tune between his teeth, a lilting melody which Kerjanian had heard before. His mind went back to that night at Chez Boris when the big blond man had stepped onto the dais and taken the bandmaster's violin. Yes, that was one of the tunes he'd played, while singing in a soft voice which did not at all go with his heavy body, *"Wien, Wien, nur du allein . . . sollst stets die Stadt meiner Träume sein."* Kerjanian had never heard the pretty tune before that night, and it seemed to him somehow right that this gay little boy should be whistling it today. He knew that henceforth, whenever and wherever he might hear it, he would experience for the fraction of a moment a sensation of undiluted pleasure.

During the week that followed, Kerjanian's life underwent a change. He still spent the long mornings lying on his bed, torn between futile speculations and equally vain regrets; his days were still poisoned by memories of past griefs and past humiliations. But now, in contrast to before, there was a glimmer in the darkness; at any moment the picture of a laughing boy would flash into his mind, and he would feel a lightness of limb, an unwonted quickening of spirit. Abruptly Kerjanian would realize that he was smiling. A little embarrassed before himself, he would pass the back of his hand awkwardly across his lips, and it would seem to him at such moments that his own skin felt softer, more youthful to the touch.

57

Then one afternoon he saw the boy again. He had gone to the bank to ask for mail—a daily formality, nowadays, as he was expecting the arrival of an important letter. They had told him at the American consulate that to get his visa he must first obtain two so-called affidavits of support. Indeed, that was one reason he had been so anxious to see the American Minister in person, this matter being extremely complicated. It seemed that it did not suffice to be vouched for by two American citizens in good standing; each of these had in turn to find other citizens to vouch for him, and the second group of vouchers probably had to be vouched for by a third. The maze of regulations had grown so prodigiously complicated as to be nothing short of ludicrous!

No wonder that Kerjanian was nervously awaiting the arrival of these all-important affidavits, which his brother in Brooklyn had promised to submit; no wonder that he had learned to know the face of the bank employee in charge of clients' correspondence. A supercilious little fellow, he looked like a weasel. Today as soon as he caught sight of Kerjanian, he began to shake his head.

"*Nada!* Nothing!" he exclaimed, evidently delighted to be able to convey bad news.

"Please look through the letters," said Kerjanian coldly. "I am expecting one of great importance."

The weasel skimmed through the meager pile of unclaimed correspondence and flung them back on the rack.

"*Nada! Nada! Nada!*"

Kerjanian began to grow annoyed. He didn't trust this little fellow—never had. How did he know that he wasn't keeping his brother's letter away from him out of spite, or maybe for an even more sinister reason? Perhaps he wanted to go to America himself and could make good use of those famous "affidavits of support." Kerjanian didn't know—he couldn't be quite sure. But one thing certain was that the man despised Kerjanian, considering him a refugee who could be treated in any way one chose. As always, it would be wisest to go directly to the top.

58

"I wish," he said, putting on an air of dignity and glaring at the clerk from across the counter, "I wish to see the manager."

"The manager?"

"Yes, the manager, the manager! Don't you understand your own language?" he asked in his atrocious Spanish. "Tell him that it is Mr. Kerjanian—Mr. Nestor Kerjanian." He searched through his pocket for his one and only calling card and handed it to the employee. "That is my card. Please don't forget to bring it back to me."

The fellow looked at Kerjanian curiously and disappeared with the card. A few moments later he came back, accompanied by a heavy-boned, dark-skinned man whom Kerjanian had not seen before.

"Are you the manager?" the Armenian asked, switching to French, both to make an effect and because his Spanish was so meager.

"The manager is busy," the heavy-set man answered in Spanish. "I am the assistant manager. What do you want?"

"Your man here says that there are no letters for me," Kerjanian explained. "But I think there are. Every time I come here, he keeps telling me, *nada, nada*. That seems to be the one word he knows."

The assistant manager exchanged a few sentences with the clerk, then turned back to Kerjanian.

"There are no letters for you! There hasn't been a letter for weeks. Please don't bother us! This is a bank, not a post office."

"I always do my business here," cried Kerjanian indignantly. "I shall leave you after this. I shall go to your competitor."

"By all means," said the manager scathingly. "In the last two months you have done no more than exchange a few five dollar bills and come to pester us about your mail. If this bank can't get on without your business, then it's high time for it to fold up voluntarily."

In a fury Kerjanian snapped up his irreplaceable calling card, which fortunately was lying on the counter, and turned his back

59

on the assistant manager. He put one hand in his pocket with would-be nonchalance and stood there glowering, not knowing what to do next, nor how to save his honor without taking the drastic step of severing relations with the bank. A delightful scent of mimosa reached his nostrils. As Kerjanian sniffed it in, trying to remember where he had known it before, he felt a light touch on his sleeve, and there was the Austrian girl who had sat at his table at the night club Chez Boris!

"Oh hello, Mr. Kerjanian," she said, and she gave him a quick smile before turning about to speak to the official. "All we foreigners seem to be in the same boat, don't we, Señor Alvarez?" she said in an assured, almost condescending manner, which Kerjanian felt instinctively had been put on for the occasion. "We're always waiting for letters which refuse to arrive. *Nada! Nada!*" She flung out her empty hands in a symbolic gesture, "But you'll be sure to look after my friend, Mr. Kerjanian, won't you? I know that he's expecting some very important correspondence from the States."

Kerjanian stood there flabbergasted, assailed by conflicting emotions of embarrassment and gratitude. How perceptive this girl must be, to have instantly grasped his situation! And how generous to have put on an act that would incline his enemies in his favor! Both the weasel and his superior were bowing and scraping as she took his arm to walk away, and the Armenian noticed to his amazement that they were bowing to him too, if in a somewhat puzzled manner.

By the glass door leading to the street the Austrian girl halted. "Oh dear!" she said to Kerjanian with a laugh. "What fools people are! There's nothing they enjoy like treating others badly, but if you just scare them or impress them the least bit, they'll begin to cringe. You must forgive me for butting in like that, Mr. Kerjanian."

The Armenian was seeking about for words to convey his gratitude, when he saw through the door a little boy skipping down the street, a pear-shaped toy balloon floating above him. Even before catching a glimpse of the fresh young face under the sombrero, Kerjanian had recognized the lad from the market place. Who else in Santa Rosa, who else in the whole world, possessed such grace of movement? The beautiful balloon bobbing at the end of its string was like a symbol of the boy's own gaiety and lightness. His eyes were fixed on it with a radiant look as he skipped along, utterly oblivious to all else.

Kerjanian, behind the bank's glass door, stood watching him spellbound, and as he watched, a smile softened the bitter line of his mouth. All at once he imagined himself back in a gallery of the Louvre that he used to visit during his brief stay in Paris. A classical statue of two children had been Kerjanian's favorite work of art, and sometimes he would stand before it for ten or fifteen minutes at a time, loving the lithe lines, the graceful postures. Those marble children had given Kerjanian the same esthetic impersonal enjoyment that he experienced today.

But suddenly a terrified little cry escaped him; his body went rigid. In the street outside a heavy motor truck was bearing down upon the skipping boy, whose whole attention lay concentrated on the balloon. Instinctively Kerjanian reached his hand out for the door, though realizing at the same time that it was too late to intervene. For already the speeding truck was clattering over the very spot where the lad had stood. In anguish Kerjanian flung open the door and rushed out of the bank—to see the blond boy standing beside the road, miraculously unscathed! Only now the balloon was no longer in his hand. With a surprised, whimsical expression, he was watching it drift up slowly into the sky.

Kerjanian leaned against the bank building, weak from the shock; his whole body was shaking. The boy turned his head and looked in his direction, then came running across the street toward the Austrian girl standing behind Kerjanian.

"Oh Marie-Té," he said, addressing her, "I've lost my beautiful balloon! It got knocked right out of my hand."

Kerjanian saw that the girl's face had gone dead-white, but

when she spoke, her voice sounded as calm, as pleasant, as ever. "That's too bad, Bubi dear," she said. "I'm sorry."

"I'm sorry too," the boy answered. "But not terribly sorry. The balloon is happy to be free. Look at it way up there, Marie-Té!" He pointed at the pear-shaped object tossing in the sky, its iridescent surface glittering in the strong sunlight.

"Is it happy, Bubi? How do you know?"

"Oh, I just know."

"Ah yes, you always just know, Bubi. And I think that somehow you are always right."

The three of them stood looking at the airy bubble that was floating away so blithely, and on each upturned face, kissed by the strong sun, lay an expression of longing. Mere humans, bound inevitably to the earth, they envied the absolute freedom possessed by that little toy balloon. And their longing for a state of happiness unrealizable as long as man's spirit is imprisoned in his body, seemed to Kerjanian to link them all together. At that moment Kerjanian realized that he was happier than he had been for months—happier than he had been for years. Yes, happier than he had ever been before!

It was all like a dream—a dream which could not last. As the balloon floated out of sight, and the boy with a laugh reached for the girl's hand, Kerjanian was flung back into reality. So this lad, who had seemed as impersonal an object as that marble statue in the Louvre, had human ties like everybody else! It was for Kerjanian a painful revelation.

"Is that—your son?" he asked, fixing the young woman with his brilliant eyes.

"My son? Oh no!" She laughed. "He's my brother."

Relieved, the Armenian gave a little smile. So she was only a sister! That was much better. For the first time at such close distance he allowed his glance to travel to the boy's face, but he withdrew it quickly. How beautiful he was! Kerjanian did not trust himself to look into that face, any more than he would have looked into the face of the sun. He remembered suddenly that his shirt was dirty and that he had not shaved for over a week.

"I'm afraid I must be going," he declared uncertainly.

"Must you really? Well, I hope we'll meet again," said the girl, studying him with her clever eyes. "I suspected that you had left Santa Rosa, Mr. Kerjanian."

"Left Santa Rosa? Oh no."

"You are still waiting for your visa?"

"Yes, waiting—always waiting," said Kerjanian, his old grievance flaring up. "They began by telling me that I had to have a letter from some relative in America. Very well, I got that. Now they talk to me about 'affidavits of support,' whatever that means. One of these days my patience will come to an end, and then I will *force* Harrington to give me my visa!"

"Well, a lot of people are in the same boat—that's some consolation. We wouldn't be here either if Santa Rosa weren't the jumping-off spot for the United States. Would we, *Bübchen*?"

There was something about the way she addressed the boy that made Kerjanian acutely aware of the great intimacy between them. It was obvious in her every word, as well as in the quick glance that passed between them. And in the meanwhile he had to stand here, occupying the ignominious position of an outsider—that position that he seemed fated to occupy, whether in relation to countries or to human beings! The mark of the refugee was on him; he would never be free of it in this life. Suddenly Kerjanian was overcome by one of those spasms of self-pity which always caused him to act rudely and aggressively.

"I'm busy," he muttered, deliberately turning about and walking back into the bank. "I'm sorry, I have business to attend to."

"Come and visit us at Pension Hilda," the girl called after him, but Kerjanian gave no sign of having heard. Not till a good moment had gone by did he venture out into the street again. Some distance off he espied them, hands clasped, legs moving in rhythm. Oh, you had only to watch those two together to realize what friends they were, had only to see how the boy looked up at her to understand what she meant to him! An agonizing feeling of loneliness and frustration seized Kerjanian.

Keeping in the shadow of the buildings, he began to follow them, eyes fastened on the boy, studying his every movement. Heedless of direction, he hurried on, bumping into blind beggars and tripping over Indians lying sleeping on the sidewalk. A cart almost ran him down, the driver cursing and cracking his whip as he went past. Kerjanian paid him no attention.

Into a brick building on a side street the boy disappeared, and for a long time Kerjanian stood across the way, hidden beside a slender acacia tree. Looking up at the row of windows, he tried to guess behind which one the boy was living. What was he doing at that moment—laughing, having his supper, playing a game? Where had he put his sombrero with the drawing of the red cow jumping over a train?

Darkness crept into the street, and one by one the lights in the brick building were switched on. Still Kerjanian stood there without moving. The southern moon rode into the sky, causing the shadow of the acacia to fall across the pitted roadway. Kerjanian's own pale shadow lay beside it. His eyes peered longingly at those lights as if they stood for all the love and beauty in the world that must remain unattainable forever.

Chapter V
Crocodiles

THE NIGHT OF THE DANCE AT THE PORTUGUESE
Legation, Harrington stopped by at Pension Hilda to call for Marie-
Té. The moment he saw her tall figure coming down the stairs, all
his doubts about having invited her were dissipated. She had done
something to herself—Harrington could not decide just what—and
she looked not only beautiful but extraordinarily elegant. Now if he
only could persuade her to behave herself tonight!

"It's going to be quite a formal party," he hinted in the car.
"You know what these diplomats are like, Marie-Té: very stuffy—
very conventional."

She glanced up at him mischievously and burst out laughing.
"All right, my dear. You needn't coach me. I understand."

"I wasn't coaching you," Harrington hastened to assure her.
"Only you can't imagine what a lot of gossiping old women there
are in this little town."

"Oh yes I can, Harrington—after knowing you."

The Portuguese Legation bordered on a tree-decked avenue on
the outskirts of the city. Here all the legations and consulates clus-
tered together, as if to gain a little comfort from each other's respectability. There was an upper-class atmosphere about this little
district which seemed utterly misplaced in an Indian town lying
segregated from the outer world in the hollow of an extinct vol-
cano. The national coats of arms upon the white stone houses were
like insignia of gentility, and no wonder that many a wealthy Santa
Rosan had been ready to pay for the privilege of an honorary con-

sulship. Thanks to this custom the size of the buildings bore little relation to the importance of the country represented: the massive structure of the Vice-Consulate of San Marino dwarfed the adjoining British mission, while the Consular Agency of Liberia towered above the German Legation—boarded up and deserted since the severance of diplomatic relations with the Axis.

As Harrington's car drew up before a brightly lighted house, there reached them a plaintive cry, as of a child in pain. Harrington smiled at Marie-Té's startled expression.

"Only one of the pumas in the town zoo," he explained. "They saw fit to put the gardens directly behind the legations—perhaps with the idea that foreigners and wild beasts would get on fairly well together. It's a little disturbing in these spring nights when the animals are restive."

But now the gay, rippling music of a marimba orchestra came to their ears. Just outside the Legation gates a large group of people had congregated and were happily listening to the music. Indians lay like gaily colored bundles in the grassy strip beside the road, while others had climbed into the trees to get a look at the festivities through the windows. Even on top of the iron gate hung a little native boy with a tattered shirt and a big frayed sombrero. As the porter swung open the gate for the new arrivals, the lad clung there precariously, his spiderlike legs wound around the iron grillwork for support.

"It's a scandal!" Harrington muttered in annoyance. "Every time there's a party in this town, the whole population gathers outside as if it were being given for them. You ought to tell that rascal to climb down from the gate, Porter. We didn't come here to see a trapeze performance."

The porter's dusky face lit up in a smile; with shining eyes he gazed up at the trespasser. "But, Señor, he likes to listen to the music—the beautiful music," he explained. "That boy is a fine singer himself. A real artist, you might say."

66

Marie-Té, looking up, recognized the little boy who had sung "The Star-Spangled Banner" the night that she walked home from Chez Boris with Siegfried Stumpf. "Hello, Paco!" she called up to him, but so absorbed was he in the music that he did not hear her. Disapprovingly, Harrington took her arm and hurried her into the house, where they found Lopez's jazz band trying to drown out the rippling music of the marimba orchestra in the garden.

An elegant party for Santa Rosa, thought Marie-Té as she glanced about the room. The men guests were wearing decorations ranging all the way from foreign orders to bronze medals issued for the benefit of the local fire brigade. Rushing about with trays of drinks was a cohort of liveried servants, while in a corner, behind an improvised bar, stood Harrington's Chinese boy, Ah Sing, who had been lent Señora de Castro for the occasion. The hostess herself had on a gold lamé dress which would have looked well on a debutante; her bosom was sensationally displayed.

"How nice of Harrington to bring you," she said, smiling insincerely at Marie-Té.

"Will you give me the great pleasure?" Old De Castro came hurrying up, screwing his monocle tighter in his eye. He put his arm around Marie-Té's waist and went dancing off with her, bouncing over the floor like a rubber ball.

"Now tell me where you found her," said Señora de Castro to Harrington, peering after the couple through her lorgnette. "Quite attractive! But then *all* Austrians are attractive, aren't they?"

"She is just passing through Santa Rosa. A young girl of excellent family," said Harrington, who had caught the *sous-entendu* in that last remark.

"Yes, no doubt, no doubt. Still, my friend, that's no reason to keep staring after her as you are doing. Manuel is harmless, you know. He couldn't seduce an attractive female chimpanzee, much less your blonde beauty."

Harrington gave one of his little nasal chuckles. So Carola de Castro really was jealous of him! Drawing his eyes away from

Marie-Té, bouncing blithely about the floor in the arms of the old diplomat, he turned on his charm.

"Do let us sit down for a few moments and have one of our nice chats," he suggested. "It is a week since I have seen you and, to tell the truth, I am dying to hear a little scandal."

They were still sitting in a corner twittering away when De Castro brought back Marie-Té from their dance. The old fellow looked ten years younger and he was tossing his monocle in his palm in a gay, devil-may-care manner.

"Ah, she dances divinely—divinely," he exclaimed. "I almost imagined that I was a young man again waltzing in a ballroom in Vienna . . ."

"Sit down, Manuel," said his wife dryly. "You are *not* a young man and you have a bad heart, as you should remember." She raised her lorgnette to study Marie-Té at close range. "What a charming dress! The same that you were wearing the other night, I believe, and also the first time I saw you, at Chez Boris."

"Quite right," said Marie-Té. "It's my *only* dress."

"One only needs one dress when one wears it as you do, dear lady," De Castro came gallantly to the rescue.

"Yes, I do wear clothes well," Marie-Té admitted blandly. "After all, I've had practice: I was a dress model for years."

An embarrassing silence followed this remark. Overwhelmed with mortification, Harrington tried in vain to force a smile. Oh why had he ever committed the indiscretion of bringing this shameless creature to the party? To make matters worse, who should turn up at that moment but the obnoxious John Camberly, his First Secretary. Simply so as to stop her from committing any more *faux pas,* Harrington asked Marie-Té to dance.

"Why are you so silent?" she asked him after they had been circling about for a moment. "You're not being nearly as amusing as usual, my dear. You are angry with me!"

"Certainly not. If you want to go out of your way to shock people, that's your own affair."

68

"Now you are being pompous again," said Marie-Té, laughing. "Anyway, it would take a better person than I to shock that aging siren."

Harrington looked about quickly. "Do at least talk in a low voice," he entreated her. "Please remember that the De Castros are one of the most distinguished families in all Europe."

"What!" Marie-Té shouted the word so loudly that Harrington danced her off quickly into a deserted corner. "Oh, Harrington, really you are too naïve! Allow me to tell you that the De Castros were still standing beside their casks bottling wine in Oporto when the Falkenborns were ruling princes. It's a little grotesque to think of a Baroness Falkenborn making up to a wine merchant's wife."

That was the first that the Minister had heard that Marie-Té possessed a title, and in one second his whole opinion of her changed. Incredible that she had hidden such a fact, while boasting openly of having been a dress model! He decided to convey the news to Carola de Castro at the first opportunity.

"Yes, she's very eccentric, as I say," he found himself telling the hostess a little later. "For instance, just think of her having been a model! A strange occupation for a Baroness Falkenborn."

At his mention of that word "Baroness," it seemed to Harrington that a transformation took place in Señora de Castro. She lost her debonair, confident manner, and a harried expression came into her eyes; her neckline sagged; she looked suddenly what she was: an aging woman with the grimmest of futures before her. Now that this rival had appeared upon the scene, she would never become the wife of an American diplomat! Perhaps, thought Harrington, she saw with her mind's eye the little villa outside Lisbon where she would retire upon De Castro's death—dull, dull beyond imagining. Outside her window, down the red earth road, the lumbering oxcarts would go creaking past the olive trees, and the only relief from the monotony would be an occasional letter from some other diplomat's wife whom she had known out in the wide world.

She cast a quick look about the ballroom, as though to take stock of what she would be leaving behind her forever.

"Well, I agree that she is eccentric," she answered finally with a little falsetto laugh. "I suppose that her eccentricity even has a certain attraction. In any case, you're not the only man to have been captured by this strange—er—baroness. Look at that morose compatriot of yours, Mr. Camberly." She pointed her lorgnette. "This is the first time I've seen him take to the dance floor."

Harrington scowled as his glance moved in the direction indicated. He hadn't even known hitherto that the man could dance—much less that he could cause someone to want to squeeze up as close to him as Marie-Té was doing at that moment. It wasn't for this that he had brought her to the party!

"Well, what do you think of our friend Camberly?" he asked Marie-Té a little later as they sat together smoking. "On the quiet side, isn't he?"

"Quiet? Yes, I suppose so. But intelligent."

"Oh, Camberly's a good enough First Secretary," said Harrington patronizingly.

"You don't like him, my dear, do you?"

"What on earth put that idea into your head?" asked Harrington, alarmed. "Though, to be sure, there are more amusing people than Camberly for you to dance with. You've made a tremendous success, Marie-Té. Everyone is talking about the beautiful Austrian girl."

As if to give point to his remark, Moffat, the British Chargé d'Affaires now came up to ask to be introduced.

"I say, what luck for Santa Rosa—having you here," he drawled, smoothing his mustaches and acting as if he were taking off the typical Englishman. "Care to have a little fling?"

Marie-Té jumped up and went twirling off with Moffat, as gay and vivacious as ever. She gave Harrington a good-by wink over her partner's shoulder, and as he smiled back at her, he decided that he had made no mistake about Baroness Maria-Theresa Falkenborn after all. Everybody seemed delighted with her, exception of course made for Señora de Castro. Harrington chuckled to himself. He was riding on the crest of the wave.

But later that evening a reaction set in. It began when he lost sight of Marie-Té and wandered about pretending to be looking for no one at all. By coincidence, the wind changed just then, bringing from the zoo that faint odor of wild animals with which he had grown familiar in Santa Rosa. Somehow it always managed to depress him, reminding him as it did that he was accredited to an out-of-the-way Central American town rather than to one of the large world capitals.

Not till he looked for the second time into the garden, where the marimba band was hammering away, did he catch sight of Marie-Té's lithe figure on a stone bench by the poinsettia bushes. With a little shock he saw that she was seated next to Camberly, and with a second shock saw that it was Camberly, the silent, who was doing the talking, while the chatterer, Marie-Té, was listening intently.

Harrington stepped back quickly into the house. He glanced about him. No, fortunately he had not been observed, and he tried to look as nonchalant as possible as he sauntered back into the sitting room. Yet from one moment to another the party had gone sour for him. Now it seemed to him that the scent of wild animal was growing stronger, and on the wind blowing from the zoo was carried the melancholy roaring of the captive puma lions. He could hear it right over the loud jazz music. Through the ballroom windows he caught sight of the ragged Indian boys clinging to the branches of the trees and staring in.

Ah, there was no point in pretending to himself any longer that this was an elegant diplomatic ball! It was only a dull little party held on the peak of a desolate plateau in a remote region of the globe. Surrounding this city in every direction were bleak, hideous mountains stretching out toward the steaming jungle strips that gave on the two oceans. And beyond that was water—nothing but

71

flat blue water which few ships traversed in this year 1943. Everything suddenly seemed to him dreary beyond words, and he realized that the gilt was wearing off the chandeliers and that Lopez's orchestra was playing out of tune and that most of the women had on dowdy dresses copied by Santa Rosan dressmakers from Paris models dated years before the war.

That was the way it had always been in Harrington's life. For a while he'd been able to keep up an illusion, but sooner or later the stark truth had struck him like a bucketful of cold water. Back in Stoneborough, for instance, he used to persuade himself that he was a New England bluestocking, but then he would go to Boston and be treated by the real bluestockings as if he didn't even exist. Or at another time he would convince himself that he was a coming power in the State Department, until one day he would get a letter from Washington that showed him that he was no more than a cog in a machine.

Señora de Castro caught him the moment that he stepped into the sitting room. "Come, Harrington, you're the very person that we want. We are going to play bridge."

"Ah—bridge," said Harrington vaguely. Though he was a keen player as a rule, the thought of being anchored to a table while Marie-Té sat in the garden with Camberly was intolerable. "A good idea. Splendid," he murmured, following his hostess to a table at which Mrs. Moffat and the Argentine Envoy sat waiting.

They began to play, and as usual Harrington had good cards, and as usual played them well. Nevertheless, he could not keep his glance from wandering to the other room, where it sought in vain a graceful figure in a blue velvet dress. This was becoming ridiculous, he told himself. He was acting exactly like a schoolboy! When the interminable rubber reached an end, he insisted on giving up his place to Moffat and stepped out into the garden as though to get a breath of air. He saw at once that Marie-Té and Camberly were still sitting on the same stone bench, and there was something about the way she was leaning forward listening that gave Harrington a sinking feeling.

He forced a pleasant smile as he sauntered across the lawn. "Hello there!" he called to them. "I've just been playing bridge."

Camberly rose from the bench in that slow way of his that always so irritated the Minister. "Won't you join us, Mr. Harrington?"

"Well, thank you very much," said Harrington, drawing up an iron garden chair. "Delightful out here, isn't it? There is a full moon, if I'm not mistaken. But then there always seems to be a full moon in Santa Rosa."

He felt presumptuous and a little undignified to break in like this, but then he remembered again that it was he who had brought Marie-Té to the party. Wasn't it Camberly who was doing the real breaking in? And when a moment had passed and he was able to establish his conversational superiority, the awkward feeling vanished. For Camberly, as always in the Minister's company, said little. With a glum expression on his gaunt countenance, he sat listening to his chief's flights of verbosity; occasionally he tugged at his ear lobe with that characteristic gesture. Before long Harrington's self-confidence returned, and as he rambled on, skirting now one topic, now another, he experienced a gratifying sensation of superiority to the taciturn Southerner. The man never had been cut out to be a diplomat, he reflected. A diplomat should be like a gull, skimming the surface of the water without ever plunging in except to spear his prey.

But now something decidedly disturbing took place. As the gull swerved about, executing his graceful arcs and bows, the painful realization came to him that the silver fish might elude him, after all. Not that Marie-Té said or did anything that betrayed her attraction for the other man. Indeed, it was to Harrington that she addressed herself, and it was at Harrington's jokes that she laughed. Yet the Minister was keenly conscious that her thoughts were not on him. Had he actually seen Marie-Té reach out and touch Cam-

73

berly's hand, he could not have been more certain that she was physically drawn to him!

All at once he began to feel quite desperate. Apparently it didn't matter in the slightest that he was volatile and witty, whereas Camberly lacked most of the social graces. Perhaps it was that very lack in him that appealed to the unpredictable girl. How humiliating it all was! Harrington laughing and making witticisms, chattering away like an old woman so as to avoid a break in the conversation, knew the whole time that he could have spared himself the effort. Camberly asserted himself through his very silence, so how was one to fight against him?

They sat on there for what seemed to him a long time, and every moment he felt that the atmosphere was growing more tense. He was seriously considering taking leave of them, when to his relief he caught sight of Señora de Castro in the open doorway. Obviously she was looking for him, just as he had been looking for Marie-Té, and she, too, made a pretense of drawing deep breaths into her lungs. How badly she does it! thought Harrington. I acted out the part much better. And it occurred to him that a person was very ludicrous when looking for someone who had not the slightest desire to be found.

Now she pretended to have caught sight of them for the first time; she raised her hand in an affected greeting, then came strolling across the garden. As Harrington went to fetch her a chair, he passed close to the entrance gate and noticed to his disgust that a number of Indians were still pressing their faces against the bars as they listened to the marimba music. On top of the gate clung the same little ragged boy.

"Psst! Hello!" he called out to Harrington in an urgent whisper. "Me sing 'Star-Spangled Banner.' You like? Yes?"

"No!" said Harrington decisively. "No like." And he walked back to his group. "If you don't mind my saying so," he remarked to his hostess, "you ought to have your man tell those natives to go away. That boy was positively impudent."

74

Marie-Té laughed. "Oh, he's a very good friend of mine. His name is Paco, and he has a truly marvelous voice."

"Really?" said Señora de Castro, and then added, to Marie-Té's astonishment, "Do tell him to sing us something."

"Oh, may I?" Marie-Té seemed delighted, and looked at Señora de Castro as if she had discovered for the first time that her hostess was a human being. She beckoned to the boy, who scrambled down from the gate and ran up to them, holding his battered sombrero. Marie-Té said a few words in Spanish, whereupon Paco, grinning broadly, darted across the garden to the platform with the marimba band. "I've asked him to give us 'Tres Cosas,'" said Marie-Té. "A lovely song. 'Three blessings there are in life.'"

"Three blessings? What are they?" asked Harrington.

"Wait and you will learn." Marie-Té's eyes were fixed on Paco, who had climbed onto the platform and was plucking at the band leader's sleeve. The man bent his head to listen, then, his brown Indian face softening in a smile, he made a sign to the musicians. Gently the music of the marimbas flowed forth, and presently the youth's voice rose into the night, pure and sweet. The sound seemed to come not from a human throat but from a skillfully played flute, and it was as if the whole beautiful garden were singing with him. Gradually the little singer gathered power as he came to the words of the refrain: "Three blessings there are in life—a few pennies, a handful of love, a little health . . ."

Marie-Té sat leaning forward with half-open lips. She had broken off one of the big red flowers from the poinsettia bush and was gazing down at it with a dreamy expression. For the first time Harrington realized that this girl had more than charm and good looks: there was real beauty in the sensitive, mobile face. When the song had wandered into silence, she raised her head, and he saw that her eyes were glistening.

"How beautifully that boy sings! What talent he has!"

"Yes, you are right," Señora de Castro agreed, and to Harrington's surprise, her usual affectation of manner was absent; she looked at Marie-Té simply and directly.

"Do you know what I would like to do?" Marie-Té's young voice sounded eager, and she took Señora de Castro's hand, as though she considered her a real friend. "I would like to find someone to train that boy's voice. He has the makings of a great singer. I feel it."

"Come, come, my dear Marie-Té," Harrington broke in, giving his little chuckle. "You're much too clever to talk such nonsense. All these boys know how to yodel a bit; they have it in the blood. Besides, what if he really did become a singer? He'd make some money and before you knew it, he'd take to wine and women, like all these natives. In five years' time he'd have drunk himself into the gutter."

Marie-Té nodded. "Yes, you're probably right—" she admitted reflectively. But then her eyes flashed. "And what about those five years?" she said. "What about those moments of ecstasy when he stands singing to people, knowing that they worship him like a god? Those moments would make up for everything. To give anyone one minute of great happiness is tremendously important—tremendously worth while."

Señora de Castro pressed Marie-Té's hand and smiled at her warmly. "Yes, yes, my dear," she said, and there was more feeling and conviction in her voice than Harrington had ever heard before.

"And what do *you* think, Camberly? Do you agree with us?" said Marie-Té, turning toward the First Secretary.

For almost the first time since Harrington came into the garden, Camberly broke his silence. "I can't tell you how thoroughly I do agree with you," he said, nodding slowly.

Harrington was surprised. Here he had known Camberly almost a year, and as far as he remembered, he had never before heard the man agree unreservedly with anyone. He felt suddenly that all of them, even the superficial Señora de Castro had a fundamentally different viewpoint on life than he. An impractical, idealistic view-

76

point, utterly unsuited to this modern age! It irritated him so greatly that he could not resist breaking his long-standing rule of never divulging an opinion.

"Personal happiness," he said, "seems to me unimportant. Just as unimportant as—let us say—personal unhappiness. Let's be realists and admit that we deal in masses nowadays and that the individual has ceased to count."

Marie-Té gave Harrington a searching look. Perhaps she would have said something in reply, but just then there reached them from the direction of the zoo the sound of frantic squealing. The wind blowing from that direction brought it as clearly to their ears as if the animal were in the Legation garden. For several seconds the sounds lasted before they grew fainter and finally died away.

"Good heavens!" said Marie-Té. "What was that?"

"Don't let it worry you," said Harrington. "One of the crocodiles in the zoo is having his dinner. You see, some of those big fellows are several hundred years old and they're fine specimens. Nothing but live animals will tempt their appetites, so they always keep a few pigs in the crocodile pens."

"Goodness! How gruesome!"

"Yes, even more gruesome than you think," Señora de Castro told her. "Manuel saw the feeding once and he says that he'll never forget the sight of that crocodile waddling after the little pig—nor of what happened when he caught it."

"Brr." Marie-Té shuddered. "I suppose that wouldn't have shocked you, Harrington, seeing that individual suffering is of no importance."

"Well," said Harrington, "if you want valuable crocodiles you have to kill swine. Can't be squeamish about it."

"No, of course not. The crocodiles are the master race, hence superior to the swine. Just as the Germans claim to be superior to the Jews and to the Poles, and you personally consider yourself superior to these Indians. Perhaps you're right—you usually are right, Harrington—but let me tell you this: I, for one, could never reconcile myself to the suffering of those pigs—nor—" her voice trembled with emotion—"to the suffering of the Jews either."

Harrington began to feel uncomfortable, aware that this discussion was going a bit too far. It was a good thing, he reflected, that he so seldom aired his views; they were not popular views in a democracy. Yet what realist could feel anything but profound scorn for the human race, and especially for its lower branches? Feed them to the crocodiles, by all means! Feed them to the crocodiles!

Abruptly the squealing recommenced. Perhaps the sight of one of their number feeding had whetted the appetites of the other beasts; now at least two pigs were squealing at the same time, and eventually the death cries of another were added. Then, before silence was restored, the wailing of the puma lion could be heard, and a second later the doleful screeching of a hyena. As if oppressed by the near presence of suffering and death, the animals one by one added their voices to the hideous concert. Before long it sounded as though all the dumb beasts in the world were protesting against the injustice of life.

Señora de Castro had risen to her feet. Her usually vacuous face was tense and pale, and into her soulless eyes had come a look of dismay, almost of panic. For a moment she stood, looking distractedly about, then clasped her hands to her ears and hurried towards the house. Marie-Té, catching up with her, spontaneously put her arm around the older woman's waist. Harrington and Camberly followed behind, and it seemed to the Minister that the atmosphere between them was even more constrained than usual. The beasts in the zoo were still howling in misery, so when Harrington passed by the musicians, he gave them a sign to play. Immediately the marimbas broke out into the "Beer Barrel Polka." It gave Harrington a disagreeable little shock to remember that that was the tune that the Nazis had ordered played to cover the sound of firing the day that they marched into Oslo.

78

Chapter VI
The Flowers May Die

SIEGFRIED STUMPF FELT THAT HE COULD NOT GO on much longer. His job in the night club, instead of getting easier, seemed every week more exhausting, more distasteful. Popoff, the proprietor, was drunk almost continuously nowadays and often became violent and objectionable. Once he knocked out a customer and Siegfried got mixed up in a fight with the man's companions; before the police arrived he had received a bloody nose, and his precious eyeglasses, brought from Germany, were shattered beyond repair. When he saw Popoff next day, the Russian only laughed and had the effrontery to suggest that his headwaiter take a course in boxing. Siegfried Stumpf felt that for a Doctor of Philosophy that was the crowning insult.

A short time before this ignominious incident he had received a second letter from the Schiller Schule, the German school of Santa Rosa. It was a politely worded missive, expressing the regret of the institute that Dr. Stumpf had not replied to their previous communication. They wondered if it would be convenient for the Herr Doktor to drop in at their office in connection with a teaching vacancy—without obligation on either side, of course.

This letter disturbed Siegfried Stumpf extremely. Despite its discreet wording, it seemed to him more of a command than an invitation, and he had never forgotten that he still had relatives in Germany. At the same time, the letter pleased him, in a way. It showed that he was not entirely forgotten, that for some people he still had a very definite existence as a German and as a cultured man.

79

They even knew enough about his past to offer him a teaching job without ever having seen him!

Siegfried carried the letter in his pocket for several days, and at odd moments he took it out and reread it. The very sight of the German script gave him a little thrill, for it was a long time since he had received a letter in his language. Apart from his sister, Hilda, he knew few Germans in Santa Rosa, and he lacked the leisure to strike up friendships with those few. Sometimes Siegfried Stumpf had such a desire to speak German that he used to stop Herr Falkenborn, or his niece, Marie-Té, on the staircase and try his best to drag one or the other into a conversation.

It was two days after the fight in the night club that he finally decided to pay a call on Dr. Hildegard, head of the Schiller Schule. It would, he thought, be better policy not to ignore this second letter, and after all, the call obligated him to nothing. He had not the slightest intention of accepting the teaching job as he brushed his thinning blond hair and for a change selected his green felt hat. Pleasurably he noted in the mirror that that hat and his best olive-green gabardine suit gave him a thoroughly German air.

It was a windy day, which meant that the rainy season was approaching, but the wind had an enervating quality making it even more exhausting than the regular still heat. Old papers were being blown about as Siegfried left the pension, and the acacia trees across the way were sighing. Siegfried recalled how his sister Hilda had planted these trees along the block shortly after their arrival in Santa Rosa, hoping to give the vicinity of the pension a pleasant air. His heart warmed toward her as he thought of the two of them fighting in a hostile world against insuperable odds. It seemed to him a great tragedy that he was inhibited by nature from ever telling Hilda how much he loved her.

As he gazed at the acacias in walking by, Siegfried noticed with a shock that behind one of them stood a man with eyes fixed on the top windows of the pension. He did not look like a native; his bearded cheeks were pale, almost sallow. Siegfried could not place the man in regard to social class or probable occupation; he was neither workman nor bourgeois, neither gentleman nor tramp. It occurred to the German that the man's lurking presence behind that tree might somehow be connected with the Schiller Schule's evident interest in himself, but he dismissed that thought as he continued on his way.

He was received in a sunny room hung with pictures of Germany, and with flowering geraniums in the window boxes. Siegfried, casting a quick glance about, was reassured to see no picture of the Fuehrer, no swastika signs, in fact no indications that this house was inhabited by Nazi Germans. Nor did Dr. Hildegard, when he appeared, give the slightest impression of being a Nazi. He was a well built, pleasant-looking man, with clever eyes and a likable manner. Instead of plunging into the subject of the call, he began by inquiring about Siegfried Stumpf's academic career, the various professors under whom he had worked, the student *Vereine* to which he had belonged. Only after some time did he bring the conversation around to the school and to the recent vacancy in the teaching staff. He was aware, he said, with a little bow, of Dr. Stumpf's admirable qualifications.

"I am honored that you thought of me," said Siegfried, feeling his heart pound, now that the crucial moment had arrived. "May I ask if you realize that I have spent several months in a Bavarian concentration camp?"

"Of course, we have heard about that," answered Dr. Hildegard with a friendly smile. "But that was long ago; no one is going to remember it against you."

"I must be frank with you, Dr. Hildegard, I have not changed. I still am not a Nazi."

"Nor are a number of us foreign-born Germans, I assure you," said Dr. Hildegard, apparently unperturbed. "Anyway, our work in the school has nothing to do with politics. Since this country broke off relations with the Reich, we have been strictly forbidden to engage in any sort of propaganda, and are subject to constant

81

government supervision. As you know, all our teaching is now done in Spanish. The only thing that interests us is to keep open our school, so that our younger generation will not grow up deprived entirely of their native culture. That would be a sad state of affairs for us Germans, wouldn't it, Dr. Stumpf?"

"Yes indeed," said Siegfried, pleased despite himself at again being addressed like a fellow German. And everything that Dr. Hildegard had said was true. He knew that were it not for this school, and similar ones scattered throughout Central and South America, the German colonies, as homogeneous entities would soon disappear; their existence was indispensable if Teutonic culture was to survive in Latin America.

"After all," pursued Dr. Hildegard, as though scenting his advantage, "we are all of us primarily Germans, and only afterwards adherents of a political party. If you had, like me, spent most of your life on foreign soil, you would realize what it means to us Germans in Santa Rosa to keep our old traditions alive. The thought of our children attending native schools and forgetting their own language is intolerable."

"I can understand that," said Siegfried warmly. "But may I ask, Herr Doktor, why you happened to think of me? There must have been other men available."

"Not as many as you might think. Besides, Dr. Stumpf, if you don't mind my saying so, your present position is hardly suitable for a man of your qualifications. Frankly, it hurt me to think of a cultured compatriot doing that sort of work."

Siegfried Stumpf could not help feeling moved at this expression of sympathy. Studying Dr. Hildegard's clever face, he found the man more and more to his liking.

"May I take it for granted that you are definitely offering me the post?" he inquired.

"After our present talk I can say definitely yes."

"Please allow me to think over the matter for a few days," said

82

Siegfried. "You will understand my difficulty in making a decision."

"Do so by all means. Now let me outline your future duties, should you decide to accept. . . ."

When Siegfried left the Schiller Schule, his brain was in a whirl. He knew that regardless of his decision, this new problem was bound to complicate his life; whichever way he acted, he would have regrets and qualms of conscience. It was no longer a question as to whether or not he approved of a regime, but as to whether he was more of an anti-Nazi than a good German. Long after the Nazis had passed into oblivion, Germany would still be there, and by saving for her some of her distant sons, he would be helping that future Germany. Would that not be a more useful occupation than selling watered whisky for the benefit of Boris Popoff?

As he walked along the Calle de la Independencia, Santa Rosa's main street, and peered into his soul for guidance, Siegfried caught sight of little Bubi Falkenborn across the way. With Siegfried, as with everyone in the pension, Bubi was a great favorite, and now as he stopped to watch the boy, his worried expression vanished. Casually Bubi was kicking a stone before him, his unconscious movements beautifully co-ordinated and rhythmical. What grace the child had! Siegfried thought. It made one realize that there was something in blood and breeding after all, even if Hitler spoke of the Austrian nobility as being irresponsible and effete.

Standing there watching him, Siegfried suddenly grew aware that another pair of eyes were on the boy. A short distance behind Bubi walked the little bewhiskered man whom Siegfried had seen standing outside of Pension Hilda. His rapt glance rested on the lad, and as he made his way along, he gave the impression of being lost to all else. Clearly, no spy shadowing a man could have been more intent on keeping him in view. Yet, curiously enough, Siegfried was not worried for Bubi's safety. In the face of the little man was a look of such pure love and devotion that it would have reassured anyone who saw it.

83

Undecided, Siegfried stood staring across the windswept Calle de la Independencia. He knew that the sensible thing was to join Bubi and accompany him back to the pension, yet for some reason felt loath to do so. One must not believe evil of man, he told himself, looking after the curious pair and thinking at the same time of Dr. Hildegard with his clever, penetrating eyes. Had not all the great ethical philosophers from Lao Tse to Immanuel Kant based their teachings on the existence in people of a fundamental goodness? Who was poor Siegfried Stumpf, follower in their exalted tracks, Doctor of Philosophy, Heidelberg 1927, to question the wisdom of the masters?

The wind was still blowing hard when Siegfried came home that evening, and it was a relief for him to hear Bubi's laughter from upstairs. He had made up his mind to report what he had seen to Marie-Té, so before leaving for the night club he went to find her in her room.

Marie-Té's little room was always in a state of great disorder. Books in three languages were piled on chairs and scattered about the floor. Stacked in a corner were a number of half-packed suitcases, crowned by a portable phonograph on which a symphony record was usually turning. Phonograph records were Marie-Té's great extravagance and she had fled halfway around the world with her entire collection, a feat of which she was very proud. She used to say that when things got really bad she would begin to sell her red-seal records one by one, the way the White Russian refugees used to dispose of rubies.

Siegfried Stumpf, standing respectfully in the doorway, half in and half out of the room, described what he had seen that day. If he had expected it to create a sensation, he was disappointed; she seemed to take the news lightly, as she took most things.

"Oh, Bubi's very special, Herr Stumpf, God watches over him. And if that man likes to look at him—well I don't wonder. There aren't so many pretty things to look at in this world any longer!"

Knowing how Marie-Té adored her little brother, Siegfried had difficulty understanding this somewhat casual attitude. The Austrians had always been a puzzle to him anyway. They held everything so lightly, it was no wonder that their hold on their own country had proved easy to disengage.

Nevertheless, for the next few days Bubi never left the pension unaccompanied by his uncle or his sister. Though Marie-Té kept her eyes open, she saw no sign of the man whom Siegfried had described. Probably she would have ended by forgetting the matter, had she not chanced to look out of her window one afternoon while giving Bubi his English lesson. Standing behind one of the acacia trees across the way was a little pale man whom Marie-Té felt she had seen somewhere before. The narrow but proud shoulders, the erect carriage, the sideways tilt of the little head, all were familiar. So was the vague lost atmosphere that he gave forth. Then he turned his face upwards toward the pension windows, and at once Marie-Té recognized him as Kerjanian, that strange Armenian. Making up her mind at once, as she always did, she hurried downstairs and walked across the street.

"Good morning, Mr. Kerjanian!"

Kerjanian gave a violent start. His face grew even paler and his eyes began to hunt about, like those of an animal at bay. Then, regaining his usual air of dignity, he returned her greeting with a sour little smile. He tapped the bark of the acacia with his knuckles, evidently to give the impression that he had stepped beside it to examine the tree's structure.

"There aren't many nice trees in Santa Rosa. This row would make the street look quite European if only they cleaned it up a bit and put in sidewalks."

"So you long for Europe, Mr. Kerjanian?" said Marie-Té, trying to avoid any implication that his presence outside the pension was not the most natural thing in the world. "I suppose we all do, even though we know that we're fortunate to be here. Why

85

don't you come to visit us some day at Pension Hilda? It's a little stronghold of Europe in the Western continent."

"I am not going out very much," said Kerjanian quickly. "I have no respectable clothes with me and no money to buy new ones. I don't usually look like this, you know."

"But what is the matter with your looks? You are wearing a very smart necktie, I must say."

"Oh, do you like it?" He put up his fingers to touch the rich crimson silk. "Yes, I am glad that I'll have at least one nice thing to wear the day I finally get to Brooklyn. That's where my brother lives; it's the most respectable place in New York. My brother's children get completely new outfits every Easter and fall. They don't have to go ragged like the children in Europe."

Marie-Té saw his eyes darken, and she felt her sympathy go out to him. "You like children very much, don't you, Mr. Kerjanian?" she asked.

"Like them? No, much more than that: I revere them. I was a teacher once upon a time, as I've told you before, and I've seen children fall down fainting over their little desks because of starvation. That was in our poverty-stricken Armenia, and in Syria. But now in rich France and Holland the children are fainting too. They don't play games any longer between classes. Imagine a whole continent where children don't play! They sit, very quiet and white-faced, saving their little strength so as to last out until the arrival of the food ships from America. They don't know that because of men like Harrington those ships will never sail."

Marie-Té's heart contracted. "Don't say that, Mr. Kerjanian!" she said. "Those ships *must* sail. They must!"

Hatred flared up in Kerjanian's eyes. "My brother in Brooklyn and his children would deprive themselves of everything to save one small life in Europe. They are Americans—real Americans—and there are millions like them. But they're forbidden to act. A big hand is stopping them, and it's the same hand that keeps the doors of the South American granaries locked. It's Harrington's

86

hand! Yes, the hand of Mr. Warfield Harrington and his friends in Washington's State Department. They're not live men with live hearts. They are machines, as the Nazis are machines. But what statesmen and diplomats don't realize is that in a few years those starved, stunted children will have turned into ferocious wolves that will turn and rend their tormentors. That's the hour when Harrington . . ."

Out of one of Pension Hilda's downstairs windows popped Hilda Stumpf's leonine head. "Mr. Harrington's on the phone again, Fräulein Falkenborn!" she shouted.

Marie-Té tried to think up a fib, embarrassed to have Kerjanian know she was on friendly terms with Harrington. "He wants to talk to me about our American visas," she told him.

To her amazement a look of pure anguish passed over Kerjanian's face. "That means that you and your brother will—be leaving here?" he asked, his black eyes wide with apprehension.

Impulsively Marie-Té stretched out her hand and gave his arm a squeeze. "No, no, not at all. Mr. Harrington's fondness for red tape amounts to a real passion and we're apt to be here as long as you. Perhaps we'll reach New York at the same time, and then you'll introduce Bubi to your brother's children in Brooklyn."

Kerjanian began to behave as if he had just received a present. He wanted to show his appreciation and became extremely affable all at once. Summoning a flower woman who happened to be passing by, he selected three branches of flowering jasmine.

"They will look nice in your room," he said, putting them in the arms of Marie-Té. He took from his pocket a tiny silver coin and handed it to the flower woman with an airy gesture.

"How lovely they are!" said Marie-Té as she pressed the blossoms against her cheek. "I'll put them in my little brother's room. Won't you come and see them there?"

"Perhaps I will come," said Kerjanian vaguely. "Yes, yes, I will come one day."

"Better not put it off too long, Mr. Kerjanian. The flowers may

87

die. You know, beautiful things are often fragile. We must appreciate them while we may."

Marie-Té hurried back to the pension, reflecting that these calls from Harrington had become an integral part of her life here. Two weeks had gone by since the ball at the Portuguese Legation, and there had been few days that he had not honored her with at least one of them.

"Good morning, Marie-Té. I trust that you slept well," he greeted her today in his usual suave manner.

"Oh yes, my dear, I always do."

"To be sure." Obviously Harrington had not even listened to her answer. He asked that question daily not out of solicitude but because it was his policy to be polite; she could have spent the dark hours in writhing sleeplessness for all that he really cared. "And how are your uncle and your little brother?" he went on to inquire.

"Very well," said Marie-Té, feeling a bit bored with this daily ritual.

"That's splendid. Splendid. And what are Marie-Té's plans for the day? I suppose that she is pretty well booked up with her numerous admirers?"

Marie-Té had come to learn that this was Harrington's roundabout manner of asking her to dinner. He never invited anyone without giving that person a chance to refuse in such a way that he, Harrington, need not feel offended. It was a habit carried over from earlier years, when he had not always occupied his present important position; it had saved him many an embarrassing moment.

"Oh well, not as booked up as all that," Marie-Té answered noncommittally.

"I'm supposed to be playing bridge. You wouldn't care to join us?"

"But you know how I loathe bridge, Harrington!"

Over the wire came Harrington's little chuckle, implying that

88

he, also, scorned the game of bridge but had to play occasionally because of the demands of his position.

"If you're not too late, give me a phone call," Marie-Té suggested. "We might meet somewhere for a drink."

"That's not a bad idea," said Harrington, his voice more confident, now that he had learned the lay of the land. "I'll make a point of not being late. In fact when I come to think of it, I might skip out of that bridge game altogether. What would Marie-Té say if I picked her up for dinner about nine?"

"I would say thank you very much."

Hardly had she replaced the receiver on the hook than the telephone rang again.

"Hello. May I speak to Miss Falkenborn?" came Camberly's voice.

"You're doing so, idiot," said Marie-Té, laughing. "Good afternoon, John."

"Hello, Marie-Té. What about a drink in half an hour?"

"That would be lovely."

"See you at the Yacht Club. Good-by."

Marie-Té hung up again, amused at the difference in the two conversations; nothing could have brought out more clearly the conflicting characters of the two men than their respective manners of speaking on the telephone. Humming a tune, she ran upstairs to finish Bubi's English lesson before slipping on a fresh linen dress and setting off to meet John Camberly at the Yacht Club.

The Yacht Club, or to call it by its local appellation, *El Club del Yates*, had nothing to do with a club, and even less with yachts. In fact, Santa Rosa was a hundred kilometers from the nearest body of water and boasted only of a meandering river which during the dry season turned into a creek. A few sailing skiffs and half a dozen rowboats were moored to the Yacht Club's pier, on which the members (comprising everyone in Santa Rosa who owned a yachting cap) could gaze while sipping their mediocre Cuba Libres.

At the Yacht Club it was that Marie-Té and Camberly usually

89

had their rendezvous, rather than in the smarter Hotel Imperial, which was, so to speak, Harrington's territory. Today she found the First Secretary sitting on the veranda when she arrived, his drink before him, his Panama hat resting on the second chair. In his drill suit and soft white shirt he looked as cool as the cubes of ice floating in his frosted tumbler. Camberly seemed to belong to the tropics, just as Harrington, the New Englander, belonged in a more wintry, less mellow atmosphere. The slow-moving, relaxed Camberly had adapted himself without effort to Santa Rosan life, which after all did not differ essentially from life in the southern state where he had his roots.

"Hello," he greeted her, rising and shaking hands. "I've ordered you a mint julep. The barman here's a clever fellow; he's taken my few hints and he certainly makes them as they should be made."

"M'm. I should say so," exclaimed Marie-Té, sampling her drink. She gave Camberly a friendly smile, delighted with the way he always gave credit to other people. "I'm sure they couldn't do them better even in your own Virginia."

"Oh, you ought to taste my Uncle James' if you think that!"

"John, the only time you act the professional Southerner is when you begin talking of mint juleps! When you sit there with your Panama hat pushed back on your head and tell me of your uncle James' mint juleps, I can almost imagine your developing into a real southern colonel—the kind you read about in books!"

Camberly laughed. He knew that Marie-Té realized that nothing was less likely, for in his way Camberly was as much in revolt against the aristocratic southern tradition as was Marie-Té against that of aristocratic Austria. She sometimes wondered if one of the reasons they got on so well was this very similarity of inheritance, to which they had both reacted alike.

He sat there quietly, taking long enjoyable sips of his mint julep, and not making the slightest effort to create conversation. This tranquillity of his appealed to Marie-Té. After Harrington's garrulousness, she found it restful to be in silent company and allowed to think her own thoughts for a change.

"I am having dinner with your friend Harrington tonight," she remarked after a long moment.

"Ah, that's something to look forward to!"

"Oh yes, Harrington can be very amusing," said Marie-Té teasingly. "Even brilliant at times."

"Of course. He has to live up to his reputation."

"It's funny how you two hate each other," said Marie-Té with a laugh. "I don't suppose one could find two men anywhere less congenial. What a joke that you have to work in the same office!"

Again Camberly didn't answer. Whenever an answer was either too obvious or too difficult, he simply kept silent, which Marie-Té had begun to think an excellent system. It certainly didn't make for rapidly flowing conversation, but then it stopped one from uttering a great many banalities.

She finished her drink, and between sips found herself stealing glances at his gaunt, tanned face which had appealed to her so strongly from the start. Not that it was precisely handsome, nor youthful either. Camberly showed all of his forty years, a fact that Marie-Té rather liked. For her the important thing was that a face should possess calm and strength and dignity, and this Camberly's face certainly did. There was breeding in the high thin forehead and maturity of spirit in the firm grooves at the corners of the mouth. His eyes, frequently downcast when he was not talking, were those of a thinker and an introvert; however, when he raised them, one saw that they were remarkably clear and full of life. His was a lonely face, yet one with capacities both for tenderness and joy.

They had ordered a second round of drinks when Marie-Té perceived Uncle Konrad walking down the unpaved street beside the Yacht Club. He had on his fine velvet jacket and bow tie, a circumstance suggesting to Marie-Té an engagement with Irène Legervais. She pointed him out to Camberly.

"Doesn't he look a darling?" she asked.

"I would very much like to meet him. Do you think we might ask him to come over for a drink," Camberly proposed.

Marie-Té hesitated. She loved her uncle so much that she was a little afraid of anyone thinking him ridiculous, knowing that in spite of his formality and old-world manners, he was not ridiculous in the least. He was genuine, and no genuine person can be laughable, even though his individual characteristics might be. It wasn't until the two men were actually shaking hands that her doubts were dissipated.

"Maria-Theresa has told me much about you. I'm delighted to make your acquaintance," said Uncle Konrad, huge straw hat in hand.

"I am delighted to make yours, Baron Falkenborn. Do have a seat, sir."

Marie-Té was pleased to see that Camberly instinctively changed his attitude when he spoke to Uncle Konrad, becoming formal and ultra-polite, as the older man would have wished. He ordered another mint julep and he made Uncle Konrad feel not only that he was not intruding but that Camberly thought it a great honor to be his host. Subtly he turned the conversation to Uncle Konrad's violin playing, and listened with absorption while the Austrian described that famous episode when as a child he had played the violin before no less a person than the Emperor Franz Josef. Later he asked a number of questions about the imperial family, which it was Uncle Konrad's obvious delight to answer. For Konrad Falkenborn the atmosphere of that royal and imperial Austria was still actual, and so well was he able to portray it that for a moment it seemed not incredible at all that an old man with mutton-chop whiskers should by the charm of his personality have kept together a heterogeneous nation of sixty million souls.

Sitting before that landlocked Yacht Club, surrounded by dusky Santa Rosans in their gold-braided yachting caps, Marie-Té suddenly began to feel intensely happy. That was the effect that Uncle Konrad always had on her. His gay, pure spirit infected those around him, making them, too, seem nicer in each other's eyes. He would rather have borne suffering than hurt the feelings of a stranger; his was a truly gentle soul.

In a near-by church tower the clock began to strike. Uncle Konrad sprang to his feet. *"Donnerwetter!"* he cried. "Six o'clock! I'll be late for my appointment. Good-by. Good-by. And thank you." Seizing his big straw hat, he went bounding down the stairs, stopped below to wave and smile to them again, and hurried off down the street.

"The angel!" said Marie-Té, her glance following Uncle Konrad. "He has found a girl friend for himself, and he is as excited about it as a schoolboy. I am so pleased for his sake."

"He is a delightful person," said Camberly. "Very gay, very youthful. Obviously a happy man."

A pleased smile came into Marie-Té's face at those last words. Leaning forward, she continued to watch Uncle Konrad until he was out of view, her expression that of a mother watching her favorite child. Then she leaned back in her chair and gazed at Camberly.

"So he really does give the impression of being happy?" she asked him. "Do you know that nothing you could have said would have pleased me more! Uncle Konrad has been through terrible things, John. That he got over them at all was a miracle."

"Yes," said Camberly. There was no implication in his voice that he wanted to be told more; he simply let her know that he was interested and that she should speak on if she wished.

"My uncle was a Royalist. That's why they locked him in a concentration camp," Marie-Té told Camberly for the first time. She always found it very difficult to touch upon these memories; she shied from them as one shies from discussing something that is personally painful, such as a past insult or a physical defect.

Camberly must have sensed the anguish behind Marie-Té's words; reaching out, he pressed her hand, and Marie-Té squeezed his back without speaking. Perhaps the day would come when she

93

could talk of the past with equanimity, but though five years had gone by, it was still as vivid as a fearful nightmare. It seemed but yesterday that she had gone to the Paris station to meet her uncle, recently freed from the German concentration camp. One glance at his face and all her joy at their reunion had vanished. He had looked the same, only a little thinner, he had tried to give her one of his old smiles, but the whole time she had kept feeling that this was not Uncle Konrad at all. All at once Marie-Té had realized why the Nazis had allowed him to depart: they had known him to be a broken man.

Now as Marie-Té sat with Camberly on the Yacht Club veranda, her eyebrows contracted in pain. When she thought back on the Marie-Té who had gone down to meet Uncle Konrad at the station, it seemed to her that she was remembering another girl—a very young girl who understood very little of life. The weeks that followed had brought about a change in her almost as striking, if not as devastating, as the change brought about in Uncle Konrad at the concentration camp.

Glancing across the table at Camberly, she saw that he was still sitting there quietly, arms folded, calm eyes fixed on his frosted tumbler. For the first time in all these months and years, she felt a desire to speak out; Camberly's lack of curiosity invited confidences. Marie-Té felt that he was the one person to whom she could have told this immensely private chapter of her life.

"Uncle Konrad lived with me in Paris during the weeks following his release," she said aloud, continuing her own thoughts from where they had left off. And Camberly turned his eyes to her and at once he was all attention. "John, that was the period that shaped my life. People often say that I seem so grown up for a girl of twenty-five. Well, I grew into a woman during those weeks, because it was then that I learned to love selflessly for the first time. I suppose that's the thing that makes a girl change into a woman. You see, Uncle Konrad needed love so badly. Without love he was lost. So I *had* to find love inside me, even if it hadn't been there before."

Marie-Té paused for a moment, but when Camberly gave her a quick nod, she went on, trying to speak in a matter-of-fact way, "The first thing I did, John, was to arrange to give all my time to him. I wanted him to feel that he meant everything to me—that it was all-important to me, personally, that he throw off the shadow of the concentration camp. I was in love with a Russian boy at the time, and we'd even spoken of getting married. Well, naturally, I couldn't have anyone else in my life when Uncle Konrad needed *all* of me. So I told Sacha that we couldn't meet for the time being—that he shouldn't even think of me as living in the same city. I don't blame him for not understanding and for finally falling in love with someone else. It was a tragedy for me, but nothing—*nothing* really seemed to matter beside Uncle Konrad's well-being.

"During the next weeks and months I tried to nurse his sick spirit back to health. He went through his days as if he were a machine, eating what was put before him, answering when he was spoken to, but performing every action as if he lacked will power of his own. At times I was afraid that the task I'd set myself was too great—that the poison had worked its way too deeply into his system. The rescuing of Uncle Konrad had become the most important thing in my life. Somehow it seemed to me that in fighting for Uncle Konrad I was fighting for all the victims of persecution in the world. That's why the outcome seemed to me so important. Can you understand that, John?"

"Yes, I do understand it," said Camberly. "Certainly I do. It was a sort of test case."

"A test case. Yes, yes." Marie-Té nodded eagerly. "That's exactly what I mean. Well, one evening—it was my twentieth birthday—I asked Uncle Konrad as a special favor to take me to a concert. Up till then he'd refused to listen to music, though he used to live for it in Vienna. He hadn't once touched the violin I'd bought for him, and he'd even seemed annoyed when I played my phonograph. Brahms' Fourth Symphony was to be performed that day, and Brahms had always been Uncle Konrad's favorite composer. But during the preliminary numbers he sat there as apathetic as usual. I remember that he kept rustling his program, and it was terribly unlike him to do that—he who'd always been so courteous and thoughtful.

"But then the Brahms began. At once I noticed a change in Uncle Konrad: his body grew tense, his breath came quicker. His glance, which had been so wandering of late, was concentrated on the violins. Oh at last, John, at last he seemed to be aware of something outside himself!

"The moment that the symphony was over, he rose without a word, and left the hall. Of course I followed him. He walked rapidly and struck out at random down a side street. I almost had to run to keep up with him. After a while we found ourselves in the middle of the big Paris markets—I don't think either of us could have said how we'd got there. It was night, but the streets were full of people and I remember that we turned a corner and almost bumped into a man with a great basket of apples on his shoulder. He cursed in the absent-minded way of French workmen, and Uncle Konrad cringed and threw up his shoulder, as though he were expecting a blow. Oh, John, if I live to be a hundred, I shall never forget the look upon his face!"

Marie-Té stopped talking; she felt that she could not go on. Never, she knew, would she be able to tell anyone about the remainder of that night—the most dreadful night of her life. As little as one can speak to another of a night of love, can one speak of a night of tragedy.

She closed her eyes, and there came before her the picture of Uncle Konrad and herself walking through the dark streets, and at last returning, still without having said a word, to his room. He had seated himself on the edge of his bed and stared into space, while Marie-Té had taken a chair by the window. Perhaps another ten minutes had gone by—perhaps much longer. And then, quite abruptly, Uncle Konrad had begun to speak. From that very first day of his arrival Marie-Té had known that this moment would have to come

96

—had known also that it was he who must determine when. If those festering wounds were ever to be healed, then the first condition was to expose them to the light of day. Now she prayed for the strength to listen without flinching. Gradually, gingerly at first, he began to touch upon the memories that had gnawed into his soul.

Every word was like a blow in the face to Marie-Té. She listened to him, feeling so sick, so overcome with horror, that at one time she was afraid that she would faint. The thought that Uncle Konrad— her Uncle Konrad—had been subjected to all this, brought home to her the reality of the concentration camp for the first time. These cruelties had not been enacted in some fantastic tale; they were actual, and Uncle Konrad himself had been their victim. He spared her nothing, and Marie-Té did not want to be spared. She submitted herself to the pain of listening as she would have submitted herself to physical pain for Uncle Konrad's sake. Though she said not a word, she wanted to call out to him, "Uncle Konrad, Uncle Konrad, I love you! Try and find some solace in my life. I would give my whole life to make up to you for your suffering, Uncle Konrad!"

Throughout that long night, Uncle Konrad and Marie-Té never slept. Once the first frenzied outburst was over, his talk was punctuated by long silences, but the thought of leaving him did not enter Marie-Té's head. Completely still, she lay on the couch with one hand thrown before her eyes, while Uncle Konrad strode incessantly up and down, up and down; if he stayed without moving a single second, the nerves in his legs would begin to twitch. Then after each of these silences he would launch forth again. Often he repeated himself; some things he told her three and four times, and those were the most gruesome of all. She had heard much before about the horrors of concentration camps, about people beaten to death and people searching frantically for the means of suicide. And yet it seemed to her that she had never until tonight heard anything. It was Uncle Konrad who had seen these happenings. He it was

97

who had witnessed the beatings and heard the screams of the tortured.

When dawn came, Uncle Konrad was still talking, but slower now, in a sporadic, exhausted way. The pent-up water in the dam had rushed out; the locks had been broken at long last. On the bed lay Marie-Té, feeling that she had turned into an old woman on her twentieth birthday, feeling that there were new lines in her face and that her body had become aged and brittle. She was tired—tired unto death. She knew that if at that moment she had been attacked by someone with intent to kill, she could have offered no resistance. It was full day when she dragged herself to her own room, adjoining Uncle Konrad's. She fell asleep immediately and slept uninterruptedly for sixteen hours . . .

Abruptly Marie-Té realized that she had been sitting opposite Camberly all this time without saying a word; calmly and patiently he was waiting for her to continue. She had never known anyone like Camberly—so silent, yet with so much to say. In gratitude, she reached out for his hand. He smiled at her understandingly, and Marie-Té felt that they had grown very close to each other that afternoon.

"And was there a change in Uncle Konrad after that night?" he asked, to make it easier for her.

"Oh yes, thank God there was," said Marie-Té, "even though it came only gradually. If I hadn't been watching him so closely, perhaps I wouldn't even have noticed that Uncle Konrad was trying to re-establish contact with life. How shyly, how fearfully he did it, ready at any second to pull back into himself! There still were moments when I doubted if I would ever draw him from the shadows."

"And when did you know you would succeed?"

"Oh, I can remember the exact day," answered Marie-Té, and now there was a joyful ring in her voice. "It was an April morning, and I was awakened by the sound of a violin in the next room. Somebody was playing Brahms. I remember that I listened for quite a while before suddenly realizing that it was Uncle Konrad. John, I hadn't ever cried since I was a little girl—not once—but this time I couldn't stop myself. I lay there on my bed and sobbed and sobbed. For now I knew that Uncle Konrad was saved! Of course the battle wasn't over yet, but the darkest days were passed. If Uncle Konrad could play Brahms, then he was rescued from despair. He could begin to live again.

"When I went into his room, he was sitting by the window in his dressing gown, the violin on the floor beside him. The window was wide open, and I remember that the sunshine fell right on Uncle Konrad's face. Perhaps it was that warm light that made his face look so young that morning. For once I didn't notice the bitter lines about his mouth, and John, even his eyes looked younger! He held out his hand to me, in a gesture that was just like the old Konrad of Vienna days.

"I walked over to him and laid my hand in his. His fingers closed around mine, and there was strength and warmth in his clasp. I didn't say anything. What was there to say? We understood each other far too well to have to speak. Do you know the thought that came to me as I stood there holding Uncle Konrad's hand?"

"What was it?" said Camberly, his eyes fixed on Marie-Té's radiant face.

"It was this: that though I'd given Uncle Konrad everything I had to give, somehow I had received more than I had given. That was strange, wasn't it? From Uncle Konrad I had had no more than a dead man can give, yet through the very fact of loving him I had become a richer person. Perhaps, John, the important thing isn't *who* one loves, nor *how* one loves, but simply the feeling of love inside one."

Chapter VII

Trouble at the "French Embassy"

AH SING, THE CHINESE BOY, COULD NOT understand his master's behavior. During the eight years since he had entered his employ in Shanghai, Mr. Harrington had never deviated so far from normal habits as in these last weeks. Instead of jumping up when Ah Sing touched his shoulder in the morning, he would lie abed, watching with his impersonal eye while the valet laid out his clothes. His daily exercises he accomplished in a less concentrated manner than usual—almost as though he were bored with them. On some mornings he gave no more than a few moments to the rite which Ah Sing could not remember his having omitted for these last eight years; the penning of the daily letter to his mother in Stoneborough, Maine.

Tradition-loving as all his race, Ah Sing distrusted out-of-the-way conduct; he knew it was a bad sign when a person of predictable actions behaves unpredictably. For instance, who would have suspected Mr. Harrington of having in his possession a photograph of a young lady in a white linen suit? One morning when Ah Sing, clad in his immaculate white jacket with the pongee silk shirt underneath, was engaged in dusting, he espied it under a paperweight. To judge from the background, the picture had been taken in Santa Rosa, and Ah Sing was sure that he recognized the subject from that party at the Portuguese Legation when he had had charge of mixing and serving the drinks. She had been very gay and very pretty, he recalled, and when he brought her a drink, she had smiled at him in such a friendly way. But what, Ah Sing would have liked to know, what was her picture doing on Mr. Harrington's writing desk?

He was still asking himself that question when the door opened and Mr. Harrington himself came in from the bedroom. Sensitive to atmospheres, Ah Sing realized at once that his master was displeased at his having seen that photograph. From the corner of his oblique eye he watched Harrington's expression, knowing from past experience that an attack of some sort was imminent.

Harrington sauntered over to the window alcove, where his breakfast was laid out on a little table. Unfolding his napkin, he remarked dryly, "Ah Sing, I thought I told you before that you were always to wear gloves when you were on duty. I don't want to have to speak to you about this again."

The eyes of the Chinese boy narrowed a trifle. "Yes sir. Velly solly, sir," he said, and went out into the pantry.

He pulled out the bottom drawer of the linen cupboard, where he kept some of his clothes, seeing that all would not fit into the wooden box in his bedroom that served as wardrobe. From four pairs of rolled white cotton gloves, Ah Sing selected the least worn, and his face was expressionless as he stood there in the serving pantry drawing on one of these gloves. But then he looked down at his other hand and slowly clenched it into a fist. Ah, what wouldn't he have given to smash it into a supercilious face that he had to look at with respect so many times each day! A face on which Ah Sing could read scorn for all people, and especially for him, because he was a member of the inferior, of the slightly repulsive, yellow race.

Ah Sing spread out his fingers again and studied them, holding them to the light. He had a beautifully shaped hand which sprang from the slender wrist as gracefully as a five-petaled lotus flower springs from the end of its stalk; through the almost transparent skin he could see the shadowy lines of the bones. Ah Sing had a theory of his own as to why Mr. Harrington was so insistent that he always wear gloves at work. For Mr. Harrington's own hands were stumpy and brutal-looking, quite at variance with the rest of his person, which passed as that of a well-bred man. Ah Sing knew that Mr. Harrington was embarrassed about those hands of his. He remembered an occasion shortly after he came into Mr. Harrington's employ when he had handed him a newspaper, and for the fraction of a second their fingers had lain side by side. He had seen Mr. Harrington gazing with the strangest of expressions at the two contrasting hands. It was from that day on that Ah Sing had orders always to wear cotton gloves in his master's presence.

Returning to the sitting room, Ah Sing noted with surprise that Mr. Harrington had scarcely touched his breakfast. He was still seated in the window alcove, neither reading his paper nor writing his morning letter, and that too was most unusual. He seemed nervous, and his eyes, fixed out of the window, followed the movements on the street below.

Ah Sing resumed his work, passing the long feather duster over one after the other articles of furniture—over the writing desk (from which he noted that the photograph had been removed), over the mantel, over the bookshelves with their heavy rows of books. Very lovingly Ah Sing's duster flitted across the leather-bound classics, the thick biographies, the works on science and history and law. Had Harrington been watching, he would have noted that Ah Sing eyed the books in quite a different way than he eyed the costly vases, or even the jade Chinese boxes: his glance was tender—almost possessive.

Yes, those books were very precious to Ah Sing; each one meant a great deal to him. Through them alone it was that he had succeeded in advancing along his arduous path. For the truth was that Ah Sing had set himself a goal as ambitious, as difficult to attain, as that of Harrington himself. Eight years ago, a poor coolie's son in Shanghai, he had taken on the gigantic task of educating himself— a task at which he was still struggling with the indomitable courage, the patience, the tenacity, of the Oriental. By attending night classes, he had learned to read and write in English and, equipped with this knowledge, had assaulted the pinnacles of learning, using the books in his master's well-assorted library as guideposts on his way.

But all this Ah Sing had kept carefully to himself. Harrington was not a man who would have approved of a member of the lower classes bettering himself, especially not an Oriental. When Ah Sing had first learned to write, and began to take down telephone messages, Harrington had looked at them with an icy-cold stare, then asked Ah Sing to repeat them orally, as if they were incomprehensible. When Ah Sing bought a cookery book and tried to surprise his master by preparing an American specialty, Harrington left most of the food untasted on his plate. As far as the Chinese boy remembered, he had never received as much as an approving word during all these years, excepting only indirectly, when he overheard people complimenting Harrington on his butler.

So naturally Ah Sing kept secret not only his browsings in Harrington's books, but even his ability to speak proper English. It was an effort for him, who had heard the language spoken correctly for eight years, to continue to say "Velly vell, sir," and "What you likee for dinner?" but he knew that Anglo-Saxons of Harrington's type expected Chinese to speak pidgin English; it confirmed them in their agreeable conviction of the inferiority of the yellow race. Harrington would have been shocked to receive proof that Ah Sing, in addition to being a good servant, was an intelligent and superior human being.

Now as the Chinese boy moved softly about the sitting room, duster in hand, he remained keenly conscious of his master's nervousness. During eight years he had grown accustomed to Harrington's fixed habits, and his sitting there, restless and inactive, on a weekday morning was as unusual as his keeping a photograph of a lady in his sitting room. The knowledge of Harrington's nervousness made Ah Sing nervous too. He wished heartily that his master would go to the Legation, or that he at least would begin to read, or to write a letter. This moody inactivity was out of keeping with his character, and Ah Sing did not like it—no, he did not like it in the least.

In the meanwhile Warfield Harrington sat there feeling even more surprised than Ah Sing at his unorthodox behavior. How could he have said why he, Warfield Harrington, had allowed his well-organized existence to be disrupted by a young girl who was not only penniless but a refugee? Or why things which used to seem important, such as his Swedish exercises and his bridge games at Señora de Castro's, nowadays bored him beyond measure? Even his work at the Legation appeared tedious at times. The only moments that counted were those few when he was seated opposite Marie-Té at a table in the Imperial, or riding next to her in his car.

Was he in love with her then? he kept asking himself, and it was exactly as if he had been trying to decide if he had caught leprosy or the bubonic plague. Always he had considered love as the cardinal menace to a public career. When he thought of diplomats he had known whose entire future had been disrupted by a woman, he literally shuddered. And yet by what other name than love was he to designate the strangely weak feeling that possessed him whenever the picture of Marie-Té flashed into his mind? What except love could have caused him to lie awake at night, thinking of Marie-Té and of himself—and even of their possible future together? A startling thought had occurred to Harrington the night of the dance at the Portuguese Legation, and since then had been recurring almost daily: that Baroness Maria-Theresa Falkenborn would be not at all unsuitable for a diplomat's wife!

Swish! Swish! Ah Sing's leather sandals whispered as he moved across the floor. Harrington turned his head to scowl furiously, then recovered himself and looked away. Strange how his nerves were getting the better of him nowadays! Of course it was his imagination, nothing more, that made it seem that Ah Sing was acting insubordinately of late. And everyone else seemed to irritate him too; a hundred times a day he had to remind himself that it was the part of the good diplomat never under any provocation to show his feelings.

There was that fellow Camberly, for instance. To be sure he always had disliked Camberly, but since the evening in Señora de Castro's garden, the very sight of the man had become distasteful; the knowledge that he was seeing Marie-Té had caused the Minister many a sleepless night. And as he lay in bed tossing, his feeling against Camberly had crystallized. Gradually he had come to hate everything about him: his slow movements and his drawl and his habit of pulling at the lobe of his ear. Nothing could have displeased Harrington more than Marie-Té's growing friendship with his colleague—a man whom he personally disliked and whose entire outlook on life he found antipathetic to a degree.

Somewhere in the town a clock struck twice. Harrington roused himself with an effort. Nine-thirty! So he had been sitting here for almost an hour, mooning and brooding like a lovelorn youth. And the result was that he was going to be late at the Legation for the first time since his arrival in Santa Rosa. How he disliked to be unpunctual! It disrupted his whole idea of himself.

"My hat, Ah Sing," he said icily, pushing away his breakfast table. "Hurry up, please."

As he emerged on the street, Harrington noticed that the hot wind of the last days was still blowing; it was picking up the dust and whipping it about in frantic circles. These hot windy days before the advent of the rainy season always depressed the Minister, and it occurred to him now that the weather might be partly responsible for his state of nerves. About to step into his car, he caught sight across the street of a figure lurking in the shadow of a doorway, and at once his mind flew back to the little man who had stood there eying him with hatred the night after his first dinner with Marie-Té. Though the car started off before he could see if it was the same person, the sight of that shadowy figure gave Harrington a peculiar, a most disagreeable sensation.

"*Pronto!* Drive quickly!" he said to the chauffeur, and as the car flew through the streets it occurred to him for a second that he was like a man fleeing away from danger.

Still feeling jumpy and ill-humored, he stepped out of his motor car in front of the Legation; without even mumbling a good morning greeting, he brushed by the porter Jesús. Once again the man had failed to shave, and Harrington remembered his decision to discharge him next time he was guilty of the oversight. Well, this would be the fellow's last chance to contravene the regulations; Baker would be instructed to find a new *mozo* today.

But no sooner had the Minister entered the Legation than he realized that he might have something more important to worry about than Jesús' untrimmed whiskers. There was a feeling of excitement in the air, and as he passed down the hall he caught a glimpse of Hermosillo, the clerk, and Señorita Baricala, the typist, whispering together. They stopped abruptly when they saw him and pretended to be hard at work. When he went into his own office, almost at once there came a knock at the door. In walked Baker, the Third Secretary, on his face an anxious yet at the same time gratified expression. He shut the door carefully behind him before turning to Harrington with a confidential smile.

"I am sorry, Mr. Minister, to have to inform you of something disagreeable. Your vice-consul is being—er—detained in a local brothel."

The "local brothel" to which George Baker referred was no other than Madame Olympe's famous establishment on the Calle de la Independencia. As a matter of fact, "brothel" was a term which only a gringo would have applied to a house of such respectability as Madame Olympe's—a house which had been frequented by the highest political figures and the celebrities of the land. No, it certainly was not a brothel in the accepted meaning of the word; nor was it a mere private residence. It was something peculiar to Santa Rosa in which its inhabitants took a justifiable pride. For there was

106

nothing shoddy nor shady about Madame Olympe's place, and besides, it sold the best whisky in the city.

So Ted Kelly, the vice-consul, had discovered in the course of his dreary sojourn in Santa Rosa, and by now it had become his favorite rendezvous. It was pleasant to loll on one of Madame Olympe's plush *fauteuils* while one sipped one's drink and played gin rummy with a fellow guest or one of the girls. For Ted Kelly the place was neither more nor less than a social club, and poor Ted needed a little relaxation after working under Harrington all day.

For of course Harrington had had it in for him from the start. An Irish American and a Midwesterner to boot, Ted knew that he was precisely the type whom the Minister would have liked to see banned from the country's Foreign Service. No wonder that he sought a little social life to make him forget his worries, and where should he have gone for it but to Madame Olympe's gilded drawing room? In all his visits he had never yet been lured upstairs, and had it not been for an attack of malaria he might never have gone to bed in an institution which after all was dedicated primarily to that purpose.

Early in the morning of the day that Harrington arrived late at his Legation, Hermosillo had received a telephone call from Madame Olympe herself. Monsieur Ted was ill, she said. Very ill. He had a high fever, accompanied by chills, and he would not be able to go to work for several days. In the meanwhile, she informed Hermosillo in a tone of authority, he was to stay where he was and would be allowed to see no one. The Minister was to be assured that Madame Olympe was looking after him like her own son.

That was the situation which George Baker disclosed to Harrington, and which Harrington, when he had had time to analyze it, found not at all contrary to his liking. What was this but the long-awaited opportunity to put Kelly on the mat! Now that this incriminating evidence had come his way, he had only to inform Washington and things would automatically take their own course.

The objectionable Kelly would get what he deserved without Harrington's involving himself in any way.

He was still feeling rather pleased with all this when a second knock came on his office door. This time it was Hermosillo, with a message from Camberly asking if he could see the Minister. Harrington knew at once that Camberly meant to put in a good word for Kelly. The fellow had an insatiable passion for what he called justice. He was forever championing people whom Harrington would have rid himself of as soon as possible—refugees without passports and stranded citizens without funds and natives without a knowledge of English. It would be just like him to try and protect Kelly, who was headed for the dismissal that he obviously deserved!

"Well, tell Mr. Camberly that I can see him for a moment right away," he said to Hermosillo. "I have appointments later in the morning."

Harrington was sitting at his desk reading through some papers when Camberly arrived. (He always made a point of being occupied when a visitor came into his room.) He flung them aside quickly, thus drawing attention to his own politeness, and smiled up wryly at Camberly.

"I hear," he said, giving his little snicker, "that our young friend has not been particularly discreet."

"No," grunted Camberly as he accepted a chair. "He certainly hasn't. You'll excuse my inquiring, Mr. Harrington, but do you intend drawing up a report of this for Washington?"

"That remains to be seen." The Minister toyed with his automatic pencil, eyes averted.

"I only ask because I happen to know that it would be a very serious matter for young Kelly's family if he were to receive a discharge."

"Yes. Well, he should have thought about that before," said Harrington.

"Of course he should have. I'm not trying to justify him in any

108

way, but after all this Madame Olympe's isn't nearly as bad as it sounds—not nearly as bad as it would sound to Washington, I mean. A good many of the diplomats make no bones about going there."

"Less than they do about visiting some of their colleagues," said Harrington, chuckling. He had learned by heart that old diplomatic trick of pretending to agree with one's opponent.

"Precisely," said Camberly. "That's why I want to enter a plea for leniency."

Harrington gave a slow nod which meant nothing whatsoever. He had already made up his mind to ask the State Department for Kelly's recall, and if anyone could have dissuaded him, it certainly was not Camberly.

"Very understanding of you to see his side of the case," he murmured. "I'll have to think about it. Of course the Good Neighbor policy doesn't extend quite so far as to encourage our staff to do business with Madame Olympe. We have to look after our reputation in these days."

Camberly saw that he was getting nowhere, so he took leave of the Minister. He knew that technically Harrington was right, as he nearly always was. That did not prevent his once again being shocked at the man's callous attitude. It was obvious to him that Harrington was going to break Kelly and that he relished the task. God help anyone who falls into his power, he thought angrily as he returned to his own office. He is going to go on like that, walking over people, until he stumbles over one of them in the end.

Camberly had an appointment with Marie-Té that afternoon and was even less talkative than usual. He would not have told her what had happened, but she felt that something was wrong and drew it out of him. At once she suggested that they pay the invalid a call, for Marie-Té had been hearing about Madame Olympe's ever since she had come to Santa Rosa and that keen curiosity of hers had been aroused. Camberly grinned.

"Afraid you don't know what you'd be getting in for, Marie-Té.

Madame Olympe's is respectable enough, but there's no ladies' entrance."

"Do you really take me for a 'lady'? Don't insult me, John."

He continued to object, but it was hard work stopping Marie-Té when she had set her mind on something. Finally he gave in and they drove together to Madame Olympe's villa on Calle de la Independencia.

A dark young lady with dazzlingly blonde hair opened the stained-glass door and gave Marie-Té an appraising look. No doubt she took her for an applicant for a job, brought here by a gentleman who made his livelihood out of such introductions. Wrapping her kimono tighter about her body, so as to outline the curves, she escorted them into the main salon.

"One moment, *monsieur et madame*," she said. "Please make yourselves at home, *s'il vous plaît*. I shall fetch the *patronne*."

Marie-Té would have been at a loss to account for the splattering of French had she not known something of the history and traditions of this institution. When Madame Olympe arrived from France forty years before, she had brought with her a number of female compatriots, who naturally were received with open arms by the unspoiled Santa Rosans. It was thanks to their charms that Madame Olympe's reception office became a drawing room, with the girls acting the parts of gracious hostesses. Many a present-day Santa Rosan matron, living, plump and bejeweled, in the bosom of her family, started her career in the "French Embassy," as Madame Olympe's marble villa is affectionately called. The old lady is godmother to several distinguished younger members of the Yacht Club.

Marie-Té and Camberly were left standing in an immense room filled with an assortment of plush furniture, a glass ceiling and murals representing familiar mythological scenes. "The Rape of Europa" occupied the most conspicuous position, perhaps because of the traditional Spanish interest in bulls, perhaps because of the appropriate nature of the subject. The Olympian animal here repre-

110

sented was a fiery beast indeed, with steam issuing from his nostrils and passionate locks curling on his brow; he looked as if he were just ready to dash into the bull ring of Santa Rosa. Everything from that painting to the kimonoed lady and the long-horned phonograph in the corner smacked of the 1900 era, when Madame Olympe had come to install herself in Santa Rosa. No changes seemed to have been effected since.

Attracted by her great hobby, Marie-Té walked over to examine the phonograph records, ranged in a great cabinet of walnut. There they all were, those favorites of another age, to which elegant Parisians in tight skirts or striped trousers had once swung in naughty rhythm. *"Très moutard," "Je danse avec mon grand frisé," "La valse brune,"* Marie-Té read on the warped disks titles of tunes which her mother used to mention with nostalgia. She would have liked to put one on, but the entrance into the room of Madame Olympe stopped her. Clad in a starched black blouse with long skirts trailing underneath, the old lady was as little streamlined as her gramophone. Dangling from her waist was a massive bunch of keys.

"Ah, I see that you are interested in our records," she remarked with an old-fashioned graciousness. Stiffly she took a few little dance steps, humming as she did so some bars from *"Je danse avec mon grand frisé."* "Those French songs are our favorites," she said, "but, alas, they are getting well worn now. We only play them on occasions, and the rest of the time confine ourselves to—American jazz." She pronounced the last two words in a tone that implied her withering scorn for anything belonging to this modern era.

"I also prefer the Parisian tunes," Marie-Té remarked, switching to French. "We have the same taste, madame."

"And the same country?" asked the old lady, her little eyes twinkling with interest. But the truth was that poor Madame Olympe was quite out of practice in her native language. After forty years abroad, her original *provençal* accent had become tinged

111

with the guttural pronunciation peculiar to all Spanish speaking people.

"No, I am not French," answered Marie-Té, "though I lived in France for some time. Haven't you ever returned there?"

"Never. I have always meant to, but you know how it is—the calls of duty." Her pudgy hands with the diamond rings effected a gesture to designate the establishment. "I haven't been able to get away. In fact I have been stuck in this *sacré* hole for forty years." Madame Olympe glared furiously through the mauve-tinted window at the houses of Santa Rosa outside. Her chins quivered indignantly above the wrinkle-concealing velvet band. She looked to Marie-Té like some great, almost extinct species of mammal, fated soon to disappear from our planet. This room was her proper environment; transported therefrom, she would rapidly wilt and die.

"I have come here to see Mr. Kelly," Marie-Té seized this propitious moment to remark.

"Monsieur Ted? No, I'm sorry." Madame Olympe's little mouth tightened behind folds of fat. "I've said before that Monsieur Ted can see no one; he is very ill."

"I know. That is just why I must speak to him. I am his fiancée."

"His fiancée! Monsieur Ted has a fiancée!" Madame Olympe was flustered. She could not imagine anyone with a fiancée coming night after night to her establishment, especially when the girl seemed the sort who should have little difficulty in holding any man. Still, she reflected, that may have accounted for Monsieur Ted's extraordinary celibacy during all his visits. "He never said a word to us about a fiancée," she muttered, not yet reassured.

"Well, that was natural, I suppose."

"Yes, I suppose it was. And what about him?" she asked with a glance at Camberly, who was standing sheepishly, hat in hand.

"Oh, he'll wait here."

"Very well. If you are Monsieur Ted's fiancée, I can't prevent your seeing him, but you must only stay a moment. Above all, don't bother him. He has enough on his mind, what with that dreadful

Harrington who hates him, and his poor mother so many hundred miles away."

Madame Olympe escorted the visitor upstairs, puffing asthmatically and dragging herself aloft by means of her two hands rather than actually climbing. The wooden banister, painted to resemble marble, swayed under the colossal pressure. In her shapeless long skirt, she looked from behind like a fat monk in his cassock; her bunch of keys could have been taken for a crucifix dangling from the rosary about his waist.

"Here we are," she said, and unlocked one of a row of doors with an object that resembled the key to a city.

Marie-Té found herself in a Turkish harem. Byzantine columns pretended to support the ceiling and through the window painted on the wall could be seen the Bosporus, teeming with sailing boats and steamers, models 1900. In the background, or rather on the opposite room wall, lolled voluptuous ladies, some with, some without, shawls. A fat eunuch, looking somewhat like Madame Olympe, squatted vigilantly beside them. Thrust into this sensuous atmosphere, reclining on a couch of love, was a very seedy-looking young man clad in a woman's lace-embroidered nightgown.

Marie-Té had only laid eyes on Ted Kelly once before, when he interviewed her about her visa. She even doubted if he recognized her, but conscious that Madame Olympe was watching her suspiciously, and offered her cue by that lady's *"Eh bien, voilà, mes enfants!"* she ran up to the bed and gave the invalid a resounding kiss. For a moment, Ted looked as if he had been shot. Through his feverish mind probably passed the thought that one of the girls whom he had been resisting for so long was taking advantage of his incapacity.

"No, no," he mumbled protestingly in Spanish. "I am too sick. Not today!"

"It's all right," whispered Marie-Té reassuringly and leaned over him as though she were telling him a lover's secret. "I'm a friend of

113

Camberly's. We're supposed to be engaged—you and I. It was the only way I could get in."

"Oh. Oh—I see," said Ted, and though he was very pale, he suddenly blushed scarlet. He fingered the lace bosom of his nightgown. "This isn't mine, you know. They lent it to me."

"Don't worry. It looks very smart."

"So the Legation is onto things? Good God!"

"Yes, Madame Olympe telephoned this morning."

"Does—Harrington know?"

Marie-Té was forced to nod. Ted Kelly groaned and closed his eyes. Lying there in the lace nightgown, he looked both ridiculous and pathetic; a shiver passed through his body; his teeth began to chatter.

"It's the malaria," said Madame Olympe, waddling up solicitously.

"No. It's Harrington," Ted muttered without opening his eyes.

Marie-Té began to laugh. She knew that it must seem unkind, but she couldn't help it. The whole situation was so ludicrous, with poor Ted lying in his lace nightie in that oriental setting of respectable vice! It tickled her fancy, and never since she was a little girl had she succeeded in checking a fit of laughter.

Madame Olympe was shocked. "Your fiancé is not at all well. Excuse me, mademoiselle, but I must admit that I see no cause for amusement."

"It's all right," said Ted, his Irish eyes glittering. "Let her laugh, Madame Olympe! I swear to God, that's the first good laughter I've heard in Santa Rosa for weeks."

Next morning when Harrington arrived at his Legation, he was greeted by a new doorman, who saluted and clicked his heels as if Harrington had been a general. The Minister was pleased to see that this was a much younger man than Jesús, and that he was not only well shaved but looked actually smart in his dark-blue uniform. Baker seemed to have handled the matter very well.

114

"What is your name?" he inquired of the fellow in Spanish.

"Carlos, Your Excellency."

"Have you done this sort of work before?"

"No, Your Excellency. I mean yes. Quite often."

Well, thought Harrington as he made his way to his office, the man's not too bright but he will do. At least he makes a good appearance and he shows respect; you can't ask more.

Calling Baker into his office, he notified him that the new man was acceptable and asked if there was any news of Kelly.

"Why yes," said Baker, not looking directly at Harrington. "Yes sir, Kelly is still there. I understand that Mr. Camberly went to see him yesterday afternoon."

"Is that so?" Harrington asked the question without great interest.

"So Hermosillo informs me," said Baker, his glance resting on the American flag attached to the miniature flagpole on the table. "He saw Mr. Camberly coming out of the place with Baroness Falkenborn. Apparently they'd been paying Kelly a visit."

Only with an effort did Harrington control his features. He knew that whatever he did, he must hide his feelings before George Baker.

"H'm. That was very thoughtful of them," he remarked. "I know what these attacks of malaria are like—I had one myself in China. Well, congratulations on finding the new doorman, Baker. You made an excellent choice."

When the Third Secretary had left him, Harrington sat for several moments completely flabbergasted. Was it possible that Marie-Té had done this thing? He could hardly believe it, even though he'd suspected before now that she would stop at nothing. But to think that a girl of good family, a girl whom he actually had debated marrying, should have put herself in such an undignified position! And put him in almost as bad a one, when he came to think of it. Oh, he was going to pay back Camberly for allowing this!

He grew calmer after a while, and after deliberating on the situation, summoned the typist, Señorita Baricala. Rapidly he dictated to her a long letter for Washington about Ted Kelly, stressing all of the young man's shortcomings, leading up to the scandal in which he was now involved. He had mapped out the letter while lying in bed the night before, but it turned out to be a good deal more biting than he had planned. He felt a little better after writing it; it was almost as if he had dealt a return blow to Camberly himself.

Next the Minister summoned back George Baker. Resuming his usual bland manner, he asked him to take a taxi to Madame Olympe's and call for Kelly; if there was any difficulty, he should get the help of the police. Whatever happened, Baker was not to return without definite word that Kelly had left the "French Embassy." As to where he was to take him, Harrington was not at all specific.

"You arrange about that, Baker," he said when the young man asked him in the semi-subservient manner that he adopted with the Minister. "I don't care where he goes, but we've got to get him out of that 'French Embassy.' A vice-consul doesn't belong in an embassy of vice, you know."

"That's right, Mr. Minister," said Baker. And he forced a laugh, knowing that his chief was rather proud of such limping puns.

A few minutes later, Harrington was standing at his window, watching Carlos, the new porter, run down the hill to fetch Baker's taxi. Things were being accomplished now, and he no longer felt quite so impotent; he had taken charge again. A tap at the door caused him to wheel about, and when he called, "Come in!" he was surprised to see Camberly's tall figure in the doorway.

"Can I have a word with you, Mr. Harrington?"

"By all means," he answered, seating himself and rearranging some papers on his desk. He smiled at the visitor politely, almost cordially. Camberly, on the other hand, seemed for once perturbed; he acted as if he did not quite know what to say, and Harrington

116

again experienced his old feeling of ascendancy over the Southerner. For a second it seemed to him quite absurd that he should have considered this heavy-footed fellow a rival for Marie-Té's affections.

"Have a seat, Camberly," he said, indicating the visitor's chair, which was always kept in such a position that the light fell full on the occupant's face, while Harrington remained in the shadow. Camberly made a sign that he preferred to stand.

"I understand that you are sending Baker to fetch Kelly, Mr. Harrington."

"Why, yes. That is correct."

"I went to see Kelly myself yesterday, and I should say that he'd be better off where he is—at least until the fever drops. He's being very well taken care of."

"Oh, I'm convinced of that," said Harrington pointedly. "However, the fact remains that he is still a member of this staff."

"There may be a scandal if you try to move him," said Camberly, tugging nervously at the lobe of his ear.

"There will be no scandal. Baker has orders to get in touch with the police in case of difficulty."

Through the window the taxi could be seen driving up with Carlos hanging on the running board. He swung his porter's cap proudly at some friends, who replied with jubilant shouts and cat-calls. While the ancient taxi was still moving, Carlos jumped off in a spectacular fashion and went bounding into the Legation. A moment later George Baker, buttoning his spruce double-breasted jacket, stepped into the car, which drove off with asthmatic wheezes.

"You said just now," remarked Camberly speaking very slowly, "that Kelly was still a member of the staff. Does that mean that he may not remain in that position?"

Harrington shrugged his shoulder. "That depends."

"In that case," said Camberly abruptly, "I ought to tell you of my intention of sending in a report of my own. I think that his side of the matter should be stated too."

117

Harrington felt that he had grown pale. His immediate reaction was fear—unreasoned fear, he hastened to tell himself, seeing that his position was impregnable. It was Camberly who would have to justify himself for his insubordination, yet this did not prevent the Minister from experiencing an unpleasant sensation, as though he were about to choke. There was no doubt that this was the beginning of a state of war, and Harrington, like the Nazis, was opposed in principle to outright declarations of belligerency.

"That will be for you to decide," he said, picking his words with care. "I'm sorry that there should be any misunderstanding between us."

"I don't think that we misunderstand each other, Mr. Harrington. We have different ways of looking at things, that's all. I am under your orders, but I can see that it is going to become more and more difficult for us to work together."

"Yes, I think that I can see that too," said Harrington.

Suddenly he began to feel quite desperate. Wasn't Camberly, by planning to go over his head, imperiling his very position as head of the Legation—that position for which he had worked so unsparingly, so unceasingly? He wanted to strike out with any weapon, and for one panicky moment was on the point of mentioning Marie-Té's visit to Madame Olympe's the day before. Yet when he spoke again, his voice was almost as cold and impersonal as usual; even in the stress of the moment he had time to compliment himself on his self-control.

"Suppose that we don't discuss the matter any more at this time, Camberly. As you say, it's a question of viewpoints."

"I quite agree. I only wished to make my own position clear."

Left to himself, Harrington paced the floor for several moments, trying to regain his calm. Finally he seated himself and took up an important paper that required his consideration; it had arrived from Washington that morning and vitally concerned the work of the Legation. Though he read it through three times, he seemed unable to assimilate its contents. Feeling thirsty, he went to the ice-

118

water container and drew two glasses of water, which he drank down rapidly, contrary to his rule. To his surprise, he noticed that his hand holding the water glass was shaking, and when he lifted the other hand, he saw that that one, as well, trembled slightly. He was unable to hold it steady.

It's too ridiculous, he thought. I really must get hold of myself. It's too ridiculous.

Again he seated himself at his desk and, taking out a sheet of his personal stationery, began to compose a letter to his mother. After he had been writing for several moments, he stopped, tore up the sheet and threw it into the wastepaper basket. He rang the bell for Señorita Baricala, and when she appeared, he told her,

"Please hold up that letter to the State Department. I have decided not to send it off today."

Chapter VIII

Mr. Refugee

LITTLE BUBI FALKENBORN HAD A GOLDEN
afternoon before him. His big sister Marie-Té had gone to a luncheon party at Mr. Harrington's, and Uncle Konrad was in the country with Madame Legervais. For once he had been let off his lessons,
which ordinarily took up most of the afternoon. Marie-Té, his
teacher, was adamant about Bubi's putting in his five hours daily;
she was as strict with him as with herself, on whom she imposed
long sessions of Spanish after getting through with the boy's classes.
Under her tutelage Bubi had advanced as rapidly scholastically as
in his general development.

He had lunch in the pension, seated beside Fräulein Stumpf at
the head of the long table. Fräulein Stumpf was writing a book, and
Bubi knew that was the reason she was so absent-minded and never
answered when one spoke to her. In spite of this annoying habit,
Bubi liked Fräulein Stumpf, with her big head and clumsy body;
Bubi had learned to judge people from their faces, not from what
they said, and Fräulein Stumpf's face, although hideous, was nice.

Lunch over, he went upstairs and played a couple of chess games
against himself, taking alternately the white and the black pieces.
He won both games and concluded that he was not such a bad
player after all, even if Uncle Konrad could give him a queen and
a knight and beat him as a rule. It was a wonderful day. The Santa
Rosan sun, falling between the slats of the Venetian blinds, painted
Bubi's leather shorts and the squares of the chessboard in warm
new colors. He looked at his big nickel watch, which he had got as

120

a present on his last birthday. Only three o'clock. Neither his uncle nor his sister would be back for hours. Bubi decided to take a walk.

Whistling a tune, he wandered up the main street to Independencia Park and struck out toward the poorer part of town, where the native cottages sprawled beside the dusty road. Bubi laughed when he looked at them, remembering that Marie-Té had once said that they were like a row of discolored teeth; some were no more than stubs, others were tall and jagged, still others had assumed uneven shapes due to the caving in of one or more of the adobe house walls. Bubi thought that it would have been difficult to chew with such a badly matched set of teeth.

As he walked along, essaying the difficult feat of kicking two stones ahead of him at the same time, Bubi became aware that someone was following behind. He began to walk quicker, and the other person walked quicker too; he stopped, and the person behind him stopped also and pretended to be tying his shoelace. Turning his head, Bubi recognized the little man whom Marie-Té had spoken to one morning outside the bank. Self-assured as always, he decided to begin a conversation.

"*Como le va?*" he asked politely, taking off his hat. "*Bonjour. Guten Tag.* Good morning."

World traveler that he was, Bubi always gave people their choice of languages. In spite of this, the little man seemed strangely embarrassed. Quickly he turned his eyes away and the blood rushed to his pale cheeks. When he finally responded, he spoke in French, fluently but with a strong accent.

"How do you do? I am pleased to meet you," he said formally.

There was a soft-drink stand beside the road and now Bubi pointed to it meaningfully. "I have money today. Shouldn't we have two drinks?" he asked with that natural courtesy which lay in his Austrian blood.

"No, no!" The little man seemed horrified by the suggestion. He took out his own pocketbook, extracted a coin, and purchased two bottles of rose-colored fruit juice, of which he handed one

121

to Bubi. Solemnly they stood there, taking swigs from their respective bottles and neither trying to make further conversation. Bubi decided that he really liked this shy little man, uncommunicative though he was. Anyway, the conversation of most people was rather boring, in the opinion of Bubi Falkenborn.

When he had finished his drink, Bubi gave an unexpected hiccough, and that made them both laugh and seemed somehow to seal their friendship. With a common accord they walked on together, still without speaking. They passed a cottage before which some pigs were lying in the dust and in whose doorway was standing a naked brown boy with a belly button that looked like a doorbell. Bubi's companion shuddered.

"Think of people living in such filth!" he said disgustedly.

"Filth?" repeated Bubi in some astonishment. He had never noticed it, but not wishing to contradict, added a French phrase of Madame Legervais' which seemed appropriate at the moment, *"Ce n'est pas Paris!"*

A little later they came upon a drunken Indian lying sprawled across their road, his face turned upwards with glassy eyes and wide-open mouth. The sensitive nostrils of Bubi's companion quivered in indignation; gesturing to the boy to follow him, he made a wide circle so as to avoid the body.

They had come into one of the shabbiest quarters of Santa Rosa, fairly near to the market place and to Kerjanian's dwelling. This was Bubi's favorite part of town, though Marie-Té had several times asked him not to go there. He had a destination in this neighborhood and even an appointment of sorts, so now he quickened his pace, with his companion following suit.

Presently they arrived at a broken-down adobe cottage surrounded by a fence of organ cacti. Pointing out a narrow opening between the plants, Bubi scrambled through with the agility of a little animal, to emerge on the other side without a scratch. He had to laugh when his friend caught his jacket on one of the long prickles, but he stopped laughing abruptly on seeing the other's tragic expression.

Of course Bubi, the refugee, understood very well that this pale-blue suit was the only one that the little man possessed. His own Uncle Konrad had only two suits of clothes, plus his velvet jacket, and Marie-Té had only three dresses, including the blue evening dress. Still he remembered the time that she'd spilled a whole glass of wine over one of them, and had burst out laughing. "Just laugh and the spots will come out by themselves," she'd said to Bubi. "Always laugh. Then everything will turn out right." So Bubi followed his big sister's advice. Throwing back his head, he began to laugh again, and it turned out just as Marie-Té had said: the little man looked at him, and slowly the tragic expression went away, and he started laughing too. And the rip wasn't nearly as bad as it might have been; it was near the pocket and really looked quite decorative.

They now found themselves in a yard inhabited by a great variety of animals: chickens, turkeys, pigs, rabbits, all were represented. Apparently Bubi was a familiar visitor, for a hideous dog ran forward barking, then, seeing who it was, walked up with wagging tail. An old woman stuck her head through the cottage's unpaned window, and her ancient face turned into a labyrinth of wrinkles as she smiled at the boy. She disappeared from the window, and a moment later came limping toward them on a stick.

This old woman had fared badly at the hands of life. Like a deserted motorcar, she had been stripped of accessories and adornments, so that now little more than the hulk remained. Hair, teeth and even the toes of one of her bare feet were gone, and every superfluous ounce of flesh had vanished from her ravaged body. But out of this scene of human devastation gleamed a pair of eyes of incredible beauty, alive with warmth, tenderness and gaiety. Giving a little cry of joy, Bubi ran forward to throw his arms about her.

For a moment they stood whispering and chuckling, like two people who share a secret. Not wanting his new friend to feel out of it, Bubi ran back to him, seized his hand and led him over to the old woman.

"She is going to give me something," he explained. "Something wonderful. A little animal that I love."

Then he took the old woman by his other hand, and the strangely assorted trio walked around to the rear of the cottage, where an extraordinary sight greeted them. Fastened to a tree by a long cord that encircled its armor-plated waist, was a creature as big as a fair-sized dog that seemed to have stepped out of a museum devoted to antediluvian monsters. His strange elongated face, which tapered out into a long greyhound's nose, protruded from the buckler-like plates of his armature; his short legs stuck out underneath, and a long heavy tail covered with scales trailed behind. The creature was as out of place in the modern world as would have been the knight in armor which his well-sheathed carcass brought to mind.

"Good God! What is that?" exclaimed Bubi's friend, and to the boy's amusement, there was real terror in his voice and in the movement with which he drew back from the animal. What a frightened little man he was, despite his superficial air of bravado!

"That's an armadillo," said Bubi, laughing. "Isn't he beautiful? The old woman's son caught him the other night, and they were going to eat him, because he is delicious. But she's promised to give him to me instead. She loves me, you see," Bubi explained simply and earnestly.

The little man looked at him with a strange smile. "Yes, I see," he said. "I see."

A few moments later the man and the boy left the cottage, Bubi pulling his pet after him on a cord. "I hope that our armadillo will like us," he remarked as they crawled through the cactus hedge to the road. Noticing the little man's pleased expression on hearing the word "our," he added, "He is *our* armadillo, isn't he? I mean, I own him, but you will take care of him. Fräulein Stumpf doesn't even allow people to keep dogs, so I'm sure she wouldn't like having an armadillo walking about her dining room! But I will come to visit him every day. You and I are friends now, aren't we?"

"Ah, yes, yes, we are friends," said the little man, and he looked at the armadillo and smiled, just as if he no longer thought it a dangerous and loathsome beast.

Their progress down the street was rather slow, for armadillos are not used to being led on cords. Presently, however, they came into the more populated quarter of the city and began to arouse attention; a group of Indian boys collected behind them, laughing and pointing to the queerly shaped animal. A dog ran out from the back yard of a cottage, barking at the armadillo and snapping at its legs. The terrified animal lashed out at him with his tail and gave a low hissing sound. At that the boys tried to sick on the dog, but to Bubi's relief, his friend took matters in hand. So loudly did he scream at the urchins that they scattered in fright, and then he shooed away the dog.

Bubi gazed at his friend with pride. He did not at all give the impression of being meek or terrified any longer, but seemed quite fierce instead, and he was breathing hard through his nostrils. Bubi's respect for him went up tenfold. He was sure that if this little man had to defend something or someone he loved, he would stop at nothing. He would even be ready to kill, if it was necessary.

At the doorway of a tired-looking house which had once been painted mauve, Bubi's friend turned in and led the way up a staircase between walls of peeling plaster. Without the slightest hesitation, Bubi bent to pick up the animal and climbed with him up the stairs. Opening a door at the top of the second flight, his host indicated the tiniest of bare rooms; there was a bed, a chest of drawers, and a wicker chair with its back broken. Bubi seated himself gingerly and let loose the animal, which went scampering under the bed, happy at finding solitude and darkness at last.

Grinning at Bubi, the little man seated himself on the edge of the bed, but then suddenly he seemed to remember what was un-

125

derneath it; hurriedly he drew up his short legs and folded them beneath him. However Bubi understood that his friend hated to sit in that undignified position. He jumped up from his chair and offered to change places with him. "Because," he said, "I am not frightened of the armadillo. I am not frightened of anything in the world!"

Bubi's friend gazed at him with wonder. Was it possible, his glance said, that in the year 1943 there existed somebody who had not yet experienced fear? He looked beneath the bed to make sure that the armadillo was not waiting to snap off his legs, then hopped down and hurried over to the wicker chair. Bubi nonchalantly seated himself on the bed and let his glance wander about the room.

"It's nice here," he said politely. "Have you lived here always?"

"Always? Oh no! I have only been in Santa Rosa for three months. Nestor Kerjanian is my name. I am—a foreigner."

"What are you doing here?" asked Bubi. "Refugee-ing?" He spoke the word as if he had been mentioning some recognized profession, such as engineering or dentistry, but when he saw that the little man looked offended, added quickly, "That is what Marie-Té and I are doing here."

Kerjanian appeared gratified at this tactful assumption that they were all in the same boat. "Yes, you are right. I am refugeeing," he said. "In fact I have been refugeeing since—let me see—1918."

"1918!" Much impressed, Bubi gave a low whistle. "Have there really been refugees ever since then?" He counted on his thin aristocratic fingers, a little dirty now because of having held the armadillo. "Goodness! That is twenty-five years—almost three times as many as I have lived."

"Yes, it is quarter of a century. Always I have fled—fled until now I hardly remember what I'm running from."

Bubi gazed at Kerjanian with admiration, as a novice at a trade looks at an old hand. He glanced down at Kerjanian's feet. "Your feet must be tired, after running all those years," he said. "Why don't you take off your boots and soak the feet in cold water? My sister Marie-Té always soaked hers in cold water and eau-de-cologne after she had been dancing all night in Vienna. She said it did them a lot of good."

Kerjanian looked impatient at this mention of another person, obviously displeased that the conversation should veer away from himself for a moment.

"I didn't mean running in that way," he explained a little sourly. "Usually I was on boats or trains or busses. After all, I'm not a tramp, you know! I am a graduate of the University of Erivan in Armenia, and I am a professional schoolteacher, second class. My parents were educated folk and when they heard that my brother in Brooklyn was selling carpets, it almost broke their hearts."

"Is your brother a refugee too?"

"No," said Kerjanian in a tone of pride, "he is an immigrant. He left of his own accord and at the right time—just before the last war."

"I suppose *you* left at the wrong time?" said Bubi.

"I did indeed. When I graduated from the University of Erivan, I got a job as tutor to two boys in a wealthy family in Russian Armenia. Then the Bolsheviki came. I fled to Tiflis—that was my first flight. Then to Kiev. It was the time of Denikin and the White counterrevolution. After the defeat of Denikin I fled back into Turkey. I crossed the Caucasus in the middle of winter—the snow lay eight feet deep. It was bitter cold, and I spent one night in an unheated hut, lighting matches to keep warm. We had to blow on each other's ears or they would have frozen off. I came back just before Easter, 1921, to my native city—to Erzerum . . ."

Kerjanian pronounced that name in an awed whisper, gazing at Bubi with eyes dark and tragic. So evident was his horror at the recollection aroused that Bubi, too, almost whispered. "Erzerum. What happened in Erzerum?" he asked.

Kerjanian's lips were trembling. He wiped them with the back of his hand. "Terrible things happened," he said, raising a long pony forefinger above his head. "Today, twenty years after the massacres, the city of Erzerum still stinks of blood. I met someone who was there quite recently and he told me so. For two weeks a thousand Armenians were slaughtered every day. The Turks broke into the houses and killed every able-bodied man. They tore out the women's and the children's nails. I saw them beat in my own father's face until it was nothing but a shapeless jelly. . . ."

Bubi gave a shudder. "How did you escape?"

"I escaped," said Kerjanian, a note of arrogance stealing into his voice, "I escaped because I was even cleverer than the Turks! I pretended to be one of them and fled to Smyrna. Not many of my people got away, for the Turks had made up their minds to exterminate our race."

"Didn't anybody do anything to help the Armenians?" Bubi asked.

Kerjanian gave a hard little laugh. "Help them! Why should they have helped them? It was the gentlemen who drew up the peace treaties that gave the Armenians to the Turks, their deadliest enemies. They knew what would happen. Men like Harrington did it—diplomats, politicians! What does Harrington care if a hundred thousand Armenians are slaughtered? At this moment men of his kind are slaughtering Jews even faster. You'll find his like in all nations. It's they—the icy-hearted—who've brought the world to the state it is in today."

Bubi interrupted him. "He has a nasty laugh, that Harrington. He-he-he, like that—eh? I know. He comes to fetch Marie-Té for parties. He keeps taking her away. I don't like him either. But I like you, Mr. Refugee. Tell me more about how you ran away from that town with all the blood. It's terribly interesting."

"*Interesting!*" Kerjanian looked at Bubi with a shocked expression, but then his face broke into a smile and its tense muscles relaxed. It was as if in relating the story of his life to this excited young listener, it had somehow come to seem less tragic—more like a fantastic adventure story. "Well, I dressed up as a Mohammedan, and made my way by slow stages to Smyrna, in western Turkey," he went on, with Bubi sitting forward intently on the bed. "For a year I lived in the greatest poverty and in constant danger of my life. Most of the educated people in the town were Greeks, so I learned Greek and finally managed to get a job as assistant teacher in a Greek school. Things were just beginning to go a little better when war broke out between Turkey and Greece. The Greek army occupied Smyrna, but a few months later it was driven out. There were terrible massacres again, this time of Greeks instead of Armenians, and I had to flee once more to save my life. I hid on a ship, and after a terrible journey I reached Athens."

"Athens! I know," said Bubi. "That's where the Acropolis is."

"Yes. But will you believe that I never saw the Acropolis till I had been there two years? Imagine it! I, an educated man! I lay ill for almost all that time in a shack made of tin sheets and rubble. I almost died from the aftereffects of what I'd gone through in Erzerum, in Smyrna. There's a whole city built of tin outside of Athens, and the poor Greeks who were kicked out of Turkey live there—thousands of them. They were moved there temporarily, until some other place could be found for them, but now twenty years have gone by, and they're still there—at least those who haven't died. It's because of people like Harrington that such things happen. They want it like that! Imagine life inside such a shack, built on the bare mud. No heating, scarcely any food . . ."

Kerjanian could not go on. The bitterness of the memories had overwhelmed him again, and his fists clenched, his face contracted in a grimace of pain. Then all at once it softened, and the tears clouded his eyes.

"One moonlit night I dragged myself to—your Acropolis," he said in a choking voice. "It took me hours to get there, I was so weak. But at last I climbed the hill. I saw it. All night I lay on the white marble steps in the white moonlight and . . ."

"And what?"

"And—wept," the little Armenian said. Two tears rolled down his cheeks, slowly, in dignity.

Bubi whispered, "Was it so beautiful then? Or were you so tired?"

"Perhaps both. But from that night I received new strength. I must leave Greece, leave my city of tin, or I knew that I would die. I longed for the great centers of culture. So I left Athens and tramped up through the Balkans, to Budapest, the gateway of the Western World." He looked down at his feet. "Yes, that is the time I really did tramp. It took me almost a year to get from Athens to Budapest."

Bubi clapped his hands. "Oh how lovely to walk over the world as if it all belonged to one! Marie-Té says that we shouldn't only be sad about being refugees, but that we should be glad too, because we see wonderful things that we'd never have seen otherwise. A refugee can't ever get stodgy, whatever else happens to him, she says. I'd never have seen an armadillo if I hadn't been a refugee. But what happened in Hungary?"

"The Bela Kun Revolution," the little Armenian answered resignedly. "Isn't it strange that I, the most harmless and peaceful person, always managed to be on the scene when a disturbance or a war broke out? Or perhaps it isn't so strange, seeing that there have been nothing but wars and disturbances and suffering in the world for the last twenty-five years. Usually I didn't even know what it was all about, but that didn't keep me from getting mixed up in it. I suppose that's the fate of a man like me in a world run by Harringtons. Anyway, they arrested me in Budapest, and I was unjustly in prison for a long time. When I got out I went on to Germany."

"Germany!" said Bubi in a voice of profound scorn. "I wouldn't stay there for ten minutes. They stole my country. I hate the Germans!"

"So do I—after what they did to me," said Kerjanian, bringing the conversation back to himself, as usual. "Someone said he recog-

nized me from the days of the Bela Kun Revolution and that I
was a dangerous character. It was a lie, of course, but I was put in
prison again and treated very badly. Fortunately my brother in
Brooklyn was beginning to do fairly well in carpets by then, so he
sent me a little money and I managed to get out."

"Does he still send you money?" Bubi asked.

"Yes, whenever he can spare some," said Kerjanian. "I am a
refugee; no one will give me an honest job and let me earn money
of my own. Anyway, I finally managed to leave Germany and to
get to France. I drifted to Paris, then to Marseille. Again I fell on
thin times. I used to go down to the wharves to buy a few fish
when the boats came in with their catch. That was the way I lived."

Bubi shook his head. "Goodness, Mr. Refugee," he said, "you
certainly have seen something of the world!" He looked at Kerjanian with admiration. His sister Marie-Té had once told him
that in times gone by young men of the upper classes were sent
on something called "the grand tour" to finish off their education.
Nowadays refugees embarked on a sort of "grand tour" too, but with
signal differences: the hotels at which they stopped were concentration camps and the tour was apt to continue until terminated by
death.

From underneath the bed they could hear the scaly body of the
armadillo scraping against the floor as he moved about; with his
hard tail he struck the bottom of the bed several times in rapid
succession, making its wire springs sing out. Bubi burst into laughter on seeing Kerjanian's horrified expression.

"I hope you don't mind being left alone with our armadillo," he
said. "You'll get used to him; he's such a nice animal. When we
get our visas and go to America together, we'll take him with us,
won't we? We'll show him the skyscrapers. I bet he won't lie and
sulk under a bed then." He took out of his pocket his huge nickel
watch and consulted it. "It's almost six. They'll be waiting for me."

"What a nice watch," said Kerjanian, for almost the first time
mentioning something not directly connected with himself.

131

Bubi beamed. "Oh, do you like it? Is it rather beautiful?" He held it up for inspection.

"Very beautiful. Very, very beautiful," said Kerjanian.

"My Uncle Konrad gave it to me in Havana. Good-by, sir. Take good care of the armadillo, please. Be nice to him—talk to him sometimes, for he must be lonely. After all, he's a sort of refugee too, isn't he?" He bowed politely and clicked his heels as he had been taught to do in Austria, and when he saw that his friend was pleased to be saluted so formally, he added an extra bow. "When can I come back to hear more about your travels?" he asked. "I want you to tell me how you tramped all over the earth. It's great fun! Is tomorrow too soon—after my lessons?"

The Armenian's eyes lit up. "No, no, come tomorrow. Tomorrow is not too soon."

Bubi waved to him, got down on his knees to have a last look at the armadillo, and then went tearing down the stairs.

"Good-by! Good-by, Mr. Refugee," he called back from the landing.

Chapter IX
Dr. Ruíz

WHEN GEORGE BAKER ARRIVED AT THE "FRENCH Embassy" to fetch Kelly, he received a much less cordial reception than had Camberly and Marie-Té. Madame Olympe was getting fed up with these unwanted calls, and she did not hesitate to say so. Poor George, who understood very little Spanish, was set upon by the old lady, who forgot all her Parisian elegance and reverted to the manners of Marseille, where she had been born. She let it be known that Monsieur Ted was a good deal worse this morning, and that even his own mother would not have been allowed to see him, much less an inquisitive *gringo*. Taking George Baker by the sleeve of his smart suit, she escorted him to the stained-glass door.

George remembered Harrington's instructions, so he told his taxi to drive on to police headquarters, meaning to put his case before Señor Pinchinchi himself. Pinchinchi, the head of the Santa Rosan police, was a firm advocate of Pan-American solidarity, and no doubt he was the right person to address. Indeed, when his country broke off relations with the Axis, he had sent a special note to Mr. Harrington expressing his readiness to be of assistance at any time. Besides, he spoke a little English, picked up in New York some years before.

At that time Santa Rosa was growing traffic-conscious, and Pinchinchi had headed a group of police officers who visited the northern metropolis to find out how the situation was being handled up there. They returned minus one of their number, who had been run over on 42nd Street, but with an American engineer and a

133

number of advanced ideas about traffic signals. The upshot of it was the erection of three magnificent traffic beacons along Calle de la Independencia, before which the puzzled cowherds and muleteers were made to halt while the lights changed from red to amber to green. As to the five hundred-odd cars roaming the Santa Rosan streets, they had long ceased to pay much attention to the Pinchinchi beacons, which functioned very irregularly since the departure of the American engineer; frequently the stop light remained on for several hours, resulting in a long line of waiting bullock carts with the drivers so soundly sleeping that they did not move on even after the signal had turned to "go."

Pinchinchi received George Baker in an elegant office hung with large portraits of the president of the Republic and of Franklin Roosevelt, side by side. Relegated to an inconspicuous corner was the calendar distributed gratis to government offices by the German pharmacy, graced with a photograph of the Brandenburger Tor in Berlin. Pinchinchi, a large florid man with a flowing mustache and sparkling eyes, looked a little like a Sicilian bandit.

"Ah, you have come to me for the help," he exclaimed. "O.K. Very, very glad. In this time, all the Americans must stick together. You agree, gentleman?"

"Of course," said George Baker.

"Our two countries are one," cried Pinchinchi. He looked as if he were about to burst into emotional sobs.

George began to explain the purpose of his call, the police chief listening carefully and stroking his long mustache. At the mention of the Madame Olympe, a worried expression stole into his face.

"But, gentleman, to take the step in this case is perhaps not so easy."

"Why not?" inquired the American.

"Madame Olympe, she is personal friend of mine. And of all the police force," he added feelingly.

"Still, you will agree that she has no right to keep Mr. Kelly against his will? It's preposterous!"

134

"Perhaps. Perhaps you are O.K. The matter is delicate, however. If you please, put yourself in my position. Madame Olympe is human, like everyone." He made an understanding gesture. "If I taking the step, she end with get mad as hell. Then it is she who taking the step. She perhaps forbid the police force come to 'French Embassy' for three, four, months. Myself included! It has happened before. That not so damned good for my position with my colleagues, apart from personal inconvenience."

George Baker could find no way of refuting this unexpected line of reasoning. He decided to emulate the example of Mr. Harrington and use the diplomatic approach.

"If you'll allow me to suggest it, Mr. Pinchinchi, a personal call from you might have effect. If you used your powers of persuasion . . ."

"Impossible, gentleman," Pinchinchi answered severely as he rose to show that the interview was at an end. "Besides everything else, my wife would not allow."

"Your wife?"

"Yes. Mrs. Pinchinchi is French lady. She came to Santa Rosa from Paris with Madame Olympe. So you will understand. Quite impossible for me to taking the step. Quite impossible. Good-by, gentleman."

George Baker left the police chief's office with the feeling of frustration that was the inevitable lot of any foreigner who tried to get something accomplished in Santa Rosa; it was like wading through a sea of honey. He dreaded to face Harrington without having fulfilled his seemingly simple mission, so decided as a last resort to seek the advice of Hermosillo, the Legation clerk. Hermosillo, a native of Santa Rosa, had various ways of his own of arranging things, which often proved more effective than orthodox methods; he was, Camberly used to say, the most valuable man in the Legation. Using the telephone in the police court, the Third Secretary succeeded after the usual delay in getting his call through

135

and was told to wait right where he was and be sure not to speak to anyone.

About half an hour later Hermosillo wandered in, just as casually as though he were making a social visit. Nodding to George Baker, he strolled over to the police captain's desk, around which progressed a card game between a number of uniformed policemen. Hermosillo slapped several of them on the back and watched the game for about a quarter of an hour, winking at George Baker to have patience. He finally drew a couple of the men aside and spoke to them in whispers. There was a great deal of discussion to and fro. In the end Hermosillo returned to the American and said urgently, "Ten pesos for these gentlemen, if you please. It is all arranged."

George Baker wanted to engage a taxi, but Hermosillo thought that the roomy patrol wagon would be more suitable. Besides, he pointed out, it was included in the price. All four, Baker, Hermosillo and the two policemen, went tearing through the streets with the bell clanging as though there was a fire, right past the three Pinchinchi beacons, which had been named respectively Magdalena, Lupita and Concepcion in honor of the police chief's daughters. The two patrolmen squatted on the floor, smiling happily and obviously enjoying the ride.

They drew up at the "French Embassy" with a screeching of brakes and a final burst of bell clanging. Almost immediately a crowd of urchins collected, while the two policemen jumped down with a stretcher and went hurrying up to the glass door. Their pounding and shouting brought the young lady in the kimono to open it, whereupon they rushed past her up the stairs. George Baker and Hermosillo followed, the American beginning to experience a few qualms because of this categorical procedure.

"*Donde está el gringo?* Where is he?" Hermosillo demanded of the young lady, who, taken by surprise, answered, "*En el palacio turco.*" The policemen, evidently knowing the place like the palms of their hands, at once headed for the right room. When George

136

reached the doorway, they were already lifting the protesting Kelly from his oriental couch and placing him on the stretcher. Feverish though he was, he kept swearing at them and trying to pull down his lace nightgown, which had crept up around his neck.

"It's all right, Ted," George called out. "I've come to take you to a better place."

"Damn you to hell!" Ted Kelly shouted back furiously. "There isn't any better place. Get out of here, will you!"

"Sorry, but Mr. Harrington sent me."

"Tell that bastard . . ." Ted's advice to the Minister remained unexpressed, for at that moment one of the two policemen picked up an imitation Turkish rug and threw it over his head to stop his struggling. Then they picked up the stretcher and scurried out with it, down the stairs and straight through the crowd of on-lookers to the Black Maria. Evidently they wished to finish their job before the appearance of the choleric Madame Olympe herself. George Baker just had time to swing himself onto the open rear end before they started off with a jerk that almost sent the invalid rolling off his stretcher.

"Where to?" said Hermosillo, lighting a *Deliciosos*, the popular Santa Rosan cigarette, and handing about the packet. He could well feel proud at having accomplished in a few minutes what the First and Third Secretaries of the Legation had both failed to do. And it had only cost ten pesos!

Indeed, things had gone so quickly that George Baker scarcely had had time to debate the next move. There was a civic hospital in Santa Rosa to be sure, but its reputation did not recommend it. Built from the proceeds of a special tax, it had suffered from graft even more than most of the public institutions. There never had been sufficient funds available to purchase beds, with the result that the patients, who could only be inducted into the house of mercy when too poor or too weak to protest, lay on straw *petates* on the unswept floor. George Baker certainly could not dump the sick vice-consul there, nor could he leave him unattended in Ted's own furnished room. The only solution, for the moment at least, was the Hotel Imperial, where everybody eventually ended up when they had no other place to go.

There seemed to be more than one person in that position today. It was lunch time when he got there, and the first person George ran into when he went to ask for a room was John Camberly.

"Hello there, George! I'm just about to have a snack. Want to join me?"

"Afraid I can't," George Baker answered. "I've got Ted in a police wagon outside."

"God almighty!"

"Yes, very complicated. I haven't time to explain it all now."

"What are you going to do with him?"

"Why, I mean to get him a room right here. Unless you have some better suggestion."

Camberly thought fast, and came to the decision that Ted had better be taken to Pension Hilda. There he would at least be sure of Marie-Té's care, while lying alone in this hotel, he could die before anybody knew it. Marie-Té had taken a real fancy to Ted when she met him at Madame Olympe's the day before. Of course, George Baker was only too pleased to have the responsibility shouldered by someone else, so the two men climbed into the station wagon, which went clanging off again in the direction of Pension Hilda.

Ted Kelly was completely delirious by this time. He seemed to have the idea that Camberly was Harrington, and kept mumbling something about not giving a God-damn whether or not a report was sent off to Washington.

"That's all right, old boy. Everything's under control," Camberly reassured him, whereupon Ted lunged out and tried to sock him on the chin. "Take that, you lying, double-crossing son of a Boston sea cook," he yelled. They had the greatest difficulty getting him calmed down.

Fortunately, Marie-Té was at home when they arrived. She at

138

once took charge of everything, spoke to Hilda Stumpf, and within a few minutes had put the sick boy properly to bed in a pair of Uncle Konrad's pajamas. As she and Camberly were trying to make him comfortable, Hermosillo came in to say that the men wanted two more pesos for the extra trip and that Mr. Baker had got tired of waiting and taken a taxi back to the Legation. Camberly gave him the two pesos.

"If you wish them to drive you anywhere, they will have to get some gas. Another peso, if you please, Mr. Camberly."

Camberly told him that he preferred to journey in a less conspicuous-looking vehicle, and Hermosillo departed, looking somewhat crestfallen. While they had been talking, Ted seemed to have dropped off to sleep; he lay, breathing deeply but unevenly, and his good-humored boyish face was flushed with fever. Leaving Uncle Konrad in charge, Marie-Té and Camberly tiptoed out of the room.

They were on their way down the spotless corridor when they passed her door, and on the spur of the moment she pulled it open to show him where she lived. Marie-Té's room was, as always, in a colossal mess, the floor positively strewn with belongings. She had been playing records before Camberly arrived and one of them was still turning grindingly on the electric phonograph. Marie-Té stepped across a few dozen books and a pile of other records to turn it off.

"I was playing Beethoven. Do you enjoy Beethoven, John?"

"No."

"Oh John, you really are an honest man," said Marie-Té laughing. "I think I like you quite a lot."

"That's good, Marie-Té."

"What should I play for you? I have a bit of everything—even jazz. Would you care to hear some jazz?"

"Play anything," said Camberly. He was standing with his tall figure leaning against the doorjamb, while Marie-Té was on her knees, going through the pile of records on the floor. She had on her thin white dress with the low neck, and from where he stood he could see the curves of her bosom very plainly. Utterly absorbed, she was examining her beloved records one by one, then laying them aside with a tenderness that was truly maternal. Her blonde hair kept falling before her eyes, whereupon she would toss it back each time with an impatient little gesture.

Camberly walked over to Marie-Té, put his hands beneath her armpits and lifted her to her feet. He looked at her a moment, and then gave her a long hard kiss on the mouth. Marie-Té did not have time to be surprised. Indeed, every other feeling was submerged in the delightful sensation aroused by that hot physical contact. It was a very satisfying sort of kiss. She realized suddenly that she had been wanting it for a long time.

Probably there were more good doctors in Santa Rosa than any city of its size in the entire world. Unfortunately one couldn't get the services of a single one of them. The specialists from Hamburg, Berlin and Vienna were all running tailor shops or dry-cleaning establishments, and woe to them if they ever dared to give professional advice; it was as much as their visas were worth. The government's comparatively liberal policy toward refugees was based on the premise that they came to the country simply as refugees, not members of any particular profession. It was as difficult for a refugee lawyer to practice law, or for a refugee architect to build houses, as if these specialists had been day laborers.

So Marie-Té learned when she tried in vain to get Herr Professor Levi for the ailing vice-consul. The professor, who once upon a time used to lecture at the Hamburg Institute for Tropical Diseases, almost rang off when Marie-Té telephoned him at his bakery. It was a matter of public information that all telephone wires in Santa Rosa were tapped, and that the refugees' conversations were the censors' particular concern.

"But if you can't come yourself, couldn't you at least recommend someone?" Marie-Té begged, but the eminent professor answered with panic in his voice, "I know *nothing*. Do you hear? Nothing! All I know is how to bake cakes and to make Vienna rolls. Don't ask me about anything else."

So reluctantly Marie-Té had to give that up and go to Hilda Stumpf for advice. "No, there's no point in trying to get a foreign doctor," answered Hilda. "Better call up Salvadore Ruíz. He's an extremely cultured man with an alert mind, though unfortunately it's so long since he studied medicine that he has lost his grip. Still he's the best doctor available. He's hundred per cent Indian, and was born in a backward mountain village, many miles from the nearest road. Those purebred Indians are wonderful men, Marie-Té."

Marie-Té thought she understood Hilda Stumpf's enthusiasm when Dr. Ruíz arrived later that afternoon and greeted her with a dignified little bow. Very erect he held his finely shaped body, but neither stiffly nor arrogantly. To Marie-Té it seemed that there was something as free and proud about this man as about a wild animal in the forest, yet his eyes had a warm glow that invited intimacy. Marie-Té instantly felt a great liking and great respect for the doctor, though she soon saw that Hilda had been right to recommend him only with reservations.

In the first place he had failed to bring along his medical kit, and this had to be sent for in a taxi. When it arrived he was unable to find his stethoscope, a bottle of alcohol or a thermometer. Puzzled, he stood gazing at the cavity of the bag, in which reposed forceps and other equipment usually associated with childbirth rather than with the treatment of malaria. He ended by restrapping the bag and placing it in a corner, where he forgot it when he said good-by. But in the meanwhile he had charmed everyone and left the impression that here was a truly good and truly humane man. The fact that he was inept was unimportant, unless one happened to consider that the lives of a great many people lay in his kind clumsy fingers.

Like all Santa Rosans, he seemed to regard a business call as primarily a social event. While waiting for his bag, he stood downstairs chatting affably with Marie-Té and Uncle Konrad, and actually looked disappointed when it arrived so soon.

When finally he made his way upstairs, Dr. Ruíz examined the sick boy with a gentleness that did not conceal his fundamental lack of interest; it was obvious that he felt it did not matter a great deal when his patient recovered—or for that matter, if he recovered at all. Only when Ted Kelly began to mumble some English phrases did Dr. Ruíz abandon his phlegmatic manner. He stood for a moment, gazing into Ted's broad Irish face, then ran his fingers over his straight black hair in an amazed gesture.

"No! This is extraordinary—most extraordinary."

"What is the matter, Doctor?" asked Marie-Té, alarmed.

"But surely I visited this young man yesterday. And in quite another locality."

It turned out that Dr. Ruíz had been summoned by Madame Olympe the day before and that he actually had attended Ted Kelly at the "French Embassy." Poor Ted did not make very much sense today, so he hadn't breathed a word about that visit. As to the doctor, he had far too many malaria patients in Santa Rosa to be expected to recognize them all.

Recovering from his momentary surprise, Dr. Ruíz now seated himself on the edge of the bed, rummaged vainly through his pockets for a prescription pad, and finally wrote on the back of an old envelope with a borrowed pencil because his fountain pen did not work. He gave the impression of a man who is repeating the identical action for the millionth time.

"Won't he need a nurse?"

"A nurse? Ridiculous! This is simply a mild case of *malaria tertiana*—we have hundreds every day. Tomorrow or the next day the fever will drop, then it will return the day following, drop again on the third day, and so on until the sickness burns itself out. Now if it were tropical malaria, that would be quite a different story; there you can easily have death within thirty-six or forty-

142

eight hours. But I'm glad to say that there are very few cases of 'tropical' in Santa Rosa."

Dr. Ruíz stayed on for dinner without much urging. He sat between Marie-Té and Hilda Stumpf at the big table, and proved an interesting conversationalist. In all the time that she had been here, Marie-Té had met comparatively few upper class Santa Rosans, who seldom frequented the public places, and did not associate with the diplomatic set. Though their exquisite manners prevented them from showing it, the well-born Santa Rosans despised all foreigners (particularly Protestants), considering themselves infinitely above them in breeding. "It's too bad," Marie-Té had once remarked to Camberly. "For all the real contact we get with the people of this country, we might as well be living in Paris or New York. My social intercourse with the Santa Rosans consists of saying 'Thank you' to Hilda Stumpf's maid, and yours in giving a morning nod to Jesús, your doorman. Bubi's the only one of us who's caught a glimpse of Santa Rosan life." Now at last Marie-Té had the chance of learning something about the country from the educated native viewpoint.

The picture that Dr. Ruíz painted for her was a tragic one, in spite of its exotic coloring; poverty, misery and disease stalked across a landscape already fouled by the devils of sloth and of corruption. He told her of the incredible misery of the rural districts—a phenomenon current in almost every Central American country. If she thought that parts of Santa Rosa had reached the depths of poverty, it showed that she did not know the tropical provincial towns, nor had she visited the coffee *fincas* in the mountain districts. Deserted by the central government, at the mercy of predatory landlords, the peasants lived ever in a state of near starvation.

That was the region where tropical malaria and typhoid raged almost unchecked, and where the dreaded *simulium* fly, whose bite causes blindness, had claimed as victims a third of the native population. Laying its eggs solely in running water, the *simulium,* said the doctor, profited from scattered efforts to connect the stagnant malaria ponds with the rivers; the slowly moving waters of the canals became its ideal breeding spot. In other words it was the same old story once again: a surge forward in one direction implied a lowering of the level elsewhere.

Dr. Ruíz leaned back in his chair and threw out his arms in a hopeless gesture. "So, you see, my friends, there is nothing to do about it. Nothing! *Nada, nada!*" he repeated, smiling almost gaily.

But surely, Konrad suggested, there was a certain progress after all. Despite disappointments, the efforts of a few well-meaning men like Dr. Ruíz himself, could not have been entirely unavailing.

He was sitting across the table from the doctor, beside pretty little Irène Legervais, clad in her one smart Parisian gown. In honor of the visitor he had produced from his private cellar in his clothes closet a bottle of Tokay wine, for Uncle Konrad was not one to let pass an excuse for a celebration. Now on his large face lay an anxious expression, as though the reply to his question really might affect him personally.

Irène Legervais laughed. "Don't take it so seriously, Konrad. Remember, this has been going on for centuries!"

Dr. Ruíz nodded. "Yes, centuries—centuries," he repeated. "In the time of the pre-Mayan Indians things were exactly as they are today—neither better nor worse. They will continue like that for a few hundred years more. Yet why should it surprise you that in our backward country there still are regions where cow dung is collected and baked into cakes for food? Even in Europe, where conditions are comparatively ideal, you have not advanced a great deal further. And now," he added bitterly, "you are all engaged in tearing down with dynamite the little you have built up through the centuries."

As she listened to him, Marie-Té became aware of the profound disillusionment of this man. He was one of those rare people who could allow himself a grimly realistic outlook without having it impair his feeling for humanity as a whole. He had a great pity

144

for the individual, struggling on in a world where injustice, stupidity and confusion reigned supreme.

Hilda Stumpf it was who enlightened them about some of the works of mercy in which Dr. Ruíz was engaged. Ever he had spoken for those who had no voice, for the poor, the ignorant. Nor did he confine himself to helping his own people; he was an active friend of the refugees, who had been trickling into Santa Rosa for the last years, always penniless, usually with shattered nerves, despairing minds. He had even helped found a Refugee Help Society, of which Hilda Stumpf was a member.

"Speaking of refugees," he said, addressing Marie-Té, "there are some more due to dock at Puerto Marques next week, en route to the United States: a Dutchman and two German Jews. Have you been to Puerto Marques, Señorita Marie-Té?"

"No, we came to Santa Rosa by air."

"Well, you ought to go there. A visit to Puerto Marques would give you a better idea of this country than residence in the capital for years. And it would mean much to those poor men to be welcomed by someone speaking their own language. Even now they might not be let into the United States." Dr. Ruíz threw his hands in the air, palms upwards, in one of those extraordinary expressive Spanish gestures. "What a terrible thing, señorita. *Quel cosa terrible!* In 1939 the United States let in almost a hundred thousand immigrants; now, in 1943, they will let in only a fifth as many. I could weep. I *do* weep! Everything is done to make the admittance of refugees impossible, especially for the impoverished, uninfluential ones who have most need of succor. The business of investigation takes so long nowadays that when the visa is finally granted the applicant is often dead!"

Marie-Té interrupted him. "And the people in America—do you think, Dr. Ruíz, that they know the situation?"

Again Dr. Ruíz threw up his hands. "Of course they do not know! Do you think they would let such things happen? Only some men of stone in Washington know—and know also how to keep the truth hidden from the great warmhearted American people, who couldn't eat, who couldn't sleep, if they realized that thousands of little, cold children's bodies were being buried in Europe's earth because of official indifference. Darling little bodies that could be saved for love and laughter if only the will to save them were present! But the politicians have duped the public into believing that to win the war it's necessary to sacrifice the children of Europe, as well as its entire Jewish population. There's a lot of talk in the democracies of totalitarian brutality, but what of the democracies' own brutality? Not one loaf of bread has been sent to the dying people of the ghettos, not one official act undertaken to help them to survive or to escape. . . ."

Marie-Té might have given little thought to her suggested visit to Puerto Marques, had it not been for complications concerning the very group of refugees that Dr. Ruíz had mentioned. Next evening, when the heat of the day had subsided, she was leaving Pension Hilda to take a walk when she saw Camberly coming toward her. Though his demeanor was as calm as ever, Marie-Té sensed immediately that he was troubled and that it was for that reason he had sought her out. The thought filled her with pleasure. So his kiss yesterday had really meant something! So their meetings these last weeks had been more for him than a pleasant way of passing the time! She felt her heart beat faster, and from one second to another the whole world seemed gayer, brighter.

Coming up to her slowly, Camberly shook hands. "I see that you are off for an engagement, Marie-Té," he said, and there was disappointment in his voice. That little note of disappointment, also, Marie-Té pressed to her breast.

"No," she answered him. "I was just going for a stroll. It's been terribly close all day." But in her heart she knew that it wasn't because of the closeness that she had run out of the pension, but to be alone and think of Camberly.

"Yes, it is muggy," he said. "The rainy season is on the way. Tell me, Marie-Té, would you mind if I came walking with you?"

146

"Mind? Oh no, I should like it very much."

He took her arm, and it was the first time he ever had done that; it wasn't in the nature of this man to make physical contacts lightly. They began to walk under Hilda Stumpf's acacias, and it gave Marie-Té a delightfully intimate feeling to be strolling with him in this casual fashion, instead of sitting in a café or restaurant. She liked having him for the moment preoccupied, unaware of her existence as a woman; today she was a friend whom he had need of at a difficult moment of his life. She didn't think of asking what was on his mind, and for several minutes they walked up and down the street without either saying a word.

"I'm sorry, Marie-Té," he said finally, forcing a little laugh. "I'm afraid I'm not very good company this evening. The fact is that our friend Mr. Harrington has been even more insufferable than usual. No, no, we've not had any more words," he added quickly in answer to the question in Marie-Té's eyes. "It's simply that I can't bear his—well, his attitude. I mean, his attitude to people. Yesterday there was the Kelly business, and this morning he showed his colors again in connection with some refugees due to land at Puerto Marques en route for the United States."

"I know," said Marie-Té. "Dr. Ruíz was telling us about them last night at dinner. Are they having—visa trouble?"

"Unfortunately, yes. It's a crying shame that these people who've gone through years of torture, shouldn't even yet be granted a place to lay their heads. There's not a single valid reason why their American visas are being withheld, but as usual the State Department is putting off the decision as long as possible. One word from Harrington and they'd be allowed to land here, and later travel up to the States when their American visas are granted. Without it, they will be sent back to Europe, which may mean the concentration camp, torture and death. It's that one word that Harrington is withholding! And why? Not because he has anything against them, but simply because three more human lives matter very little when there are already so many millions of refugees in the world. What *does* matter is that Warfield Harrington, on the road to an ambassadorship, might possibly annoy some individual in Washington by allowing into the United States immigrants whose entry can't benefit anybody but themselves. Therefore three men will have to jump off their boat tomorrow night in Puerto Marques harbor and drown."

Camberly stopped speaking for a moment. Marie-Té had never heard him talk so long in one stretch before, nor had she ever seen him as serious as he was now. He kept tugging at the lobe of his ear, and in his eyes was a strangely remote look—the look of a visionary, thought Marie-Té. Instinctively she knew that this man would one day be of great importance in the world, and she felt a thrill that it was she whom he had sought out today in a mood which he surely showed to but few people.

"I am speaking to you like this," he went on, "because I want you to know exactly how I feel about things, Marie-Té. It isn't only because of those three men that I take this case so to heart, but because in my opinion the attitude of Harrington and his likes is—a shame for my country! You mustn't think that it's an attitude typical of America. It's a Fascist attitude! And I, personally, am out in a war to the death against Fascism. We're fighting it on four continents, and by God, Marie-Té, I mean to fight it when I recognize it at home."

"American Fascism!" said Marie-Té. She clasped her hands together, like a child that is scared. "So there really is such a thing?" she asked, remembering how Kerjanian kept comparing Harrington to the European "man of power."

"Of course there is. For the moment it chooses to masquerade under another name, but it's the same thing at root. We Americans are gullible, you know. Put a synthetic concoction in a can, call it by a fancy trade name, and we'll clamor for it. And in the same way, put Fascism in national dress, call it Harrington, and most of us will take it with no questions asked. But not I! I'm ready to fight the Harringtons with the last breath in my body. I'd stand up against them even if I were unsure of the final outcome and if I thought that they would win. But they shan't win! Fortunately for us, we can still check them in time. We Americans have the advantage of knowing how they gained control in other countries, and there is an army of men like me, ready to fight to the hilt for—the *real* democracy."

"Thank God there is," said Marie-Té, feeling a tremor go through her. For some reason she was immensely moved, and because she would have been ashamed to have the tears come to her eyes, she asked quickly, "And what are you going to do about those three refugees, John? Of course you *are* going to do something."

"Yes. I am going down to meet that boat tomorrow," answered Camberly. "If I find it possible, I'll fix things on my own responsibility. Harrington had intended to send Baker. He's always sending Baker to do his dirty work—Baker, the coming Harrington, the embryo Fascist! You'll find his like in every legation, and, for that matter, in every large business concern throughout the world. But I told Harrington that I had to go to Puerto Marques in any case, so he had no choice but to let me handle this."

"You know, John," said Marie-Té, "it's a strange coincidence. Only yesterday Dr. Ruíz was telling me that I ought to have a look at Puerto Marques myself."

To her surprise, Marie-Té saw a deep flush go over Camberly's countenance. For a second he was silent, then said abruptly,

"Will you come with me, Marie-Té?"

That question was asked in a voice so intense, so serious, that Marie-Té was taken aback. She knew that it wasn't possible to laugh it off, as she would have done with anybody else, yet she instinctively sought to postpone the issue.

She said, "Oh, I really am almost tempted. It's silly to live in a country for months and never see more of it than a European pension and a yacht club . . ."

But then she felt that she could not go on. She couldn't make believe with Camberly, especially not this evening when he had come to her in such a grave frame of mind. She knew that he was going through something like a spiritual crisis, and that with a complete person like him, such a crisis involved the whole being, body as well as mind. Emanating from him she felt a physical desire for her which differed from the desire of all other men whom she had known. It was an uncontrollable urge, like that of a cataract that throws itself down the mountainside.

And suddenly she felt her own body answer, calling out to his in a way which she never had experienced before. So strong was that call that for a moment Marie-Té actually felt frightened. If her soul had grown into a mature woman's soul the night that she lay listening to Uncle Konrad, so did her body become a mature woman's body now. She realized that even her looks had changed: her eyes had grown dark and brilliant and tender, for they were the eyes of a woman in love.

Camberly put his hand on her shoulder. "But Marie-Té," he said, "how beautiful you are all at once. I've never seen you like this before."

"I know," she answered simply. "I know."

Chapter X

Evolution of a Nazi

LIFE HAD TURNED A SOMERSAULT FOR SIEGFRIED Stumpf. Strange how a man can go on for years with the most uncongenial of existences, yet never seriously contemplate a change. Then from one day to the next his course is altered; abruptly he finds himself caught up in a new life, and it is as if the old life had never been. Thinking back afterwards, Siegfried could not remember just when he finally made up his mind to join the Schiller Schule, or if he ever actually had made up his mind. One day he was not a member of the school; the next he was. That was all.

And yet this step, taken after so many hours of self-searching, so many weeks of vacillation, had changed everything from his position in society to his everyday routine. Nowadays instead of dropping into bed at six o'clock each morning, that hour saw him drawing on his clothes; instead of dispensing *aguardiente* and whisky, he dispensed learning, meant to stimulate the recipient in quite a different way. For boss, instead of the sodden Popoff, he had the authoritarian Dr. Hildegard, who inspired respect and a certain amount of terror.

For the first time Siegfried realized how greatly he had missed being the member of an organization taking commands from a common Fuehrer. Standing alone, as he had done for years, he had gone against the dictates of his very nature, and he now rejoined the herd with a sensation of relief. Had he been a member of another race, his lonely fight might have fortified him; being, like all Germans, highly gregarious, it had proved a soul-shattering ordeal which had bade fair to break him in the end. A disciplined herd existence was right for him, even though it entailed a compromise of principles on his part. He belonged here, in the congenial setting of the Schiller Schule, a recognized member of an organization. The ticktock of the big clock in every room was as soothing to his ears as the sound of music. It meant that once again life was proceeding in orderly rhythm, purposefully directed toward a goal.

It was like a nightmare to think back on the chaotic period connected with the night club. Occasionally he actually did dream about it, sleeping in the trim little room which Dr. Hildegard had placed at his disposal after he left Pension Hilda. He would see Boris Popoff in these dreams, reeling about on bare feet with a damp cigarette clinging to his lips, a half-empty bottle of *aguardiente* in his hand. Several times there was re-enacted in his sleep that ignominious fist fight which had resulted in the breaking of his glasses.

He had a new pair now, with gold rims and special bifocal lenses, which Dr. Hildegard's friend, the German-born optician, had made for him. They suited him very well, giving him that air of a wise owl so appropriate to a schoolteacher. Generally he looked better than he had for years; he had taken on weight, held himself more erect, and had once again begun to speak in his old didactic manner. His new well-being extended even to his sparse blond hair, which in the space of a few weeks had practically ceased falling out.

Unfortunately these blessings did not come free of charge. He had had to give up many precious things for them, including the respect of others, and, what was even more important, of himself. How infinitely desirable small things become when one is deprived of them! No longer could he saunter down the streets of Santa Rosa and meet the eyes of his fellow men unabashed. Nowadays when Siegfried chanced to see a brother refugee, he realized with a spasm of self-loathing that the word "traitor" was written over him. He shunned the places where he might meet these threadbare compatriots, who preferred to bake bread or to dry-clean people's clothes, rather than to soil their hands as he had done.

But the worst suffering of all was his gnawing longing for his sister, Hilda, whose wounded eyes he so dreaded to meet that he finally gave up leaving the Schiller Schule altogether. Those eyes! When he told her of his decision to join the German school, something irreparable had happened to them: their light had died, as the light dies in the eyes of a wounded doe while looking, looking at the person who has dealt the death blow. Siegfried had heard of men giving up hunting after seeing that. And he—he had groaned aloud while Hilda looked at him with that stricken gaze of hers, and then had thrown his hands before his face. Five minutes later he had fled from the pension, utterly shattered and in the deepest anguish of soul.

Now Siegfried found his thoughts going back to Hilda many times each day. He missed her not as one misses a dear friend whom one has lost, but as one misses an amputated member of one's body. Always he had gone to her for help in his most difficult moments, always had relied on her instincts rather than his own, atrophied as they were from an overintellectual existence. Henceforth he would no longer have her to turn to, however desperately he might need her. His anguish at that thought was at times almost too great to bear, yet through sleepless nights he would raise his despairing hands and pray, Oh Lord, don't let my sister Hilda ever change! Protect her blessed single-mindedness. Let the flame that is Hilda burn, oh God, for a whole world is crying for the sight of it!

But there were other times when he tried to argue with himself that in spite of what had happened, he still was not a Nazi. Technically, of course, that was true. He didn't teach Nazi ideology; he didn't make the Hitler salute; outwardly he was a free man. But in joining the Schiller Schule he had effected a compromise, and compromises are fatal nowadays. One must stand on one side of the fence or the other, and to straddle it is equivalent to being on the Nazi side. He who is not with the forces of freedom is against them.

Could it have been his new gold-rimmed spectacles that gave Siegfried such clear sight nowadays? He saw right through that idealistic haze with which he had surrounded many things, himself included. For instance, he saw Dr. Hildegard as he really was: a true Nazi, even if he displayed no swastika emblems in his rooms and spoke of this Central American nation as his country. Like so many Germans, the cultured doctor may have shuddered at various Nazi practices, but disapproval of a party's rule does not imply disloyalty to one's country. Circumspection was necessary in the present difficult situation, but when Germany triumphed, the time would come for him to play a more active role. In the meanwhile it was his task to antagonize no one and to keep the Schiller Schule from being closed.

Despite it all, Siegfried admired Dr. Hildegard; his first favorable reaction to the man had not proved wrong. Nor had he been mistaken in thinking that the doctor reciprocated his friendly feelings. Time and again the principal demonstrated that he had a high regard for the new assistant, both by entrusting him with responsibility and by letting him feel that he was a member of the Hildegard family. Since he was living in the house, he was often asked to meals, and Frau Hildegard, a Santa Rosan by birth, began to take a marked interest in the young man.

The Hildegards struck Siegfried as typical of all those thousands of German families who had made their home in Latin America, and it interested him to study them as such. Through them he understood why Germans had always been welcomed in these countries more heartily than either the business-minded Americans or the supercilious English. For whereas Anglo-Saxons came here with the avowed purpose of making money, nearly all Germans came to settle permanently, and frequently, like Dr. Hildegard, married women of their adopted countries. Siegfried had met American engineers who had lived in Latin America for twenty years, yet still knew nothing of its traditions and its history, and seemed to find pleasure in murdering the classically beautiful language. But

Germans like Dr. Hildegard not only appreciated Spanish culture, but had adopted it as their heritage. They were all loyal to Germany, it is true, but their love for their new countries was genuine also.

Yes, thought Siegfried as he sat at a dining table on which German specialties alternated with native dishes, the United States would have to do more than talk about Pan-American friendship and send down ravishing movie stars and Middle Western professors as good-will emissaries. Friendship—Pan-American or other—is a plant that requires much cultivation; it never springs up overnight. And the Germans, who had watered and tended that plant for generations, certainly had a better chance of eventually plucking its fruit.

The jewel of the Hildegard family—the mother's love and the father's pride—was Clara, the elder daughter. While her brother Davilo, dark-haired and flashing-eyed, was a pure Spanish type, Clara took after her father entirely. With her blonde braids, blue eyes and scrubbed rosy cheeks, Clara was the sort of a girl whom every German longs at heart to have as wife. Complementing her good looks, she had the advantage of being goodhearted and not unintelligent.

Siegfried felt himself violently drawn to her. Apart from Marie-Té Falkenborn, whom he considered infinitely above him in station, she was the first woman in Santa Rosa to arouse his instincts as a male. In the last harassing years, the physical side of the man had lain dormant; now it reasserted itself with a vengeance. Clara had only to touch Siegfried while handing him the saltcellar for him to feel a shock of desire; the sight of the young girl tending the plants in the patio caused his concentration to wander while he was teaching classes.

Of course Clara soon realized how the wind was blowing. Obviously she did not find the new assistant unattractive, and it was not long before she was taking advantage of her physical appeal for him. Assuming a bantering air of ownership, she began to order

155

him about and generally to treat him in a motherly manner. Siegfried, who was used to being mothered by Hilda, enjoyed this; it made him feel a bit less lonely.

Unfortunately, of all the Hildegard family, Clara was the most outspokenly pro-Nazi; Siegfried had to keep his wits about him to steer their conversation from controversial ground. Almost daily they had little squabbles, and he would decide that he must cease thinking of the young girl's desirability. But next day Clara, sensing that she had momentarily lost her prey, would refrain from saying anything that might upset him. As if by accident, she would brush against him as they passed in the narrow corridor, or else let him catch her looking at him as they sat at table. The blood would rush to Siegfried's head, and later he would take advantage of the first opportunity to patch up their quarrel. Siegfried realized that his position as an anti-Nazi was growing more and more impossible. Pressure seemed to be bearing down on him from every quarter, gradually weakening his resolution to resist.

One evening when they were having after-dinner coffee in the Hildegard sitting room, one of their usual misunderstandings broke out. Its origin was the announced arrival of two more German-Jewish refugees at Puerto Marques, and Clara happened to drop the remark that if the boat on which they were traveling went down, everybody might be better off.

"A Christian attitude!" remarked Siegfried, trying to control his resentment.

"I am a German first and a Christian afterwards," Clara pointed out. "Every Jew is an enemy of my country—of *our* country, Siegfried. Have no illusions about that."

"I have no illusions any more—about anything," said Siegfried bitterly.

"Come now, children, stop bickering," said Frau Hildegard, smiling benignly first at one, then the other. "*Clärchen,* turn on the radio. It's time for the musical program from Berlin."

Clara switched on the radio, whose dial was already adjusted to

156

the family's favorite short-wave station, and presently the sooth-ing words and music of German "Lieder" soared through the air.

"*Röslein, Röslein, Röslein rot . . . Röslein auf der Heide . . .*" trilled a dulcet voice wafted to them over the Atlantic from their faraway homeland.

Heine, the non-Aryan, the expatriate, had composed that song, yet it was as German as any melody ever written. Glancing at Clara, kneeling on the floor before the radio, Siegfried saw that a rapt look had come into her handsome but usually placid face. Was it his imagination, or were her blue eyes glistening as she listened to that sweetly sentimental old tune which reminded her of the fatherland that she had hardly ever seen? He moved his glance to Dr. Hildegard, and here there could be no mistake: two tears were actually sliding down the cheeks of the hard and disciplined school head.

The "Lieder" came to an end, and now the strains of a tran-scribed Wagner record filled the room. As though the national anthem itself were being played, Clara rose to her feet and stood by the radio with arms folded over her high breasts, gazing fixedly before her. Even the expression of her eyes had changed; intense, almost fanatical, they had become as she listened to the sweeping music of the "Götterdämmerung." Siegfried could easily have imag-ined Clara herself as an ancient Walküre, riding out with her sis-ters to battle against all the other peoples of the world. And in the violent chords of Wagner, it seemed to him that he heard expressed the whole intensity and glory and intolerance of the German race.

What a vastly complicated people we are, Siegfried thought as he watched her. And yet foreigners are always trying to make us out so simple. We have in us veritable labyrinths of emotion. Our thought world has the most intricate pattern; our hearts are brim-ming over with conflicting emotions.

Suddenly he felt elated and proud to be German, of the same race as Wagner and Bismarck and Dr. Hildegard—dedicated, like them, to the holy task of making Germany great. He felt united with the people in this room, and especially with his own Clara. Was she not the very personification of Teutonic womanhood?

But now, as if she sensed her victory and wanted to exploit it, the girl switched the dial to another short-wave station, and instead of music there poured out words—crass German words, almost as familiar as the notes to which they had been listening. Propaganda from Berlin boomed out at them—condemnation of the Jewish enemies, boasts of Nazi power, invocations to hatred.

Somehow this act of tactlessness on Clara's part struck Siegfried as typically Teutonic also. It was unfortunate that she shared with most of her countrymen a veritable talent for doing the right thing at the wrong time! In one instant his warm feelings for her had changed entirely; all his former resentment and annoyance flooded back. Forgetting his usually impeccable manners, he jumped to his feet, glared at her, and then tore out of the room without even making his good-bys. This was the end, he thought. He would resign from the Schiller Schule tomorrow!

Outside, the hot night wound itself around him; it laid fingers to his throat, making it difficult to breathe. The rainy season was at hand, thought Siegfried as he slid his thumb under the stiff collar encircling his neck. But it seemed to him that there was another cause as well for the oppressive atmosphere tonight. In the world, just as in his own life, sinister things were happening; a thick blanket of depression lay over the town of Santa Rosa.

He walked along, apparently at random, but presently found himself in the near vicinity of Pension Hilda, which he had left so precipitately a month before. With a feeling of elation he quickened his step. A wild thought had occurred to Siegfried—a wild but wonderful thought. Why did he not go in and see his sister Hilda *now*, this very night, before he had time to weaken? Throwing himself at her mercy, he would confess that he had been guilty of a terrible mistake, and beg her for forgiveness. She would weep, that he knew, but by those very tears his betrayal would be washed away; he would become again that most glorious of all God's creatures: a free human being.

Now he was passing beneath the row of acacias that fronted the pension. The lights were burning in Hilda's study and when Siegfried came a little nearer, he saw to his surprise that people were seated in a semicircle about the writing desk. Behind that familiar desk he saw a woman's figure and could recognize Hilda's big shaggy head as she bent over a sheaf of papers. By her side was a small table with a row of coffee cups and a huge cake smothered in whipped cream.

For the first moment Siegfried could not understand what was happening, then the thought came to him that this must be Hilda's annual reading of her novel, to which he and she had both looked forward with such hope. Oh that row of Dresden china cups, that sherry decanter, that huge cake from Herr Professor Levi's bakery! Everything was the same as on every other year, the only difference being that he himself was not among the listeners. Instead he stood here, an outsider, a pariah, and there was no question of his joining the loyal little group of friends. As though a leper had come into their midst, they would one by one have got up and gone away, leaving him alone with Hilda—and with Hilda's eyes. No, no, he could not go in there! This strangest of coincidences—his return on the very night of Hilda's reading—was like a sign from heaven.

The sweat was pouring down his face, whether because of the sultry atmosphere or because of his own anguish Siegfried did not know. Standing beneath a tree, he took out his pocket handkerchief to wipe his streaming temples. Ah, how nice and clean was this handkerchief, how well pressed his suit! In his mind's eye he saw himself again as he used to look a bare month ago, ludicrous in his soup-spotted full dress, with a soiled napkin tucked under his arm; he saw himself reading his volume of Kant behind the bar, quarreling with customers, helping the drunken Popoff to his room. What humiliations he had had to bear, what loneliness he had suffered!

And at that moment Siegfried knew with certainty that he could never again return to that sordid life; between being a waiter and being an outcast, he preferred the latter. As to an actual solution, there was none—unless it were the obvious solution of self-destruction. But even if he debated suicide, as he had done so often before, he knew in his heart that he would never accomplish it. He was too weak to kill himself, just as he had been too weak to stand alone. Always hitherto it had been Hilda's strength that had sustained him, and he had deluded himself into believing that her strength was his—that her magnificent convictions were his also. She was one of those rare people who could live in loneliness, without the approval of other men. He couldn't. A true German, he existed only as one member of a whole, was strong only in the knowledge of the great mass of his countrymen behind him.

Facing the lighted window, Siegfried took off his hat and stood there for a moment in a gesture of reverence. Good-by Hilda, he said. Good-by, my sister. God grant you the strength to go forward along your path. If there were more people like you, our beloved Germany would not be on the road to perdition.

He felt utterly miserable and dejected as he trudged back through the darkness to the Schiller Schule.

Next morning when Siegfried was preparing for his history class, Frau Hildegard poked her head in the schoolroom to inform him that two visitors wished to see him. On entering the reception room he found it empty, but when he glanced into the schoolyard, whom should he espy but his little friend Bubi Falkenborn, and beside him the pale man whom Siegfried had once seen following Bubi down the Calle de la Independencia.

Bubi looked more enchanting and lovable than ever. Standing there with his hands deep in the pockets of his leather shorts, he seemed so much at home in life that it was sheer joy to watch him. Delighted with this visit, Siegfried hurried to the yard.

160

"Hello, Bubi!" he called from the top step. "I'm so glad you came to see me."

"Good day, Mr. Stumpf." Bubi took off his sombrero and went up to shake hands in his rather formal way. Switching from German to Spanish, he went on, "I only came to see you because I wanted you to do me a favor. My friend Mr. Kerjanian here is a very great teacher from Aleppo in Syria. He would like to be a teacher here. Can he begin right away? He talks Armenian and Syrian. He could teach everyone Armenian and Syrian."

"I see," said Siegfried. "Well, I'm sure that would be very useful."

"Oh yes. I can say a few words in Armenian already. Mr. Kerjanian has taught me. *Hiress miress espanvatz en eem polor yergeress pejatsvadze.* That means, 'My mother and father were murdered and my whole nation was wiped out.' " Bubi translated this with a radiant smile.

Siegfried was slightly taken aback, but he turned to Kerjanian politely and extended his hand. To his surprise, the Armenian only touched the tips of his fingers briefly, then let them drop. Strange fellow! thought Siegfried. Any other person introduced in that fashion by a child would have given one a knowing smile, then proceeded to explain his case in a sensible way. Not so Kerjanian. He made no attempt to expound on Bubi's introduction, but in a self-important way took out his pocketbook and extracted a sheaf of incredibly dirty papers for inspection.

"This is from Aleppo," he explained. "This is from Baku, in Russia. This is from Smyrna. As you see, they are affidavits showing that I am a fully qualified teacher, second class."

"Yes, yes," said Siegfried. "I see." He made an effort to appear impressed by these torn bits of paper scribbled over in incomprehensible languages, and handed them back with a formal German bow. "Won't you step into our office, Mr. Kerjanian?" he suggested. "This way, please."

Kerjanian didn't budge an inch. A scowl rose to his face. "No," he answered. "I don't like offices. I've sat waiting in too many offices in my life, and been kept off with words—words—words. I want a plain answer now: can you use my services—or can't you?"

Bubi interrupted before Siegfried could compose an answer. "It's very important for us, Herr Siegfried. Mr. Kerjanian has to earn some money and get a larger room, near me. You see, we are keeping an armadillo."

"A what?"

"An armadillo. You know, it's a sort of animal. It belongs to both of us. Mr. Kerjanian lives near the market place, and Marie-Té says she isn't going to allow me to go there any more because there's so much malaria about. Of course she'd be angry if she knew that I'd come here today. Simply furious! She'd never think of letting me visit a Nazi school!"

Siegfried was flustered, and said quickly, "Oh, but you're wrong Bubi. We are not Nazis here."

"That's what *you* say," answered Bubi knowingly. "But you are Nazis all the same. Everybody knows it."

Kerjanian seemed most upset. "If you'd told me that, I never would have come here," he burst out. "I spit on every Nazi."

"I spit on them too," Bubi said. "Do you know why? Because: *Hiress miress espanvatz en eem polor vergeress pejatsvadze.* That's just what they did to us: cut people's throats and wiped our whole nation from the earth. But Herr Siegfried isn't a Nazi really. He's nice, like Fräulein Hilda, his sister, whom I was telling you about. She's the lady who read aloud from her wonderful book last night."

Siegfried, greatly excited, grasped Bubi's shoulder. "You must tell me about it, Bubi. How was the reading? Did it go—all right?"

"All right!" Bubi stuck his hands deep in his trouser pockets and laughed loudly. "I should say it did go all right! It was a terribly huge success. Marie-Té told me that everybody cried like anything, and afterwards Herr Publisher Apfelbaum from Leipzig, who'd come to listen, said that our Fräulein Hilda was the greatest writer alive. He sent a cable to a friend of his who is a famous publisher in New York and he says that the book is going to be translated in the English language and that Fräulein Stumpf is going to become terribly famous almost right away."

Siegfried stood there as if thunderstruck. "This is my sister Hilda's book you are talking about, Bubi? Are you sure?"

"Yes," said Bubi. "Of course I'm sure. The book is about Fräulein Hilda and about you, Herr Siegfried, and it tells everyone that it's very fine to be a refugee, not awful, as stupid people say. Herr Publisher Apfelbaum told Marie-Té that Fräulein Hilda's book is going to make all refugees feel happy and proud. It says that refugees are refugees because they were too wonderful to live like slaves. They are terribly free people and they want everyone else to be proud and free, and they are going to help everyone be the same as they are. It's an awful long book. I think it ought to have a red cover, don't you, Herr Siegfried? Red—or perhaps blue."

"Oh Bubi, Bubi!" Siegfried shook his head in bewilderment. "I can hardly believe it. It's like a fantastic dream. To think that this has happened to my own Hilda! Hilda—a real authoress at last. . . ."

Siegfried was still talking when the main door of the school building flew open. It was recess time, and like a cataract the boys poured into the yard, laughing and calling to each other in their harsh German voices. Before the war a number of Santa Rosan families used to send their boys to the Schiller Schule, but since the break of relations with the Axis, practically all had been withdrawn. As a consequence the school membership had dwindled to a handful, but those remaining formed an aggressively Teutonic little group. With a tactlessness typical of their race, they gathered around Siegfried and the two strangers, and stood there staring curiously at the shabbily dressed Kerjanian. Siegfried tried again to lead his visitors indoors.

"If you please," he said. "We can talk easier in the office."

Kerjanian's dark eyes met his in an icy stare. "No," he said. "I'm not going in. I've even decided to withdraw my application for the post." With indignant fingers he thrust back his papers into his wallet. "Now that I know that this is a Nazi school, I shan't put my foot here!"

Uneasily Siegfried looked about, and noticed that the group of boys were pressing closer, Hans Holtzapfel, an overbearing young Teuton, at their head. Assuming his best authoritative manner, Siegfried clapped his hands. "Move away, boys. What are you all gaping at? Move away!"

Surlily the boys broke up, several casting dark glances at Kerjanian. One of them started to strut about like Charlie Chaplin's eternal tramp, feet out, an imaginary cane swinging in his hand. Meanwhile Hans Holtzapfel took a ball from his pocket and began throwing it against the school wall, then catching it. Gradually he aimed the ball nearer and nearer to Kerjanian, until, on bouncing back from the wall, it grazed the Armenian's black hat and knocked it right off his head. A gale of laughter swept over the other boys, but Hans Holtzapfel, pretending to be unaware of what had happened, continued nonchalantly flinging his ball against the wall.

Quivering with fury, Siegfried stepped toward him. All his dislike of this arrogant boy and what he represented rushed to the fore. For one brief moment he felt that he again was on the other side of the fence—on the side of the shabbily dressed, of the Charlie Chaplins, of the Kerjanians. He was on the point of reaching out to seize Hans Holtzapfel's arm, when he felt a touch on his own sleeve. He turned his head to look into the eyes of Clara Hildegard.

"Siegfried," she said, "Father wants to see you. He is in his study."

For a wild moment he hesitated, and it seemed to Siegfried himself that he stood at the final parting of the ways. Desperately he looked about for Bubi, but saw that the boy had taken Kerjanian's hand and was walking off with him. How terribly young he looked, now that he was frightened! No more than a little kid. And how shabby and miserable was that so-called schoolteacher from Aleppo. Yet Siegfried realized that there burned in those two a fire which he would have given his soul to feel blazing inside him. It was the fire that had burned so fiercely in his sister Hilda that it finally had consumed her altogether, making of the whole woman one glowing flame. It was part of the great fire which burned in all free men, and without which the human race would soon become nothing but a herd of dumb scared beasts, huddling together on a rapidly cooling sphere that whirled senselessly through space.

Siegfried opened his mouth to call out to Bubi to wait. He, Siegfried, was about to break the bars of this Nazi prison, to go out and join the company of free men again! The words were actually on his lips, yet no sound issued forth. Suddenly he realized with a finality that frightened him that he had forfeited forever the right to intimacy with this gallant little fellow, Bubi, and—yes, even with that shabby and ludicrous Armenian who had spurned a position in a Nazi school. A wave of despair swept over him, so intense that he actually swayed a little sideways.

Instantly the firm hand of Clara Hildegard was on his shoulder; there swept into his nostrils the odor of her clean, light hair, which curled a little at the temples from sheer youthfulness and health. The feel of her full high breast against his arm caused him to swing about to gaze at her. Even in that moment of crisis the desire for her rose within him, and it was that which put into his eyes the question which he never had dared ask before.

Her answer was frank. Very widely she opened her blue eyes, and she looked at him fully, giving herself to him without doubt or reservation. Her nostrils quivered a little, and her breast, pressing against his arm, seemed to him to become fuller, as if the sap of life were surging upwards in her body. In that instant the relations between them became as intimate, as complete, as if they already had consummated the final act of love. Siegfried made an instinctive movement to take her in his arms, but Clara stepped back, a tiny smile of triumph on her lips.

"Father wants you, *Siegfriedchen*," she repeated gently, making

165

a little gesture toward the house. "I'll be waiting for you in the garden. Go now. Go."

Without another glance in the direction of the gate, Siegfried turned, and with bent head made his way into the schoolhouse. Though his blood was pounding in spasms of desire, the heart which pumped it had already died. A cold flaccid object lay in the spot where for thirty-five years a living heart had been beating— beating often in sorrow, it is true, sometimes in anguish, but ever beating. As he knocked at the door of Dr. Hildegard's study, Siegfried lifted his hand and laid it on his breast, as if to warm that poor dead object that had abandoned its functions. A futile gesture.

Chapter XI
Torrid Journey

FOR SIX HOURS MARIE-TÉ AND JOHN CAMBERLY HAD
bumped their way over the sinuous mountain road that led to Puerto
Marques. Time after time Marie-Té had called out in fright, or
else had just gritted her teeth and clenched her fists as they negoti-
ated hairpin curves with drops of a thousand feet on either side.
But in between she had stared about her, open-eyed, awed by the
brutal beauty of the landscape. Here man counted for nothing, she
had thought. Were he to disappear forever, destroyed by his own
overclever inventions of poison gas and incendiary bombs, these
sierras and ravines, these roaring torrents and whispering jungles,
would not change an iota. Everything here was built on a violent
scale and built for eternity. Only men themselves cut to a generous measure would feel at home in this vast countryside, thought
Marie-Té, and she glanced curiously at John Camberly beside her.

He sat at the steering wheel bareheaded, his shirt sleeves rolled
up over his strong brown arms. Coat, tie and hat had long since
been discarded, and the onrushing breeze swept back his dark hair
and fluttered his shirt, open on his chest. And now, as they turned
another corner and the whole expanse of the Atlantic unfolded
itself before them, sapphire-colored and glittering, she heard him
draw a deep breath into his lungs. Watching him, Marie-Té knew
that she had been right about John Camberly; he was a man without
a grain of pettiness inside him—a man who ever would respond
spontaneously to the noble, the majestic.

This long day alone with him in the intimacy of the little car had awakened in Marie-Té feelings never experienced before. The very sound of his low voice excited her; if he as much as grazed her knee in changing gears, her blood leaped high. At the top of the hill he stopped the car and leaned forward to gaze at the immense vista spread out before them. Surreptitiously Marie-Té studied his profile, and his hands lying on the steering wheel, which had become as familiar to her today as the hands of Uncle Konrad, for instance, or of her brother Bubi. What beautiful hands! she thought. Sensitive and strong. How different from the nervous, grasping hands of a man like Harrington! Phrasing a question that had occurred to her many times before, she blurted out,

"John, why on earth did you become a diplomat?"

Camberly slowly slipped the car into gear, and as it started rolling down the slope of the last hill, he turned to Marie-Té, smiling. "Now why do you ask that? D'you think I make such a bad one?"

"Not at all," she answered. "You'd be good at anything, but best—well, just doing nothing! I can see you drinking your mint juleps and letting the days slip by pleasantly on your Uncle James' plantation in Virginia."

"So can I," Camberly admitted. "I'm naturally lazy, Marie-Té, and that's why I've always worked so hard. You see, I have a theory that lazy people understand life better than others, so they ought to force themselves to take an active part in it. After all, that's what you do yourself, Marie-Té! The Viennese have the reputation of being indolent, but one wouldn't ever think so, to judge from the way you drill poor Bubi at his lessons five hours every day, and then plug away two hours more at your own Spanish. You've mastered the language through sheer determination. Isn't that so?"

"Yes, I suppose it is. The young woman of 1943 is a hard worker, not a languid charmer, and thank goodness for that. There's no time nowadays for dawdling, excepting for brief moments now and then."

"I agree with you absolutely. If we lazy people left things to the go-getters, our world would soon become altogether impossible.

That's why I decided to override my inclinations as a young man; I took one deep breath and embarked on a career in the Foreign Service, where, if I did no other good, I could at least counteract the Harringtons and Bakers. Does that sound—a little pretentious?"

Marie-Té reached over and squeezed his arm. "Yes, terribly. As if you ever could be pretentious, John Camberly! It ought to be plain to any idiot that you're doing your country as much good—as a man like Harrington is doing it harm."

"I wish that the powers that be in Washington were as sure of that as you are, Marie-Té. I'd like to think that the tide has turned against the Harrington type of diplomat at last—the self-seeker, the calculator, the potential Quisling. Our country can't afford to be represented by such men any longer, but at the present moment, and I'm afraid for some time to come, the Harringtons are in. They're firmly ensconced in their seats, and by the time the great American public realize the fact, it may already be too late."

A few moments later the first adobe houses of Puerto Marques came into view. Identical to the barren plain in color and consistency, they rose out of it like hideous protuberances; one could well have imagined a tropical rainstorm dissolving the whole town and washing the rubble into the sea. Marie-Té and Camberly drove down the main street, wending their way between groveling pigs and naked children who sat pouring dust into each other's hair. Here and there lay high piles of cocoa beans, and men with brooms were solemnly spreading the brown beans across the roadway. Marie-Té was beginning to wonder if the heat had gone to the poor fellows' heads, when they passed a string of women squatting in the street, engaged in sorting out the unripe and broken beans.

"That is their job," Camberly explained. "They get paid the equivalent of fifteen American cents a day."

"Why not get hold of a few monkeys and train them to do it? They'd be more effective."

"But you'd have to feed the monkeys, Marie-Té. These women work at wages that actually wouldn't keep an animal looking healthy.

169

And those of us who aren't Harringtons know that they are real human beings, despite their battered looks—stouthearted, full of feeling, even intelligent. That they and their ancestors have been kept down by a grasping church and a corrupt business system isn't their fault."

The sweetish odor of the cocoa beans spread over the whole town, mingling in some places with the smell of refuse, in others with the saline smell of the sea. The damp heat was so intense as actually to be visible; it hung in a vapory cloud above the streets. In the shadows of the houses slept scores of loafers, for the most part clad solely in cotton jeans; their dirty flesh, dark brown or black, was visible through the rents. Among them were to be seen negroes, not a few Mongolians, and some pure European types. But it would have been impossible to state accurately any man's antecedents; granted that he knew his own parents, it was fairly sure that he could have done no more than hazard a guess as to their racial descent.

They dropped their bags at the little brick hotel, and then drove straight to the boat pier, where the ship bringing the refugees from Havana was due to dock at any moment. However, there was no sign of it, nor evidence that a vessel was expected. A group of porters lay sleeping on the hot planks of the jetty with their straw hats pulled over their faces. Tied alongside was a tugboat, its three sailors lying stretched upon the deck; through the window of the steering room could be seen the captain, cap on head, sleeping in an armchair before his wheel. Even the animals had been unable to stay awake: curled up inside a coil of rope, a dog and cat were enjoying companionable slumber, the cat's head resting on the dog's hindquarters. Marie-Té thought that the whole scene had about it a quality of unreality; it was like the enactment of a fairy tale in which all the characters have been artificially put to sleep and wait for a magic signal to resume their everyday activities.

Beside the jetty was an open-air *cantina,* and Camberly suggested that they park their car and have a drink before the ship arrived. There was no one in sight, but at his call, a figure stirred on the floor behind the bar and eventually rose to his feet. The proprietor came forward, wiping the dust off his white apron.

"*Qué quiere?*"

"I believe there is a boat docking this afternoon?" suggested Camberly.

"*Quién sabe?*" said the man. "It may be."

"You're not sure?"

"Who knows?" repeated the proprietor, and he yawned prodigiously, leaving his mouth wide open.

Marie-Té squeezed Camberly's arm, "I love Puerto Marques," she said. "If I stayed here three days, I'd forget my own name. *Quién sabe?* I'd say if you asked me, and go to sleep with my head on the table."

With drinks before them, they sat side by side beneath the sun-bleached yellow awning. A stone's throw away lay the blue Atlantic, huge pelicans floating on its surface like inflated rubber toys; banana trees stretched along the shore, and incredibly colored birds skimmed between them on secret missions. Since leaving Santa Rosa everything had been so strange, so exotic, that she had almost forgotten that she was traveling alone with John Camberly in a thoroughly unconventional fashion. By all the rules a young girl in her position should have felt shy and constrained, yet Marie-Té was as much at her ease here as if it had been any other afternoon, and she and Camberly had been sitting drinking Cuba Libres on the Yacht Club terrace!

"Well, Marie-Té," he said after one of their long silences, "here we are in Puerto Marques. You don't regret having come?"

She shook her head. "I made it a rule long ago never to regret anything."

"An excellent rule! Especially for someone with such sound instincts as you."

Marie-Té smiled at him. "How nicely you say things. I'd ever so much rather be told that I had sound instincts than be told that

I had a pretty nose or did my hair attractively. By the way, John, have you ever noticed *how* I did my hair?"

"Of course I have," said Camberly, looking sheepish. "You do it—very nicely."

"Oh, don't try and fool me, John! Admit that you're not even sure if I have long hair or short. Some women would be annoyed, you know. I'm really quite attractive."

Camberly grinned at her. "I realize that. I realize also that plenty of people have told you so." And then he asked one of those brusque questions that Marie-Té had grown used to: "How often have you been in love, Marie-Té?"

"In love?" She laughed. "Oh, I've been in love all my life. When I was ten I was in love with all my cousins, and later I was in love with my friends' brothers, and later I was in love with the officers in my father's regiment. And they were all in love with me! I suppose I've been in love literally hundreds of times, but really in love— not once."

"And how about Sascha—that Russian boy in Paris?" suggested Camberly.

"You're right, John. Sascha was different from the others. I wasn't really in love with him either—I mean not really, *really*— but if Uncle Konrad hadn't arrived in Paris at the crucial moment, I've often wondered what would have happened." For a second a shadow passed over Marie-Té's fine features and her eyebrows knit together. But then she shook her head and laughed again. "Anyway, all that seems terribly distant now. Ancient history!" She stretched her hand toward his across the table, and their fingers met and closed around each other. "All that counts is the present. And the present—is wonderful!"

Suddenly, without the slightest warning, a great burst of activity descended on Puerto Marques. One might have thought that the fairy prince had kissed the sleeping beauty and brought everything back to life. Shouting people were running down the streets, deserted a few minutes before; on the pier the porters woke up and

172

immediately began to jabber and for no apparent reason to push about empty luggage carts. The tugboat's captain in his steering room was shouting orders and blowing his siren in a frenzy. Even the dog and cat inside the coil of rope woke up and began to fight. The proprietor rushed up to their table, on his arm a napkin with which he excitedly flicked the dust from the marble top.

"The boat! The boat!" he shouted, with the joyous expectancy of a little boy. "The Spanish ship 'Santander' is in port."

At the pier everything was in a state of intense confusion; the porters with their carts were bumping into each other and swearing; an army of uniformed officials had sprung up from nowhere. On the end of the jetty stood a growing group of onlookers, and officials were constantly running up and shoving someone to one side. A few of the more sophisticated spectators had brought along fishing tackle; they were squatting on the pier with their lines dangling through the rotted-away sections of the planks. Several people were plowing about trying to sell lottery tickets, an invariable accompaniment of any public gathering in Latin America.

"How do you do, Mr. Camberly. I scarcely expected to see you here!"

Camberly swung about on hearing himself thus addressed by a young Chinaman in a well-fitting Palm Beach suit. There was something very superior about this young man; he had an air of culture which was accentuated by his intelligent eyes and unobtrusive manner. When Camberly failed to recognize him, he smiled nervously and lifted a hand to finger his discreet necktie. At once Marie-Té remembered having seen before that exquisite hand with the thin, sensitive fingers.

"Why, Ah Sing, I'm glad to see you," she said cordially. "Are you down here to meet someone also?"

The young Chinaman nodded. "A friend of mine, madame—a compatriot whom I used to know when I was staying with Mr. Harrington in Havana. I only hope that he will be able to land. They don't make immigration easy—especially not for us Orientals."

173

"Why didn't you ask Mr. Harrington to arrange it with the immigration authorities?" suggested Camberly.

But at the mention of that name "Harrington," all life seemed to go out of Ah Sing's face; his brown eyes hardened. "I never ask favors of Mr. Harrington," he said in a flat voice, and then he tipped his hat, first at Marie-Té, then at Camberly, and moved discreetly away.

"Well, that was a surprise," said Camberly, watching him as he vanished in the crowd. "I've always liked Ah Sing, but I never knew before that he could speak anything but pidgin English. How different he is today from the man one sees in Harrington's apartment! Something tells me that he likes Mr. Warfield Harrington even less than I do."

As they spoke, the "Santander" had come into the bay, and now with a great rattling of chains was dropping anchor. Infected with the meaningless excitement that prevails at such occasions, Marie-Té pushed her way to the end of the pier, where she stood on tiptoe, trying to peer over people's shoulders. There was something thrilling for her in the thought of the big ship lying there at anchor, the Spanish pennant fluttering from its masthead. Hundreds of years ago a galleon bearing the same name, the same colors, might have lain in the harbor of Puerto Marques, loading gold and precious stones for Aragon. Now its successor had sped here under steam not to remove treasure but to unload a seedy group of immigrants: a Dutchman, two German Jews and possibly a Chinaman.

Already a number of rowboats and small motor launches were traveling between the jetty and the ship, and after a certain amount of bargaining, Camberly succeeded in coming to an arrangement with a piratical-looking boatman. A few moments later Marie-Té and he were climbing up the side of the "Santander" and were being accosted by a government official who stood near the ladder's head.

"Your permits, please!"

"I am from the American Legation," Camberly began to explain, but the official cut him short.

"It doesn't matter. Nobody can come on this ship without a permit. I order you to leave at once."

Camberly was about to reach into his pocket for the currently accepted substitute for a permit, but at that moment, the official lost interest and began shouting something to one of his colleagues. Presently he hurried off down the deck, gesticulating wildly, and left the two visitors free to step inside the boat.

They found themselves in a roped-off smoking room in which a number of officials were sitting about a desk. Before these men lay numerous documents, and each official had a leather portfolio that he kept opening and closing as he took out papers and a moment later put them back again. Facing the officials stood the four prospective immigrants. It was easy to tell which of them were the two German Jews: Marie-Té recognized the ravages of the concentration camps in their wavering eyes and nervous movements, and she was filled with pity, coupled with that wild feeling of indignation that the knowledge of injustice always aroused in her.

"What is going to happen now? Must we pay again?" she heard one of them ask the other in German.

"We must but we can't," was the answer.

"*Guten Tag!*" said Marie-Té, walking up to them. "I have come down from Santa Rosa to meet you."

Both men jumped as if they had been shot at, and even their companion, a florid Dutchman, looked thoroughly alarmed. Only the fourth immigrant, the Chinese, fixed her calmly with his inscrutable oriental gaze.

One of the officials suddenly rose from his chair, took up three of the four passports lying on the desk, and waved them in the faces of the European immigrants. "These papers are not valid," he said in the querulous voice used by petty officials the world over. "You are attempting to enter this country illegally. You have no United States visas, and we can't let you in here without them. They don't want you in the United States. They have no room for you, nor for anyone. How do you expect our impoverished little country to harbor you when great wealthy America refuses to?"

The smaller and more terrified-looking of the Jews was wringing his hands, and the immigration official, looking at him, began to shout in the angry tone of someone overcome with sympathy who yet realizes his inability to help. "Don't look at me like that! It is not my fault! We small nations, used to deprivations, have hearts. Do you hear me—hearts—*corazones!*" He banged himself on his narrow chest, then tilted his head sideways as though listening. "Hear my heart tick? Yes? And America's heart?" He threw his head to the other side, as though listening to an invisible heart suspended in mid-air beside him. "Hear *that* tick? No! And why? Because America's heart is dead, and a dead heart doesn't tick. A dead heart's no good—only fit to throw to the cat. Pfui!" He pinched his nostrils with his delicate, grubby fingers. "America has taken in less refugees than even the small neutrals of Europe. This is a fact—this is written in a book." He pointed at the book in front of him.

"What does he say?" asked the small Jew of Marie-Té. "How much does he want?" His face had taken on a completely demented expression, and now he thrust his fingers in his mouth and bit frantically at the tips.

Overcome with horror, Marie-Té tried to calm the miserable man. "Everything is going to be straightened out," she told him. "We are here to help you."

"We paid for our passage! We paid good money—American money," wailed the immigrant, still chewing at his fingers.

The Dutchman jumped up, his face completely red, and began pounding on the table. "*Incroyable!*" he shouted. "Such a scandal. *Unverschämt!*"

"Just as usual," remarked the taller Jew resignedly. "I knew that it would come to this."

The Dutchman began to speak very rapidly in three languages at the same time. "To get into America," he said, "you have to have

176

the strength and resistance of a tank. No one else can manage it. I am a scientist—a well-known scientist specializing in biological research—and it is two years now since I applied for my visa. It hasn't yet been granted! At the United States consulate in Lisbon they told me that I had to present a military discharge first. How can I get a military discharge from Nazi-occupied Holland, I ask you? Then they told me that I had to have a certificate that I had paid my taxes in the past. How can I get such a certificate when the buildings with the files have been bombed to atoms? Finally they said I mustn't have a single relative in Axis-occupied territory. How can I, a Dutchman, not have a relative in Holland? Is it that they only let into America someone whose entire family has been annihilated—brothers, sisters—even distant aunts and cousins? Does this make sense? The Nazis said that one mustn't have one drop of Jewish blood to be allowed to exist, but America says that one mustn't have one living relative! That's just as cruel, just as inhuman, isn't it?"

The Dutchman turned to the official, who had been listening attentively, but who now regretfully shook his head.

"I have not understood one word," he remarked.

Marie-Té took it on herself to translate, but the official kept shrugging his shoulders and pointing at the passport.

"No one can land in our country without an American visa. Besides, how do I know who this fellow is? Scientist? Biological research? We do not need any scientists. We have scientists of our own."

"He says that he cannot return to Europe and that he has no money for another voyage," Marie-Té translated for the Dutchman, but the official, like most Latin Americans, found it boring to pursue the same topic for long. Already he had picked up the passport of the Chinese and was studying its queer characters with interest.

"What is your profession?" he inquired in a polite manner.

"Laundryman."

"Laundryman? Ah, that sounds better. There are plenty of dirty clothes in Santa Rosa. Still, I'm not at all sure that we can let you land either—we're very particular about taking in Orientals. As to the other three, they will certainly have to go back where they came from."

Though it was unlikely that he had understood, the smaller of the two Jews suddenly began to tremble. His eyes stared; his face twitched; alternately he stuck into his mouth the fingers of his left hand and of his right.

The tall Jew turned to Camberly in embarrassment. "It's his nerves," he explained. "You see, he couldn't get out of Germany until 1939, and he was in *nine* concentration camps. He had all his fingernails pulled out by a Nazi guard, and every time he gets upset the nerve pains start again. Please excuse him. It will pass."

But it didn't pass. With dismay Marie-Té watched the trembling man as he began to rummage through his pockets for his papers. One of the inner pockets was fastened with a safety pin, which he fumblingly tried to unfasten. Then with shaking fingers he drew out some torn documents, only to drop several of them on the floor. Flinging himself down with a cry of dismay he began to gather them together. One of the papers had fluttered under the table and when he found that he could not reach it, he burst into agonized sobs.

Marie-Té closed her eyes, feeling that she could bear no more. And suddenly, instead of this little Jew, she saw in front of her the face of Kerjanian, whom she had come to think of as the symbol of all refugees. For a quarter of a century Kerjanian had been treated as this man was being treated today, and with him despair and indignation had mounted to such a peak that anyone should have understood that it needed but little to turn him into the path of violence. Multiply Kerjanian by several million and you had that multitude of wronged and desperate men who nowadays stood ready to avenge themselves on their tormentors. Was it possible that no one understood their plight? Was no one willing to *act,* instead of merely voicing sympathy?

As if he had read her thoughts, John Camberly stepped forward.

Marie-Té opened her eyes to see him bend down and pick up the fallen paper, then he looked the shaking little man straight in the eye.

"Everything is going to be taken care of," he said. "You are not to worry. Do you understand? I am in charge."

Camberly was indeed in charge. Swinging about, he addressed the head official in his authoritative but polite manner, explaining that as Secretary of the American Legation, he assumed complete responsibility for the eventual admittance of the refugees to the United States. So positive was Camberly's manner that the official immediately acquiesced, and one could see from his demeanor that this little Latin American with the big *corazon* was delighted to do so. It struck Marie-Té how easily things could be accomplished if in high places there were a few more men of good will.

Now the passports had been stamped, and the official was handing them back to the immigrants. The smaller of the two Jews seized his booklet and clutched it to his breast; then his face began to work and again he burst into those dry, raucous sobs. Collapsing on a bench, he sank his head in his hands. His friend turned to Camberly and held out his hand.

"You don't know what you've done for us. You can't possibly know. If it hadn't been for you, we would have been sent back to Europe, like so many thousands before us. My friend and I have seen men tortured and killed before our eyes. Our only wish is not to be killed or tortured. It is ten years now that we have been dreaming of America. . . ."

Oh God, thought Marie-Té, what small blessings men have come to ask! Kerjanian wants only half an acre of land on which to grow his vegetables, and here is someone who wants even less: merely the assurance that he will not be tortured. Surely America, great and wealthy, cannot refuse people with such modest desires!

She sat down on the bench beside the little Jew. He was still trembling, and now and then a long shudder passed through his body. Marie-Té reached for his hand, then felt a momentary repulsion at the thought of touching that mutilated hand with the crooked,

179

half-formed nails. But when she held it in hers, a wave of pity flooded over her. She experienced that awed respect for suffering which had brought her to maturity so early in her life, and it seemed to her that it was a great privilege to be allowed to hold this hand that had been branded in torture. Very close she felt at that moment to John Camberly, who, she felt, had accomplished a great deed that day. For men's and women's individual lives *did* matter, whatever the Harringtons said. They mattered more than all else, and this was recognized by many a man like Camberly, who was going to help shape the world of the future. The thought filled Marie-Té with exultation.

She was still feeling in an elated mood when they left the ship a little later and took their places in the rowboat. Even as they traversed the short distance to the shore, the quick dusk of the tropics descended, imparting harmony and beauty to everything. The boatman's oars plashed in the water with a rich soft sound, propelling the little bark gently forward. Once they passed a canoe with a lantern gleaming at its bow and a brown boy, stripped to the waist, standing beside it with upraised spear. Then they saw the boy plunge his spear into the water and bring it back with a large eel-shaped fish dangling on the tip. Lights were beginning to twinkle along the shore, and when they turned about, they could see the dark form of the "Santander" outlined against the sky. High up on the mast shone a little yellow light, and presently another light, almost identical, showed up beside it: the first evening star.

They stepped out of the rowboat onto the pier, which was deserted now. Darkness had brought little relief from the day's heat, but it had cloaked the ugliness of the town: the adobe buildings looked less wretched; the streets that they passed through seemed sordid no longer, but strange and romantic instead. Marie-Té put her arm through Camberly's, and it occurred to her that she did this naturally now, as a woman takes the arm of her lover.

"Where are we going, John?"

"Not far," he answered. "There's a little place only a few minutes walk from here. You wouldn't believe that there's anything so nice in Puerto Marques."

In an open-air restaurant at the edge of the town, its tables set among mimosa bushes, Marie-Té and John Camberly dined that night. Above them was the star-sprinkled roof of heaven, and at their feet stretched the black carpet of the sea, bisected by a broad streak of moonlight. The breeze blowing in from the Caribbean carried a spicy tropical scent. Everything had an exotic quality that night: the sound of the breakers in the distance; the tart heady wine; the saffron-hued dish of sea food that was set before them. It all seemed to have been made to order for a pair of lovers, and Marie-Té knew instinctively that this was to be a night among nights for her. Young though she was, she had learned already that a golden day or a golden night are rare in a person's life. One must savor them to the full. Sliding her warm hand into John Camberly's, she sat looking up into the jumble of stars above their heads.

The twanging of a guitar reached their ears, and when Marie-Té turned her head, she caught sight of the waiter lying in a yellow hammock under one of the mimosa bushes. He was singing lazily and strumming his guitar, whether for his own pleasure or for theirs, his only clients, Marie-Té did not know. The breeze shook the branches of the mimosa and sent a few yellow blossoms fluttering down onto his face, but the player did not brush them away; he let them lie there, where, without turning his head, he could breathe in their fragrance.

"Do you know, John," said Marie-Té, "that waiter is as wise as Solomon. All he owns is a soiled suit and a guitar, but he is a happy man. He knows that he can get drunk on the smell of flowers and feast every night on the skyful of stars above his head."

John Camberly put his arms around her, and as his shoulder knocked against the bush, it brought down another shower of yellow blossoms. Now they, too, had flowers in their hair, flowers on their faces, and they let them lie there and kissed and kissed while the music of the guitar mingled with the distant beating of the waves. Pressed in his arms, Marie-Té felt oblivious to all else but the near presence of the man she loved. Slowly she drew her mouth away from his and leaned her head backwards so that she could look into his face.

"John," she whispered, "do you see how my eyes look now—now that I really love for the first time? They will always look at you like that . . ."

It was late when they left the restaurant and sauntered back toward the hotel. They passed the *cantina* where they had sat that afternoon, and stopped a moment to gaze out at the "Santander," riding gently on the harbor's swell. Somewhere on that boat three refugees were lying sleeping—men torn from their old lives, just as Marie-Té had been, to be flung into a strange environment. Once again she remembered that it was thanks to John Camberly that a new life lay before them. Would they, she wondered, have the strength to live it? Tremendous handicaps all three would be called on to overcome, but Marie-Té had learned through her own Uncle Konrad that men already dead could live again. Today those refugees had had proof that there still were people fighting on their side, and Marie-Té was certain that the knowledge would give them new strength, new hope.

"Poor devils!" said Camberly as they walked on, arm in arm. "To think that there are tens of millions in their position, not to mention more millions of Chinese—homeless, penniless, futureless. Marie-Té, when I think of the problems that we'll be called on to solve when this war is over, I feel dizzy."

"So do I," said Marie-Té. "But not as dizzy as I'd feel if there weren't men like you to struggle with them—men of intelligence—men of good will. There are thousands of your kind, and thanks to you, decency and kindness will not perish."

Camberly said nothing. Head sunk in thought, he walked on beside Marie-Té, and it was only the pressure of his arm against hers that told her that he understood her meaning and that he would not disillusion her. Never had Marie-Té felt so confident of the future as at that moment, never had she been so certain that the world was headed for a better, saner era.

And this new feeling of happiness about life mingled with her own personal happiness because of being with John, and conscious of being loved by him. Completely natural it seemed to her to be walking with him in this tropical night, completely natural to enter the same hotel and to go up the staircase arm in arm. Through the window at the end of the hall she could see the dark ocean and a section of the beach, lying as white in the moonlight as if it had been composed of snow instead of sand. The sight of the waves surging powerfully up the long beach made her think of her own blood surging through her body with an urge that was equally elemental, equally irresistible. He put his arms around her, and Marie-Té came into his embrace eagerly, without reserve; their lips found each other and clung together as if they wished never to live apart. When, a moment later, he opened his door, she walked unhesitantly into his room, and it was she who pushed shut the door behind them. And even that seemed to Marie-Té completely natural . . .

But late that night she woke up knowing that she was weeping, with John shaking her by the shoulder. He was looking into her face, and at once she began to smile and threw her arms around him.

"What is it, Marie-Té? Don't weep," he said, stroking her soft long hair. "You mustn't ever be sad when you and I are together, sweet."

"No, no, I'm not sad, John. I'm so happy." She rubbed her warm cheek against his. "I'd rather be here with you than anywhere in the world. If I wept now, it wasn't because I was sad—it was—well, I suppose it was just because of everything. Because of that Jew on the boat. Because of Kerjanian. Because of my own Uncle Konrad. Oh, John, there's so much sorrow in the world today—so much stupidity and misunderstanding! One would have to be terribly insensitive not to feel like weeping even in one's happiest moments."

Chapter XII
Diplomatic Procedure

NEXT AFTERNOON WHEN MARIE-TÉ LEFT CAMBERLY in front of the pension, the first person she saw was Paco, the newsboy. "Big news!" he shouted as he ran up, waving a paper. "America has taken England. Very big news!" He aimed an imaginary gun at her and imitated the sound of shooting. "Pang—pang—pang. *Ahora está muerta.*"

"All right," Marie-Té agreed. "I am dead." She felt very pleased with the world today, and, bending down, gave Paco such a hug that his big sombrero fell off and went rolling down the street. Singing at the top of his lungs, Paco raced after his vanishing sombrero.

Marie-Té glanced at the headlines of the paper in her hand. Well, America had not taken England, but her troops had landed in Europe, which a year before would have sounded almost as sensational. Yes, the tide of victory had turned at last, and Marie-Té was feeling lighthearted as she ran up the steps of Pension Hilda. She was in love—wildly in love, she admitted to herself. It gave her a sensation of overpowering happiness to say those words over and over and to accept the idea that she, Marie-Té, had given herself wholly to one man.

In the hallway under the picture of the majestic Goethe, stood Hilda Stumpf. One look at her and Marie-Té knew that something had happened in her absence; instinctively she turned her eyes away and her thoughts flew to those she cherished most on earth—to Bubi, to Uncle Konrad. She had an impulse to run out of the building so as not to have to hear anything that would spoil her happiness.

184

Don't let her say that something has happened to Bubi! Dear God, please stop her from saying it! She breathed a prayer.

"You had better hurry upstairs," Hilda Stumpf's voice came to her ears. "I have bad news, Marie-Té: your little brother has fallen ill."

Marie-Té tore up the staircase and ran down the corridor to Bubi's room. When she pulled open the door, she saw that Uncle Konrad was standing by the window, while the little boy lay in bed with flushed face, brilliant eyes. "Oh darling, darling!" cried Marie-Té as she hurried up to him. "Little Bubi! *Liebchen!*"

"Marie-Té, are you back? I thought that you would never come." He threw his arms about her neck and she could feel them burning against her skin. "Have you brought me something from Puerto Marques?"

"I have, my angel. I've brought you a fish that looks as if it had been blown up, with lots of spikes on it. It has an idiotic round little mouth." Marie-Té puffed up her own face and pursed her mouth to make Bubi laugh. "And what have you gone and caught yourself?" she said, pretending to joke as she laid her hand on the hot dry forehead.

"Dr. Ruíz says that it's malaria, but Uncle Konrad says that the doctor is an idiot." Bubi began to shiver and threw out his arms spasmodically. "O-oh! They ache," he said, drawing them back gingerly to his sides.

"You'll feel better soon," said Marie-Té, pushing back the fine blond hair, which had a way of falling down upon his forehead. "Poor *Bübchen*."

Bubi was still shivering; he had closed his eyes and lay there with chattering teeth, just as she had seen Ted Kelly lying such a short time before. She wondered if it was only her imagination that made it seem that his handsome little face had already shrunken.

"What did the doctor tell you?" she whispered to Uncle Konrad.

He motioned her to come over to the window, and then said, ruffling his hair, "This is bad, Maria-Theresa—yes, terribly bad.

Malaria! And in its worst form. Oh, Maria-Theresa, what are we going to do?"

There was something desperate about that question that would have terrified her, had she not been already terrified. But Marie-Té always had had the faculty of forcing calmness on herself in moments of crisis; she knew that it devolved on her to take charge, for Uncle Konrad, the impractical, was of exactly as much help as the chest of drawers. When there came a low rap upon the door, it was she who called, "Come in" in a voice so even that it surprised herself.

Medicine kit in hand, Dr. Ruíz walked into the room. He bowed politely to Marie-Té, then put down his bag and stepped over to the bed. "And how is the patient?" he said, giving Bubi a cheerful smile. He took the boy's hand and held it for a moment as he felt the pulse, and it was exactly as though he were holding the hand of his beloved. "H'm. Fairly rapid," he said, replacing the hand gently beneath the sheet. "That is how these sicknesses always develop—high fever, neuralgic pains, trembling. Poor little boy," he said, and gazed down into Bubi's face with an expression of great tenderness.

"May I speak to you for a moment, Doctor?" asked Marie-Té.

Dr. Ruíz gave a start; he seemed to have forgotten that there were other people in the room. "Speak to me? Why, certainly," he said, and joined Marie-Té by the window.

"Dr. Ruíz, isn't there somewhere that we could take him—some good hospital?" asked Marie-Té, gazing earnestly at the doctor. "Surely this is no place to take care of a sick person."

"But we went through all that in connection with the young American. Things haven't altered since the other day."

"So there isn't any place?"

"No. I am ashamed to say it, but Santa Rosa, with a population of a hundred thousand has only one hospital. And that is a hospital with straw mats instead of beds. He is better off right here."

"Is it—serious?"

"Yes, no doubt about that. You see, my dear friend, this is not the usual *malaria tertiana,* such as the young American contracted. Unfortunately it is the tropical variety."

"Yes, I see," said Marie-Té, and now she made up her mind that the situation called for honest speaking. "Don't think," she said, "that I doubt your capacity, Dr. Ruíz, but may I ask you a frank question?"

"By all means."

"Would you advise me to take my brother away from here by airplane? To the United States, I mean?"

The doctor hesitated for a long moment before answering. Reflectively he passed his hand over his straight black hair, while his glance sought out Bubi on the bed. It occurred to Marie-Té that he might very well be standing like that a few days hence, looking with those same wise, understanding eyes, not at a sick person, but at a corpse. How could he be affected by the death of one more patient when he realized so keenly that every day thousands were dying stupidly, painfully, needlessly on battlefields and in the overcrowded hovels of Santa Rosa? Perhaps, she thought, it was a mistake for a doctor of medicine to have far vision.

When Dr. Ruíz spoke at last, there was in his soft voice an infinity of kindness. Yet at the same time she could detect a note of resignation that was like an acknowledgment of defeat.

"Dear Fräulein Falkenborn, if you love your little brother very much, then it may be best for you to take him away tomorrow. He would get better attention in the United States—and perhaps a better doctor. Though, in the last analysis, it is all a question of luck," he added with a bitter little smile.

Marie-Té decided at once to go and see Harrington about their visas.

Warfield Harrington was in a crotchety humor. Commencing with the Ted Kelly affair, everything had been going wrong, and the climax had come the day before with Camberly's insistence on handling that immigration matter in the place of Baker. But as if all this were not enough, Ah Sing's train had to be late in getting in from Puerto Marques, with the result that lunch was not yet ready though it was past one o'clock. One thing Harrington insisted on was prompt meal hours, and as he sat in his sitting room listening to Ah Sing patter about the kitchen, he fumed inwardly. He had a bone to pick with Ah Sing anyway; it gave him a certain satisfaction to think that after all these years, he at last had a legitimate cause for attack.

"It's about time. Please don't let this happen again," he said when the valet, immaculate as ever in his white jacket and striped dark trousers, finally announced luncheon.

"No, sir. Velly solly," said Ah Sing, pulling out Harrington's chair. "I make chicken chow mein for lunch."

Harrington had lived long enough in China to have acquired some oriental tastes in food. He particularly liked chow mein the way Ah Sing prepared it, which had little to do with the ignominious substitutes often served under the same name. Nevertheless, Harrington always made a point of passing a little criticism of some sort; it was a matter of principle with him never to offer whole-hearted praise to a member of the lower classes—a dangerous practice, in his opinion, which led to communism and related evils.

"You don't think that a bit more celery might help next time?" he asked with that suave politeness he affected to camouflage his commands.

"Velly vell, sir," Ah Sing responded.

Harrington selected a dainty-looking morsel and transported it upwards with the chopsticks in whose use he had perfected himself in China.

"And a few more chives, perhaps?"

"Excuse me, Mr. Hallington," said Ah Sing in his pidgin English. "Last time you tell me not to put in any chives at all."

Harrington checked a scowl. Yes, he remembered that very well, now that Ah Sing mentioned it, but he particularly disliked being put in the wrong. Once again he had the unpleasant feeling that had come to him several times of late that Ah Sing was being insubordinate. He glanced up at him suspiciously, but the Chinese was standing respectfully beside the table, a snow-white napkin folded on his arm, the usual enigmatical expression on his face.

Suddenly Harrington was overcome with a violent feeling of antagonism for Ah Sing. Damn the boy, he thought. He would teach him who was servant and who was master, and nothing would have given him greater pleasure than to teach the whole race the same lesson. One of the very worst things this war had done was to give them a feeling of equality with white men; if it wasn't checked in time, it might lead to no end of trouble. He was overcome with his old hatred of Orientals, and had he been a man of violence, he might very well have jumped up and struck the boy. However, when he spoke, his voice was as dry and precise as ever.

"Ah Sing," he said, "I am very disappointed in you."

"Sir?"

"What you have done is neither more nor less than thieving," said Harrington without looking up from his chow mein.

"What do you mean, sir?" asked Ah Sing, his face gone completely white. His hand flew up to the collar of his jacket, where it lay like a pale flower—like an exquisite object meant to adorn rather than perform humdrum functions. It was as if all of old China—its culture, its deep wisdom, its love of beauty, had contributed to the fashioning of those perfect fingers, of that slender wrist. The very possession of this hand seemed to Harrington an act of insolence on Ah Sing's part. Instinctively he put down his chopsticks and thrust his own hands into his lap. Speaking deliberately, he said,

"I went into your room yesterday, Ah Sing. I consider that an employer's prerogative," he added, as one of Ah Sing's black eyebrows rose a fraction of an inch in esthetic horror. "Well, evidently it was a good idea, for there, lying on the table, was one of my finest books: a translation of Lao-Tse in a beautiful calf binding! Yes, Ah Sing, I really am disappointed in you," he went on, picking up his chopsticks. "After all, we belong to different races. You ought to understand that I don't enjoy having my books touched by you."

There passed through Ah Sing a movement that was like a shiver without yet being one; one might have thought that a live nerve had been touched, causing a spasmodic reflex. Then his body became quite rigid and his eyelids closed; he stood there like an oriental statue, not a muscle stirring, not even his nostrils moving. So still did he remain that Harrington finally grew nervous as he finished transferring the contents of the plate to his mouth. Why didn't the fellow say something, or at least give a sign of emotion? Nothing was as irritating to a white man as this impassive attitude, adopted by Orientals in the same way that certain breeds of animals adopt protective coloring.

Finally, simply so as to break the tension and *force* Ah Sing to speak, he said, "Oh, I meant to ask you: what happened to your friend yesterday at Puerto Marques? Did they let him in?"

Then Ah Sing spoke, but to Harrington's utter astonishment, he employed instead of pidgin English, the most smoothly flowing grammatical language.

"Yes sir. Thanks to Mr. Camberly, everyone was let in. Mr. Camberly was extremely kind, and the young lady with him was very helpful also. They succeeded in convincing the authorities."

Now it was Harrington's turn to change his face into a mask. A quarter of a century of diplomatic training stood him in good stead, and not even Ah Sing's perceptive eye could have detected the tremor of a feature at that mention of a young lady in connection with John Camberly. His curiosity was excruciating, yet stolidly he continued to maneuver the chow mein into his mouth, performing the operation with remarkable deftness considering his clumsy-looking fingers. Was it possible that Camberly's female companion had been Marie-Té? Ah Sing seemed determined to keep him in suspense. With the impassive expression of a Chinese torturer who is turning the knife inside a wound, he stood watching Harrington

190

from across the table. Not until he had served the chow mein for the second time did he break his silence.

"It was very hot in Puerto Marques, sir," he remarked in his most respectful manner. "It was really quite oppressive."

Harrington said nothing, fully aware that the final stab was about to be administered; he waited in an agony of suspense.

"Mr. Camberly and the young baroness found Puerto Marques very hot also," Ah Sing went on. "That is why they decided to spend the night there and drive back early this morning, before the worst heat of the day."

From between Harrington's uplifted chopsticks, a few particles of the chow mein slipped out. The Minister saw Ah Sing's eyelids give the tiniest flutter, as if he had waited for this evidence that his blade had found its mark. And the Minister understood that Ah Sing had scored a triumph—in fact so great a one as almost to avenge the insult inflicted. This was his first thought, before the full implication of what he had heard grew clear to him.

After Ah Sing had served coffee and retired, Harrington sat on for several moments at the dining table. From the kitchen he could hear the sound of soft footsteps as the boy moved about, putting things in order; by straining his ears he could just make out the tuneless Chinese song with which Ah Sing accompanied himself at his task. Fearing that the servant might return and find him still sitting there, Harrington presently moved over to the writing desk and took some papers from a drawer. He spread them carefully before him so that he could pretend to be reading if he were broken in on.

In the meanwhile his thoughts had gone skimming through these last weeks, right back to his first meeting with Marie-Té. How well he remembered that afternoon when she came striding into his office, sunshine in her hair, warm color in her cheeks! She had been wearing the same white linen dress which was to become so familiar to him, seeing that she wore it almost every day. It must have been washed and ironed at least a thousand times, yet in it she always

191

looked incredibly fresh and springlike. Her blue and white striped shirtwaist had been open at the throat, and as she sat there in the big leather chair, slender legs crossed, red lips curving mischievously, she had seemed like an apparition from another world blown straight into his office. There had been about her something so youthful, something so vivacious and bright, that after she had left him, the room had seemed positively murky; he had sat there for a moment, just sniffing in the faint aroma of mimosa lingering behind her.

Then he saw her dancing round and round the ballroom of the Portuguese Legation. Regal in her blue velvet dress, her blonde hair worn like a golden crown, high on her head, she had waltzed about, giddy and flushed and beautiful. How angry he had been with her that evening for having boasted about her modeling career, and how amused she had been when his anger turned to surprise on his hearing that she had a title!

"Oh Harrington, you're so funny!" she had said, dancing close to him, seductive and brazenly flirtatious. "I really think you feel that you ought to have a little more respect for me from now on."

Well, that was one time when she'd been wrong. He always had had respect for her, even if unable to understand why she played the *enfant terrible* and why she insisted on being introduced simply as "Miss Falkenborn." He had respect for her even now, after she had spent the night with Camberly in Puerto Marques, but he knew that she would never again figure in his life. The period that centered around Marie-Té was over, brought to an abrupt end by Ah Sing's revelation; she had ceased to exist as far as he was concerned. The same will power with which he had fought his way to success enabled Warfield Harrington to put Marie-Té out of his life for good.

And having done that, it seemed to him that he had known always that it would finally come to this. He had known it before Camberly met her at the Portuguese Legation, indeed even before he himself met Marie-Té. A presentiment of this coming defeat had

192

lain in his mind long before, perhaps ever since he was an unpopular boy at school. He understood, through all his pain and disillusionment, that his fate was fulfilling itself again: his very nature
forbade his attaining a warm human relationship.

After all, this thing that had now befallen was no more than a
re-enactment of earlier tragedies: of the election of another as
school valedictorian, of his rejection by a college fraternity. In
other words, everything was following the old pattern. It was even
typical that Camberly, whom he disliked above anyone, should
have been the instrument of his defeat. In position, in wealth, probably even in intelligence, he was the other man's superior, yet it was
clear that Camberly possessed something in which he, Harrington,
was lacking. What was it? The ability to feel? A talent for loving?
Or simply the quality of being completely human? Harrington did
not know. He knew only, keenly and painfully, that there was this
lack in him which had condemned him to loneliness his whole life
long.

In the kitchen the soft Chinese humming had ceased. When Harrington heard the click of the door which connected with the servant's bedroom, he opened his desk drawer and took out the photograph of Marie-Té that she once had given him. It was, she had
told him, the work of her brother's little camera, but it was not bad
at all. Taken outside the Pension Hilda, it showed Marie-Té standing smiling with her arm around an acacia tree. It had seemed to
Harrington that with that gesture she was doing more than embrace
the acacia; she was taking in her warm arms the whole of nature, and
life itself, that she loved so well.

Harrington sat studying the picture for several moments. Then
he quickly tore it across, again and yet again, and dropped it in the
wastebasket; the glossy bits of paper shone as they fluttered through
the air. He went to get his hat, but, about to leave, changed his mind
and came back to the writing desk. Gathering up the torn photograph from the basket, he carried it into the bathroom. First he tore

193

it into smaller pieces, then dropped these down the drain and watched carefully until the last scrap had disappeared.

He drove to the Legation in his Packard, sitting up very straight on the leather seat, and feeling that his whole body was peculiarly taut and rigid.

Carlos, the new *mozo,* ran to open the door of the car, and stood saluting as Harrington alighted. Every button of his uniform was gleaming, and his handsome stupid-looking face was beautifully shaved. Well, he's an improvement, that's certain, thought Harrington. It's a good thing I got rid of Jesús, even if he did hold this post for twenty years.

Gratified by the *mozo's* salute, Harrington entered the Legation. He was walking through the vestibule when he caught sight of Marie-Té Falkenborn in the reception room. He was told that she had been waiting for him for over an hour.

And another half hour passed before Marie-Té was summoned. In agonizing nervousness she paced up and down the little room, counted the steps from wall to wall, added up the precious seconds and the minutes that she was spending here while Bubi lay wasting in the grip of the disease. Once or twice she stopped to look at the colored poster of Niagara at which she had seen Kerjanian gazing with such longing on her first visit to the Legation. Now better than ever she understood the desperate yearning of refugees for those United States—the country that spelled happiness and safety.

George Baker came hurrying down the corridor with some papers in his hand. "Oh Mr. Baker," said Marie-Té, stepping out into the hall, "does Mr. Harrington know I'm waiting?" George Baker, officiously polite as a rule, did not even bother to come up to her today. "Yes, yes, he knows, Baroness Falkenborn," he called as he disappeared into his office. "The Minister is busy."

Marie-Té gave a frown. It was only too clear to her by now that there was something wrong, for Baker was like a weather vane that always pointed with the prevailing wind. If "young Harrington," as Camberly called him, dared to be off-handish, then weather conditions must have been far from favorable.

Finally the new *mozo* appeared in the entrance, saluted twice, and asked Marie-Té to step into the Minister's office. Harrington greeted her with even more than his usual politeness.

"Delighted to see you, Marie-Té," he said, drawing up the visitor's chair. "Be seated."

"I have come to ask you a great service, Harrington," said Marie-Té, going straight to the point. "You know my little brother? You've met him at the pension several times."

"Yes, of course. Little chap about three or four—is that right?" asked Harrington, who never remembered anyone unless they could be of direct use to him.

"Exactly," agreed Marie-Té, not troubling to point out that Bubi was a big boy of eight. "Well, he has caught malaria and caught it badly. About as badly as you can catch it! The doctor says that it may save his life if we fly him to the States at once. But *literally* at once. Harrington, you've simply got to help me!"

She was aware of the note of anguish in her own voice, and she let her eyes speak for her, entreating him not to fail her. For a moment Harrington did not answer. Sitting with his thin lips pursed, he seemed to be deliberating the situation; unceasingly his fingers played with the little American flag upon his desk and with the miniature flagpole to which it was attached.

"I presume that it's a question of visas?" he inquired at length.

"Of course."

"Well, I would like to help you, Marie-Té. Unfortunately it's not so easy."

"Not so easy! Surely you have to do no more than authorize temporary visas."

"Oh, I wish that it were as simple as all that," said Harrington, and his customary little chuckle sounded particularly mirthless today. "These matters are extremely complicated—you know that from your own experience. Though you all made your applications months ago, your visas have been held up by innumerable complications."

"But what has that to do with it?" asked Marie-Té, and she looked at Harrington uneasily. "What I am asking for is emergency visas, not immigration visas. The authorities can send us back here later on."

"Yes, yes, but Washington has been cracking down on us in all passport matters," said Harrington, smiling blandly. "As you may have heard, Marie-Té, our country is at war. Of course I need hardly assure you that I'd like nothing better than to help you."

"For God's sake don't be diplomatic, for once," cried Marie-Té, beginning to feel desperate. "What good are assurances? We've had four years of them, unaccompanied by actions, and we refugees don't take much stock in the assurances of the democracies any longer. This is a matter of my brother's life. I came to see you as a friend in fearful need. As it happens, you alone can help me."

"But my dear Marie-Té, what should I say? I'm not a private individual now, but an officer of my government. The proper regulations have to be observed."

"Regulations! The boy may be dying, and you talk to me about regulations. Really, Harrington, I just can't understand you."

She sat there with eyes fixed on the floor, biting her lips to control herself. Obviously a flare-up would do as little good as a further appeal to his sympathies; Harrington being what he was, the human equation simply didn't count. Like the Nazis, he disregarded such factors as kindness, generosity or even decency in coming to his decisions.

"So it's definite that you can do nothing?" she asked him after a moment, her voice calm again, but icy.

"I didn't say that," Harrington hastened to point out, reluctant as always to make a concrete statement. "I'll have to think about it. But don't look so serious, Marie-Té. It doesn't suit you."

As Harrington emitted another of those characteristic sniggers, Marie-Té raised her eyes and looked straight at him. Suddenly she had made up her mind that, whatever happened, this would be the last time they met. Ever since her girlhood, she had felt that she belonged on the other side of the fence, yet up till this day she had always compromised; she had flirted with Harrington and with what he represented, not because she liked him, or liked those things, but because she was lighthearted by nature and inclined to take the easiest way. Now the time of compromise was over; never more would she have to do with him or with his kind.

Marie-Té stood up. She realized that she was wearing the same white dress as the first time she came to this office, and that Harrington, too, had on the same clothes and even the same necktie; it was precisely the same time of day. Yes, outwardly everything was identical, but a great transformation had taken place within her. She was a mature woman now, a woman who knew her path and would never veer from it.

"Good-by, Harrington," she said. She was stretching out her hand when she changed her mind and drew it back. To shake hands with Harrington now would have been a betrayal of Bubi and, what was worse, a betrayal of everything she stood for. For a second she and Harrington stood looking each other in the eye. Then without another word, Marie-Té turned and left the office.

Chapter XIII

The Beautiful Bubble

W HEN KERJANIAN HEARD FOOTSTEPS ON HIS STAIRS, he hurried out onto his landing. Those sounds had been made by leather shoes—he knew it instantly! Quite different was their step from the shuffle of *huaraches*, and who beside his little friend Bubi ever came to this house wearing shoes? But then he saw that he had been mistaken, and a look of disappointment and hostility swept into his face. Coming up the staircase was the Austrian girl, Marie-Té.

"He isn't here!" he called down to her, for Kerjanian's first thought was that she meant to forbid him the boy's visits. With his foot he pushed shut the door behind him to prevent the armadillo from running out.

The Austrian girl raised her head, and now Kerjanian saw that her face was tense and harassed. Stopping on the top flight, she talked up to him.

"Oh Mr. Kerjanian, excuse me for breaking in like this. Bubi asked me to come and fetch you. He is ill."

"Ill!" Kerjanian repeated the word in a tone of fright.

"Yes, very ill indeed. He has caught malaria. He says that he wants to see you—and the armadillo."

Kerjanian felt a pang go through him and his legs suddenly grew weak. Instead of answering, he made a vague gesture that might have been interpreted as a command to wait. Then he went back into his room, shutting the door behind him.

He began to walk about, passing his hand nervously across his

198

chin. Malaria! Was it really possible that the boy had caught that dreaded disease? Here in Santa Rosa he had seen plenty of its victims on the streets, shuffling along listlessly with that cadaverous expression that distinguished them at first sight. Would it strike at Bubi in the same way, pushing in his cheeks and sucking the vigor from his sturdy limbs? No, no, there must be some solution! He, Kerjanian, would take charge and insist on obtaining the services of the best doctor in Santa Rosa. The important thing was to go to the top—the very top. He would make inquiries as to who treated the President of the Republic.

Momentarily relieved by this decision, Kerjanian went to fetch a clothesbrush, which he passed over his jacket and felt hat; with great care he straightened his crimson necktie. Then he got down on his knees beside the bed, and began feeling beneath it for the armadillo. When his hand touched the carapace, he instinctively drew it back, but then he conquered his aversion and pulled out the wretched animal by the tail. When he joined Marie-Té a moment later, he had fastened a cord to one of its diminutive legs.

"I am ready," Kerjanian announced impressively.

They set out through the market place, the armadillo following behind and occasionally tugging at its cord in an effort to get at the refuse piles. It had become quite tame during the weeks that it had been living with Kerjanian; it even had grown used to being led about on a lead. The Armenian strode along in a concentrated manner, paying no attention either to the armadillo or to the usual little crowd of urchins that soon collected and followed behind, laughing and pointing at the animal. Constitutionally lacking in a sense of humor, he saw nothing stranger in having a pet armadillo than in having a pet dog.

"I suppose you have engaged a good doctor?" he asked as they passed the glass-covered market hall. "I always believe in going to the top."

"Yes, but there are tops and tops. The truth is, Mr. Kerjanian, that we have been advised to take Bubi to the United States."

Kerjanian reacted as if he had received a physical blow. He stopped dead in the street and his fanatical black eyes began to roam about, like the eyes of a hunted man. So it had come at last, this thing that he had dreaded for so long! Moreover, it had come in such a way that he would not even wish to stop it, seeing that the boy's welfare depended on his departure. One glance at Marie-Té's face had dissipated the suspicion that this was nothing but a plot to take the lad away from him.

"When are you leaving?" he asked, twisting the armadillo's cord in his nervous fingers.

"We don't know," said Marie-Té. "We don't even know if they will give us visas."

"But surely they can't refuse you in such a case!" His voice wavered between hope and indignation. Perhaps after all the boy would be staying on! And yet under the circumstances might that not be the worst thing for him? "Have you gone to the top?" he inquired anxiously. "Have you seen Harrington himself?"

"Harrington refuses to do anything about it."

Those words produced a violent explosion in Kerjanian. All his old hatred of Harrington seethed up, and it seemed to his over-wrought mind that the man's guilt extended much further than refusing visas; at Harrington's doorstep could be laid responsibility for this entire catastrophe, and the pain that it was bringing to Kerjanian.

"He has no right to refuse!" he shouted, standing in the middle of the street and gesticulating. "How dare he refuse? Who is this Harrington, anyway, to treat everyone like dirt? I tell you that he is going to pay for it one day!"

"Do let us hurry, Mr. Kerjanian. Bubi is waiting," Marie-Té exclaimed impatiently. It was growing dark and they were still some distance from the pension.

"Yes, yes, we mustn't keep him waiting. Let us hurry," said Kerjanian, giving the cord such a tug that the poor armadillo hissed in protest. "So Harrington doesn't want you to leave, eh? Wants to

200

keep you here!" he muttered as they hurried along. "Oh, I know that Harrington. A low fellow, take my word for it. He may hold the rank of Minister, but that doesn't matter. He's lower than that armadillo! The animal has a little feeling—it can suffer—it feels gratitude when it is being fed. But Harrington has no real feelings at all. Is there anything lower in this world than a living being without feelings?"

As they entered the pension, Hilda Stumpf ran up to meet them. Her rosy face was beaming; she exuded an atmosphere of cheerfulness and goodness.

"I have splendid news," she cried. "The fever has gone down." And then, on catching sight of a prehistoric-looking animal walking across her best carpet, *"Gott im Himmel!* What is that?"

"It's Bubi's armadillo," explained Marie-Té. "And this, Hilda, is a friend of his—Mr. Kerjanian."

The big woman shook the Armenian's hand and her candid glance met his. Ah, this was a real woman, Kerjanian thought—warm and friendly. He liked her at first sight. Rare indeed, were the people who laid no stock in appearances—who could evaluate a person by looking not at his shabby clothes but straight into his eyes.

Tucking the armadillo under his arm, Kerjanian followed Marie-Té upstairs. As they reached the first floor landing, music came to his ears—the airy notes of a violin. Ah, where was it that he had heard that gay lilting melody before? Kerjanian could not recall, but for some reason a wave of happiness swept over him. An utterly delightful association stirred in his subconscious. In his mind's eye he saw a beautiful bubble floating in mid-air, pearshaped, iridescent in color. The bubble was blown backwards and forwards gently in time to the music; then it exploded with a frivolous little sound that was like a young boy's laughter. Suddenly for a single moment Kerjanian felt youthful and light; it was as if all his worries, including this new one, had been lifted from his shoulders.

Halfway down the corridor the boy's sister stopped and opened one of a row of doors; still carrying the armadillo, Kerjanian stepped into a room behind her. On a bed lay the boy, his cheeks red, his eyes glittering. As his glance met Kerjanian's and then traveled downwards to the animal, his face broke into a smile. He began to stretch out his arms, then pulled them backwards, grimacing. But a moment later he was smiling again. On the edge of the bed sat a big man in a velvet jacket, playing the violin. Though his back was turned to Kerjanian, the Armenian recognized the player from his solitary visit to the night club, Chez Boris. How long ago had that been? he tried to remember. It seemed to him like a century.

The violinist's concentration did not wander as he played on, *"Wien, Wien, nur du allein. . . . . sollst stets die Stadt meiner Träume sein. . . . ."* Only when he had reached the last note did he gently lower the bow and turn his head.

"Ah, delighted that you have come," he said to Kerjanian in an old-fashioned, courtly manner, and made a little bow. "As you see, I have been playing for the invalid. I read somewhere that there's nothing like music to help the body's recovery. I don't know about that, to tell the truth, but at least it can't do much harm. It's a terrible feeling just to sit by, doing nothing."

Kerjanian nodded. He felt very ill at ease, standing by the doorway with this ridiculous animal under his arm, and when the big man unobtrusively pulled up a chair for him beside the bed, he seated himself quickly. What natural graciousness this family had! thought the Armenian. They made one forget that one was a refugee in a shiny suit and without a passport; in contrast to most upper-class people he had met—typified for him in the figure of Harrington—they treated one in a friendly, natural way, as though they actually *believed* that one was as good as themselves. Yes, these people were genuine aristocrats, he thought—aristocrats of the heart.

In the meanwhile, the armadillo had begun squirming in his arms, and when he put it on the floor, it at once scrambled to its favorite hiding place—beneath a bed. Relieved of the animal, Kerjanian sat with a stiff smile on his face, without speaking. He remembered the jasmine branches that he had once given the boy's sister, and his nervous eye roamed the room in their search. But then he recalled that that had been several weeks ago. No doubt the flowers had died before he paid this visit, just as the boy's sister had predicted that they would. He saw before him their bright young petals, so fresh and confident on the graceful stalks. How beautiful they had been that day! As he thought of them, a sensation of sadness, sweet and nostalgic, crept over him. No more could Kerjanian have explained it than he could have explained the brief feeling of happiness that had come to him a short while before.

He knew that he was expected to say something and searched about for the appropriate words. Never before with the boy had he been forced to make conversation. Abruptly he blurted out, still looking about the room rather than at Bubi, "How are you, *amigo mio?*"

"Oh, very well," was the answer. "Very well indeed."

Kerjanian nodded wisely, as though he were ruminating on this statement. However, his heart felt so heavy that he could not go on with the conversation. Ah, how he wished that he were alone with the boy now! He was sure that somehow he could have helped him. The presence of strangers, however sympathetic, broke the great bond between them. Subtle as it was, maintained by intuitive understanding rather than by words, it was inevitable that it should snap when exposed to the emanations of other people.

As if she had read his thoughts, the Austrian girl turned to say something to the man in the velvet jacket, and then she addressed Kerjanian. "Would you mind," she asked him, "staying with Bubi for a few minutes? If you need us, we will be in the other room."

Kerjanian nodded. What could he say in appreciation of such a wonderfully tactful gesture? Immediately the door was closed, he leaned forward in his chair and looked long and searchingly into Bubi's face. They were all alone now, but even so he couldn't find a word to say. His throat felt all clogged up. It was clear as daylight that the boy was desperately ill, and, worst of all, Bubi seemed to know it himself. He made no attempt to speak, and he wasn't even interested in the armadillo, which could be heard crawling about beneath the bed. He just lay there with flushed cheeks and eyes glistening with fever, gazing up at Kerjanian.

The quiet in the room was very deep. Through the wall came a low murmur of voices as the boy's sister and the man who had played the violin conversed together. Outside the window a train of burros passed by, their little feet making a pattering sound on the mud-baked street, gentle as the drip of falling tears. One by one the seconds were ticked off by Bubi's silver watch, lying face up on the bedside table. As he sat there, no more than dimly aware of these outer sounds, or of the darkness that was creeping into the room, a feeling of sadness, gentle as a mother's caress, enveloped Kerjanian.

Then at last Bubi spoke. Looking straight into Kerjanian's eyes, he said something which the Armenian did not remember ever having heard before. Perhaps it had been said to him in his own country, in that long-distant past, the very memory of which had been washed away by the bitter waters of time; for Kerjanian it was as if he were hearing it for the first time.

"I love you, Mr. Refugee," he said. "You know, I love you very much."

Kerjanian felt that he had been waiting all his life for someone to say just that to him. The tears rose to his eyes, almost blinding him, and there mingled with his sadness a feeling of utter bliss. Now that he had been given those words that he had always longed for, he knew that nothing could ever take them from him again; they were his forever, to cherish as his most precious possession.

Ah, now he felt that he could speak and that there was much he wished to tell the boy! He looked down at Bubi—and saw to his horror that a fiery color had come into the cheeks and that Bubi's mouth was open, as if he were having difficulty breathing. "Oh, I am choking—I am choking!" he called out in an anguished voice.

Terrified, Kerjanian rushed into the corridor and pounded on the neighboring door. The Austrian girl hurried into her brother's room and ran up to the bed. "It's all right, Bubi. It will pass in a minute," she said, making him sit up and putting her arm around his shoulders. "Don't be frightened, darling, darling."

Kerjanian walked about the room, twisting his fingers. He felt his own breath coming in gasps, as though his lungs were reacting in sympathy. Yet all the while a fatuous smile lay on his face. One might have thought that he considered all this the greatest joke imaginable! Knowing that he was smiling, he could not stop himself. The presence of strangers ever had made him painfully self-conscious and called forth unpredictable reflexes.

Now Bubi's breathing began to come a little easier. He lay back on his pillow, exhausted, and little shivers passed through his body; his teeth chattered. Seating herself on the edge of the bed, Marie-Té wiped his forehead with a damp cloth. Then she sat holding his hand, on her face an expression of such tenderness that it struck even Kerjanian in his distracted state.

And suddenly he wanted to get away. After what had happened between the boy and him, he did not want to stay on in the presence of other people who could understand nothing of their great friendship. He himself was unable to understand, nor did he endeavor to understand, why the boy's existence had become for him the most important thing in the world.

Without warning, he flopped down on his knees and began to rummage for the armadillo's cord beneath the bed. He hauled out the animal, whose scaly body scraped against the floor.

"But please do not go yet. Stay a little longer, Mr. Kerjanian," said the violin player in his courteous way.

"No, no. I am meeting a very important person in a little while. I must go."

Kerjanian did not trust himself to say good-by, but marched

straight for the door. Perhaps they would think him ill-mannered—boorish. It didn't matter. He could not bear to stay on in this room where the boy was suffering and he had to sit by unable to help, unable to relieve his pain.

At the door he turned to look back, and for a flash his eyes met Bubi's. What a strange look he saw in them, just as though the boy were endeavoring to send a message! Had they been alone, he was sure that he would have understood. As it was, he could not even tell if the boy was asking for something or if he was trying to give something to Kerjanian.

Late that evening there came a low knock on Marie-Té's bedroom door. When she failed to answer, the door was opened from the outside and John Camberly stepped in. Marie-Té's room lay in darkness, but the connecting door to Bubi's room stood ajar, and in there a night lamp was burning. In a deep armchair by the bed sat Uncle Konrad, his violin clasped in his arms, his glance fixed on the face of the sleeping boy. Marie-Té was sitting on the edge of the bed with her head sunk in her hands. Her soft blonde hair had fallen down over her face, and her white linen dress was crumpled, as if she had been lying down in it. For once she didn't look like the elegant Marie-Té but like a very tired little girl.

John Camberly made his way up to her on tiptoe and laid his firm hand on her shoulder. "Marie-Té," he whispered, "please come downstairs and have a cup of coffee. Fräulein Stumpf tells me that you haven't eaten a thing all day."

Marie-Té had given a start when he touched her. Now she looked up at him and shook her head. "No, no. Bubi has just fallen off to sleep. I shan't leave him."

"But Marie-Té, you must keep up your strength if you're to help him. Come with me now. I'm sure your uncle will call you if you're needed."

With reluctance Marie-Té rose to her feet. Her movements, usually so alert and limber, were tonight as stiff as an old woman's.

206

Without a word she accompanied John Camberly along the corridor and down the stairs. He reached for her hand and squeezed it; it lay in his like an inert object.

At the end of the deserted dining room Hilda Stumpf was making coffee in the percolator. The standing lamp shed a circle of light around her, but in that big black room it looked as if it was Hilda herself who was radiating the light, creating a bright corner in a world of darkness. Startling indeed was the change that had come over Hilda Stumpf in the short period since the reading of her book. She was like a person who for years has been forced to wear unbecoming clothes, but now finally has a suit cut to his true measure. The knowledge that her way as a writer lay broad and clear before her had straightened her shoulders and put confidence in her gaze.

"You look exhausted, child," she said, peering anxiously in Marie-Té's face. "You mustn't let yourself get discouraged. You're not one of those defeatists who gives up when things go wrong. That's never been your way, my dear."

Marie-Té tried to give Hilda a smile, then sank down in a chair by the table. Hilda and John Camberly exchanged glances. With a common accord they began to speak of things that had nothing to do with what was on their minds.

"I can't tell you how happy I am about your book, Fräulein Stumpf," said Camberly. "Marie-Té tells me it's the most stirring novel she has ever read. Beautifully written too. And now they want you to go up to the States on a lecture tour!"

"Yes. I can hardly believe it myself," Hilda answered in her strongly accented English. "I feel like a butterfly not yet used to being out of the chrysalis. Madame Legervais keeps telling me that I will have to buy a new dress and do my hair in a more chic fashion. Yesterday she came into my room with a comb and a pair of scissors and wanted to get to work on it right away. I shall have to keep my door locked at night for fear of waking up next morning with a giddy bob!"

207

John Camberly laughed, and it was clear that he had taken to Hilda Stumpf as quickly as she to him. Now the coffee was ready, and Hilda poured out three cups and set one of them before Marie-Té, together with some coffeecake. Automatically Marie-Té began to eat and to drink.

"I wonder if you've heard about the plans that I've been hatching with Irène Legervais," Hilda Stumpf asked Camberly. "I want Baron Falkenborn to take over Pension Hilda while I'm away—and perhaps indefinitely, if I decide to stay in the United States. After all, I have no more ties in Santa Rosa," she said, and for a moment an expression of sadness crossed her face as her thoughts went to Siegfried.

"Excellent! What do you think, Marie-Té? Would your uncle do it?"

But Marie-Té was not listening. She had put down her coffee cup after a few swallows and sat gazing through the window into the dark night outside. When she spoke, her words were unrelated to Hilda's question. John Camberly had never heard her speak in such a dreamy, faraway voice before.

"I don't see how anything bad can happen to Bubi," she said. "Not anything *really* bad. Bubi has always been so—so special." She stopped talking for a moment and a little smile came to her lips as though it moved her just to think back on Bubi's past. "Even when he was a very little boy we used to let him go out alone," Marie-Té went on, "and it was strange, but nobody felt anxious about him. 'Oh, Bubi—he'll be all right,' we used to say, and somehow we were all pleased to think that he could look after himself so well. Danger might threaten him, but somehow it could never touch him —we knew that. Did I ever tell you about that incident with the snake, Hilda?"

"I wish you would," said Hilda Stumpf, putting her arm affectionately around Marie-Té's shoulder.

"Well, we used to spend the summers on my great-aunt Stephanie's estate in Styria—this was before the *Anschluss*, of course.

Bubi had his breakfast each morning on the front lawn while the rest of the household was still in bed. One day my aunt came downstairs, and to her dismay found Bubi sitting happily at the table with a huge snake coiled up before him. And the snake was drinking out of his bowl of milk! Of course the poor woman was terrified, and she almost fainted when she saw Bubi pick up his spoon and hit the snake right on the head. She was sure that the animal would strike out at him, but instead he just looked at Bubi—affectionately, my aunt said—then after a moment slithered off into the bushes. 'Oh, he comes here every morning and I always give him a little milk,' Bubi told us later. 'I hit him this morning because he took too much.' My aunt said that he looked so wonderful sitting there in the sunshine on the green grass—as if he was a friend of all the world and afraid of nothing."

"Oh, what a beautiful story, Marie-Té!" said Hilda Stumpf, her face radiant. "Not to be afraid, never to experience fear in any of its forms, is the beginning and end of wisdom. And why wasn't Bubi afraid of the snake? Because he *liked* it. He likes everything and everyone, and so he is completely free of fear. Bubi, for all his youth, is wiser than anyone I've ever met. Ah, when I think of my poor brother Siegfried—always so terrified, so unsure . . ."

Hilda stopped herself. Never before had she mentioned in public her brother and his betrayal of all she stood for. Nor would she have gone on now, had she not been aware of a feeling of warm intimacy and friendship reigning about this little table. Passing her hand over her broad forehead, as if to brush away something that hovered over her, she went on,

"Oh Marie-Té, I have such a different memory of my brother Siegfried as a little boy! Do you know that I always see him standing, thin and shivering, on a rock fifty meters or so from shore in the lake near our parents' home in Bavaria. He had swum out and he could easily have swum back, but he didn't dare. 'I can't do it! I can't! I'll drown!' he cried, and his whole face was twisted with fear. If there had been ten other boys with him, he wouldn't have hesitated to take the plunge, but alone—no! Never to dare act alone, never to trust oneself, never to rely on one's own judgment—that's the great weakness of our German race, Marie-Té. But you Austrians are different; you're individualists. And little Bubi is a real Austrian."

Perhaps it was because Marie-Té, too, felt that she was in the presence of people who loved and understood her that she now let go of all restraint. An utterly miserable expression swept into her face, and she put her head on the table, and her shoulders shook with sobs.

"Oh John," she said, reaching out her hand for his across the table, "I love Bubi so. I love him so."

John Camberly laid his hand over Marie-Té's, oblivious of Hilda sitting there beside them. They were three good friends together—three people who liked and respected one another in a world where such groups of friends were rare. For a long moment they sat on silently like that, John Camberly and Hilda trying to convey their love, their sympathy, without the clumsy intermediary of speech. Then Hilda Stumpf rose and slipped out of the room, so silently that only a moment afterwards did John realize that she was no longer there. He brought his chair next to Marie-Té's and raised up her head and looked into her eyes.

"I know what you are going through, darling. Believe me, I know. I realize what Bubi means to you, and that is why I have done what I could to help. I can't go over Harrington's head in the visa matter, but I have arranged for a good doctor to fly down from Panama. Martin is his name, a specialist in malaria. I've been in touch with him by telephone today, and he'll be here tomorrow morning."

Marie-Té looked into John's face without speaking. Slowly she shook her head. "You did that for me, John?" she said at last. "You really did that for me?"

"Oh Marie-Té, don't you know that I would do anything in the world for you? Don't you understand that yet?"

210

Then they were in each other's arms and their lips were seeking each other with the same eagerness as in Puerto Marques the day before. But tonight there was in Marie-Té's kisses a certain desperation, a fervor that was tragic in its intensity. Did it spring from the knowledge that life has a habit of snatching away with one hand at the same time that it is bestowing with the other?

Chapter XIV

The Weaponless

KERJANIAN AWOKE NEXT MORNING IN AN EXALTED state of mind. Though he could not for the first moment recall his great decision of the night before, he was aware that something unusual, something altogether momentous, was to happen. What was it? From his bed he frowned upwards at the brown stain upon his ceiling, which always reminded him of the picture in his childhood schoolbook of Don Quixote tilting with the windmill. The knight's expression this morning seemed especially desperate, as if the Spaniard realized the heartrending futility of this joust in which he was involved. Ah yes, now Kerjanian remembered! His features hardened. He was going to see Harrington and demand an American visa, not only for Bubi, but for himself. One way or another, everything was to be settled.

Kerjanian leaped from his bed and, completely naked, began to pace the floor, arms folded on chest in his favorite gesture. His brain was afire. He thought of a dozen different things to say to Harrington, discarded half of them, thought of a dozen more. He must make it quite clear what Bubi meant to him, and how essential it was that the boy be allowed to proceed to America. Kerjanian was convinced that if only he was eloquent enough, even Harrington would be moved. The man was low, it was true, but after all, there were limits to human lowness. If anything happened to Bubi, it was Harrington whom he would hold *personally responsible!*

Not until he had memorized his speech word by word did Kerjanian begin to dress. Over his head he pulled a clean shirt, and he removed from under the mattress his one and only pair of trousers, which he had put there the night before to press. Though it was still dawn, his every movement was as hurried as if he had not a moment to spare. About to put on his shoes, he first took his customary precaution of tilting them upside down and, sure enough, a big brown scorpion dropped out of one of them and lay writhing on the floor. But Kerjanian was much too excited this morning to feel upset at the sight of an everyday scorpion. As he automatically raised his shoe to crush the animal, he noticed that its tail, instead of being lifted to strike, trailed docilely behind him. Oh, that was a propitious sign! On a day when even scorpions were friendly, Harrington, too, might feel well disposed. Gratefully Kerjanian lowered his shoe, allowing the scorpion to scurry to safety through a deep crack in the wall.

Striding over to the washbasin, he proceeded to work up a lather on his face by means of two fingers and a cake of yellow soap. As Kerjanian possessed neither brush nor shaving cream, the slicing of his wiry whiskers with a rusty razor was always something of an ordeal. A stream of soft Armenian curses poured forth when he administered the inevitable cut, and Kerjanian quickly took his eyes from the glass, for he was unusually squeamish about blood; like many gentle people, the very sight of it caused him to feel faint. Holding a rag to his lacerated cheek, he seated himself on the bed and waited impatiently for the bleeding to stop. Then he squeezed the rag into a little ball and, taking great care not to look at it, threw it out of the window.

When the din of the market place told him that the morning was beginning to advance, Kerjanian gave his cracked shoes a final polish, took his black hat, and double-locked the door behind him, though apart from the armadillo, there was little in the room to steal. As he passed through the market place with its squabbling vendors, its frantic buyers, its assembly of stray dogs, cats and pigs, the Armenian felt his usual disgust of this objectionable locality. Directly beside a stall lay a couple of tattered Indians, dead drunk even at that inappropriate hour of the day; people were stepping over them rather than taking the trouble of moving them aside. Vultures hovered over the refuse piles, or landed on top of them with lazy flaps of their big wings, followed by a couple of ungainly hops. Some of the birds had particles of decayed matter clinging to their beaks. With difficulty Kerjanian fought back a shiver of repulsion.

Well, if all went well, he would be leaving here soon, he consoled himself. In the United States there were no filthy markets, but everybody bought his food in cans in drugstores. There was no dirt, no poverty and the only Indians to be found were out in the Wild West. And even these were not like their Santa Rosan brothers, downtrodden and degenerate. No, they were imbued with the great American spirit of democracy; they drank ice-cream sodas, and rode about in Ford cars. All people, even the Indians, were happy in that wonderful free country; everyone there was considered as good as everyone else.

This reflection, so agreeable to Kerjanian, was hardly verified by events to follow. Having arrived at the Legation, which he had always thought of as a bit of America transported onto foreign soil, he was received even less graciously than on his former visits. Little success though he had had with them, he at least had been treated politely by the porter—a man with a pleasant smile and a gentle manner. But the new *mozo* who opened the door this morning was surly and bore on his face a stupid, arrogant expression. He did not hide his scorn as he tried to usher Kerjanian into the same waiting room where the Armenian had already spent several dozen hours of his life.

But today Kerjanian had the courage and resourcefulness that come to those who love greatly. He could not afford to wait for hours, only to be told in the end that his interview with Harrington was impossible. Making a quick decision, he put his hand into his coat pocket and brought out a small packet of *Deliciosos* cigarettes which by good chance he had with him.

214

"*Quiere?*" he asked in a casual tone. "Will you have one?"

The *mozo* cast a sly look about before reaching out to snatch one of the cigarettes.

"Have them all," said Kerjanian quickly. "I don't need them." And he shoved the packet into the porter's hand. Watching him anxiously, Kerjanian saw one of his eyelids come down in a sly wink and he realized that he had judged the man correctly. Acting at once, before the fellow had time to gather his wits together, Kerjanian stepped past him and through an open office door.

At a large desk by the window sat the young man with whom Kerjanian had had dealings on one of his former visits. As bad luck would have it, it was at his feet that Kerjanian had spat on learning that Warfield Harrington was the head of the Legation. The Armenian hoped fervently that he would not be recognized as he advanced to the desk, and tried to conjure up a smile.

"Please pardon me," he launched forth in English, speaking in an ingratiating way, though it was against his nature. "I know that it is irregular for me to come here without an appointment, but the urgency of the case is my excuse. It is a matter of life and death."

"Who are you?" said the young man, scowling. "The porter had no right to let you in."

"I made bold to walk in," said Kerjanian in his stilted schoolteacher's English. He whipped out his pocketbook and began searching through it for his solitary calling card, then changed his mind and shoved it back in his pocket. Seeing that card for a second time would certainly remind the fellow of their previous encounter. "I have forgotten my visiting cards. Please forgive me," he announced formally. "Accept my assurance that it is of great importance that I see Mr. Warfield Harrington at once."

The young man gave Kerjanian a close scrutiny. The urgency of the visitor's tone and the half-frantic expression on the intense, pale face seemed to have impressed him, but at this favorable moment Kerjanian made the mistake of overplaying his hand.

"I am a personal friend of Mr. Harrington," he declared. "I have known him a long time."

The young man's eyes narrowed and their glance rested on the badly repaired rip near Kerjanian's pocket, suffered the day that he had clambered through the cactus hedge. A sarcastic smile lifted the corners of his mouth.

"Excuse me, but I don't believe you," he said brusquely. "You can explain your business to me. Otherwise write a letter to the Minister asking for an appointment."

"Appointment! But I told you that it is a matter of life and death. Every minute counts," cried Kerjanian distractedly.

"I'm busy," said the young diplomat, glancing at the papers on his desk. "I must ask you to leave."

Kerjanian grew desperate. He was like a lion in the zoo that realizes his inability to break down the iron bars, and howls agonizingly in protest. There really was no more for him to say—obviously words would be futile—but, beside himself, he began pounding on the desk.

"I insist on seeing Mr. Harrington. Do you hear? I insist on it!"

The young man jumped to his feet. Over his self-satisfied face had spread a look of anger, not unmixed with fear. He backed away a few steps, interposing the whole length of the desk between himself and Kerjanian.

"Hermosillo!" he called out. "Hermosillo, come here!"

The sound of typewriting in the next room stopped abruptly, and a stocky fellow hurried into the young man's office.

"This person has no business here. Please escort him out," said the secretary drily, all his *sang-froid* back now that he had the situation in hand.

Before Kerjanian had time to say any more, his arm was seized in a firm grip and he was yanked out into the hall. He tried to resist but long undernourishment had sapped his strength; he was no match for his tough opponent. Within a few seconds he had been pushed out on the street and the Legation door had banged shut behind him.

He stood on the street, stunned, unable for the first moment to grasp fully what had happened. So this was Harrington's reception! He had gone to see him, ready to humble himself for the boy's sake, and the result was that he had been thrown out of the Legation. Well, he supposed that he might have expected it!

Suddenly a feeling of exhaustion assailed Kerjanian, so intense that he had to lean against a building for support. It was as if his fatigue, which had grown with every harassing and humiliating interview, with every hour of futile waiting, finally had overmastered him like a virulent disease. Only gradually did the spasm pass and Kerjanian was able to think clearly again. It frightened him to realize how close he stood to complete prostration. He would have to rally what remaining strength he had, if he was to get the boy and himself to America. Once there, he could let himself collapse, as he was sure that thousands of refugees had collapsed the moment they had reached their final destination.

Straightening up, he began to rub the sleeve of his pale-blue suit, which was covered with chalk from the house wall. He must try to look smart and spry, he thought, remembering his own precept that a refugee should always maintain his dignity. Whipping up his courage, he reminded himself that it was not Harrington himself who had had him shown out, but merely an underling. Granted that he could not see the Minister at the Legation, what prevented him from waiting for him at his hotel? Undoubtedly his best plan was to go to the Imperial at once, and pass by Pension Hilda on the way to ask how the boy was getting on.

Curiously enough, this was the first time that morning that Kerjanian's thoughts had turned to the boy's illness. Now, as he directed his steps towards Pension Hilda, all his anxiety flooded back. Quicker and quicker he walked, until he was almost running. He bumped into people without noticing it, and when an importunate vendor of lottery tickets tried to intercept him, Kerjanian waved the man angrily aside. As he hurried past the acacia trees which so often had hidden him as he stood looking up at the boy's window, grim forebodings seized Kerjanian. Though for years he had prided himself on being an atheist, he could not resist muttering beneath his breath a little prayer in Armenian.

The big blonde woman whom he had met here yesterday opened the door in answer to his ring. He had only to look at her to know that his apprehensions were justified; her features, so cheerful the day before, seemed ravaged; she looked at least ten years older. Had it been her own son who was lying ill, she could not have manifested greater distress.

"He's—very bad?" said Kerjanian, hardly trusting himself to speak, yet realizing that the inane smile which had a way of creeping into his face at such moments made the question sound nonchalant.

She nodded without answering, and as she did so, Kerjanian felt that his whole world was toppling about him. Involuntarily he pressed his hands together behind his back, squeezing them so fiercely that he could hear the bones crack. His heart pained him as if someone were contracting it in a fist.

Other questions were on his lips, but he could not get them out. And now his one desire was to flee from here before she told him more than he saw written on her face. Still smiling idiotically, he backed down the front steps, and when he reached the street level, he put his hat on his head and started walking off. Only when he had taken a few steps did he turn his head to call out as explanation— "An important appointment. Please forgive me"—then he hurried off as fast as he could walk. Kerjanian realized at that instant that if anything bad—really bad—happened to the boy, he did not want to go on living.

Three hours had passed and Kerjanian sat in the lobby of the Imperial, waiting for Warfield Harrington to come home for lunch, according to his usual habit. Over a period of several weeks, that is to say, until he came to know Bubi personally, he had checked on the Minister's daily routine, not for any specific purpose, but simply because the person of Warfield Harrington held for him a violent fascination. Many an afternoon or evening he used to station himself outside the hotel and wait for a sight of his "enemy" alighting from his limousine and then stepping aloofly across the sidewalk to the entrance.

As he waited today in the darkest corner of the lobby, Kerjanian suffered throes of nervousness. He kept fidgeting in the deep leather chair, twisting his hat in his hand, biting his fingernails; with the greatest difficulty he controlled an urge to walk about so as to move his twitching legs. He realized that the suspicious eye of the desk clerk had traveled his way more than once; obviously he could not afford to disclose his shabby attire to closer view. Every time that the man looked in his direction, he forced himself to fasten his glance calmly on the banner that streamed down from the balcony, inscribed with the words *"Vivas las democracias!"* He tried to look like a bored gentleman awaiting the arrival of an unpunctual friend.

The human brain has a fortunate capacity for self-deception. Even now, after his visit to Pension Hilda, Kerjanian refused to acknowledge the desperateness of Bubi's case. Far from asking himself whether the boy was still well enough to fly to the United States, he clung to the conviction that the moment the visas were issued, everything would be all right. They would all board the airplane that very afternoon—Bubi and Marie-Té and the man with the velvet jacket and himself. Before evening the boy would be in a clean American hospital, under the care of American doctors who, like everything else American, were the best in the world. All that stood in the way was the sinister person of Warfield Harrington, who, as if to spite him once again, refused to arrive for luncheon. Already it was almost one by the big clock on the balcony, and people were trickling into the lobby and seating themselves at the little marble tables for drinks.

Frantically nervous though he was, Kerjanian still felt curiosity as he surveyed these members of a world so different from his own. The women, in their expensive dresses and smart hats, were chattering to one another like monkeys. As to their dandified escorts, they had as little to do with real men as figures from a fashion plate come to life; their suits were perfectly pressed, their shoes gleamed, and as they walked into the lobby, nearly each one stopped at the hotel flower shop to buy a red rose or a white gardenia for his buttonhole. But the thing that struck him most about these wealthy people was the unhappiness and restlessness of their faces and the unpleasant expression of their eyes: scared and miserable they were, yet at the same time hard and demanding, like the eyes of people forever unsatisfied, forever unsatisfiable.

Kerjanian, set apart from other people through his great oriental loneliness, studied in amazement the jabbering, cocktail-drinking crowd. To think that this agitated life went on about him every day, while he was lying in his lonely room debating in a desultory way whether it would be worth while to get up and dress, or even whether he should put an end to things for good! Never had he felt so definitely an Easterner—moody and introverted and sad— as he did now in comparing himself to these Western people with their soulless and insistently demanding faces.

A lady who had swept into the lobby and seated herself at a table almost within touching distance of Kerjanian; agitated, futile and petulant, she seemed to Kerjanian completely typical of all the people in this room. This woman had taken with her a whole array of possessions to identify herself and establish her position. On the table before her she proceeded to range her golden cigarette lighter, a great tortoise shell case with a jeweled monogram, a jade cigarette holder, and finally a pair of long, pale-green gloves. Her restless hands kept rummaging about among these objects, now extracting a cigarette, now drawing forth a lipstick, now opening and again closing the clasp of the case. Kerjanian found her performance positively eerie, much like that of a lunatic who ceaselessly tears up little bits of paper with fingers whose movements are no longer controlled by a conscious mind. As she pursued her inane activity, her glance kept flying to the revolving door, and when the expected friend eventually appeared, she emitted a little yelp of delight, as though she had been a person on a desert island who at long last had come across a fellow human being.

"Don't scold me, dear Señora de Castro! I know I am late," cried the newcomer, who, like the occupant of the table, was an overdressed lady of uncertain age. "Here boy, bring me a Martini," she ordered the waiter as she subsided in a chair. "And now you must tell me at once if this dreadful news is true. Has your poor husband really suffered a heart attack?" She turned to her friend with an affectedly anxious gesture.

"Alas, it is true," said the lady referred to as Señora de Castro. "Manuel is an ill man. It's even doubtful if he'll be able to stay on in the service. He speaks of resigning and of our returning to Portugal."

"What a catastrophe!" said the second lady, trying to impart to her voice a note of distress. But she flew to a new topic as inconsequentially as her friend's hands had flown from one trinket to the next. "My dear, I do look forward to our bridge game this evening. You can't imagine my surprise when I heard that Harrington was coming. It's weeks since anyone has enticed him to a bridge table. Things can't be going so well between him and the young Baroness Falkenborn!"

But Kerjanian was no longer listening. At the mention of that name, Harrington, his heart had given a leap and then begun to pound furiously in his body. Yes, he'd suspected it: this world of superficial people with icy eyes and predatory hands was the world of Harrington; these cocktail-drinking men and women were his friends. In all the countries where this diplomat had held posts, it was only with the smug, the well-dressed, that he had cared to associate. He had lived in Syria, but had he known one real Syrian? No, not Mr. Warfield Harrington! He'd known a handful of rich businessmen from Beirut, a handful of smart society women who gave dinner parties while the Syrian children fainted with starvation and the Syrian men grew so desperate that they killed and became bandits and sank lower than beasts. It was with people like these that Harrington played bridge; it was with them that he dined and danced and talked politics.

But they had better look out—Harrington and his friends! thought the Armenian in a fury. They had better remember that human beings, if goaded too far, would finally turn on their tormentors—they would crush the Harringtons, the care-nots, the men of ill will. He, Kerjanian, wasn't scared of these people, even though they did rule the world. He loathed them! Yes, he despised them so thoroughly that he refused to sit in their midst. Jumping up with a spontaneous movement, he stood there glaring angrily about him.

"What do you want? Whom do you wish to see?"

The Armenian swung about, to find the desk clerk confronting him with that pompous mien typical of people wielding a limited authority.

"I am waiting for a friend," the Armenian answered airily. But the desk clerk remained unsatisfied.

"You have been here since eleven o'clock," he said, following Kerjanian, who had turned on his heels. "There is no use in your waiting any more. Your friend will not show up."

Kerjanian had reached a dark corner of the lobby, where he hoped that his shabby clothes would be less conspicuous. Reaching into his pocket, he seized the unopened packet of *Deliciosas* with which he had supplied himself.

"Have one?" he said, prepared to repeat his maneuver of that morning.

The hotel clerk looked at the cigarettes disdainfully. He shook his head. "I don't smoke."

"You don't smoke?" repeated Kerjanian in distress, realizing at once that his stratagem had done more harm than good. He had

222

shown his cards, and that was a fatal thing to do when they were so very weak. "Well, I will wait a few minutes longer," he pronounced with dignity.

"We will see about that," answered the clerk offensively. "Kindly tell me whom you are waiting for."

"I am waiting," said Kerjanian, and he raised himself to his full height, "for Mr. Harrington, the Minister of the United States."

For a second the clerk was taken aback; his pompous façade seemed about to collapse. But then the same thing happened as that morning in the Legation: an appraising glance took in the pale-blue suit and came to rest on that unfortunate rip beside the pocket. When the fellow spoke again, his voice was insolent.

"Sit down here," he said, pointing to a wooden bench destined for the use of tradespeople and messenger boys. "I shall find out if Mr. Harrington wishes to see you, Mr.—Mr.—"

"Kerjanian."

"Kervanian," said the hotel clerk, repeating the name incorrectly, probably on purpose.

Disdaining the bench, Kerjanian stood while the clerk made use of the desk telephone. He was assailed with a crushing sense of impotency. How humiliating to think that he himself could not even get in touch with this Harrington, in whose hands lay the decision as to whether or not the boy should live! By means of a regiment of underlings—porters, secretaries, hotel clerks—Harrington had cut himself off from Kerjanian, and incidentally from life in general, with which he likewise scorned to have dealings. As always, Kerjanian was weaponless—that was his great weakness. Without a weapon in his hand, a man could not demand even the right of speech in the modern world!

The hotel clerk put down the telephone before turning to Kerjanian with a gratified expression. "Mr. Harrington is not coming home for luncheon. What is more, his secretary tells me that Mr. Harrington doesn't even know you. So get a move on now! Get a move on, my man!" Stepping over the doorsill of the flower shop, he spoke to the vendor, busy making up boutonnières from the basket of gardenias and roses at his feet. "By the way," he said, addressing him, "Mr. Harrington's secretary has just ordered a bouquet of roses sent to the Baroness Falkenborn from the Minister. Not red ones, as usual, but white. It seems that someone in her family died this morning—her brother, I believe. So don't go and make a mistake with the colors now. Not red, for love, remember. White, for death."

He turned to go back to the hotel desk, but finding Kerjanian still standing in the lobby, stopped and scowled at him. "Didn't I tell you to get out of here? In one second I'll send for the police and have you put in jail, you—you refugee!" he shouted, using the worst term of abuse that he could find.

Over Kerjanian had come a calm so deep that it seemed that his very soul had settled into impassivity. Not a muscle moved in his deathly pale face, and the big dark eyes looked like the hollows in a mask. "White—white, for death." He had heard those words and nothing would obliterate their memory; they would be with him forever more.

Even the hotel clerk must have realized that a change had taken place in Kerjanian; the glance that now rested on the clerk's face had in it something austere—almost majestic. Instead of moving toward him, the fellow instinctively backed away. But Kerjanian hadn't finished with him yet. With the deliberateness of someone entirely sure of himself, he unbuttoned his coat, took out his pocket-book, and extracted his precious visiting card. Glancing at it, he read the name aloud as though he had never heard it before, then he held out the card to the hotel clerk.

"Give this to Mr. Harrington," he said. "Tell him that I waited for him, and for his help, for four whole hours. Tell him that I have waited for him, and for his help, for twenty-five years. Tell him that millions of us refugees have waited for him and for his help, but that we can wait no longer. Be sure to give him that message. It's a personal message from me to him, but please tell him also that it isn't going to remain a personal message much longer. The millions of other refugees will see to that, and when they do, it is going to be an evil day for Mr. Warfield Harrington. But listen! Before you give him the card, take a good look at my name yourself. It is a name that is going to be known all over the world. The name is Kerjanian. Not Kervanian, mind you, but Kerjanian. K-E-R-J-A-N-I-A-N. You will never forget it. *No one will ever forget it!*"

Chapter XV

Disruption of a Career

EARLIER THAT SAME MORNING WARFIELD
Harrington had awoken with the sensation of a man come out of a
long fever. All his reactions were different since his final break
with Marie-Té—more positive, more normal. No sooner had he
opened his eyes than he sprang from his bed to begin the Swedish
exercises; for the first time in many weeks he accomplished them
with concentration and efficiency. He had got into the habit of letting his shower run lukewarm—a testimony to the softening influence that had crept into his life. Now he turned on only the
cold tap and subjected himself stoically to the icy spray. When
Ah Sing brought his breakfast, he sat munching at the driest and
crispest piece of toast that he could find. Even in this minute matter, Marie-Té's influence had made itself felt; recently he had
found himself selecting the softer pieces, and once had even contemplated telling Ah Sing to butter his toast a bit more generously.

In quick time he accomplished the remainder of his early-morn-
ing routine: the brief perusal of the newspaper, the issuing to Ah
Sing of orders for the day, the penning of the letter to his mother.
Before leaving his apartment, he opened the Venetian blinds and
glanced out to ascertain the state of the day. As usual, it was a
real scorcher! Spirals of mist were rising from the asphalt, and
curling around the bus of the Pan-American Airways, which stood
loaded before Harrington's hotel, about to leave for the airport.
Despite the withering heat, one passenger was carrying a light
overcoat, no doubt equipped for his arrival in cooler climes. Lucky

226

devil! thought Harrington, squirming a little inside his own sticky clothes. He could do with a bit of cool weather himself,—a change generally from Santa Rosa, now that the Marie-Té episode was over.

And over it certainly was, he reflected as he closed the blinds and came away from the window. It was really strange to think that a relationship which had dominated a man's life for months could be eternally dissolved in a few minutes. He congratulated himself on having acted so wisely, and particularly on never having tried to make physical love to Marie-Té, which would have made his present position far more embarrassing. Fortunately, the idea of a physical love tie between them had always remained for him extremely vague, even at the time that he was contemplating marriage. If he was to be honest, he would have to admit that he doubted his capacity, physically or spiritually, for the wholehearted love that a girl like Marie-Té demanded. His life would be a little gray without her—a little savorless, perhaps; he would have to get used to normalcy again. Still, it was better thus. Oh, far better thus!

Getting to the Legation even earlier than usual, he at once seated himself at his desk and proceeded to examine his engagement sheet for the day. As his glance passed down the list of names, the old feeling of self-satisfaction flooded back. They were not nonentities, these people who nowadays left their offices to keep engagements with Warfield Harrington! He wondered what some of his old college classmates who had failed to elect him to their fraternities would have said. The Minister of the Interior was coming in at ten o'clock; at noon there was to be a conference with the British Chargé d'Affaires; the representative of the United Fruit Company was paying a call at half past three. Taken all in all, not so bad for a single day!

He let his eye travel to the bottom of the sheet and saw that he had a dinner at the De Castros', to be followed by bridge. That, also, pleased him. His bridge must be getting quite rusty lately,

227

for he had never played so little as during these last weeks since he had known Marie-Té. And he quite looked forward to seeing the Portuguese lady, whom he had been neglecting shamefully these last few months. Now that Marie-Té had faded from the picture and old De Castro with his bad heart was apt to fade, it might be good policy to renew their friendship. After all, she was a chic woman, thought Harrington, and he made the additional reflection that if Carola de Castro had entered his thoughts again, then life must be normalizing itself fairly rapidly.

Nevertheless, the morning was punctuated by a thoroughly abnormal, not to say unheard-of, occurrence. About an hour after his arrival, just before the Minister of the Interior paid his call, he was disturbed by sounds in the next room: someone was banging a fist on a table and calling out Harrington's name in fury. A second later a brief scuffle seemed to ensue. Harrington, listening nervously, felt just as he had felt that night when he caught sight of a shadowy figure lurking in the doorway opposite his hotel. The atmosphere in his room suddenly grew tense, ominous, and he was overcome with a sensation of fright. Not till quiet had been restored did he regain his self-control and go to open the door of Baker's office. He found the Third Secretary standing at the window, apparently watching someone in the street, while the clerk Hermosillo was adjusting the collar of his jacket.

"What's happened here?" asked Harrington, his voice quite cool.

"Crazy fellow break in," explained Hermosillo. "I put him out all right O.K."

"Just a crank, sir," Baker elaborated. "Gave his name as Kerjanian and insisted that he knew you. He became quite violent when I told him to write for an appointment. Dirty-looking chap."

Kerjanian—Kerjanian, Harrington repeated to himself as he went back to his own office. The name did seem vaguely familiar, now that he thought of it. He had always prided himself on his infallible memory, which, like his other gifts, he had developed not for its own sake but because it was a useful attribute for a diplomat. He certainly had had dealings with someone called Kerjanian before.

Other surprises lay in store for Harrington that same morning. Scarcely had the Minister of the Interior taken his departure, than in came Baker to inform him that Marie-Té's little brother had succumbed to the malaria attack; Mr. Camberly had just received a telephone call from the pension and had left in a taxi posthaste. Uninterestedly Harrington gave a nod, reflecting that Marie-Té hadn't exaggerated the seriousness of the boy's illness after all. No wonder that she had been so anxious to get those temporary visas!

He was about to tell Baker to send flowers, as etiquette demanded, when the desk clerk at the Imperial rang up to say that a shabby-looking individual who gave his name as Kerjanian was waiting in the lobby. Of course he had Baker give orders to get rid of the intruder, at the same time taking the opportunity to order flowers for Marie-Té. But no sooner had he hung up than a little bell started ringing in his mind. In a flash that whole episode from Syria unrolled itself before him: the drive from Aleppo to the country house of Colonel de la Baume, his picking up of a pedestrian to show the way, the final incident when the fellow had thrown back the five-franc note with the words, "I am Kerjanian!" Instinctively he knew that this was the same man, even though there were many thousands of miles of sea and land between Aleppo and Santa Rosa.

At the moment that this realization came to him, Harrington experienced a pang of uneasiness, irrational yet sharp. For some reason the knowledge that the fellow had popped up again after all these years came as a distinctly unpleasant shock. He seemed unable to banish that old memory from his mind, and gradually detail after detail of the episode in Syria recurred to him. Plainly now he remembered the man's tormented, fanatical expression as he crumpled up the bank note and threw it at Harrington's feet. Yet he had only wanted to reward him for his trouble, and actually had given him more than he deserved because Colonel de la Baume

229

and his wife were looking on. For some reason the fellow had taken it as an insult. He had looked poor enough to be grateful for fifty centimes, to say nothing of a five-franc note, but Harrington recalled a remark made by Madame de la Baume at luncheon when they were discussing the incident afterwards. "You never know in these regions who belongs to the gentry and who doesn't," she had told him. "You can't judge from clothes, because practically everyone is indigent. Look into the man's face next time, *Monsieur le Consul!* Look into his face!"

Yes, perhaps that had been the trouble. He had not looked into Kerjanian's face, because he never did look into the faces of the people with whom he came in contact. Faces meant nothing to him, and the people behind the faces meant nothing either. He frankly admitted it to himself. He was only interested in people for what they represented; as individuals they left him cold, if they did not actually disgust him. If you were a Harrington of Stoneborough, Maine (of the better and poorer branch of the family), you had a special attitude to people who differed from yourself—people who smelled unpleasantly, who did not take showers, and who were apt to bear family names like Kerjanian.

Not until he was seated at the bridge table that evening did he completely forget the episode. Despite De Castro's recent heart attack, the atmosphere at dinner had been cheerful, the conversation witty; Harrington, in his best form, felt duly appreciated. It was true that none of these people had Marie-Té's cleverness, nor her superlative sense of humor, but at least they looked up to him, which was more than she had ever done. He had put on a stiff collar and a regular evening shirt with a boiled front, abandoning the soft type usually worn in Santa Rosa. He knew that Marie-Té would have made fun of him for that, but no one that night seemed to think it in the least unusual; indeed, he was complimented twice on his gray pearl studs.

At cards he had as partner Carola de Castro, and was pitted against the wife of the British Chargé d'Affaires and his host, who played remarkably well for a man who looked as if he was at death's door. But Harrington excelled himself that evening, ending up with a declared grand slam, doubled and redoubled, which he succeeded in completing through his favorite play: a tricky little finesse. On the way home in his car he suddenly began chuckling to himself. Well, well, he seemed capable of getting on very nicely without Marie-Té after all!

Next morning dawned even hotter, more humid, than the one before. Harrington, dabbing at his damp forehead, decided that the rainy season could not be more than a few days off, and he scowled irritably at the prospect. The climate of Santa Rosa was bad enough at any period of the year, but in the wet months rain often fell steadily for days on end; then suddenly it would let up, and the glaring sun would draw clouds of steam from the saturated earth. The whole city would be turned into a communal Turkish bath for a few hours, until, without warning, the downfall would recommence. Again it occurred to Harrington that he would like to leave Santa Rosa for a few weeks to let the atmosphere clear of moisture—and perhaps of other things.

"I think I'll put on my short morning coat instead of this sack suit," he told Ah Sing after breakfast. "And lay me out a white shirt with a stiff collar please."

"Stiff collar, sir?" queried Ah Sing, glancing out of the window.

"Yes. That's what I said," confirmed Harrington, whose usually suave manner toward Ah Sing had altered a bit since the episode of the book.

He changed his clothes and stood at the mirror attaching the ends of the tight collar to the stud with a button hook. Ah there! That was better. He had always felt more at his ease in clothes that had some shape—clothes that gave a person character instead of demanding that the wearer impart his own character to the clothes. It would be a good idea to stick to his morning coat—for the time being at any rate.

231

He had seated himself at his desk, drawn out a sheet of stationery, and had written "My dear Mother," when there came a ring at the apartment door. As Ah Sing went to open it, Harrington paused with pen in air; it was rare indeed for him to receive calls at that hour of the morning.

"A cableglam for you, sir," said Ah Sing putting the yellow envelope before him. Harrington split it open, unfolded the sheet and read,

VERY SORRY INFORM YOU YOUR MOTHER DIED LATE TONIGHT FOLLOWING AN ACCIDENT STOP ONE OF THE OLD ENGLISH TILES SLID OFF THE ROOF OF HER HOUSE AND STRUCK HER AS SHE WAS PASSING UNDERNEATH STOP DEATH INSTANTANEOUS ACCEPT SINCERE CONDOLENCES HER SOUL IS IN HANDS OF HER MAKER

UNCLE CALEB

Harrington's first thought was that Ah Sing was in the room and that it behooved him to behave in a fitting manner, seeing that the servant would later learn the contents of the wire. He put his hand before his eyes and sat for a moment completely still, thinking of nothing at all. He expected Ah Sing to say something, but instead, the Chinese boy picked up the breakfast tray and silently withdrew. Not till he had been gone a full moment did Harrington realize that he was sitting in the room alone.

His brain began to function again. He reread the cable, noting the fact that it had been sent as a night letter, and counted the words. Yes, as he'd suspected—fifty! Trust Uncle Caleb not to exceed the minimum rate. He could imagine the old fellow's satisfaction at getting in that smug remark about the "Maker" without its costing him an extra penny!

Harrington caught himself up abruptly. Here he had just received one of the greatest blows that can come to any man and he could think of nothing more important than Uncle Caleb's stinginess! For some reason he seemed unable to visualize his mother at that moment; he could not summon to mind her face, much less resurrect her personality. Taking her snapshot from his writing desk, he sought her eyes, for of course it was in the eyes that one could see a person's character. Fixedly he peered at them, and they peered back at him as blankly, as glassily, as the eyes of a blind person.

There came back to him then that remark of the French colonel's wife which he had remembered yesterday after all these years: "Next time look into a man's face, *Monsieur le Consul.*" Yes, that was all very well. But how was one to look into a face with eyes that could not see? They used to say that he took after his mother in everything. Perhaps he also had inherited from her those blank, unseeing eyes.

He let his glance pass over the photograph to the roof of his mother's house, covered with the precious tiles which henceforth would have other associations for him besides their link with the Harrington family in old England. How proud of them his mother used to be! They had been brought over by his grandfather from the Dorset estate of the English Harringtons that was being dismantled for debt (though this last detail remained unmentioned by his mother when she showed visitors about her place). Despite her habit of talking about them, Harrington had sometimes wondered whether his mother was really quite as fond as one might think of those famous English tiles. They were of an extremely unattractive color for one thing—a splotchy pale ochre—and nearly all of them were badly chipped or broken. He even had a lurking suspicion that she doubted their genuineness, for there was a rumor that the original tiles had been stolen in transit and replaced by cheap imitations. At any rate, it seemed somehow appropriate that his mother, who had seldom been able to distinguish sham values from genuine, should have found the instrument of her death in one of these famous tiles of doubtful authenticity.

Glancing at his wrist watch, he saw that it was well past nine. Well, he supposed that he ought decently to stay at home this morning, though he supposed that it would be permissible, even well seen, to go to the office in the afternoon. It occurred to him to tell Ah Sing to get out his morning coat, then realized abruptly that he already had it on. It gave him a very strange sensation to find that he foresightedly had put on his mourning garb in advance.

Then he saw the sheet with the words "My dear Mother," and took up his pen before remembering that there was no point in his continuing that particular letter. It would feel strange not having to write those daily letters—actually not being able to write them! They had meant a great deal in his life, even if his mother herself had meant but little. By maintaining this undemanding pen-and-ink relationship, he had rid himself of the psychological necessity of entering into more intimate relationships with other people; his well-nurtured feeling of duty to the old lady in Stoneborough, Maine, had been a substitute for the flesh and blood feelings that he had never had. In the last analysis, he had written those several hundred letters to himself, and he might as well have sent them off to himself also.

So the fact was that this event would change his life; somehow he would have to find a substitute for what was already a substitute. Immediately his thoughts turned to Carola de Castro. How pathetically pleased she had been when he turned up for dinner and for bridge last night! Perhaps the critical condition of her husband's heart had had something to do with it, still it really was touching how grateful she was for just his company, how little else she demanded of him. Undoubtedly she would be the ideal wife for a busy diplomat, and even when his life ambition of becoming an ambassador was achieved, he need never feel ashamed of a woman like Carola, who looked well in black and played a respectable hand of bridge. With the Marie-Té affair over, he looked forward to an emotionally tranquil future; his life would be safe and satisfactory with George Baker in his office, Ah Sing in his kitchen, and Carola de Castro in his bed.

But then he remembered that old English tile falling on his mother's head. Yes, there was always the risk of a loose tile, of

234

course, and nowadays when so many structures were getting wob-bly, the danger was much greater than before. It struck him as a bad sign, a disturbing sign, that his mother should have been sig-naled out for such an end. Perhaps the time was coming soon when all the old English tiles on all the colonial roofs would come clat-tering down on the owners' heads. About that there was nothing to be done but to pray to God and avoid the neighborhood of earth-quakes.

Abruptly he decided that he would take the opportunity pre-sented by his mother's funeral to ask for leave from Santa Rosa. The rainy season was at hand; he felt that his life had reached a period's end.

It was three o'clock when the Packard with the coat of arms drove up to the United States Legation. Harrington stepped out, nodded absently to Carlos, who saluted him, as usual, and made his way directly to his office. Seating himself, he read through the notices on his desk, none of which were of great importance: there was a telephone message from Moffat, the British Chargé d'Af-faires, inviting him to an informal dinner; another from Police Chief Pinchinchi, who wanted to see him on a matter connected with the German school; a memo from Señorita Baricala, the stenog-rapher, reminding him that she was still holding up the letter to Washington about Ted Kelly. Well, he knew that without her tell-ing him, reflected Harrington. It was devilishly ticklish—that Kelly business—and he preferred to attend to it personally when he went to the United States on leave. In spite of Camberly, he would see to it that Ted Kelly got what he deserved: his expulsion from the service.

Among the letters on his desk was an air-mail special delivery, postmarked Washington, D.C. He split it open, and had not read two lines when he was bending forward in absorption. Harring-ton's correspondent was a man high in diplomatic circles, a former superior of his in China. Now he wrote to inform his colleague that Harrington would soon be appointed to a larger and more important post, probably—Harrington read the words with a wildly beating heart—*to an embassy*. Although it had not yet been made official, everything was as good as settled, he assured him. The diplomat stressed the fact that Harrington had many friends in Washington—men of the old school, who not only appreciated his work but sympathized with his general attitude toward contemporary problems—and he predicted with authority that such a change was imminent.

Letting the letter drop, Harrington leaned back with closed eyes. So it had come in sight at last—the goal toward which he had been struggling for so long. He, Warfield Harrington, was to be Ambassador of the United States! He was to take the rank of a national figure, and henceforth there would be no limits to his possible achievements. Representing as he did the views of an influential faction in the State Department, he could count on stanch support as he struggled to the pinnacles of leadership. He had good confidence that he would attain them, while men of John Camberly's type were left to languish in obscure outposts like Santa Rosa. After all, Harrington's friends were still in the saddle in Washington, as were their likes in London, Berlin, and most of the large capitals of the world; it would take more than the efforts of a few dreamers to displace them. They would remain in power until the common man took matters in his own hands—a thing which had never happened hitherto, and which Harrington and his friends back home could manage to prevent indefinitely.

As this pleasing thought passed through his mind, Harrington heard a rush of footsteps in the corridor. With the usual instinctive movement, he took up the letter to show that he was busy, and assumed an expression designating displeasure and surprise. Then he raised his head, and his glance, ever coldly disdainful, met—a leveled pistol and a pair of burning eyes. Today he could read in them the same hatred and indignation as on that distant day in

236

Syria when their owner had flung a five-franc note at Harrington's feet.

Now I will never be ambassador after all, the thought flashed through his mind. It was all useless—yes, it was all a farce.

He could hear the sound of his terrified blood pounding in his ears. Then came the great explosion.

Chapter XVI

Catastrophe Due

KERJANIAN LOOKED AWAY BECAUSE HE COULD NOT bear the sight of blood, and fired again twice at random. Then the automatic jammed, so that he was unable to pull the trigger. As he dropped it to the floor, he caught sight of the dark-clad figure slumped across the writing desk, one well-tended hand still holding the letter. Someone was shouting just outside the door, and there was the sound of hurrying footsteps in the corridor. Circling the desk, Kerjanian ran to the open window, on whose sill stood a miniature flagpole, a tiny American flag at its peak. As a man might seize a precious object while rushing from a burning house, so Kerjanian snatched up that beloved emblem before he leaped upon the ledge; it was in his hand when he landed on the lawn outside.

The Legation garden was bordered at one end by a high brick wall, at the other by a cactus hedge that separated it from the street. Picking out the spot where the bristly plants grew thinnest, Kerjanian ran toward it, and he never stopped running but flung his body right through the hedge. As the sound of ripping material reached his ear, Kerjanian's thoughts flew back to another cactus hedge, to another occasion when he had struggled through at the cost of damage to his suit. There had been a laughing boy watching him that other time, knees bare, hands deep in the pockets of his leather shorts. Suddenly a sense of loss swept over Kerjanian, so agonizing, so devastating, that for a moment he felt literally

238

paralyzed. He stood there at the top of the hill, unable to move in any direction.

On either side of him the street lay calm under the heavy sky; of the few pedestrians in sight, none seemed to have been startled by the pistol shots. At the foot of the long hill he could see an intersecting street down which a row of laden burros was passing. The whole scene, with the ambling burros, the sun-bathed buildings, the sleepy Indians, seemed particularly peaceful and agreeable. But then he chanced to catch sight of the flag in his hand, was seized with panic and began to run. As he ran, the silk material made a fluttering sound in the breeze.

When he reached the bottom of the hill, no one had yet started in pursuit. Shaking in fright and with the sweat pouring down his face, Kerjanian darted behind the line of burros so as to shield himself from view. For a few steps he walked alongside the animals, then darted off into a side street, cut across a dusty plot in which turkeys were rummaging, and presently found himself in sight of the first stalls of the market place.

He was quite exhausted by now and had to stop running so as to catch his breath. Standing there panting, it occurred to him that the flagpole which he was still holding might arouse curiosity. He looked around for a place to hide it and caught sight of a wooden fence across the road, giving on a vacant lot. Kerjanian carefully pulled off the beloved flag, folded it and put it in his pocket. Then he broke the pole in two and threw it across the fence.

Strangely enough, he began to feel ravenously hungry all at once, the sight of food making his mouth water. Crossing over to his favorite stall, he selected two little corn-flour cakes and told the vendor that he would pay next day. The purchase of the revolver had taken all his ready cash, but this woman knew him, and she gave him a friendly nod. Putting the cakes into his pocket, Kerjanian crossed the market place to the mauve-colored house where he had his room.

When he opened the door, the armadillo, lying sunning him-

239

self, scurried into a corner. Kerjanian seated himself on the edge of the bed, whence he absent-mindedly followed the animal's movements. What an empty feeling he had today! Had he found himself on a desert island, he might have experienced the same sensation of loneliness that had been with him ever since he heard the hotel clerk ordering those white flowers. Out on the market place were people—swarms of people milling about and getting in each other's way. Yet it seemed to Kerjanian that he was alone in the whole city; it was as if he and the armadillo were the only two living creatures in the world. He wondered if there was such a thing as dying of loneliness, and how long the process required.

Suddenly he remembered the corn-flour cakes in his pocket, took one out and began to munch it. But though a moment before he could have consumed it in a swallow, now the crumbs stuck in his throat. Giving up the effort, he threw what was left to the armadillo. He took out his handkerchief and painstakingly wiped his fingers.

As he put back the handkerchief in his pocket, his fingers rubbed against the silk material of the flag. Kerjanian drew it out and smoothed the wrinkles against his knee. A strange smile came to his face as he studied that little flag and absently counted the white stars in the blue field. He could not have explained why he felt so pleased to have saved this bit of silk from Harrington's office and to have it in his possession at this moment. He would never get to America—that was certain now—but by killing Harrington and rescuing the flag, it seemed to him that he had done America a service that had earned him honorary citizenship at least. For had not Warfield Harrington repudiated all for which America purported to stand: personal freedom and respect of man for man and brotherly love? He was not worthy to lie dead beside the emblem of the country whose principles he had betrayed.

He laid out the flag on the dresser, where its bright colors gleamed in the sunlight, and resumed his seat on the edge of the bed. There he remained for almost an hour without moving, without thinking of anything in particular. He no longer felt either fright or apprehension—nothing but that gnawing, devastating loneliness.

Finally, without actually having decided anything, he went to get his black felt hat, brushed it, and placed it carefully on his head. From the tin box beneath the mattress he drew out the remainder of his capital. Just before going out, he picked up the American flag from the dresser, folded it into a little square and replaced it in his breast pocket. It was much too precious to leave behind him here, where it would come into possession of the first stranger who wandered into the room.

Striking out through the market place, Kerjanian walked slowly, looking neither to right nor left. The atmosphere was very tense today, it seemed to him; all of nature seemed to be waiting in anguish for some tremendous happening. As he skirted Independencia Park, the branches of the eucalyptus trees were giving forth sigh after plaintive sigh; the very cobblestones in the street seemed to be awaiting something. And Kerjanian felt that his own body, too, was tense and expectant. Then without warning, a long rush of wind passed down the street, sweeping the dust with it and almost carrying away Kerjanian's black town hat. As the first heavy drops began to fall, he felt his taut body relax, and a sensation of physical satisfaction, utterly illogical at that moment, swept over him.

Now in a rush, like wild tears after emotional stress, the hot rain came down, pelting the roadway and pattering on the roofs of the pastel-colored houses. Ah, how relieving was this rain, which had been gathering in the air so long! To Kerjanian its arrival seemed connected in some way with the momentous event that he himself had brought about: the death of Warfield Harrington. It was as if nature, gratified by the disappearance of an evil force, was breathing deeply in relief.

The water was coming down in sheets by the time Kerjanian reached Calle de la Independencia. Without accelerating his step, the rain pouring off the brim of his hat and trickling down his

241

neck, he walked on till he found himself in front of the red brick building where he had registered on the day of his arrival in Santa Rosa. Going through the swinging doors, he entered a large room where a number of uniformed policemen were playing cards about a table. None of them looked up at Kerjanian's entrance, and not until the hand was over did he have a chance of stating that he wished to see the chief of police on an important matter.

"Señor Pinchinchi is busy," said one of the policemen, picking up his new cards one by one and arranging them in his hand. "There has been a big murder. Come back tomorrow."

"It is very important. I must see him today."

"Please keep still. You are disturbing our game," said another of the policemen. "Señor Pinchinchi isn't here. Someone has been killed at the American Legation and the chief is out with twenty men looking for the criminal."

"And he'll find him—never worry," said the first policeman. "Even though the wily devil has got away for the time being. He must have been planning this crime for months."

"Oh yes," declared another of the men. "Pinchinchi will nab him, all right. We aren't going to let this rascal slip through our fingers."

Even as he spoke there came the whirr of a siren from the street, and the policemen jumped to their feet and flung the playing cards into a drawer. Several of them ran off in different directions, while the others rushed to a bench and seated themselves stiffly in a row. A second later a number of police officials walked in, headed by a big burly man with a waxed mustache, whose picture Kerjanian frequently had seen in the papers.

"Excuse me," said the Armenian, going straight up to him. "May I have a word with you?"

"No, you may not! Who is this man?"

"He has been bothering us and interfering with official business," said one of the policemen.

"I think I can give you some information on the murder," interrupted Kerjanian. "I would like to see you alone."

"What makes you think that you know anything about the murder? Well, go up to my office. I will talk to you in a little while."

In a little while. How often had not Kerjanian been put off before this with that glib assurance! And how often had he not waited while the wearisome hours dragged by, in anterooms as drab and depressing as Police-chief Pinchinchi's office! Even now when his visit was motivated by a desire to give himself up for punishment—maybe for execution—his purpose was being thwarted by the same spirit of uncivility, the same love of procrastination, which had barred him and countless other refugees from safety. Suddenly the irony and absurdity of it all struck Kerjanian. In what a stupid manner man behaved towards man! No wonder that the desire to insult and humiliate one's brother had led to the current attempt to exterminate him in a universal war.

It was almost dark in the little room by the time Pinchinchi rejoined Kerjanian. Seating himself pompously at his desk, he scowled, pulled his moustaches, and asked in a conversational way, "Well now, what have you got to say, Señor?"

"I shot Harrington this afternoon."

The big man burst out laughing and laughed till he shook. "You?" he said. "You look as if you couldn't harm a fly, *amigo mio*. You shouldn't joke with me. I am a busy man."

"I would find something better to joke about," said Kerjanian icily.

Pinchinchi studied his visitor for a moment. He shook his head.

"I don't believe you. You will have to prove what you say. This is police headquarters, you know—not a place for old women's gossip."

Kerjanian took out of his pocket the little American flag and handed it to the chief without a word. Pinchinchi examined it carefully.

"H'm. Well, you may be right at that," he said. "Why did you take this flag? Are you a Nazi spy?"

"No."

"That is what *you* say. You will have to prove that too. This is no time to go around murdering North Americans. What effect do you think such things have on the good-neighbour policy? I am a believer in Pan-American solidarity. Such a murder is completely against my principles."

This speech had proved too much for Kerjanian's Spanish. Besides, it had always irritated him extremely not to be believed.

"I give myself up for arrest," he announced tersely.

"Arrest? I'm not so sure. You can't demand to be arrested; it's for me to decide—not you. If we arrested everyone who wanted to spend a few comfortable nights in jail, we would have our hands full."

"I killed Harrington!" cried Kerjanian.

"I forbid you to shout. This is my private office, please remember."

"I shot him three times!"

"You have no respect for the police," said Pinchinchi angrily. "In the future if you feel like brawling, kindly go out into the street. I officially order you arrested for disturbing the public peace—and for murder."

Bubi's death had thrown the whole Pension Hilda into a state of consternation. It had been so sudden, so incredible, that even days afterwards no one could quite face the truth. People still passed on tiptoe the door of the room where he had been lying ill; when they entered the pension they found themselves listening for the sound of his running footsteps.

Less than anyone could Marie-Té comprehend that her brother would never again run laughing toward her— that he would never again throw his arms around her waist and bombard her with a barrage of questions. Convinced as she had been that he led a charmed life, she had believed until the last that a miracle would be worked by Dr. Martin, the American specialist who had flown down from Panama at John Camberly's request. Suddenly Bubi would begin to smile again, and the fever would go down, and he would leap from his bed, as healthy and as beautiful as ever. Miraculously he would avoid the wheels of death, as he had avoided them the day that the truck almost ran him down before the bank, and those mornings in Styria that the snake came to drink from his bowl of milk. Even when Dr. Martin turned from the sickbed and silently shook his head, she refused to believe the message lying in his eyes.

However, as the days passed, Marie-Té gradually forced herself to acknowledge the tragedy. At home in Vienna, it would have taken many months for her wild grief to be assuaged, but this was the year 1943 and people's mentalities had changed. With young boys of every nation dying on the battlefields by the thousands—dying as suddenly and as senselessly as Bubi—one had come to accept the idea of death more readily than ever before.

The whirl of events likewise contributed to keep Marie-Té from brooding on her sorrow. The Kerjanian trial was set for an early date, and she had taken it on herself to see that the Armenian obtained the best legal help available; there were frequent conferences with Dr. Ruíz, whom she had interested in the case, and with Señor Solora, the famous lawyer whom Dr. Ruíz had persuaded to undertake the defense. So far it had proved impossible for her to get permission to visit Kerjanian in jail, but through Señor Solora she was able to remain in touch with the prisoner. Not a day passed that she did not send him a new message of hope and cheer.

Then there were many business matters to be settled before Hilda Stumpf's imminent departure for the United States, when Uncle Konrad would be taking over the pension. Despite Bubi's death, Marie-Té was determined that Hilda's moment of glory should not pass entirely uncelebrated, and hence suggested that a farewell party be arranged before the authoress' departure. It was decided to hold it in the garden of the Pension Hilda, and of course during the early afternoon hours so as to avoid the rain, which, now in the wet season, invariably started falling toward midafternoon.

The day of the celebration found Uncle Konrad and Irène Legervais rushing about distractedly with trays of cakes from Herr Professor Levi's bakery and dripping jugs of ice-cold lemonade. All of Hilda's and Marie-Té's friends had been invited, not excepting Paco, the newsboy, clad in a new pink shirt and an especially huge sombrero that Marie-Té had bought for him. The nucleus of the gathering was the little group of refugees who had attended that first famous reading of the novel, among whom Herr Apfelbaum, the ex-publisher from Leipzig, was very much in evidence. He had felt a proprietory interest in Hilda ever since the day that he "discovered" her, and as the enthusiastic cables about her book kept arriving from the United States, his pride in this aging *wunderkind* of his had steadily increased.

"Hilda Stumpf is a great woman," he now was telling John Camberly, to the vast embarrassment of the authoress herself, who kept making signs to him to stop. "As yet we are the only ones who realize it, but all America will acclaim her by the time she has finished with her lecture tour and made personal appearances in half a dozen cities."

At that moment Irène Legervais came hurrying up with a tray of sandwiches, cut very fine by her own dainty hands in the pension kitchen that morning. "Did I hear you mention personal appearances? That reminds me—the dress I've ordered for you will be ready this evening, Hilda. *Très simple mais très chic, vous savez.* You mustn't forget, *chèrie,* to powder your nose and look your best when you step off the airplane. The first impression one makes is so important."

Everybody began to laugh. The idea of big absent-minded Hilda remembering to powder her nose was too ludicrous—she who rarely even thought of passing a comb through her tousled hair!

"Ach, kindlichkeit!" cried Herr Apfelbaum. "This publicity business is too childish—too vulgar. It's her good books, her sound words, that the world needs—not her well-powdered nose. Mind you begin thinking of your new novel right away, Hilda."

"Oh, I have done that already," said Hilda, smiling. "If you want to know the truth, I have my new book all planned out, though I admit that the plot presented itself to me ready-made. Can any of you guess its subject?"

"No. Do tell us," said Herr Apfelbaum eagerly.

Marie-Té shook her head and leaned forward with interest.

"It's about—Harrington," said Hilda Stumpf after a little pause which showed that she had the true writer's appreciation of dramatic suspense. "About Warfield Harrington, and his murder."

A silence fell on the people in the garden; each person seemed to have sunk into himself. How strangely the thought of that murder affected everyone! thought Marie-Té. It was as if all felt that here was a mystery which demanded solution; no one was crude enough to believe that it had been just an ordinary murder, inspired by ordinary motives. The murder, one felt, was only the final link in a long chain of events—only the culmination of a cycle. One by one the eyes of everyone again sought Hilda Stumpf, as if she, in her role of creative artist, held the key to the mystery.

When Hilda finally spoke, it seemed to Marie-Té that she worded the question which was in the minds of all of them. "Why was Harrington murdered?" she said. "Why did Harrington *have* to die? I've been unable to think of anything else ever since it happened, even though my own life has been so turbulent. I keep analyzing the circumstances—from an abstract point of view, that is. There's a story here—I feel it. And it's a story with a moral that has import for us all in this year 1943."

"You mean," suggested Dr. Ruíz, "the old moral that pride

comes before a fall? I knew Mr. Harrington. He was a man of overweening pride."

"Or," said Dr. Gottlieb, an ex-professor of history who now ran a tailor shop, "that the little man will sooner or later rise up and slay the official who's misgoverned? That's the way it's been through all the ages."

"Of course," agreed Hilda Stumpf. "But this case isn't as simple as all that, is it? After all, Warfield Harrington didn't really 'misgovern.' He filled his official duties in the most meticulous manner. What's more, he hadn't, as far as one knows, done anything against Kerjanian personally. Yet he was punished by death, and the queer thing is that everyone who knew him feels that the punishment was somehow deserved. In other words, he must have broken higher rules than the ones he so carefully observed.

Ted Kelly leaned forward, his dark Irish eyes alive with interest. His reddish hair had been cropped close to the skull while he had malaria, giving him the appearance of a clever little monkey.

"That's what I've been thinking these last weeks," he said earnestly. "Mr. Harrington was punished for—well, just for being what he was. Perhaps I shouldn't say it publicly, but it's no secret to most of you what my feelings for Mr. Harrington were. And still I can't deny that he always behaved toward me in a perfectly correct fashion; he even went out of his way to be polite. My knowledge that he despised me for being Irish was instinctive. I came from what he probably considered an inferior race, though he wouldn't have dared say so openly. For him I was never an individual—I was just a 'shanty-Irishman,' and that's what made me dislike him, and work so badly for him. It was his disregard of the individual that brought about his downfall in the end. Of that I'm positive."

Hilda-Stumpf nodded. "Well, however we analyze it," she remarked, "the case has plenty of interest. To you, Marie-Té I shall have to come for detailed information. My biggest handicap is that I never knew Kerjanian personally, in fact I only saw him once. And obviously, he will be the hero of my book. You will have to tell me all about him."

Marie-Té shook her head. "I'm afraid I won't be able to help you much, Hilda. Kerjanian would never let me really know him— would never let anybody know him, when it came to that. He had been too much hurt—that's why he shut himself away from every-one." She paused a moment, and her eyebrows knit together as they had a way of doing when she was pained or troubled. "They call him a murderer," she said. "A murderer! They should have seen the expression of tenderness in his eyes when he looked at Bubi that last day. Bubi loved him. Bubi never would have loved anyone who wasn't fundamentally good, Hilda. Never!"

Her eyes filled with tears, and she raised them to meet the eyes of Uncle Konrad. For a second those two friends, who shared be-tween them the secret of a great love and of a great grief, looked at one another, and in that look was complete understanding.

"*Pauvre petite chérie,*" said Irène Legervais, squeezing Marie-Té's hand. "We all love you so much. You're among real friends, my darling, if that's any consolation to you—among your own sort of people, not strangers."

"Thank you, Irène." Marie-Té gave her hand an answering squeeze. "I know that what you say is true. Do you realize that we're half a dozen different nationalities here today? And yet any-where in the world we'd have found each other: in America, in France—yes, even in Germany! There are no Harringtons among us. That's why the thought of Kerjanian locked up in prison, await-ing sentence for a crime that was no crime, must make you all as sad as it does me." She looked at Dr. Ruíz pleadingly. "Don't you think that Señor Solora will be able to convince them of the wrong-ness of putting Kerjanian to death? I know that a long prison sen-tence is inevitable, but for God's sake, Dr. Ruíz, don't let them kill Kerjanian!"

"We will do all in our power," the doctor answered in his calm dignified way. "Señor Solora has put his heart in this case. If anyone can save your friend Kerjanian, it is he. And I really think," he added, his serious eyes moving from face to face, "that when so many good and true people are wishing for his safety, it must have some effect."

At that moment an old man with a snow-white beard, seated on a donkey, could be seen the other side of the hedge that surrounded the little garden. Paco came rushing up to Marie-Té delightedly. *"Abuelito! Abuelito!"* he explained proudly. "It's my own great-grandfather, the postman, who's a hundred years old. Do you know, señorita, *he can read!!* That's how he got the job, because he could tell what it said on the envelopes. Look, he's waving a letter. It must be for you."

Marie-Té put some ice cream on a dish for the old man and went to get her letter. She opened and read it by the fence, and when she returned, there was a whimsical smile on her face; in her hand was an official-looking envelope with a red seal on the flap.

"They've come—at last," she said, turning to her uncle but addressing all the members of the little group. "Our American visas! Isn't it typical that they should arrive just today, when they're no longer of any use? I'm sure they've often come when the applicants were already hanging dangling by the necks, having given up waiting in despair! As to us, Bubi is with us no longer; Uncle Konrad is staying here to take over the pension; and I also shall not be leaving Santa Rosa, seeing that John and I are to get married . . ."

She stopped short, and then sat back, blushing to the roots of her hair. Because of Bubi's death she had wanted to wait a little longer before announcing her engagement, but now it was out, and there was nothing to do about it. Everyone was looking at Marie-Té delightedly, and her friends crowded about to embrace her. Hilda Stumpf threw her arms around the young fiancée and kissed her resoundingly on both cheeks, while Ted Kelly patted John enthusiastically on the back. In the excitement, Uncle Konrad slipped away without anybody's noticing it, but a moment later he came running back with a bottle of Tokay in his hand.

Hilda Stumpf burst out laughing. "Ah, the Herr Baron can always find a bottle at the appropriate moment! And invariably it's his last bottle. He's like a squirrel who hides away his nuts."

"Well, this is positively my last bottle of Tokay," said Uncle Konrad as he drew the cork. "There is not another in Santa Rosa. I doubt if there is another in all Central America. Only such an occasion would warrant its consumption."

"May I drink"—Hilda Stumpf raised her glass and looked happily about her—"to the most charming couple I know. They are distinctly modern people—as modern as the day after tomorrow. They are not cynics, but they are not sentimentalists either; they are just two sincere human beings with hearts and understanding, determined to make this world of ours a better place to live in. A real American couple they will be, for although Marie-Té is a foreigner, no one has ever understood and lived the democratic ideal as well as she—so gaily and so naturally. So let's drink to John Camberly and Marie-Té—and to the new world that is full of promise!"

Ah Sing's reaction to his master's death was very different from what might have been expected: far from finding satisfaction in the demise of a man by whom he had been humiliated for so long, he saw in it cause for profound reflection. Like every Oriental, Ah Sing knew that effect follows cause as inevitably as night follows day, so it did not surprise him that Mr. Harrington had met death in so violent a fashion. Judging from the way Mr. Harrington had treated Ah Sing himself, he had treated others as well with insolence and disrespect, for it is a fact that a man is either uniformly courteous, or uniformly discourteous. And of course it is as dangerous to be rude as to walk about with a lighted torch among kegs of dynamite! Thinking back, it seemed to Ah Sing that Mr. Harrington had arranged the pattern of his own death as systematically as if he had deliberately planned it.

251

The two days following the murder Ah Sing spent in meticulously going over the apartment, dusting and again dusting every corner, polishing the floors, beating the carpets. Things should be left not only as clean as when Mr. Harrington moved in, but doubly as clean. For the former would be but to fulfill one's duty, which is very low, whereas the latter would be to maintain one's self-respect and thus show courtesy to oneself—an essential politeness.

Then at last came the evening when everything was packed and there was no more work to do. Very quietly Ah Sing went into his own room, took off his trousers and his white linen jacket and hung them in the cupboard. Opening the wooden chest which held his clothes, he took out a black silk mandarin coat, a pair of white socks and some Chinese slippers. These he laid out on a chair. After bathing himself very thoroughly, brushing his teeth and washing his hair, Ah Sing put on the Chinese clothes and made his way onto the little grillwork balcony which gave on the serving pantry. He seated himself on a stool and gazed out over the roofs of Santa Rosa toward the chain of blue mountains in the distance.

But it was the mountains of Asia that Ah Sing saw in his mind's eye—the rugged mountains of the Central Chinese province where he had been born. Then the panorama narrowed, as it might upon a moving picture screen, and he saw one particular mountain, then the valley at the mountain's foot, then a small stream running through the valley, then a great golden flower nodding its head above the stream. As Ah Sing sat there gazing across the Central American landscape which had become for him the landscape of China, his eyes half closed, and his body began to sway gently back and forth.

Eight years had passed since he had entered Harrington's employ, and this was the first time that he had allowed the memories of that stream, of that flower, to rise into his conscious mind; ever he had suppressed them, aware that there was no place for revery and contemplation in the active life to which he was dedicated. He had been very young when he started out—only sixteen—but already he had known that hard years lay ahead of him, not because service was hard by its very nature, but because Ah Sing invariably set himself arduous tasks. It was not enough to be a perfect servant; that was only his duty and was no more than could be expected of him. Ah Sing wanted to achieve something greater—something that would show that he respected not only himself, but his father and his grandfather and his grandfather's father. It was for this reason that he had taken on the vast task of self-education and had finally raised himself to the level of a cultured man.

Now for the first time in all these years he would permit himself a few days' rest—a few days of relaxation while he contemplated that great flower nodding its golden head, and attuned his ears to the sound of the gurgling stream. The little house beside the bamboo rushes he did not try to visualize; in all likelihood it had been deserted and burned to the ground long ago, seeing that the Japanese army had passed that way. But the stream was there even to this day, just as it had been in his father's time, and in the time of his grandfather and of his grandfather's father; it would be there a thousand years from now. And the flower would blossom again this summer, no matter what foreign hordes had tramped across the countryside.

Hour after hour Ah Sing sat there on the little balcony beside the serving pantry, arms folded on chest, eyes fixed on the distant mountains. He felt his body and mind gradually relaxing after eight years of incessant work; he felt his soul growing limpid once again, like the soul of a little child. Not once did worrying thoughts of the future assail him, as would have happened had he been an Occidental. New and great tasks lay before him—would always lie before him, seeing that his very nature called out for them. Yet, aware of those future tasks, he did not allow the knowledge of them to disturb him. The great Fates which took care of everything, which had sent Harrington to his death and Kerjanian to a prison cell, would send Ah Sing also where he was meant to go. As the days and nights slipped by, merging almost imperceptibly into each other, a great calm and contentment settled on the young Chinamah.

Then on the fourth morning, the telephone in the apartment gave a ring. As Ah Sing went to answer it, something told him that this little peaceful interim was already over.

"Good morning, Ah Sing," came a calm, low voice across the wire. "This is Mr. Camberly at the American Legation."

"I know your voice, Mr. Camberly," said Ah Sing. "I would know it anywhere."

"I'm sorry not to have telephoned you before," said the man at the other end. "As you can imagine, there's been a great deal to attend to since Mr. Harrington's death. But Miss Falkenborn, my fiancée, and I were talking about you only last night, and we decided that if you have no other plans, we would like you to come to us. Believe me, Ah Sing, that we don't only think of you as a perfect servant, though we know you are one. We like you—and respect you very much."

Ah Sing made no answer for a moment. Slowly he lifted one slender white hand and covered his eyes, and when the room was shut out, he again saw before him that great golden flower, and the stream running between the mountains of China. Now he knew what he had to do. A man must always set himself tasks greater than he can be expected to accomplish; a man must always live so that his ancestors can be proud of him, and so that his grandchildren can be proud of him, for what is he but a ripple in the river of eternity? When he heard his own voice, he was glad that it held not the slightest trace of indecision.

"I am most honored at your kind offer, Mr. Camberly," he said. "Nothing would give me greater pleasure than to work for you, but the fact is—that I must return to China. If you'll allow me to say so, sir, this is a time when every country needs its sons. I've been working very hard for years, Mr. Camberly, trying to educate myself. I never really knew why I was working, but now I know: it was to make myself useful to my country. It may be very difficult

254

for me to get there—it may take me many months—but I feel that my path lies Eastward."

Now it was Camberly's turn to remain silent, and when his answer came, his voice, usually unemotional, sounded strangely moved. "I have an idea that you are doing exactly the right thing, Ah Sing. Yes, exactly! If you need help, be sure to call on me; I'll do what I can to facilitate your journey. Good-by, Ah Sing. Good luck."

Ah Sing put down the receiver, and as he took a step away from the telephone, he felt that his colossal voyage had already started. Doesn't the old Chinese proverb say that the longest journey commences with the very first step? Going to his own room, he took off the black mandarin coat, the white socks, the sandals, and put them all away carefully in his chest. Then he dressed himself once again in Western clothes, drew out his little suitcase from beneath his bed and swiftly began to pack it. How very few material possessions he had accumulated during the period that he had been with Harrington! The suitcase closed as easily as it had done eight years before. He had received no gifts during all that time, had not even received an increase of salary, and now that he was leaving, he would rather have died than keep a handkerchief that did not belong to him.

Only one of Harrington's possessions did he decide to take with him, and that because he knew that it was rightly his; the wisdom of Lieh Tzu was Ah Sing's own heritage, handed on to him from his father and his grandfather and his grandfather's father, but only now come into his actual possession through the medium of Harrington, the deceased.

Standing there beside his packed suitcase, Ah Sing opened the beautifully bound volume at a familiar page. It had occurred to him that one of the parables fitted perfectly the case of Warfield Harrington and his mother, who had met death almost simultaneously in such singular and uncalled-for fashions. At that very moment people would be asking themselves why Harrington had been murdered by a man whom he had never injured, nor even known personally, but Lieh Tzu, writing over a thousand years ago, had already supplied the answer.

Mr. Wu [wrote Lieh Tzu] was a wealthy man of the Liang state. His household was rolling in riches, and his hoards of money and silk and other valuables were quite incalculable. It was his custom to have banquets served, to the accompaniment of music, in a high upper hall overlooking the main road; there he and his friends would sit drinking their wine and amusing themselves with bouts of gambling.

One day, a party of young gallants happened to pass along the road. In the chamber above, play was going on as usual, and a lucky throw of the dice evoked a loud burst of merriment from the players. Precisely at that moment it happened that a kite sailing overhead dropped the carcass of a rat in the midst of the company outside. The young men held an angry consultation on the spot.

"This Mr. Wu," they said, "has been enjoying his wealth for many a long day, and has always treated his neighbours in the most arrogant spirit. And now, although we have never offended him, he insults us with this dead rat. If such an outrage goes unavenged, the world will look upon us as a set of poltroons. Let us summon up our utmost resolution, and combine with one accord to wipe him and his family out of existence!"

The whole party signified their agreement, and upon the evening of the appointed day, they collected, fully armed for the attack, and exterminated every member of his family.

When Ah Sing had read through this little story, he nodded his head slowly and laid the book face upwards on the table. Using a thumbnail of that hand which Warfield Harrington had so scorned, and yet so envied, he made a tiny groove beneath the words that formed the title of the parable: "The Catastrophe Was Due."

256

Chapter XVII
The Faithful Heart

FROM THE MOMENT OF OPENING HER EYES ON THE day of the Kerjanian trial, Marie-Té had a strange feeling of expectancy. Through her bedroom window she could see the top branches of the acacias, with the hot rain streaming down on them from a sky which seemed to have moved very close to earth. It had been pouring for almost a month, and everything she touched felt damp: the bed sheets, the towels in her bathroom, even her black linen suit, which nowadays seemed a more appropriate garb than the white dress she used to wear. There was good cause for grief, what with her still-recent bereavement, and the prospect of the coming trial, yet instead of being depressed, Marie-Té had this inexplicable sensation of expectancy.

It was still with her as she and Uncle Konrad taxied to the courthouse that afternoon, even though there mingled with it now an excruciating nervousness; her face in the little mirror of the taxi was drawn and pale, and it occurred to her that these last weeks had put years on her age. Had either of two people been present, she could have drawn assurance from their calm and strength, but John had been made *chargé d'affaires* and felt it inadvisable in his new position to attend the trial, and Hilda Stumpf was already on another continent.

Marie-Té wished also that she had had a chance to say a few words to Kerjanian. He was such an unpredictable man, and he always made the worst possible impression with that surliness and arrogance of his which derived from his desperate efforts to maintain his self-respect. Señor Solora, the lawyer for the defense, had told her that Kerjanian's hope of escaping the death penalty depended partly on his own conduct at the trial. She dreaded to think that through a show of pride, he might jeopardize his chances.

When their taxi drove up to the courthouse, Marie-Té could not believe her eyes; it was like arriving at a theater just before a gala performance. Every private car in Santa Rosa was parked in the square, and taxis, howling like lost souls, kept darting up to disgorge passengers. The regular afternoon rain had not yet started, so a number of enterprising people had set up little kitchen restaurants on the sidewalk and were stuffing *enchiladas* with mad haste, while their children ran around selling the finished product, impaled on sticks. Lottery vendors were doing a thriving business, and as usual trying to tempt everyone in sight, including beggars, with glib promises of ten-thousand peso prizes. An Indian from the mountains had come to town with a stock of parrots in wooden cages. One of the birds had got loose and was fluttering around the square with bedraggled green feathers, screaming, *"Arre burro! Arre burro!"* which means "Giddap, donkey!" and is the Spanish equivalent of "Polly wants a cracker." To add to the confusion, two organ grinders were hard at work, one playing "Rio Grande" and the other an aria from Tosca.

The hubbub was maddening, but through it all one felt the pulse of life beating strongly, joyously, imperatively, just as it beats in a teeming jungle. And near by, somewhere in the recesses of this stone structure, sat a little silent man awaiting sentence—perhaps awaiting death, thought Marie-Té with a tightening of her heart. Yet she had the feeling that this, too, was somehow right; where there was life, death also could not be far away. That was one thing that Latin America had taught her: the acceptance of death as an integral part of life.

Uncle Konrad stepped out of the taxi and with old-fashioned courtesy helped his young niece alight. Immediately two sellers of lottery tickets and an ice-cream vendor pounced upon him, but

Uncle Konrad, who had learned to check his spontaneous reaction to buy anything offered him, waved them politely aside.

"Let us get in quickly, *Liebling*," he told Marie-Té. "It is going to start raining in a moment."

Indeed, no sooner had they stepped inside, than the heavy drops began to fall, landing with little hisses on the charcoal fires of the sidewalk kitchens. In the courtroom itself they found the wildest excitement prevailing; the atmosphere was the same as at a bullfight when the President is attending. There was the murmur of voices and the shuffle of impatient feet, and every second people were jumping up to peer about the room, then nodding and waving to acquaintances. Heightening the tension was the semidarkness and the loud sound of the rain beating on the glass roof. As usual, the Santa Rosan power station had chosen an inappropriate moment for a breakdown, and the oil lamps on the judge's rostrum gave out a flickering light in which people's features looked unreal and tense.

Marie-Té and her uncle found seats on one of the rear rows, whence they had a good view of the whole courtroom. Despite the dimness of the lighting, Marie-Té recognized a number of familiar faces, and it was apparent that Santa Rosa had turned out in force for what was undoubtedly the most important trial in the city's history. Seated discreetly at one side were Señora de Castro and her friend Mrs. Moffat, the former wearing black veils, although whether she was mourning her deceased admirer or her own ruined life it would have been hard to say. At least three members of the government were attending, not to mention Señor Pinchinchi and his French-born spouse. As Marie-Té watched her, she saw the buxom Señora Pinchinchi give a friendly nod to her former employer, Madame Olympe, who, swathed in black silk like a dowager, sat in the front row, as befitted her dignified position.

Suddenly with one accord everyone rose to his feet. It was impossible for Marie-Té to see what had happened, but when the audience with equal abruptness reseated itself, she perceived that the judge's chair was now occupied by a portly individual in a crimson gown, wearing on his head a peculiarly constructed square hat somewhat resembling the Uhlan headgear. He slowly cast his eye about the courtroom, nodded as if he were satisfied with the attendance, and whispered something to one of the officials.

"Bring in the prisoner!" called out an announcer, but the rain almost drowned out his words. As nothing happened, he shouted again, "Bring in the prisoner!" Finally the door at the side opened, and Kerjanian was ushered in in charge of two policemen.

He was wearing his old pale-blue suit, but Marie-Té noted that it looked wrinkled and dirty, as if he had slept in it; the crimson silk necktie was conspicuously absent. With his manacled hands he kept trying to smooth down the ruffled lapels. To make matters worse, he apparently had been unable to shave for several days; a heavy stubble covered his cheeks and chin, giving his face a more than usually fanatical look. Even from where she sat, Marie-Té could see the glitter of his eyes as Kerjanian cast a quick glance about the room before stepping up into the prisoner's box. While one of the guards undid the handcuffs, the Armenian looked on with a rather bored expression. No sooner were his hands free than he folded his arms on his chest in his favorite gesture and defiantly stared down at the whole court from his elevated position.

In the meanwhile the judge had been sitting slumped in his chair, without looking at the prisoner. Marie-Té could not be sure, but it seemed to her that his eyes were closed. Perhaps he had even gone to sleep, for when the announcer struck a gavel on a table, the man in the crimson robe started and looked around. He saw Kerjanian for the first time and let his glance rest on him; for a moment the criminal and the judge stared into each other's eyes.

"The state against Nestor Kerjanian," chanted the announcer. "Prisoner, you are accused of murder. Do you plead guilty or not guilty?"

Kerjanian nodded vigorously. "Yes, yes, I did it. I shot Harrington. I shot him three times."

260

"Answer my question," interrupted the announcer. "Are you guilty or not guilty?"

"Not guilty!"

Señor Solora, the defense lawyer, jumped to his feet and threw up his arm. "My client does not understand Spanish. I demand an interpreter."

"That's not true," said Kerjanian. "I understand Spanish very well."

"The prisoner mustn't talk!" shouted the clerk of the court.

"How shall I defend myself if I can't talk!"

"Keep still!"

"I shall not keep still."

While this exchange of politenesses was going on, Señor Solora's sensitive face assumed an expression of concern and chagrin. He shook his head at the court, and gave a wry smile, begging their indulgence for his client's behavior. Remembering what he had told her about the importance of Kerjanian's making a good impression, Marie-Té's heart sank.

But now the judge was fixing the clerk of the court with a watery eye. "Read the charges," he pronounced pompously and went to sleep again.

The man began to read in a singsong voice almost inaudible to Marie-Té at the back of the room. The rain beating on the roof, the uncertain light, the sleeping judge, all gave to the scene a quality of unreality; it seemed to have as little to do with actual life as a distorted dream or a fantastic ghost story. Only Kerjanian himself seemed real, standing there with arms folded on chest like the Man of Destiny. His head tilted to one side, the top part of his body leaning forward, he gave the impression of listening to an interesting document which did not concern him in the slightest. Two or three times he nodded, as though in agreement, but suddenly he shot up his arm with three fingers extending skyward.

"That's a lie! A lie!"

"Keep still, prisoner!"

"It says that I shot at him twice. I shot *three* times. Three!" He said waving his fingers frantically.

Señor Solora put his head in his hand and swayed back and forth in anguish. Then he jumped up again.

"This is cruel! My client doesn't understand a word that is being said. I demand an interpreter."

"Prisoner, do you want an interpreter?" said the judge, apparently in his sleep.

"No."

"Very well. Proceed."

The clerk read on in his droning voice, his words becoming more and more unintelligible, while the judge dozed and Kerjanian cupped his hand around his ear and listened with concentrated attention. An audible murmur of relief swept through the courtroom when the man had finally finished. People leaned forward in their seats, as they do at the theater when the prologue is over and the curtain is about to rise on the real play. The prosecuting attorney, a stout little man with a huge bald head, bounced up, pronounced a few introductory words, then without further delay called on his first witness. Saluting in a military fashion, first to the judge, then to the prosecutor, finally to the courtroom as a whole, Carlos, the ex-*mozo* of the Legation, stepped into the stand.

Despite the absence of uniform (for he was no longer doorman, Camberly having recalled Jesús to the post), he was still very smart and spruce. His hair had been newly trimmed and was plastered down on his head; he even had a red flower in his buttonhole. But one thing he had been unable to do much about was the expression on his face. He looked as stupid as a burro, and no sooner had he begun to answer questions than he tripped over his own feet. He found it impossible to explain why he had let Kerjanian through to the Legation offices on two consecutive days without inquiring his business. When it was tactfully hinted that he had been bribed, he began by making a vigorous denial, but a moment later accused

262

Kerjanian of having cheated by giving him a half-empty package of cigarettes.

Marie-Té, listening to Carlos, reflected that Harrington had certainly arranged his own death without knowing it by hiring this incompetent dolt. That was a strange thought. The old *mozo*, Jesús, lacking Carlos' smart appearance, had had a heart as faithful as a dog's, not that that was an important asset in Harrington's eyes. Only over his dead body would Kerjanian have broken into the Minister's office on the fateful morning. What poetic justice that the very love of outer show and disregard of inner worth which was typical of the diplomat should have proved so costly to him in the end!

Hermosillo, the next witness, made a much more favorable impression. With that gift of dramatic oratory possessed by every Latin American, he described how Kerjanian had broken in the day before the murder and stamped and screamed and generally misbehaved himself until he, Hermosillo, proceeded to evict him. He would have done the same the next day, he announced with confidence, except that he unfortunately happened to be paying a visit to the water closet in the basement when the assault occurred. "It was while I was there that the two shots were fired," he explained regretfully. "If that isn't fate, then I'd like to know what is."

Kerjanian in the prisoner's box again began waving his hands frantically. "Three!" he shouted. "Why do they all keep lying? I fired three shots, and would have fired again, only the pistol jammed."

"Keep still, prisoner. The next witness!"

George Baker stood up. Oh how correctly dressed he was! thought Marie-Té. How superior-looking and how obviously pleased to testify against a representative of the unwashed classes! The first two rows, occupied by the wealthiest members of the audience, sat up a little straighter in their chairs. Here was someone worth listening to at last, a member of their own world whose duty and pleasure it was to protect them against the forces of unrest loose in the world today—the forces personified in the unkempt, disreputable figure of Kerjanian.

He made a little bow to the judge, a studiedly correct bow which acknowledged the judge's superior position, yet at the same time implied that it was he who was really superior to this gentleman with the rather dusky skin. Yes, he was as clever as she'd thought, reflected Marie-Té. No wonder that Harrington had chosen him as his disciple. He'd go far in his career—perhaps even further than his master.

"Have you," asked the prosecuting attorney, "seen the accused before today?"

"I have," George Baker answered, and he leaned toward the judge so that the light of the oil lamps fell on his clear-cut features. "He has been to the Legation several times and always acted rudely and unseemingly. When told that he could not see the Minister, he would come forth with all sorts of threats. The day before his cowardly crime, he broke into my office and had to be evicted by main force."

"Have you reason to believe that he contemplated the murder already then?"

"Yes. When he mentioned Mr. Harrington's name, I could read murder in his eyes. Never before have I seen such a look of hatred."

"And what, in your opinion, was his motive?" asked the prosecutor, tilting his large head sideways so as to be sure to hear the answer above the rain.

"In my opinion," answered Baker, "Kerjanian decided on his crime simply because Mr. Harrington occupied the position that he did. As the court knows, Kerjanian was a refugee—one of that army of fugitives from the old world which has invaded us like a swarm of locusts. Naturally they arouse our pity, but we shouldn't forget that among them there exists a dangerous element—a desperate element—an element influenced by subversive propaganda! What better evidence of this could we have than the murder of the official representative of the United States?"

264

"In other words," said the prosecutor pointedly, "you are convinced that there was no personal motive in this crime?"

"How could there have been," answered Baker, "seeing that the accused did not even know Mr. Harrington?"

"Thank you, Mr. Baker," said the prosecutor. "That is precisely what I wanted to establish. My next witness is Dr. Siegfried Stumpf of the Schiller Schule."

In the dim light Marie-Té had hitherto failed to notice the tall figure of Siegfried on the witness bench. Not having seen him since he left the pension, she was struck at once by the transformation in the man: his manner, once diffident, today was assertive, almost aggressive. Marie-Té wondered which factor was most responsible: his new position at the school, or his recent marriage to Clara Hildegard, daughter of the Schiller Schule's head. Marie-Té's surprise that Siegfried should have been called as witness was heightened by the prosecutor's first question:

"I understand, Dr. Stumpf, that the accused, Nestor Kerjanian, was in the habit of paying visits to the Schiller Schule."

"No sir, that is not correct," answered Siegfried, standing rigidly at attention in the witness box. "He came once, no more."

"Well, you admit that he came once, and that you interviewed him?"

"Yes. He was applying for a post in the school."

"I see. That is very interesting. You would have us believe that Kerjanian, who with all due respect to him, looks more like a brigand than a schoolteacher, applied for a position at the Schiller Schule?"

"That is what I said," corroborated Siegfried, gazing at the prosecutor haughtily.

"And you are sure that the position he applied for was the innocent one of instructor?"

"Excuse me, but I don't at all see the point of all these questions," Siegfried exclaimed in a loud didactic voice. "Surely we at the

265

school cannot be held responsible for every twopenny Armenian who comes applying for a post!"

The prosecutor became red in the face. "Mind your manners in this court!" he shouted. "You will please remember that you are no longer *persona grata* in this country, Dr. Stumpf. The time is passed, thank God, when you Germans could take an attitude toward us."

Marie-Té saw Siegfried bridle and noticed that his glance sought out someone in the audience. Following his gaze, Marie-Té caught sight of a very pretty, blonde young woman whom she recognized as Clara Hildegard, now Siegfried's wife. As if strengthened by the ever-necessary support of a fellow countryman, Siegfried let a sullen, utterly disdainful expression creep into his face—the typical expression of every German when faced with enemies stronger than himself. Marie-Té remembered how she had walked home with this same Siegfried one night from Chez Boris, and what a humble, puzzled creature he then had seemed. Yet it had required no more than a few weeks in the company of his compatriots to turn him into an arrogant, race-conscious man!

"Now I want you to tell me this, Dr. Stumpf," said the prosecutor, standing below the witness box and talking up at Siegfried. "At this interview which you admit having had with Kerjanian, did the name of Mr. Harrington ever enter your conversation?"

"No. Not that I remember."

"Not that you remember! Allow me to suggest, Dr. Stumpf, that your memory is somewhat weak. Allow me to suggest that the subject of Mr. Harrington was discussed quite extensively between you and his future murderer! Please rack your memory, Dr. Stumpf."

"I don't know what you are insinuating," spluttered Siegfried.

"Oh, so you don't know what I am insinuating! With your Teutonic superman's intelligence I should think you would have grasped it by now. Well, I will let you know in due course, Dr. Siegfried Stumpf. You may step down. I have finished with my witnesses for the present." The prosecutor made a bow to the judge.

At once Señor Solora sprang to his feet. He was very handsome as he stood there, tall and slender in his sleek black gown. Marie-Té noticed that several women in the audience, Señora de Castro included, began to powder their noses and to set their hats straight.

"Though I sympathize," began Solora, "with my learned colleague's efforts to throw new light on this case, I cannot help feeling (and I think most of you will agree) that his method of doing so is somewhat involved. Why, we have been wondering, should he have called as witness someone whose relationship with the accused was as flimsy as that of Dr. Stumpf? I, on the contrary, wish to put in the box someone who knew Kerjanian personally. She is a lady whose breeding and connections place her on the top rung of the social ladder and whom I have not officially summoned simply because I did not want her honored name to be involved in a murder trial. But the person I refer to is in court today, and I think will be willing to testify to the good character of Mr. Nestor Kerjanian. I ask the court's permission to call as witness the Baroness Maria-Theresa Falkenborn."

Marie-Té's heart was pounding as she rose to her feet and started down the aisle. It had never occurred to her that she might be called, but now that it had happened, she felt that she had unconsciously prepared herself for just such an eventuality. Perhaps it was in order to talk convincingly today that she had painstakingly drilled herself in Spanish, day in and day out for months! Supremely self-confident she was, knowing that the old Marie-Té had changed during the last weeks into a woman of mature intelligence and firm convictions—a woman of 1943 who had something to say and would say it in the face of everyone. Without waiting to be interrogated, she started speaking the moment she had stepped into the stand, and it seemed to her that the words sprang forth of their own accord.

"Señor Solora has told you that I knew Mr. Kerjanian," she said, one hand in the pocket of her suit, her eyes fixed calmly on the judge's face. "It is true. And though I did not really know him well,

267

I feel that he and I are very close because we belong to the same category of people—a category which, for want of a better word, is called the dispossessed. Mr. Baker doesn't seem to have a very high opinion of us. He told you that there exists amongst the refugees a desperate element threatening your institutions—an element represented today by my friend—by Nestor Kerjanian."

Marie-Té saw a disapproving look come into the judge's drowsy face; she half suspected that he was on the point of stopping her. Of course she knew full well that she was not giving evidence in the strict sense of the words, yet so important did she feel it to say what she had to say, that she now turned from the judge and proceeded to address herself directly to the crowded courtroom.

"Please look at Nestor Kerjanian," she said, her voice vehement, her cheeks flushed with emotion. "Is he an element, as Mr. Baker says? I don't think so. I think he is just a man, as each one of you is a man—as Mr. Baker himself is a man—only a man tried beyond endurance by frustration and suffering. He is a man who has become frantic because for thirty years he has tried vainly to establish himself somewhere in the world. From country to country he has traveled, hoping to find refuge, hoping to be treated like a human being instead of a pariah. And when he finally tried to enter America, the Land of Promise, again the door was slammed harshly in his face. You know what happened afterwards."

Marie-Té halted for a second, instinctively sensing that she held the audience in her power. But how false even the best-chosen words sounded when one was crying out against injustice! Kerjanian, little Kerjanian! Why should he have been made the center of this legalistic tussle, with people defending and attacking him and a black-robed judge ready to pass sentence? She turned her head ever so slightly to glance at the pale, lonely little man, then turned quickly away, afraid of breaking down. There was a sob in her voice as she went on:

"I know that Nestor Kerjanian is not an important man, and that he is not a powerful man either. Of course not. But multiplied by thousands, and by tens of thousands, he *is* important! So important, indeed, that people in authority may have to protect themselves against him by bombproof rooms. Perhaps new wars will have to be fought because of him. He is more than just a refugee; he is the eternally downtrodden, demanding the justice that has been so long refused. What good will it do us to execute one Kerjanian when there are millions of others almost as desperate? As little good as it did the Kerjanians of the world that one of their number killed Harrington, who was not really an individual but the representative of a clique.

"Oh, if I could make you all see how important it is to take to heart the moral of this murder! The shabby man is tired of waiting. He is rising up, and we had better not deceive ourselves about that. Heavens, how little he asks: only the minimum of security, the minimum of happiness. But if it is kept from him much longer, then he will act at last. Oh, I'm sure of it! And he won't act criminally and blindly, like Kerjanian. He will act en masse, and with a power that is irresistible."

There was much whispering and craning of necks when Marie-Té stepped down from the stand. Was it her youth and beauty, or the wide scope of her understanding that so obviously impressed everyone? Even the eyes of the people in the front rows followed her with admiration as she made her way back to her place. Someone in an aisle seat reached out and pressed her hand as she walked by. It was Ted Kelly, and Marie-Té could see even in the dimness that his eyes were shining.

As if frightened of spoiling the effect of her impassioned speech, Solora declined to call any further witnesses, and now the defense rested. The prosecutor again took control of the case. His big bald head wagging nervously, he proceeded to make his summing up. He described with a catch in his voice how Mr. Harrington, a good kind man, beloved by the entire population of Santa Rosa, had been seated at his desk working at improving the understanding between his country and the United States, when the criminal sneaked in and

269

shot him. What was the man's motive? Ah yes, that was the crux of the matter. Kerjanian had been cleverly advised to keep his mouth shut on that point, but to anyone who had eyes to see, it was perfectly obvious. The prosecutor waited a moment, and Marie-Té understood that he was about to explode the bombshell that he had been preparing all afternoon. With a sudden, dramatic movement he seized two objects from a table and waved them in the air: one was the little American flag from Harrington's office; the other Kerjanian's red silk tie.

"These are the clues to the mystery!" shouted the prosecutor, thrusting the pieces of material under the face of Kerjanian, who neither looked at them nor twitched a muscle. "The man is an active Communist! What is more, he is a secret Nazi agent in the employ of the Schiller Schule! It is they who ordered him to destroy the American Minister and to steal the flag."

The prosecutor's announcement created a flurry in the court. Everybody turned to each other to say a few words, and several people nodded wisely, as if to imply that they had known all along that the case had a political flavor. Even Kerjanian looked a trifle startled. He threw a quick glance at his cherished necktie, which the prosecutor was still waving about his head, then quickly recovered himself and set his gaze on the other end of the room. His lips curled in a disdainful smile.

"You see, he admits it," cried the prosecutor eagerly. "If you don't deny a thing, you admit it. You yourself have heard Dr. Stumpf of the Schiller Schule describe his meeting with this paid minion. No doubt they plotted together that very day to murder poor Mr. Harrington! But even more incriminating than Kerjanian's Nazi affiliation is his bond with Communism. I understand that he regularly wore this red tie, the recognized emblem of party membership."

"Because it was the only necktie he possessed," cut in Solora.

"Ha, ha!" The other lawyer laughed. "That's a good joke. And are you going to tell me that he took the American flag because he needed a handkerchief?"

"An unthinking reflex."

"Oh really? Do you suppose that it also was an unthinking reflex that he kept an armadillo locked up in his room? Tell me that, Señor Solora! Politics, dirty politics!" Marie-Té failed to see very clearly what the armadillo had to do with politics, but the court seemed suitably impressed. "We must stamp out this spy racket in our country!" screamed the prosecutor. "It's getting worse and worse. Lately there have been new revelations about the German school. It seems that there is not one single member of its staff who isn't an ardent Nazi! Are we going to permit things like that to go on in our country: spy centers, German schools, rooms with armadillos and Communists? Shameful! Let us stamp it out, and begin by stamping out this foul Bolshi-Nazi, this monster in sheep's clothing you see before you today!"

There was no doubt to Marie-Té that the prosecutor had scored with his attack. The court clerks exchanged glances, and two friends of the prosecutor came up to shake his hand in congratulation; it was obvious that by conjuring up that old Communist bogey, he had swung to his side everyone left cold by his accusation that Kerjanian was a Nazi; the contradiction of thought seemed to trouble no one. Yes, the case was going badly for Kerjanian, very badly. Marie-Té looked despairingly toward Señor Solora, and understood at once that he was on the point of playing his trump card. His sensitive actor's face took on a sorrowing expression. He stood with head bent, frowning, like a man reluctant to speak, yet aware that he must do so.

"Dear friends," he said, talking very loudly so as to be heard above the rain, which by now was beating a tattoo on the glass roof, "as I gave ear to the various speeches made today, I couldn't help feeling moved. Yet I also felt a little saddened that so much eloquence should have been mistakenly directed. No one present seems really to have understood this case, which is, my friends, much less sensational than made out, but likewise more tragic. For the fact is that Mr. Nestor Kerjanian, my client, belongs to those unfortunate people who—" his sorrowing glance sought the judge's face "—belong in an asylum rather than in a criminal institution!"

Again a wave of whispering swept the courtroom. Suddenly the case had taken a new turn, and Marie-Té's wilting hopes revived. As things now stood, a plea of insanity was obviously Kerjanian's only chance.

Señor Solora went on, growing so moved that one could imagine the tears standing in his eyes. "I have spared no effort to ascertain facts about my client's life in Santa Rosa during the months preceding his—his final breakdown. Believe me, my findings prove my contention beyond the shadow of a doubt. How it amazed the simple folk of his neighborhood to see this man sitting day after day at the window of his room, his head sunk despondently in his hands! Then suddenly he would spring up and begin to pace the room, precisely like that noble character of literature, Prince Hamlet. To be or not to be—the question beat in his poor disordered mind.

"One day the desire for companionship swept over him and he sought an animal to share his solitude. But what sort of animal do you suppose he chose? A dog, you say, who with wagging tail would lick his master's hand and gaze up with canine trustfulness? Or perhaps a cat, whose graceful movements would give pleasure to the eye? Oh no, nothing so normal for my poor client! He dashes up the mountain slopes, and seizes for pet a beast so loathsome that our blood congeals at the very sight of it, a beast hideous beyond belief with its armour covering, its tapering snout, its absurd undersized legs. No other than a giant armadillo!

"Friends, Santa Rosans, picture this modern Hamlet striding up and down his lonely room, debating suicide, debating death, and only occasionally stopping his mad pacing to bend down and stroke the scales of this ghastly reptile! Tell me, fellow citizens, what should we decree for this poor man: the supreme penalty that his demented crime seems at first sight to deserve—or the shelter of an asylum, where the keeper's kindly word will cheer and comfort him as he leans his tired head against the window bars, and gazes out at the blue sky from which merciful God gazes down at him . . . ."

"Imbecile, shut up!" Those three words called out by Kerjanian brought Solora's peroration to an expected end. The Armenian, glaring down from his box, was waving his fist at his defender. "How dare you imply that I am crazy, you—you lunatic! I'm a qualified schoolteacher, I would like you to know. I have my official certificate—second grade. I'm saner than anybody in this room, and I tell you all that I am glad that I killed Harrington. I planned it all out carefully and did it with great skill. I am proud of myself! Perhaps through my deed America, the America I love, will wake up to what is being done in her name by Fascists like Warfield Harrington. I'm afraid if she doesn't wake up soon, it will be too late, for there are thousands of his kind in America, as there are in every country—power-hungry men, enemies of the human race, enemies of everyone from whom they have nothing to gain.

"And just because I say that doesn't mean that I'm a Communist!" Kerjanian shouted, turning to the prosecutor furiously. "Communist! That's what they call every poor devil who doesn't let himself be stepped on. Why should I be labeled Communist simply because I ask the right to get into the United States and be given a chance to work? I love America, I tell you! I love it and I love what it stands for. Why, I even know the Declaration of Independence by heart— I can recite it from beginning to end without leaving out a single word. Is there anyone here who can do that? Can you do it, Mr. Baker, who once had me put out of the American Legation? Of course you can't. 'All men are created equal'—that's what it says in the Declaration. But the only men your type think of as equals are those with power to help you on with your careers! *I* am a real American! And this flag that I rescued from Harrington's office is something that I would fight for—something that I would give my last drop of blood for . . . if only I had the chance."

For several seconds complete silence succeeded Kerjanian's speech. Marie-Té had the feeling that everyone here present realized that words of purity and truth had been spoken, even if with those words Kerjanian had pronounced his own death sentence. Now there no longer was any doubt about the coming verdict. Even Solora seemed to have given up hope; after an initial effort to silence Kerjanian, he had sunk into a chair and had sat listening to his client without interruption. Despite it all, Marie-Té experienced a wild elation. She understood that her forefeeling of that morning had proved justified; the past minutes had been among the most momentous in her life. As long as she lived, she would never forget the tragic yet exultant eyes of Kerjanian as he pronounced his declaration of love of a country that he had never seen and realized that he would never see.

But now a commotion broke loose in the courtroom. Some people in the back rows began to applaud, while others in front stood up and whistled. Gradually the entire audience took sides for or against Kerjanian, and the judge awoke at last and pounded with his gavel on the table. Several people climbed up on chairs so as to get a better look at the prisoner; others crowded forward, pressing against the cord that separated them from the front part of the room. Kerjanian began to speak again, although little of what he said was audible in the confusion. In vain the clerk shouted to him to keep still, and finally the judge, exasperated, signaled the policemen to snap the handcuffs back on and to lead the prisoner from the room.

Kerjanian refused to be silenced. His eyes burning like coals in his white face, he raised his voice higher and higher so as to be heard in the room's farthest corners. Through the prevailing darkness, the impassioned voice of the little man went out, explaining again and again to everyone who would listen that he was glad that he had done this deed, that Harrington, the man of evil will, the enemy of humanity, had had to die. His voice rose to a final scream of denunciation, and he stood there in the circle of light with accusing forefinger lifted high. Suddenly Marie-Té remembered that once before the resemblance had struck her between Kerjanian and a Biblical prophet of doom.

Kerjanian had been moved to the cells of the condemned in an isolated section of the prison. From his tiny window he had a view of the housetops of Santa Rosa, with the trees of Independencia Park in the distance. By moving far over to one side, he was able to espy the glass roof of the covered market, and sometimes in the early afternoon when the sun was out, he could see a corner of the old mauve house where he used to live. But most days it poured unceasingly; all he could make out was the roofs of the neighboring buildings, with the sheets of rain falling down upon them against a background of mud-colored sky.

His favorite position was sitting cross-legged on the straw *petate* (for he had no bed), his back resting against the angle of the wall. His thoughts were totally unimportant. Sometimes in the past he had speculated upon his mental processes with the knowledge that he had only a few days to live. Now that the situation had presented itself, he found them no more interesting than his thoughts at any other period. For instance he might ask himself whether there would be *frijoles* again for supper, or whether the guard had started in his present profession or had, so to speak, been graduated into it. Occasionally it occurred to him to wonder what had happened to the armadillo, and what they would do with his few possessions later on. He would have liked to think that no one else would ever wear his red silk necktie, but had to admit that his wish was unlikely of fulfillment. Whole hours slipped by in a state of half sleep during which he could not later recall having had any thoughts at all.

Then he would doze off, and almost invariably would be transported to America in his dreams. Waking from them, he would feel refreshed, secure, almost carefree, and in his mind he would go over those long happy talks he used to have with Bubi concerning the land of their yearning. "There are often great festive holidays in America," he had told Bubi, and the little boy's eyes had

275

shone. Kerjanian and he had actually *tasted* the gorgeous fat turkey that they would have at Thanksgiving, and when they talked about the Fourth of July, they had *heard* the rockets sizzling and exploding, and the happy free American people shouting hurrah in the warm summer night. In their fantasy they had walked hand in hand through Central Park in New York amongst all the other "Americans"—solid and respected United States citizens both of them.

Loudspeakers hidden in the trees boomed forth warm, generous words—words telling them that that old negro sitting on the grass with his coffee-colored wife was as good an American as the young sailor sauntering down the path with his blonde sweetheart; that the little fat Greek playing with his children had as much right to live and to work in this great free country as the Russian immigrant buying peanuts from the peanut vendor. As Kerjanian sat there on the *petate* in his Central American prison, he remembered with delight how he had taught his friend Bubi the great Declaration of Independence, and had imagined Bubi's reciting it aloud as he and Kerjanian walked slowly hand in hand through the city of parks and skyscrapers.

Then in the evening they would return to their home in Liberty Street in Brooklyn—that wonderfully friendly street where people liked and respected Kerjanian, who in his turn liked and respected his neighbors. He would lift his hat to them, and they would lift their hats to him, and they would all feel like brothers. Liberty Street, America—how far away it was from him now—how far away it was from millions of other longing hearts!

In a near-by building, its roof one of those visible from his cell, was a loudspeaker. When the wind blew from that direction, Kerjanian could sometimes hear music, or a metallic radio voice making an announcement; then the wind would veer, and the sounds would once more be carried off. The instrument neither annoyed him nor gave him pleasure; he never consciously listened to its emanations.

But one afternoon he woke up from sleep with a sensation of pure bliss. He had no idea why he felt so happy; it was exactly as he used to feel when he was a youth in Armenia, in love for the first time. Then he realized that there was music in his ears—the sound of a lilting melody. *"Wien, Wien, nur du allein . . ."* the violins were singing.

Suddenly that beautiful, pear-shaped bubble appeared before his eyes, as on the day when he had gone to see the boy in the pension. It danced about Kerjanian's cell, rebounded from the walls, hovered tantalizingly above his head. He could almost reach up his hand to seize it . . . . The music grew fainter, fainter, until in the end he could detect its presence only by straining his ears. Simultaneously the bubble floated off into the sky, but the feeling of great joy lingered with Kerjanian.

In the same way, he thought, his own soul would soar away in a day or two, after that stupid execution, unfettered, released. A smile flooded into his face as he remembered Bubi's eyes the day that he stood watching his beautiful balloon float up into the blue. "It is happy to be free," Bubi had said. And he had said also, "I'm sorry about losing it—but not terribly sorry." Nor would he, Kerjanian, be terribly sorry to leave this life tomorrow or the next day. His soul would be happy—happy to be free at last.

There was the sound of approaching footsteps in the corridor. Directly outside his gate they stopped, and then came the grinding noise of the bars being swung open. In the dark entrance stood a woman, and the familiar odor of mimosa reached Kerjanian. Advancing into the cell, the Austrian girl held out her hand.

"I have come to pay you a visit," she said. "It has been hard to get permission."

Kerjanian slowly rose to his feet, looking about for a chair to offer her. There was none. Standing in the middle of the bare cell, he shook hands in an embarrassed manner.

"They will only let me stay for a few moments," she said, speaking quickly. "We must not waste time. Is there anything that I can do for you? Have you any message?"

Kerjanian passed his hand over his stubble-covered chin as he reflected. "When you go to America," he said finally, "please look up my brother in Brooklyn. You mustn't forget the address: 399 Liberty Street, Brooklyn, America. Give my love to my brother. Give my love to America."

"And is there no one else? You are all alone?"

"Yes, alone. I have always been alone."

"I am afraid that there is no hope for a pardon. The President has refused."

"Yes, yes," Kerjanian nodded uninterestedly. "That is how I want it. Men are dying everywhere nowadays—senselessly, stupidly —simply because the Harringtons of Europe so decreed it. But *I* know why I die. It's in protest against the injustice of those who rule the world, and who always will rule the world in spite of wars and revolutions! I shall go to my death joyfully, for I have vindicated my honor."

"You mean that you had to kill Harrington to do that?"

"No, no, that is not why I killed Harrington," said Kerjanian quickly. "The personal factor played no part in it. I did it simply because—because Harrington had to die."

"But why? Why? I feel that you're right, Kerjanian, but I want you to tell me why in your own words: why did Warfield Harrington have to die?"

Kerjanian heard the note of urgency in her voice. He had the feeling that his answer was of great importance, and he hesitated a long moment before he spoke. Why, really, had he killed Harrington? he suddenly asked himself. Apart from Bubi's death, apart from that ten-year-old insult, there had been a deeper reason. The murder had been right, that he had never doubted, but not till now had he tried to figure out its justification. He knew that his next words would be in the nature of a final self-vindication.

"I had to kill Harrington," he said at length, "I had to kill Harrington because—he was a man without respect for human dignity."

As soon as he had pronounced the words, he knew that he had spoken rightly; that was the reason, the fundamental reason, why

278

Harrington had had to die. It merely happened that he, Kerjanian, had been chosen as the instrument of accomplishment.

The guard took hold of the iron gate and rattled it.

"Time is up," he called. "You must leave now."

"Yes, yes, I must leave," the girl repeated, and a little tremor passed through her body. "You are sure there is nothing else that I can do for you?"

"Ah yes," said Kerjanian, suddenly remembering. "I owe ten centavos to a woman in the market place. A fat woman—a seller of cakes. Will you pay her back for me? Wait, here is the money."

He went to fetch the rolled-up handkerchief in which he was allowed to keep his few centavos; when he came back, he was untying the knot.

"Kerjanian, let me pay the ten centavos. I beg you not to give them to me."

"No, no, I want to die in debt to no one."

"But Kerjanian, if I ask it! Let me do you this one service in Bubi's memory. And in Bubi's memory, as well, I want to give you a little gift. He loved you. He would have wished you to have it."

She took from her bag the big nickel watch that had once belonged to her brother; Kerjanian used to see it on him every day. As he looked at it lying in his hand, Kerjanian's expression softened and the tears rose to his eyes for the first time since he had come into that prison. He said nothing, but stood gazing down, first at the watch, then at the coins that she had refused to take.

"Bubi is dead," said the girl. "Bubi who loved you. But perhaps something of him lives on in me, and that is why I also love you, Nestor Kerjanian. In the hours ahead when you are feeling lonely, remember that you will be in my thoughts at every moment. So we will be together, even though they won't let us see each other again. Yes, we will be together till the last minute."

She looked deep into his face, then with a quick movement leaned forward and kissed Kerjanian on the forehead. It was not really a kiss, more like a mark of benediction. She turned and passed through the gates just as the sun flashed between the clouds. In one second that dark cell was flooded with light, and as Kerjanian stood there in the brightness, he felt a glow inside him as if one of the sunbeams had pierced right through his breast. Eagerly his hand closed around Bubi's watch, in which a little heart was beating—beating for him alone. Long after his own life was quenched, long after his hand grew cold, that staunch heart would go on ticking in its solid case—faithful and indestructible forever.